pretty little mistake

Willow Creek bonus content
Home for Christmas

Light in the Dark Series

Rae of Sunshine
When Stars Collide
Dark Hearts
When Constellations Form
Broken Hearts
Stars & Constellations bundle

Stand-Alones

Beauty in the Ashes
Bring Me Back
The Other Side of Tomorrow
Desperately Seeking Roommate
Desperately Seeking Landlord
Whatever Happens
Sweet Dandelion
Say When
The Road That Leads to Us
The Game Plan

pretty little mistake

MICALEA SMELTZER

Text copyright © 2023 Micalea Smeltzer
All rights reserved.

Published by Montlake, Seattle

www.apub.com

Amazon, the Amazon logo, and Montlake are trademarks of Amazon.com, Inc., or its affiliates.

ISBN-13: 9781662514128 (paperback)
ISBN-13: 9781662514111 (digital)

Cover design by Emily Wittig

Cover images: ©Mihai Simonia / Shutterstock;
©Bokeh Blur Background / Shutterstock

Printed in the United States of America

*For Stephanie,
agent extraordinaire and all-around amazing human.
Thank you for believing in me. This one's for you.*

Chapter One

LENNON

Standing on the sidewalk outside *Real Point* magazine is the most sur-real thing I've experienced in my almost twenty-four years of life. I've spent the past year since graduating from college interning for a gossip magazine for next to no pay and at the cost of my brain cells. It was a learning experience, that's for sure, but the vapid nature of the people I worked with was a bit too much. It wasn't even the talk of makeup and clothes that was an issue—there's nothing wrong with liking those things; I do too—it was the catty behavior and backstabbing maneuvers that got on my nerves.

Real Point is my fresh start. They've been in existence only three years, which is practically a newborn in the print world, but their will-ingness to push boundaries and not dance around delicate issues, while also covering lighter topics, isn't something every magazine is capable of. It's why they've been able to grow rapidly in a dying industry.

Taking a deep breath, I smooth my charcoal pencil skirt and adjust my pale-pink silk blouse. There's no need for the gesture—my outfit is perfect and not out of place in the slightest—but my nerves are cer-tainly getting the best of me.

This is what you've dreamed of, Lennon.

For as long as I can remember, I've wanted to write. It started with me writing about my everyday life in my childhood diary. Tales of my adventures with my brother and his friend. We called ourselves the Three Amigos for the longest time. That was the beginning of my love of writing.

My parents are disappointed that all I want to do with my life is be a writer—their words, not mine—but I know if they'd gotten their wish, I'd be married to one of their friends' rich sons and pregnant by now.

I'm constantly dodging calls from my mom trying to set me up on a blind date with some poor unsuspecting soul. She wasn't a very attentive mother while I was growing up, but now that I'm an adult, she sure does care about who I end up with.

I know I come from a privileged background, and the last name Wells carries a lot of weight in certain circles, but I've always wanted to make something of myself on my own. As much as I can, at least. This feels like my chance to do that.

After pushing open the doors to the renovated building that was once a warehouse, I take the elevator up to the top floor.

I love that the office is in Brooklyn and not in some shiny brand-new skyscraper in Manhattan. This place has character, just like the magazine itself. It's not cold and clinical; it has charm and life.

With a whoosh, the doors open, and I step out in my stilettos.

The loft space is filled with long tables with brightly colored desktops set up at intervals. Conversation buzzes as employees mill about. I have to tamp down the urge to smile. The energy here is infectious.

I head to my right, toward the glass-enclosed office of my new boss.

Jaci George started this production all on her own from the ground up. At only thirty, she's built her empire herself. She started online when she was at NYU, with no employees but herself. Now here she is, running her own company with numerous employees. It's an inspiration to me, how her determination and work ethic have paid off.

I knock on the door, and she looks up from her pink computer, smiling brightly and waving me inside. Her red hair is held back with a light-blue claw clip, her matching dress somehow both cute and professional. I look down at my own attire, worried I've overdressed.

"Lennon." She stands, extending a hand. "I'm so happy to have you on board. Sit, please." She motions for me to take the tufted lime-green chair. The entire office space is infused with color. No dull work environment here. "You look lovely. Would you like some coffee? Tea?"

"I'm good, thank you." I tuck my skirt under me, taking a seat.

Jaci surprises me when she takes the matching chair beside me instead of sitting behind her desk in the place of power. I already know this place is where I belong—a collaborative and supportive work environment is what dreams are made of. Well, at least my dreams.

"I like to welcome all my new hires personally on their first day. I think of you not as employees but as my extended family."

I smile, nodding along. My hands sit daintily in my lap, one leg tucked behind the other. Studying her posture, I realize she's much more relaxed than me, her body language at ease. She leans toward me, one hand lying gently on my arm.

Clearing my throat, I try to alter my posture as inconspicuously as possible. When I was young my mother sent me to etiquette classes— yeah, *etiquette classes*—so things like posture and table manners have been drilled into me. Sometimes it's hard for me to let go of that stiffness and relax around others.

"It's wonderful that you have such a personal relationship with your employees." I plaster on a smile. I hope it doesn't come across as stiff. Even though I already have the job, my nerves are getting to me.

"Well, you know me, I believe a hands-on approach makes for a healthier work environment and happier employees." I do know. It was one of the things that drew me to wanting to work for her. Word of Jaci's unique approach has gotten around. Some find her to be a tad eccentric. But what's wrong with wanting to handle things differently? "Before you join the morning meeting, let me know if you have any concerns or if there's anything you'd like me to address."

She laces her fingers together, waiting.

"Oh." A piece of hair has escaped from the bun at the nape of my neck, so I tuck it behind my ear. "No. I'm good."

When I'm put on the spot, my brain completely empties of any and all words, so even if I had anything I wanted to discuss with her, it's off floating in the abyss of my mind now, never to be seen or heard from again.

"Well, if you ever have any issues, please let me know, and I wish you the best of luck on your first day."

She extends her hand and I shake it. "Thank you so much."

"We better get out there so Brendan can start the meeting." She stands and I follow her out. "This way. Brendan handles most of the day-to-day things. He's who you'll report to, but I'll introduce you to everyone before we begin."

I nod along, taking a deep breath when we round the corner to meet my new coworkers. It's a group of about fifteen people, a small staff but the perfect number for a magazine that's still growing, like this one. They eye me with welcome smiles.

"Good morning, everyone. This is Lennon." Jaci motions to me, and I lift my hand to wave. Nerves take flight in my stomach. "She's our latest hire and comes to us after an internship at *Pulse* magazine. I'm excited to see what she brings to the table. Let's all introduce ourselves."

One at a time, everyone greets me, giving their name. I know I'll never remember all of them and instantly feel bad for it, but I know I'll settle into place here in no time.

After the last person has spoken, Jaci addresses Brendan—the red-haired guy at the head of the group with a pair of glasses perched on the end of his nose—and asks, "Where's Sulli?"

No sooner have the words left her mouth than, behind us, the elevator chimes.

I swear it's like time slows down as I turn, watching those doors open to reveal the last person I ever thought I'd see again.

A startled gasp flies past my lips before I can stop it. My pulse quickens. Dampness forms beneath my arms.

I can feel my fight-or-flight senses kicking in, and I've never wanted to flee more in my life. For a split second I imagine running away, teetering in my heels, but the problem is he's standing in the direction of escape.

Icy-cold blue eyes like the depths of the Arctic Ocean meet mine. I see the slight widening in them, the way the coffee cup in his hand trembles just slightly. His lips narrow like he's tasted something sour as those eyes scan me from head to toe. My skin pebbles beneath the intensity of his gaze.

Beckham Sullivan.

Once upon a time, he was my friend; for the briefest of moments, he was my lover; and then, like a shock of lightning, he became Public Enemy Number One.

The irony of the fact that I just thought of him this morning, of how he and my brother inspired me to start writing, isn't lost on me.

It's like the universe heard my thoughts: the first time I let this man cross my mind in a very long time, the cosmos decided to show me just how cruel the world can be.

I lift my chin haughtily, going through the motions as Jaci introduces us like we've never met before. Like I don't remember the scared thirteen-year-old boy the Sullivan family adopted. The boy who taught me not to fear the ocean and how to drive my car. The boy who stayed up late with me watching movies and reading all the stupid stories I scribbled in notebooks. The boy who took my virginity and shattered my heart like I was *nothing* to him after.

He takes my hand, electricity shooting up my arm. His eyes narrow to slits like he's felt it, too, and thinks I did it on purpose. He immediately drops my hand, his flexing at his side like he's trying to rid himself of the feel of me. I wonder if he'll run off to the restroom after our introduction to wash away my stench.

"Sulli," he says, like going by that makes him so different now. "Lead photographer."

So, we're pretending we don't know each other?

I smile, but there's nothing nice in it, and with the way his eyes narrow even further, he knows. "Lennon."

Something tells me things are about to get interesting.

Chapter Two

BECKHAM

What the fuck is Lennon Wells doing here?

I've perfected the art of keeping my cool, of not letting my emotions show, and it serves me well here. Normally, nothing shakes me, but the last thing I expected was to walk into the office today and find that the new hire is her. Out of all the billions of people in the world, what are the fucking odds?

I let her hand go, mine dropping back to my side. I shake off the zip of energy that's radiated up my arm, looking her up and down in the process.

She looks exactly like I'd expect.

Brown hair pulled taut in a prim bun, a pert nose that she lifts haughtily in the air like she's unaffected by me, soft pillowy lips, and a riot of freckles.

I called her *plain* once. Lennon Wells is anything but, and it pisses me off.

For me, she was always utterly irresistible, but times change and now she's nothing but a reminder, a fucking shackle to another time—a part of my life that doesn't exist anymore.

Her eyes narrow upon me, and I wonder what she's thinking.

Hate me, I think. *You should. I want you to.*

I was never supposed to see her again. Not after I went off to college. But here she is standing in front of me. Not only that, but we're going to be working together.

Someone, somewhere, has to be laughing at my predicament.

Jaci says something, but I miss it, too lost in my own spinning thoughts. I move away from Lennon, away from the smell of her sweet perfume.

"Morning," I say to Brendan, lifting my coffee to my mouth.

I definitely don't take an inconspicuous look over my shoulder at the one girl in the world who's off limits—or supposed to be.

I touched her once, tasted the forbidden fruit. I won't make that mistake again, despite how tempting it might be. I'm older, mentally stronger, and hopefully a bit wiser. The likes of me don't belong with women like her.

I might be a Sullivan, but it's in name only.

"Yeah, good morning," Brendan replies, flipping through a stack of papers. "Where's my coffee?"

"I'm not your errand boy anymore," I rib him.

Brendan's not so bad, and possibly one of the only real friends I have. I'm not good at letting people in. I've always been guarded; I guess being in foster care for so many years is a major contributing factor in that. Keeping people at arm's length is easier. If you don't let them in, then they can't hurt you.

"You're late again. You're lucky Jaci is so lenient."

I shrug, looking down at the old wood floors. The narrow planks gleam with whatever cleaner was used to shine them overnight. "I had something to take care of."

Before he can respond, I take my seat, setting my messenger bag on top of the table. Everyone slowly takes their own seats. When I search for Lennon, I find her at the end, speaking with another writer, Ethan.

My jaw grinds at the sight of the two of them, her *smiling* at him. When he touches her arm, I fix my gaze back on Brendan.

After he's gone over the day's assignments and dismissed everyone, I head back to my private office. Only a few of us have them, and I'm grateful for my personal space. I'm not a team player, even though that's what Jaci likes, but luckily for me she tolerates my bullshit since I'm her best photographer. And I'm not just saying that. I'm good, and I'm not in the habit of not acknowledging my own talent. After all, it's something that's entirely mine. A name can't give you talent; you either have it or you don't.

I pull up the photos I need to have edited by the end of the day.

The fingers of my right hand still feel electrified by Lennon's touch, and that pisses me off the longer I sit there in the confines of my office.

I've gotten only about an hour of work done when I decide it makes sense to take a break and grab a drink.

Scanning the open office space, I quickly zero in on Lennon seated at a pink desktop. I hate how fast I find her, how I've always been able to sense her, even in a roomful of people.

Brendan is beside her, pointing out something on the desktop. I can't hear what he's saying, but it's not important anyway.

As I grab a bottle of water, a prickling awareness has my shoulders clenching.

One more look won't hurt.

Doe-brown eyes collide with mine. I narrow my gaze, daring her to look away first. She raises one brow.

A challenge.

Oh, Lennon, you don't want to do that.

I love a challenge. I always win.

Chapter Three

LENNON

The apartment in the Park Slope neighborhood is way more expensive than anything I could afford on my salary. When my parents insisted on making the purchase, I was against it. I wanted to do this on my own, even if it meant living in a shoebox, but then my father made some very important points, mostly about safety. It was definitely the way to get through to me, even though I know that wasn't his motivation at all—rather, this is him wanting to control his status. He will always view my brother and me as extensions of himself instead of as the individuals we are.

The Wells name is best known for real estate development, with a bit of dabbling in politics. My family has put their stamp across this country since the 1800s, most notably in New York City. My dad's given me a full brief on all the details of our family history multiple times—it's one of his favorite topics—but I usually zone out less than five minutes into the conversation.

After letting myself inside, I set down my bag and grab a bottle of water from the kitchen. I gulp it, feeling ridiculously parched. Nothing has been able to quench my thirst today.

Beckham Sullivan in the flesh.

I never thought I'd see him again. I've tried to forget about him.

But there he was, and now we're working together. Surely we can both be adults about this and not dredge up the past. Besides, if anyone has a right to be mad, it's me. After all, I'm the one who was used and discarded like a dirty napkin.

I set out the to-go boxes, open them all up, and spoon everything I want onto a plate.

Are we that predictable that we order Chinese every week?

Yes, yes we most certainly are. There's comfort in routine. Sue me.

"Laurel!" I call out when the shower cuts off. "Food's here!"

"Food!" she shrieks back like some little goblin.

She joins me only a minute later, her hair twisted up, a few scant pieces escaping to frame her face. She's wearing a muumuu that's better suited for a granny than someone in their early twenties, but she swears they're the most comfortable things ever.

She dumps her rice, chicken, and sauce into a bowl, stirring haphazardly. A chunk of rice lands on the floor. She smiles impishly, shrugging. "Oops."

I clean up the rice, since I can't stand a mess, and we sit down on the couch with our food and wine.

"Okay, girl. Time to spill." She shoves a bite of food in her mouth. "Don't keep me in suspense any longer." I'm only able to understand that last part because I have years of practice listening to her talk with her mouth full. Much to her mother's dismay, etiquette classes didn't have an impact on Laurel.

I decide to get right to the point. "Beckham is a photographer at *Real Point*."

Her mouth drops open. At least she's finished chewing. I'm worried she's in need of a reboot when she finally composes herself. "You're lying."

I trace my pinkie finger around the rim of my wineglass. "I wish I were."

She stares at me for the length of three heartbeats, then her head falls back, and she laughs.

"Why are you laughing?" I would throw a pillow at her, but I don't want to risk food or wine ending up on the couch.

"Because this is the most hilarious thing I've ever heard. Like, there's no way. You're totally pulling my leg." I blink at her, and her smile falters. "You're serious? The douchebag who took your virginity and ran is your coworker now?"

I nod. "Yep."

"Whoa." She sits stunned into silence. A feat I didn't know was possible for Laurel. "So, what are you going to do? Knee him in the balls?"

"I don't think that would win me any points at my new job." I reach up to brush a stray hair behind my ear, a slight shake in my hands. I hate that after only one encounter, he's managed to get to me. It's not like he really even said anything. His presence alone has left me slightly unhinged.

"Ooh. Right." She ponders, biting her lip. "Laxative in his coffee?"

"Ew." I wrinkle my nose. "No. Besides, I'm pretty sure that's illegal."

"So, if you're not going to sabotage him, then what are you going to do?"

I stare down at my plate of kung pao chicken. "I guess I'll deal with it. What other choice do I have?"

She gives me a pitying look, and I gulp. We both know this probably isn't going to end well for me.

Walking into the office the next day, I try not to think about the fact that I'll be facing Beckham yet again. At least today his appearance won't take me by surprise.

My heels clack against the floors as I find my seat. After turning on the computer, I spin in my chair. The woman a few feet down from me at the communal table smiles.

"Hi," she says warmly, extending a hand. "I'm Claire. We met briefly yesterday, but I wanted to properly introduce myself."

I take her hand, her palm soft against mine. "Lennon. I'm sorry I was so focused on settling in yesterday that I didn't get to talk to anyone. How long have you been working here?"

"Almost a year and a half."

"Do you like it?"

She looks around with an almost-conspiratorial smile. "I love it. It's a much more collaborative environment than I was used to. Jaci is very open to listening to our ideas and input. She values us, which I appreciate. My last job . . ." She actually shudders, like the memory alone leaves her horror-struck. "Well, let's just say it was a very different environment."

My skin prickles on the back of my neck. I rub at it in annoyance.

"And"—another one of the girls across from us pipes in—"sometimes the view is very nice."

Claire and I both turn to see what she's looking at.

It's Beckham.

Of course it is.

He's oblivious to us, filling up his mug with coffee from the pod maker.

I quickly force my gaze back in front of me, but that does no good, either, because he's visible in the reflection of my screen.

"He's looking at you like he wants to eat you," the woman in front of me hisses. Layla, if I'm remembering her name correctly. It's a bit of a blur from being introduced to everyone.

Beside me, Claire murmurs, "He totally is."

In the reflection, I see him take his mug and leave.

"Sulli never looks at us like that," Layla says.

My brows furrow. "I'm sure you're mistaken."

I think of the way he looked at me yesterday, that brief flash of surprise that was quickly replaced with something dark. Not quite hatred, but I felt like I was something gross he wished he could scrape free from the bottom of his shoe. There's no way he's looking at me in the way they're implying.

"Trust me, we're not." Claire snorts, wiggling her mouse to bring her screen back to life. "Sulli is . . . nice enough to everyone here, but he does his job and leaves. He doesn't try to make friends with us, except Brendan, and he certainly doesn't look at any of us women in a hungry way like he did you."

"I thought he was gay for a long time," Layla interjects, opening the wrapper on a breakfast bar. "Then I saw him on a date and realized that wasn't the case: he just doesn't like any of us in that way."

I hate the way I bristle at the idea of him on a date. The last thing that should matter to me is him going out.

"Or," I say, clearing my throat and trying to shake myself free of the sticky feeling of . . . annoyance? Jealousy? "Maybe he doesn't want to date a coworker?"

"Then why did he look at you the way he did?" Claire volleys back, arching a brow.

I shrug like this conversation isn't getting to me in any way. "Maybe he just needs to get laid?"

The girls burst into peals of laughter.

Recovering, Layla takes a bite of her bar. "I doubt he's hurting for it," she says around a mouthful. "Who wouldn't want a piece of that?"

I try to tune them out as they continue to chat about Beckham, instead opening my office email and reading over the list of objectives that Brendan sent.

I get to work researching the topic and scribbling notes before I start a draft.

The prickly sensation on the back of my neck returns a second before Layla hisses, "He's back."

Don't look. Don't look. Don't look, I chant to myself.

I fail epically when I peek over my shoulder. He's stealing a banana from the snack bar, his eyes glued to me with a look that's a mixture of annoyance and puzzlement.

When my eyes meet his, he quickly lopes back to his office.

"He rarely comes out to the main office," Claire explains to me in a hushed tone. "He requested his own office because he likes to keep to himself. So this . . ."

"Is unusual," Layla finishes for her.

And it's only my second day.

Clearing my throat, I try to regain my focus on the article I'm drafting so I can send it off to Brendan and Jaci for their input.

Stupidly, my thoughts keep drifting back to that infuriating man.

I hate myself for giving him even a moment of thought.

Chapter Four

BECKHAM

I'm hearing what Brendan's telling me. The words make sense. But I don't believe them. Or I just refuse to.

"No," I say, almost on a growl.

"No?" He arches a brow.

It's the start of Lennon's second week, and Brendan wants to partner *me* with her? Fuck no.

"She's a newbie," I argue, though that's not the reason I'm so adamantly against this. "You know I'm the best photographer you have here. Why would you want to stick us together?" Tension has my shoulders practically climbing to my ears. I force myself to let them drop, to appear as calm as I can in this situation.

In the short time she's been here, I've done my absolute best to avoid her, to be unaffected. As much as I'd like to think she can't get under my skin anymore, I'm not sure I'm ready to test that theory by being forced to work with her in such close capacity.

Brendan shrugs. "It's not me. It's Jaci. She sees something in Lennon. Potential or whatever. She was pleased with the articles Lennon wrote last week and with her input on things. I guess she might see her as some potential protégé or something."

He looks over to where she sits at her computer. Hair in that stupid, too-tight bun. I want to rip it out and watch her hair cascade down her back, then take that hair and wrap it around my fist. Force her mouth to mine.

That bun doesn't suit her. It looks like something her prim mother would make her wear to events when we were younger. The real Lennon isn't uptight like the bun leads one to believe.

"And what exactly am I supposed to do with this potential?" Ice drips from my words, so much so that Brendan takes a step away from me, eyeing me peculiarly. I'm letting my emotions show too much. When I'm here, I'm Sulli, and right now I'm letting too much of *Beckham* show through—the guy who was never good enough in some people's eyes, certainly not the right kind of guy for Lennon.

"She wants you two to work together to come up with a unique concept. Something groundbreaking that makes people stop and think. Her words, not mine. She's giving everyone until January to come up with something and present a proposal; then she's picking the best one to be refined and go to print in the spring."

It's July now. "She never gives us this long." I narrow my eyes on my friend, wondering what the catch is. This has to be some kind of trick. A test, perhaps? Maybe I haven't appeared as indifferent as I thought, and now Jaci has cooked up some kind of half-assed idea to figure out what my problem is.

No, that can't be it.

Jaci believes in a collaborative work environment, sure, but not even she would come up with something like this just to get a reaction out of someone.

"You know Jaci, she's always thinking up something."

I rub my clean-shaven jaw. I'm never one to shy away from a challenge, but working with Lennon?

"Why is she sticking me with the newbie?" It would make more sense for her to pair me with one of the more seasoned writers. I'm trying to get an understanding of where she's coming from, of what her thoughts are, because right now nothing is making sense.

"Like I said, she sees potential in her. She must think you can take her under your wing and make something great happen."

I stifle the urge to snort. What a load of bullshit. But I can't exactly say no. This is my job, and if Jaci wants me to work with Lennon, then what choice do I have?

"Fine," I growl, not happy about this outcome, but if I want to keep my job, I can't complain too much, or it'll raise suspicion. I could go any number of places, make a lot more money, too, but this is what appeals to me. I have no interest in fashion magazines, and I already traveled the world taking photos after college. When I first met Jaci through a mutual friend, I was inspired by her drive to create something different in the market that couldn't be pigeonholed into one category. I view working here as an opportunity to grow with something that will likely become huge one day. Jaci doesn't want to write about only politics, or world issues, or fashion. She wants to put a focus on *real* people and bring light to your average citizen, highlighting the fact that there's more to every single person out there than what we see on the surface. Not that the magazine doesn't touch on other things, but that's quickly becoming her main focus. For me, getting to meet these people and hear their stories is something I won't find anywhere else. "I'll see what I can do with her."

He claps me on the shoulder. "Go easy on her."

Why does he assume I won't?

I stride toward Lennon and stop beside her, letting my shadow fall over her body. She freezes, her fingers stilling on the keyboard. I know she feels me at her side.

She doesn't acknowledge me, forcing me to speak first.

"Come with me." It's an order and she knows it, based on the way her hands clench involuntarily. I might be well schooled in keeping my emotions in check, but not Lennon. No, she's always been an open book. Easy to read.

She tilts that elegant neck back, brown eyes narrowed on me like she wishes she could render me dead on the spot. A part of me wants to smile. But I won't give her the satisfaction.

"Did you hear me?"

Her lips twist and I know, I just fucking know, there's a sassy retort on the tip of her tongue. But unfortunately for me she swallows it back. *How disappointing.*

She glances at Claire a few feet away from her at the long table, seated at another desktop.

"Why are you looking at her? She's not the one talking to you."

Red blooms on her tanned cheeks, and I wait in eager anticipation for her to finally say whatever it is I know she wants to. But I'm left in disappointment when she shoves her chair back—forcing me to step away so she doesn't run over my foot—and stands, glaring haughtily at me.

That fire. A part of me wants to stoke it, watch it grow, while another part wants nothing more than to extinguish it.

I don't say anything, just turn and walk away, knowing she'll follow.

Sure enough, I hear the telltale clicking of her heels behind me. I open the door to my office, letting her inside first. If my eyes drop to the sway of her hips, it's completely by accident.

I sit down behind my desk and roll up my shirtsleeves. She smirks about something, my eyes zeroing in on her lips. Dammit if I don't want to ask her what's so amusing, but I keep my mouth shut. About that, at least.

I drop the bomb on her, no preamble. "Jaci wants us to work together on a project."

She sits up straighter, running her hand over her perfectly coiffed dark hair like she's afraid a strand is out of place. "Us? Why?"

I flatten my hands on my desk, spreading my fingers. Her eyes follow the gesture, the tiniest catch of her breath the only sound in the room for a moment.

"She's under the assumption there's something special about you. I wish I could tell her you're perfectly average in all ways, but that's not my place." She glares at me like she wishes she could light me on fire. "Apparently everyone's getting partnered up." I wave a dismissive hand. "And you and me, we're together." I expect her to say something, anything, but she sits there in stone-cold silence. I go on: "We need to come up with a compelling story and put together a proposal by January. From there, Jaci is picking her favorite idea to go to print in the spring. I don't like to lose, so we will be chosen."

She shakes her head, looking baffled. "You say that so definitively."

"Because I believe it."

She stares at me like I'm both a stranger and the most familiar person on the planet. I suppose that's true. We used to know each other inside and out. She was the person who knew me better than anyone, even more than her brother, my best friend at the time, did. Lennon was the person I could share my darkest worries, my deepest thoughts, with.

She looks at me doubtfully. "Why is she putting me with you?" I can see her mind sorting through thoughts, and I know exactly what she's thinking when surprise flits over her features.

I lean back in my chair. Cool, calm, collected. If there's anything my adoptive father taught me, it's to always have the upper hand. "I know what you're thinking, and no, I didn't ask to be paired with you."

She tries to hide her emotions, but I see the tiniest downturn of her lips and know I've struck a nerve. Steel infuses her once more, and I hate to admit it, but she just might be a worthy opponent. I want her to fight back. I want to see how much of a spine she has.

"When do we start?"

I smile on the inside. "Right now."

Chapter Five

LENNON

"Can you slow down?" My legs struggle to keep up with Beckham's stride. I'm not that short, at five foot six, but he's still nearly a whole foot taller, and his imposing presence sends even New Yorkers scrambling out of his way. Which is a true feat, since New Yorkers are not easily scared.

"Hurry up," he gripes, heading for the coffee shop on the next corner.

If I took my heels off, I'd be able to go faster, but I'm not that desperate. Besides, the only way I'm removing one is if it's to bludgeon him in the head with it. It takes a lot to rile me up, but Beckham—excuse me, *Sulli*—has always known which buttons to push.

He comes to a stop at the crosswalk, tapping his foot impatiently.

"Why are you tapping your foot? Is your suit too tight? Is it cutting off blood circulation to your brain?"

"My circulation is just fine, honeybee." His eyes widen the moment the old pet name passes through his lips, and for a moment I'm taken back to summers at the cape, running barefoot through the grass, the smell of a bonfire crackling through the air. Beckham gave me the name the summer I was fourteen, because he said I reminded him of honeybees—I was always looking for something sweet, but I could stab you if you looked at me wrong.

Clearing his throat, he ignores me by looking over the top of my head as if I'm so insignificant to him that I don't even deserve to have something as basic as eye contact.

Whatever. I'm not going to let his hot-and-cold attitude get to me. Before getting this job, I hadn't seen him in years, and I'm just fine pretending our paths will never cross again.

The crosswalk signals that it's our turn, and like he can't help himself, his fingers gingerly cup my elbow to guide me along. A part of me wants to rip my arm from his hold, but for some reason I don't. He doesn't release his grip on me until we're on the other side of the street.

As he holds open the door to the coffee shop, he pauses like he's going to let me enter first but then seems to change his mind and almost bodychecks me in an attempt to get inside before I do. So much for manners.

There's a line, which I promptly join by skirting past him, because if I'm expected to get through this lunch meeting with Beckham, then I need caffeine.

He gets in line as well, but not behind me. Oh no, the prick steps up right beside me, his arm brushing mine. Warmth radiates from him, my body flushing from his proximity.

"What are you doing?"

He arches a dark brow at me, eyes narrowed. "Standing in line."

"The line continues behind me." I point over my shoulder in case he's too dense to understand where *behind* is.

"We're here together, therefore we order together."

"We're not together," I snap, moving up in line and a bit to my left so that his arm won't brush mine, but the jerk just closes that little bit of distance I put between us.

"I didn't say we were together," he says slowly, looking over the menu despite the fact that I'm almost positive he already knows what he

22

wants. "I said we were *here* together. Meaning, this is a working lunch." He angles his chin down in my direction, his icy-blue eyes gluing me in place. At one point in time, light and playfulness danced in those eyes, but it looks as if true happiness hasn't been in his gaze for a long time. "Doesn't it make the most sense that we'd order together?"

He has a point, and if it were anyone else, I never would've said anything to begin with. But this is Beckham of all people. I know I need to remain professional, but it feels impossible with our history.

Finally, it's our turn to order, and he waves his long fingers in a gesture that shouldn't come across as elegant but does.

I order an iced espresso and an avocado toast. He snickers at that, and I swear I hear him mutter "Predictable" under his breath. I would love nothing more than to stomp on his foot or elbow him in the gut, but I don't.

He gives the barista his order of an americano and a roasted turkey sandwich. Before he can pass his card across, I'm already giving her mine instead.

No way in hell am I letting him pay for my food and drink. I have no doubt he'd find some way to make me feel indebted to him, and I'm not in the mood to play that game.

"I was paying for it," he says in a gruff voice, his mouth lowered toward my ear as we move out of the way and go in search of a table.

"Well, I *did* pay for it."

He lets out a burst of grudging laughter, eyes widening in surprise, like he didn't mean to laugh.

After sitting down at one of the few empty tables, I cross my feet at the ankles.

I will not let this man ruffle me. Getting under my skin is clearly what he wants, and I can't give him that satisfaction.

Beckham drops into the chair across from me, tugging on the sleeves of his dress shirt to roll them up slightly. We're the only two people who seem to dress up at the magazine. I guess some habits are hard to break.

His dark hair curls loosely against his forehead, the stubble on his cheeks well groomed. The subtle spice of his cologne reaches me from across the table. I loathe the fact that I like the scent. It's strong. Manly. Entirely too tempting and suits him all too well.

Beckham Sullivan is a gorgeous specimen of a man—but he's not the man for me.

He smooths his fingers through his hair and finally looks at me. I wish I knew what he is thinking. This has to be weird for him too. I don't think either one of us ever expected to see each other again.

There were times initially, in my heartbroken state, when I wondered what had happened to him. Why he took my virginity and ran—not just from me, but from his friendship with my brother and all the ties we shared—but after a while I stopped caring.

But now that I'm faced with him again, I'm wondering the same thing. I'm older now, my heart has healed, and I can acknowledge that the whole thing is rather weird. The Beckham I knew then wouldn't have taken my virginity for sport, which is what it felt like for so long, so what happened?

I could ask him, but somehow, I know I won't get a straight answer, and we need to keep things professional anyway, which means focusing on work.

Beckham laces his fingers together, then lays them on the table in front of him.

"Do you have any ideas for this project?"

His lips twitch slightly. "Not really. It's difficult with no real parameters."

I know what he means: with no direction other than "something unique that will make people stop and take a look at the magazine," there are endless ways we could do this.

My name is called, and I move to grab our order, but Beckham is already up and going to get it.

Fine, if he's willing to get it, then so be it. I make myself comfortable in the chair once more, waiting for the infuriating man of my past to return.

He walks back with a suspicious lack of items.

He sets down one cup and one wrapped sandwich, arching that annoying brow at me.

He doesn't say a word as he pulls out his chair, slipping into it. After a moment, he finally deems me worthy of his time. "Are you not going to get yours?"

Well played, asshole.

With a sigh, I get up and collect my stuff. For a moment I allow myself to imagine showering him in my coffee. I wouldn't do it, but man is it fun to think about.

After setting my stuff down on the table gently, so I don't betray any sort of irritation, I smooth my skirt beneath me and take my seat.

Beckham sips his coffee. Lips set in a straight line, he watches me, and I see the hint of a satisfied grin in his gaze, one he won't betray by actually showing it.

"We should brainstorm," I say, reminding him why we're together.

"We should."

I wait for him to pull out his laptop, or a notebook and pen, if that's more his speed, but he does nothing. I know what he's doing, trying to get me to cower beneath him like some lowly little servant, but I won't. I'm not the same girl he knew, just like he's not the same boy I knew.

Instead, I start speaking out loud. If he doesn't want any notes, that's fine; I can write down whatever we discuss later.

"We need something interesting, eye catching, something that will gain buzz and make people want to pick up the magazine." Even though *Real Point* has an online edition, Jaci has made it abundantly clear that she wants to push print editions, to get people away from electronics.

But in today's bustling world, that's a hard ask. "Something that could potentially go viral, and not in the way some things do these days where it gets a lot of views for one day."

Beckham brushes his fingers over his lips, perhaps trying to get rid of any lingering crumbs from his sandwich, though there aren't any that I can see.

He offers no words, and I want nothing more than to huff in exasperation, but I refuse to give him the satisfaction.

I pick up my toast and take a bite. If he has nothing else to offer, then I'll just enjoy my lunch and coffee, all while pretending that His Highness isn't sitting across from me.

After a while, he says, "All you've done is state the obvious, not give any good ideas."

As I gather up my trash, I steadfastly ignore him, even though he tries to keep me glued to my chair with his icy stare.

When I stand, I glower right back at him. "This lunch was . . . enlightening."

And with that, I leave him behind in the coffee shop, though I can feel his presence hovering mere feet behind me the entire walk back to the office.

Chapter Six

BECKHAM

I pace my agitation across the short length of the white room, my fingers flexing at my sides as I go.

"She infuriates me like no one else can. She pushes my buttons without even trying. All she has to do is exist, and I'm pissed off." I stop with my hands on my hips, facing the frail man in the hospital bed. His eyes are tired, but they cease tracking my movements as I still; then his eyes trail carefully to the chair in the corner, and I know without him uttering a word that he's telling me to sit my ass down.

So I do.

I found my birth father several years ago. I'd always had a burning desire to find my birth parents, so as an adult, I put the Sullivan family money to good use and did it. My birth mom passed away at only nineteen in a car accident, the same car accident that left my father with spinal cord damage and confined him to a bed, where he can't do much of anything except watch and listen. He can speak a little, but it's obviously difficult for him, and he gets frustrated easily.

When I first found him, he was in a long-term-care facility that left a lot to be desired. I wasted no time in moving him somewhere better, cleaner, with staff actually equipped to handle someone with his needs.

He might be paralyzed and have trouble communicating, but he's still a person and deserves to be treated as such.

He was surprised when I found him. He wept openly the moment he saw me. I didn't even have to introduce myself. One look was all it took. That first encounter was emotionally draining, for sure. Despite his struggle with speaking, he managed to tell me I looked like Mom.

Hearing that filled me with this overwhelming sense of belonging. Even if she was gone, she'd been real, and I was a part of her—of him.

At first, I didn't want to tell my adoptive parents that I was looking for my birth parents. A part of me felt ashamed for even caring about them. They gave me up, after all, and I ended up in and out of homes until the Sullivans adopted me. I still don't know what they saw in me, what made them choose to adopt a boy who was starting his teenage years, but whatever the reason, I'll always be grateful to them. I finally found my birth father through newspaper articles the private investigator located, detailing his time as a high school hockey player and on through the accident.

"I'm ranting again, aren't I?" I ask my father.

He blinks once, slowly and deliberately. He gives a strangled "Yes" in answer.

"Sorry," I mutter. "Do you want me to put the TV on?"

"N-no."

I cross my ankle over my knee. "You want me to keep going?"

"Yes." I detect the tiniest hint of exasperation in his voice and have to fight a smile. It's amusing, the times when he sounds so much like an annoyed father with me.

With a shrug, I continue to fill my father in on all things Lennon Wells. To no one else would I say a word, but to him I feel comfortable speaking about her—not because he can't tell my secrets but because he doesn't come from that elitist world.

From the information I was able to gather, James Conroy and Elizabeth Adams were high school sweethearts who got pregnant with me when they were practically kids themselves and gave me up for the chance at a better life. I'm sure there's more to the story than that, especially since no one from his family has ever bothered to visit him, but I've chosen not to delve into the murky waters of family secrets. Besides, I've accomplished what I wanted: I found him and my mom, too, even if I'll never get the chance to meet her.

A whole hour goes by of me telling him about Lennon, and he absorbs every detail eagerly. This is probably the most exciting information he's ever gotten from me, since most of my daily visits include me filling him in on the basics of my day, which are almost always the same, and watching hockey games together.

I stand and stretch my body, which has been scrunched in the chair for too long. "I better go. I need to grab dinner before I head home."

His eyes have grown heavy through my talking, and I know he needs a nap. After squeezing his hand, I head out, letting the nurse know I'll be back tomorrow.

After leaving the building, I step out onto the busy evening street, headed to the subway station a few blocks away. I'm already placing the order for dinner on my phone.

I've taken this same route every evening for years now.

That's never bothered me before, but tonight the monotony of it feels tiresome.

Is this all I am? All I have to live for? The same thing day in and day out?

I spend the subway ride thinking about how I've let myself get to this point. I don't go out much; my friends in the city are sparse; and I don't date, either, instead opting for a meaningless hookup when I have an itch to scratch. I don't want to get attached.

I did that once, and look where it got me.

After getting off the subway, I swing by the restaurant and grab my dinner, adding a generous tip to the jar.

"See you next week, Sulli," the owner, Joe, calls after me, only reaffirming what I've already realized tonight.

I tip my head at him, otherwise giving no response. I'm too busy having an internal crisis to form words right now.

My apartment is only a block from here, so it doesn't take me long to get to the building.

Flicking the light on when I get inside, I'm immediately greeted by a low, growly meow.

"Hey, Cheddar." I set my food down on the side table and bend to scoop up the chunky cat.

I had no intentions of ever having a pet, but when my elderly neighbor could no longer care for him, I decided to adopt Cheddar, and he's been in my care ever since. I feel bad that I'm gone a lot, leaving him home alone, but at least he knows he's loved. The thought of letting him go to a shelter had made me feel physically ill. It reminded me too much of myself, how I'd ended up in foster care just waiting and hoping for someone to come along and take a chance on me.

After I set him down, he follows me into the open-layout kitchen. I pay a pretty penny for my apartment, but it's worth it. The views are great, and while it's small, it has an open floor plan that makes it feel larger than it is. I could afford something bigger, sure, but I'm usually working late, so what's the point?

As I take my food out of the to-go boxes and set it on a plate—trying to give myself the illusion of a home-cooked meal—Cheddar circles between my legs, purring. I grab his food, pop the top on the can, and dump it in his bowl. He meows happily when I set it on the tile floor and then goes to town on the wet food.

I carry my dinner to the couch, then sit down and turn the TV on. Cheddar joins me on the couch, licking his paws.

Scratching him behind his ears, I say, "It's just me and you, bud."

And never before has a statement felt so completely and utterly lonely.

Chapter Seven

LENNON

A shadow falls over the table I occupy, and I know from the way the hairs stand on the back of my neck who's towering above me.

"We need to talk."

I tell my body to stay relaxed, to not react to the sound of his voice, but apparently my body isn't listening. My spine straightens, my shoulders curving inward slightly in a protective gesture.

Across from me, Layla's eyes nearly bug out of her head.

I know exactly why he's glowering behind me and barking such an order. I didn't expect him to take this lying down, of course, but I guess I naively thought he'd just glare from afar and not actually confront me.

I swivel around in the chair, and he should be forced to step back but he doesn't, because why would he? He's Beckham Sullivan, and he lives to intimidate me.

Perhaps I should feel afraid, with the way he's glowering, his big body looming over mine. There's something in the depths of his eyes besides the anger. A simmering heat . . . lust, maybe? It seems that he might not be as indifferent to me as he tries to appear.

Interesting.

I lift my chin in the air, meeting his angry eyes. "No, we don't."

"It wasn't a question." He bites the words from between his teeth. "Get your ass up and come with me to my office so we can talk in private."

I look him up and down, from his crisp black dress pants to the smooth white button-down tucked neatly into them. His dark hair is brushed back away from his forehead, but there's one stubborn curl trying desperately to escape and hang free.

"Give me one good reason."

He doesn't even hesitate. "Because, *Lennon*," he says, spitting out my name like it's poison on his tongue, "if you don't, I will throw you over my shoulder right here in front of everyone. So help me God, I'll do it."

Behind me, Layla lets out an undignified squeak. I'm pretty sure she's about to raise her hand and volunteer.

By some instinct I know he isn't bluffing. I reach for my coffee mug and stand, sidestepping his looming figure.

"I need a refill."

He stomps after me—okay, he doesn't actually stomp, but he might as well. He's like a sulky toddler not getting his way.

I take my time filling the mug with fresh coffee, then adding a dash of cream and sugar. Beckham crosses his arms over his chest, leaning his hip against the counter. I'm trying my absolute hardest to ignore not only his stare but the stares of those around us as well.

"Now, Lennon."

I glower, heat infusing my cheeks. "I'm not a dog."

"No, but you are being a bitch." My jaw drops in shock. He did not just say that. "Don't look so surprised. You might be able to bat those pretty eyes at anyone else and get your way, but not me. I'll always call you on your bullshit." He takes the mug from my fingers before turning on his heel and striding toward his office. "Come on."

Simmering, I follow after him. I close the door behind me so no one can hear us. He stunned me before, but now I face him with hands on my hips, fire igniting in my veins.

He sets my coffee on his desk and takes a seat behind it. I know he's trying to establish some sort of hierarchy with that choice.

If he thinks I'm going to let his out-of-line comment slide, he's got another thing coming. He might treat me like a dog and call me a bitch, but I'm not about to roll over.

"Don't ever speak to me like that again." The words come out clipped. "I get it: you don't like me, despite the fact I've done nothing to you." I can feel my cheeks growing red with anger. Anytime I get angry, it's like my internal temperature rises twenty degrees. "But that doesn't give you the right to say such things to me, and at my job no less."

His cheeks hollow. "I was out of line." I'm shocked he's admitting it. "I'm sorry."

I try not to let the surprise at his sincere apology show on my face. Gripping the back of the chair in front of me, I refuse to sit down and instead try to get to the point. "What do you want?"

It's a stupid question: I knew from the moment he crowded over me at the computer what was up.

"You know what you did." His voice is icy calm, just like his unwavering blue eyes. Yeah, I do, but I stupidly want to make him say it. He clucks his tongue. "Now, now, Lennon. You certainly had no problem using your words when you complained about me, so do me a favor and stop playing dumb."

I cross my arms over my chest, his eyes narrowing on the defensive gesture, so I immediately drop them loosely back to my sides. It doesn't matter, though, because from the self-satisfied smirk on his lips, he's already noticed.

"You have to agree, we're not a good match."

"That's not what you used to say."

It's the last thing I expected to come out of his mouth.

I have never, in all my life, wanted to smack someone more. "For the project. You wouldn't even talk when we went to lunch to discuss it, and if you think for one minute I'm going to be the only one contributing to this, then you're in for a rude awakening. So, yes"—I pause, inhaling a breath—"I went to Jaci and told her I didn't think we were a fit for this project. Do you have a problem with that?"

He squares his shoulders, his crisp dress shirt pulling taut over his muscular torso—not that I'm checking out said shoulders. "Yes, I have a problem with that," he states bluntly. "You went above my head to my boss—"

"Our boss," I correct.

"Our boss," he repeats through clenched teeth, "and now I'm being reprimanded for my attitude when I did nothing wrong." His hands flex where they rest on his desk. It appears to be an unconscious gesture.

I scoff, shaking my head. "You're delusional."

His eyes spark. "Are you still holding prejudice against me because I wouldn't date you?"

He's really gone and lost his mind. "I can't believe what I'm hearing right now. I don't give a fuck what happened in our past. I've worked hard for this job"—I point forcefully behind me at the workspace beyond his doors—"and I'm not about to let you sabotage it for me."

"Worked hard? Are you sure Daddy didn't buy your way in?"

His mark hits and I flinch.

A scream builds in my throat, but I tamp it down, because the last thing I need is to be labeled as the hysterical new female hire.

"Absolutely not," I respond, standing up straight. *I will not cower.* "My parents would much rather I not work at all." I smooth my top down, needing to busy my hands to steady the shake that's developed with his accusation. "I got this position on my own. What about you, Sullivan? Can you say the same?"

He doesn't hesitate. "Yes."

"Now that we've established that—"

There's a knock on the door, quieting us both. It opens a second later to reveal Jaci. Her lips are pinched, her normal carefree smile missing, and I know it has everything to do with us.

Shame overwhelms me, the feeling of being a small child who has done something explicitly wrong and now must suffer the consequences.

"Good, you're both here." She steps inside, then closes the door behind her. "I've been thinking long and hard about what to do with this . . . predicament." She wrinkles her nose at that. It's obvious Jaci loathes any type of animosity, and Beckham and I have it in spades. I hold my breath, waiting for what she'll say next—if I'll be fired. It would make sense: clearly there was no problem with Beckham—I'm sorry, *Sulli*—before I arrived.

Beckham leans back in his chair, his expression almost serene.

I wonder if that's what he suspects—my termination, thanks to this dilemma.

"I want you both to go to Chicago next weekend. I had a contact I was going to meet with, but I want you two to handle it instead. Maybe it'll go a long way to teaching you to work together. I see potential with this pairing." She wags a finger between us. Her wording irks me, because I can't help but think about the swoony teen I once was who thought I'd marry Beckham. In my young eyes he was some sort of knight in shining armor, come to whisk me away from the castle I was trapped in. "I'll have Jessica transfer my ticket to one of you and book another, so watch for her email. She'll send all the information you need on the meeting."

I wet my lips slightly with my tongue, my throat going dry. Clearing my throat, I stand a bit taller. "Understood. We can handle it."

Thankfully my voice sounds stronger than I feel.

I don't dare look at Beckham, but I can feel the weight of those blue eyes.

After what feels like an hour of silence, he says to her, "You can count on us."

She smiles, but it doesn't quite reach her eyes. I can tell she's worried, that maybe she did make the wrong call with us, with *me*. I have to prove to her that I deserve to be here, even if it means working with Beckham Sullivan, of all people.

"Good." She lifts her chin, looking exactly like the young CEO she is. "Don't disappoint me."

And then she's gone.

Chapter Eight

BECKHAM

I've always felt a particular kind of comfort in the water.

I suppose that's why I find myself in the apartment's pool doing laps at a ridiculously late hour. I'm not nearly as pissed off as I was this morning, when I learned that Lennon had gone to Jaci to bitch about me, but I am still frustrated at the whole convoluted situation. I know it's my fault, not hers, and I have to accept responsibility. I haven't given her any indication that I'll be easy to work with. If I were in her position, I would've done the same thing. She certainly doesn't owe me any sort of loyalty, and I haven't acted like I want it. So why does it feel like she's betrayed me in some way? I can't wrap my head around how I feel. I thought I was over her, that I'd moved past that part of my life, but clearly, I didn't resolve things as easily as I believed.

Why, of all the places in the entire world she could end up, did she have to get hired at the same place I work? It feels like the universe is mocking me.

Back in the day, Lennon Wells was the girl of my dreams.

She was smart, with a sassy tongue, and the most beautiful girl I'd ever seen.

There was one big problem, though: she was my best friend's little sister.

All it took was one night to lose them both. I went off to college and never looked back. I couldn't. There was nothing left for me there.

Never in a million years did I expect to have Lennon Wells shoved in my face during business hours five days a week.

I must've really pissed someone off in a past life to deserve this.

My thoughts begin to spiral as I wonder what she thinks of all this. What were her immediate thoughts when she saw me again for the first time? Maybe she was happy to see me, and I shat all over that?

I've been selfish, not even stopping for a moment to consider her feelings in all this.

I let my anger over the past overshadow actually being a decent human being.

Fuck, I've done enough in this life to deserve this punishment, but damn if I don't wish the universe would cut me some slack.

Another three laps in the pool and my body can't take any more, which means I should have no problem passing out the moment my head hits the pillow.

Forgoing the stairs, I heft my body out of the water and grab my towel off the chaise I tossed it on earlier. After drying my torso, I secure the towel around my waist.

Upstairs in my apartment, Cheddar meows angrily at being abandoned shortly after I got home. He meanders through my legs, yowling as loudly as possible.

"Sorry, bud." I grab his treat bag off the counter and give him two. That seems to appease him.

After a quick shower, I make myself a sandwich, then scarf it down like I haven't eaten all day. Which, come to think of it, I haven't, except for breakfast this morning. After being reprimanded by Jaci for being unwelcoming to Lennon and not demonstrating team-player qualities, it never crossed my mind.

Cheddar's extra-fluffy paws pad against the floor behind me, following me to the bedroom.

The first night I had him, I steadfastly told him that he would never, under any circumstances, sleep in my bed.

No one ever warned me that one simply does not tell a cat what they can and can't do. He's the boss and I go along with it, which means he sleeps in the bed like a spoiled prince. I guess the old guy deserves it.

I lift him up on the bed before he can start yelling at me for that, then grab the remote to turn the TV on.

Climbing into bed, I swear my whole body does a sigh of relief. I definitely pushed it too hard in the pool tonight, but I can't bring myself to care. That's a regret that tomorrow's Beckham will have to deal with.

Even though my body is at the brink of exhaustion and it's way past the hour when I'd normally go to sleep, my mind won't shut up. I'm thinking about Lennon when I shouldn't be.

Her face appears in my mind, but instead of her womanly appearance of today, it's the teenage Lennon I see. Her face was a tad rounder, her eyes just as dark and slightly slanted, lips round and full but smiling, not the permanent half frown she seems to wear now. Back then she looked at me with such adoring trust, like I walked on water, and I never took that for granted. Her brother, Hunter, was my best friend, but Lennon was special. I adored her in a way I never had another person. I loved her, wanted to protect and cherish her, but it wasn't my place, and Hunter wasted no time in reminding me of that.

I was a Sullivan in name only, and Lennon Wells shouldn't have been sullied by a no-name bastard.

◆ ◆ ◆

Brown eyes dart up to meet mine with suspicion and surprise as I release the cup of coffee I've set down beside her.

I cluck my tongue. "Don't read into it. I got coffee for everyone."

A snarl forms on her lips, and I know there's a sassy retort at the ready on her tongue. "Shh," I hush, pressing a finger to her mouth. A spark zips from the pillowy-soft feel of her lips to my finger and all the way up my arm before it fizzles out. "Just say thank you." I let my finger fall away, shaking off the strange, electric feeling.

Steam practically rushes out of her ears. I move away before she can say anything.

Not that I wouldn't love to spar with her, but now's not the time, not when Jaci is already perturbed with me. I spare a glance behind me, in time to see her trembling fingers hesitantly touch her mouth, where my finger was only moments ago.

A smile curves my lips. Almost instantly I wipe it away, silently cursing myself. Why the fuck am I smiling over this? I shouldn't be happy that she obviously felt the same as I did.

I finish handing out the coffees I picked up this morning before sequestering myself in my office. There's an endless task list waiting for me. I'm behind on my photo editing, and on top of that, I need to get some proposal layouts to Jaci today for this month's magazine so we can begin fine-tuning things.

I've been at it a few hours when I sense a presence in the doorway.

I want to ignore her in the hopes that she'll go away, but it's as if something else is controlling me. There's a need to look at her, acknowledge her presence. It's the same feeling I had as a boy. I called Lennon a honeybee, and to me that's what she was, but I never told her the rest, that I was the flower dependent on her for survival.

Sure enough, I look up from my computer to find her hovering there like she's not sure whether she should stay or flee.

I arch a brow, giving a gruff, "What?"

"I wondered if you've gotten anything from Jessica. From what Jaci said we should have an email by now, but I don't." She inhales a shaky breath. "I thought I'd check with you before I—"

"Before you what? Asked Jessica? She's the one sending it—wouldn't the logical conclusion have been to speak with her first?"

She rolls her eyes with a huff. "Forget I asked."

Why do I do this? Why am I constantly pushing her away?

It's like I have this need to self-sabotage myself when it comes to her. It's easier to make her hate me than to show her the scarred man I am beneath all the layers I've built around myself.

She turns to leave. I sigh out an agitated plea: "Wait."

She hesitates. Her feet shuffle nervously. I don't think she's even aware that she's doing it. Nails tapping lightly against the side of her gray skirt, she waits for me to speak.

"No, I haven't gotten anything either. I emailed Jessica this morning, and she said she was still working on it. I figure we'll hear from her soon, possibly after lunch."

She nods. "See, that wasn't so hard, was it?"

"Don't push your luck, Lennon."

When she leaves, I can't help but watch her go. Not only because the view is nice but for the mere fact that, despite my better judgment, I'm fucking helpless not to.

Sure enough, after lunch I get an email from Jaci's assistant with all the information we need. Even though Lennon is cc'd on it, I still can't help myself from being a smart-ass and forwarding it to her with one line: Here's that itinerary you so desperately needed.—B

She responds right back through our team's instant messaging system.

Lennon_Wells: The lengths you'll go to, to be a smart-ass.

Beckham_Sullivan: Careful, L. The boss can read all messaging correspondence.

Lennon_Wells: Good. Maybe she'll realize what a jerk you are.

Beckham_Sullivan: You're the only one who seems to think so.

Lennon_Wells: Does that mean you're only this pretentious prick with me? I'd say I'm honored but I'm not.

Stupidly I find myself smiling. I rub my hand over my lips, trying to get rid of it.

Beckham_Sullivan: Give me your address.

Lennon_Wells: Whoa, whoa, whoa. Firstly, WHY? Secondly, NO.

Beckham_Sullivan: Because I'll pick you up for our flight.

Lennon_Wells: Ew. No.

Beckham_Sullivan: Ew? Are we five?

Lennon_Wells: I'm not but you are.

Beckham_Sullivan: Real mature. Give me your address. I have a car, I can easily pick you up.

Lennon_Wells: I said no.

This woman is the most infuriating human being I've ever had the displeasure of dealing with. I rub my jaw in an ongoing attempt not to smile.

Beckham_Sullivan: Even you have to admit it's silly for us to arrive separately. We're going to be together the whole trip anyway.

Lennon_Wells: Exactly—I'll use the time in the taxi BY MYSELF to prepare for being stuck with you.

Beckham_Sullivan: You're impossible.

Lennon_Wells: So are you. Besides, like you've already pointed out, you don't know where I live, so picking me up might be completely out of your way.

I pinch the bridge of my nose. How the fuck am I going to survive an entire weekend with this woman? She pushes all my buttons like no one else can.

Beckham_Sullivan: Fine. I'll meet you at the gate then.

Lennon_Wells: Good. See how much easier it is when you see things my way?

I don't respond; I just exit the chat and say a silent prayer that I make it out of this trip unscathed.

Chapter Nine

LENNON

Laurel watches me lug my suitcase to the door. Sure, I might've over-packed, but ever since that one time I didn't and my dress ripped right on the ass, I've refused to be caught off guard without backup clothes.

"I can't believe you're going to Chicago with Beckham." She looks torn between annoyance on my behalf and amusement over the whole situation.

"Believe me"—I push my hair out of my eyes, but it promptly falls back where it was—"I can't either." Giving up, I pull my hair into a ponytail, securing it with an elastic. I'm dressed for comfort in a pair of leggings and an oversize tee. I won't be surprised if Beckham shows up to the airport in a suit, but I can't bring myself to dress up for a flight.

"Well." She pulls me into a hug. "I wish you luck."

"Thanks." I squeeze her back. "I think I'm going to need it." My stomach churns at the thought of being stuck with him all weekend. Being around him leaves me unbalanced. He's someone I used to know so well, but now he's practically a stranger. It's a weird juxtaposition to get used to, because when I look at him, I see the grown-up version of the boy who was my friend. But I have to remind myself that I don't know the man he's become. I suppose I could do a better job of trying to get to know him again, but he's so utterly infuriating.

"You can handle him," she assures me, dragging me from my rambling thoughts.

I'm glad one of us is confident in that fact, because I'm not sure.

The ride to the airport is a quiet affair—in the sense that my driver never speaks to me, but he does spend a fair amount of time yelling at other drivers.

It shocks me that Beckham has a car. Most people I know in the city don't bother, choosing to walk or use the subway. But I guess, since he's such a control freak, it makes sense. I bet his car is just like him, probably something big and intimidating but polished at the same time. Sleek. Maybe a Mercedes or Porsche. I'm betting on a Porsche. Not that I'll ever know.

The driver lets me out, and I text Laurel to let her know I've made it to the airport in one piece. She always worries that something bad is going to happen with the way cabbies drive, so I try to ease her worries.

Inside, the security line is long and arduous, but I eventually make it through. Luckily, there's enough time until the flight that I can stop and grab coffee and a bite to eat near my gate. With extra coffee in my system, I won't be as much of a grump on the flight. It might've been entertaining to go without it just to torture Beckham, but since I'd be punishing myself in the process, I'd rather just have the coffee.

I scarf down my food inside the little café. Since I'm starving, I swear it's the best thing I've ever tasted. For some reason I haven't been able to eat all day, and it's nearly two in the afternoon already. It might be nerves with having to deal with Beckham for a whole weekend, but I would prefer not to give him any credit for making me feel any type of way. Good or bad.

After tossing my trash, I go to my gate and spot a familiar dark head already sitting there waiting. His leg jumps up and down restlessly,

AirPods secure in his ears as he looks around. When he spots me, some of the tension visibly eases from his body. Curious.

"You're late," he says when I plop my butt into the vinyl seat across from him.

I look at the gold watch on my wrist. "No, I'm not."

His jaw clenches, his leg back to bouncing up and down. It's then that I realize he's in a pair of jeans and a T-shirt. Not at all what I expected. And damn if he doesn't look good. The more casual attire makes him look younger, more his age.

"You're later than me," he says after an extended moment.

"Actually," I say as I pull my phone out of my purse, "you're wrong. I grabbed some lunch first, and you weren't waiting here when I checked the gate." He wrinkles his nose, looking mildly appalled that I could've beaten him here. I watch his restless, jumpy movements with a frown. "You still hate flying?"

"No," he scoffs, moving to tug on the sleeves of a dress shirt that he's not wearing. When he realizes his mistake, he rests his arms on the seat.

"The flight should be less than three hours," I say to try to reassure him.

"I know," he bites out, his knuckles turning white where he grips the arms of the chair. "I'm not afraid of flying."

My lips twitch with the threat of a smile. "I never said you were afraid." He makes some sort of garbled noise of protest. "Do you want a snack or something?"

"No!" he practically shouts. "No," he says, softer this time. "No food."

"All right." I riffle through my bag and pull out my own AirPods. "I'll leave you to it, then." I wave a hand at his restlessness. His lips pucker like he wants to say something, but he chooses not to.

I put on the audiobook I've been listening to and do my best to block out the annoyed man across from me. I'm not sure I've ever come across someone quite as surly as Beckham Sullivan. He was adopted by the Sullivans when he was thirteen years old, having been in foster care before then, and I'm sure getting thrust into such a lavish lifestyle overnight involved a rough transition. But the Sullivans are good people—better than my parents, at least.

I pluck out one earphone, and he raises a brow. "How are your parents? I haven't seen them in a while." The last few times I was home, my mother was too busy sending me here and there on horrid dates she'd set up for me, so there was never time to catch up with the Sullivans.

He gives a small jerk of surprise at my sudden question. "Good. They're good."

"I feel bad that I haven't stayed in touch."

His parents were like a second family to my brother and me, especially once they adopted Beckham. Hunter and I spent a lot of time at their house.

His lip curls. "Why?"

"Why haven't I stayed in touch?"

"No, why do you think you need to?"

"Because they were always kind to me. Isn't that reason enough?"

Long fingers tap against his knee. "I suppose." He looks away, and I feel as if I've been dismissed.

Popping my earphone back in, I listen to my book until we're called to line up for boarding.

Once we're seated on the plane, it becomes even more obvious that Beckham genuinely does not like flying. As the flight attendant goes over the safety instructions, a sweat breaks out over his forehead. I'm sure he's had to fly a decent amount with this job, but clearly it hasn't helped him get over his fear.

I don't know what makes me do it, but I slowly inch my pinkie finger over to his closed fist, lightly touching his heated skin to say, *I'm here.*

Ever so slowly he unfurls his fist, his pinkie moving to touch mine.

It's such a little thing, but it feels like a big thing.

When the plane lurches during takeoff, he grabs my hand fully, wrapping our fingers together. Startled, my gaze shoots to his.

"Don't say a word." There's a pleading, vulnerable tone in the way he says it.

I mime zipping my lips and throwing away the key, but that does nothing to stop my growing smile.

The car lets us off at the hotel, and we step out into the mid-August heat. Color is finally beginning to return to Beckham's face. I feel bad for the guy. He spent the entirety of the flight a putrid shade of green, swaying slightly in his seat like he was on the verge of passing out. There was a moment there where I wished I had a better grasp on what to do, whether he should nibble on a cracker or suck on a peppermint, or maybe just close his eyes and pretend he was somewhere else. But then I reminded myself that it wouldn't matter. There's no situation in which Beckham is ever going to listen to my advice.

"I need a drink," he mutters, wheeling his suitcase behind him. He twists his neck back and forth, cracking it loudly.

I follow behind him into the lobby. "Are you sure a drink is a great idea right now?" I can't help but think about how off his color still is. Surely alcohol wouldn't be the best idea.

He looks back at me, a single dark brow arched. *How does he do that? There's no way I'd be capable of moving just one brow.* "It might not be, but it is a necessity." He sighs like he's been carrying around an immense weight and exhaustion is setting in.

I don't protest further, because even *I* feel like I need a drink. Thankfully, we don't meet with the woman we're interviewing until tomorrow. One drink shouldn't be a problem.

The lobby is a mixture of exposed brick, concrete floors, and marble accents. There's a uniquely rustic-modern style that I find myself instantly drawn to. I wouldn't mind curling up on one of the green couches and reading a book—you know, if this weren't a work trip.

We get checked in and ride up together to our rooms, which turn out to be side by side.

Beckham lets out a small, humorless chuckle, shaking his head. "Jaci really took this whole forcing-us-together thing seriously."

"I'm surprised she didn't get us one room," I say, swiping my key card to open the door. "Do you mind if I join you for a drink?"

"It's a free country, Wells," he replies in a weary tone, letting the door fall shut behind him.

I stare at the closed door for a few seconds before letting myself into my own room.

I unpack the contents of my suitcase, grabbing the simpler dress I brought with me just in case I go out at all. It'll certainly look better than the leggings and T-shirt combo I'm currently in.

I hop in the shower and wash up, knowing it'll make me feel better after being on the plane. I touch up my makeup and brush out my hair before slipping into the dress. I don't have Beckham's number, so I head straight down to the lobby bar in the hopes that he's there.

The bar is busy when I reach the lobby, and I guess I shouldn't be surprised with the hour and the fact that this is a city. My eyes scan the area for Beckham, coming up empty. He could've chosen to stay in his room, I guess, or maybe he hasn't come down yet and I'm early.

With a sigh, I approach the bar to place an order. I'm not much of a drinker, but after dealing with his close proximity today, I feel like I need one. I shouldn't let him, but somehow he manages to get under my skin.

A prickle of awareness shoots through me. That's when a heavy, warm arm snakes around my middle and tugs me in close. I'm about to scream, throw up my hands, do *something*, when there's a gentle pinch on my hip and I see that it's Beckham. I relax, feeling foolish. He's seated at the bar, jaw clenched as he stares at someone. He's changed out of his jeans and T-shirt, opting for his typical attire of a dress shirt, tie, and pants.

I swing my head in the other direction, finding an attractive brunette in a sleek pencil skirt and blouse.

"As I was saying," Beckham continues, his voice strained, "I'm here with my girlfriend."

His fingers tap lightly against my belly in a little dance, encouraging me to go along with this.

Smiling, I hold out a hand to the woman. "Hi, I'm Lennon. It's nice to meet you." Then, for good measure, I lean my body into Beckham's spread thighs, my lips grazing his cheek when I ask, "Did you order me anything yet, baby?"

His eyes jump to my lips. He seems almost transfixed for a moment. "Not yet," he murmurs, his thumb coming up to stroke beneath my lip. My whole body feels that touch, and I both hate and love it. How can someone I haven't seen in years still affect me so easily? "What do you want? You can have whatever you'd like."

Something about his tone and the words has me thinking about things that don't involve drinks. I squeeze my legs together, silently cursing my lady bits for feeling anything close to desire for this man.

He might be one of the best-looking men I've ever seen, with that dark hair and intense eyes. He reminds me of a cross between Henry Cavill and Heath Ledger, and apparently that's exactly my type.

I give myself a mental slap. *Stop it! This is a game. That's all.*

I can admit that I'm attracted to him—there's a reason I only had eyes for him as a girl—but I have to keep my wits about me and not let myself get any wild ideas.

I turn back to the woman, having completely forgotten for a moment that she is even here. I'm going to start calling it the Beckham Effect, the symptoms being loss of one's mind.

She gives me an annoyed smile. "I'll let you two enjoy your evening."

She moves away to the other side of the bar. I start to pull away from Beckham, but his hold on me tightens. "Stay."

I look over my shoulder at him. "What game are you playing?" There's no way he's drunk yet. I wasn't in my room long enough for him to get drunk down here, but I can't help but question where this is coming from.

"No game." He reaches for the glass in front of him, ice clinking the sides when he swallows.

"On a scale of one to ten, how drunk are you?" I have to ask, to be certain, though I'm positive there's no way he is.

He glowers, my question having apparently offended him, and he sets the glass back down. "Not drunk."

"Fine, how many drinks have you had?"

He hesitates. "Not nearly enough." He motions lazily to the drink in front of him. Despite his admission, I make no attempt to move from between his thighs. My breath catches when his warm finger snakes up my bare back. That finger latches around the strap of my dress, and he uses that hold to tug himself closer to me. His lips brush the shell of my ear when he whispers, "I like this dress."

He says it in that raspy way where I know what he really means is, *I like this dress, but I'd like it better on my floor.*

My breath stutters between my lips. *What the hell is happening?*

I motion for the bartender and place an order when she stops. I make to move away from Beckham, to give myself room to breathe, because I certainly can't when his front is pressed all up against my back, but he tightens his hold. "Stay, honeybee."

I think I internally choke and die. My pussy clenches at his tone, at those words. I can't believe he's requesting me to stay right here again.

Sweet Jesus, this can't be happening. *I'm* the sober one, not one drop of alcohol having passed my lips yet. I have no excuse not to pull away and put an end to this.

But then my eyes catch on those of the woman across the way as she glares at us, and I realize this is just another game for Beckham so he won't have to deal with being hit on.

When the bartender places my drink down, I swipe it up and drink greedily, hoping it'll help rid me of the sting from the realization he's only using me to stave off unwanted attention.

"Are you that thirsty?" Beckham rasps, dragging his finger down my spine. I shiver in response.

I really wish he'd stop touching me, but I also dread the loss of it. Why is my body so weak for this man?

My brain—oh, my brain remembers the hurt and pain he caused me, but my body has always been attuned to Beckham Sullivan.

"You didn't answer my question." His thumb draws slow circles against my stomach, making me wiggle against him. Despite the fact that we're adults now, that time has separated us, he still manages to know exactly how to touch me.

"Y-yeah. I was thirsty."

He's quiet, but I swear I can *hear* him thinking. He doesn't say anything, just motions for another drink for each of us.

After we each have another drink, he orders us some food. He still hasn't let me move from my spot cradled between his legs, and I've since stopped trying.

"Beckham," I warn when he plays with the strap of my dress, letting it delicately drop over my shoulder. "We're in public."

He flashes a smug grin. "Does that mean you're going to let me dirty you up in private?"

My breath catches at his insinuation. "You hate me." I don't know whether I'm reminding him or myself.

He chuckles like I'm oh so amusing. "I can hate you and still want to fuck you."

Oh my.

Chapter Ten

BECKHAM

I'm drunk, but not *that* drunk.

I know exactly what I'm doing when I pull Lennon into my hotel suite. She's not that drunk either. It's been at least an hour since her last drink. But we're both pretending, using drunkenness as an excuse for what's about to happen. Neither of us batted an eye when I bought condoms from the lobby store.

Lennon's cheeks are flushed, watching as I toss the pack of condoms down on the bed.

This woman is my downfall, and I know, I fucking know, I should stay far away from her.

But right now?

I need to sink my cock into her sweet pussy more than I need my next breath.

I've been keeping her at arm's length ever since I first stepped off that elevator at work and saw her, but that doesn't mean I'm not attracted to her. Lennon has always been beautiful, but somehow, in the years since I've seen her, she's gotten even more gorgeous. It's in the way she carries herself, the confidence she exudes.

I pull out the chair from the desk and swing it around as I loosen my tie. After dropping into the chair, I remove my shoes and set them aside. Lennon watches, her pink tongue wetting her lips. She looks nervous, skittish almost, but she doesn't try to flee. I can see her thoughts warring in her brown eyes. She must have come to some sort of decision, if the way her spine straightens is any indication. Her lips pucker slightly, the unease bleeding from her eyes, to be replaced by lust.

We might not like each other, but that doesn't change the fact that despite everything, there's still attraction beneath the surface.

Seeing her standing there in front of me in her floral dress, I'm transported back in time, to when she wore a similar dress at my parents' party to celebrate the Fourth of July. Her dark hair was pulled into a low ponytail, her lips lacquered in some kind of sweet-smelling gloss.

I had wanted to kiss her so badly that night. I thought about it practically every second of the party. It wasn't until I was tasked with the job of taking her home, her brother distracted by his girlfriend at the time and passing on the responsibility of taking her to me, that I finally got the guts to do something.

I remember walking her up the stairs that led to the massive front door, which had to be at least ten feet tall, since I was already nearly six feet tall at the time. Her skin glowed warmly from the lights illuminating the front of the Wells mansion. I was nervous, my voice shaking as I told her good night.

She was pushing the front door open when I gripped her wrist, halting her movements.

She looked back at me, eyes wide with wonder as I murmured her name. I lowered my head, eyes on her lips. She inhaled the tiniest shocked little noise before I pressed my lips to hers.

It was a soft kiss, just the touch of our mouths, but it went on for a long moment before I stepped back.

I grinned and said, "Good night, Lennon."

Before I got in my car, I turned back to see her fingers grazing her lips.

I smiled the whole way home.

The memories fade away, bringing me back to the moment.

I stroke my hand over my cock through my pants. A breath hisses between my teeth. Fuck, I want her. "Strip," I command, the word raspy thanks to my suddenly dry mouth. But I need to get her naked and under me. Over me. All around me. I need to fuck her out of my system. If I get my fill of her, then maybe she won't be nearly so alluring.

Her lips part, and she seems surprised by the command. "What?"

I loosen my belt. "You heard me. Strip for me."

I can see it—the flash in her eyes, the desire to rebuke my demand. But then something settles inside her, a shiver racking her body, because she *likes* it when I boss her.

Maybe not outside the bedroom, but here, most definitely. That fact surprises me. Little Lennon wants me to take charge.

"You want a show?" she asks, a slight quiver to her voice, but she remains steady.

"Yes," I grit out between my teeth. My erection is almost painful, but I'm determined to drag this out as long as possible.

"Do I at least get some music or something?"

"Jesus Christ, Lennon." Sitting up, I grab my phone and flick through some songs before I settle on one. Arching a brow, I ask, "Does that suffice?"

She nods, slowly swaying her hips to the beat of the song. Playing with the hem of her long dress, she raises it up, exposing her tan, smooth calves. She lets it drop, dancing closer to me. Moving behind me, Lennon crawls her fingers over my shoulders as she sings the lyrics quietly, more to herself than me.

She spins back in front of me, drawing her dress up again. "I have to warn you," she says, fighting an amused smile, "this isn't going to be much of a striptease."

My lips quirk in surprise at her statement, and I squeeze my dick hard enough to almost be painful, but I can't come in my pants like a horny teenager—not when I haven't even touched her yet.

"Why is that?"

"I'm not wearing much under here."

I wet my lips, watching as she peels the straps of her dress down, revealing her small, rounded breasts with perfect brown nipples. Then the smooth slope of her stomach appears. When the dress lands on the floor, she steps to the side, leaving her in only her heels and a tiny nude thong.

Lennon Wells is my own personal hell. I vowed to stay away from her for that reason—but tonight I'm throwing away all sense of logic. All I want is to let her burn me.

She lifts her leg to take off her heel, and I growl out, "Leave them on. Come here." I point to where I want her to stand in front of me. Like a good girl, she listens.

She pauses, waiting for me to instruct her further. I can see the shock in her eyes when I get up from the chair and kneel in front of her. I can't sit still any longer.

I force her to spread her thighs more, and she complies. Moving her thong to the side, I rub my fingers against her shiny pink pussy. "That got you wet, huh, baby? Did you like dancing for me?" I stroke her soft and slow, watching the way her lids fall heavily over her eyes. Her lips pout as she moans, her eyes popping open like she didn't mean to make that noise.

I don't wait for her to reply—I already know the answer. She inhales a surprised breath, her hands grasping my hair when my mouth finds her. She tugs almost painfully, but I don't mind it. It helps ground me, reminding me that she's enjoying this as much as I am. It might be the poorest idea either of us has ever had, but at least we're both here, in this moment. Choosing this. Choosing us.

"Beckham." My name is a prayer. A plea. It's the sound of her asking for more.

Pleasure zips through me at the sound of my name, breathy on her lips. I lick and suck her sweet pussy, looping my hands around her legs to hold her in place until she comes on my mouth. Her hands clutch my shoulders as she bends forward, her hair shielding our faces. She stares at me with hazy, pleasure-filled eyes. It's like she's at a loss for words, maybe even for thoughts themselves.

I'm still on my knees, holding her legs, when she takes my face between her hands and kisses me. It's a long, slow kiss. The kind where you linger, just tasting each other, although I'm sure all she can taste on my lips is herself.

Slowly, I stand, not breaking the kiss, just changing the angle. My hand goes around her throat, using it to guide her backward toward the bed.

Releasing my hold on her, I pull away, taking in her swollen mouth. I can't help myself when I glide my thumb over her plump bottom lip.

"Undress me." I have half a mind to be embarrassed over how shaky my voice sounds, how out of control she makes me, but when her eyes flare with the heat of lust, I choose not to dwell on it.

She doesn't hesitate. Her nimble fingers make quick work of loosening my tie. She struggles a bit with the buttons, but when I go to help her, she swats my hands away. I can't help but smirk down at her. She's oblivious to my amusement, too focused on getting each button. Her tongue sticks out slightly between her lips, her concentration so focused.

When she finally gets the last button, she pushes the fabric impatiently off my shoulders. I shrug it the rest of the way off. My shirt's barely landed on the floor among the disaster of our other garments when she undoes my belt and tugs it through the belt loops.

That's when she hesitates.

Brown eyes slowly meet mine, her hand hovering at the button of my pants.

"Are we really going to do this?"

My heart stutters a beat in my chest. It's fear, I realize. I'm afraid she's going to walk away from this, and right now I need to fuck her more than I need my next breath. But while I might be an asshole most of the time, I'm definitely not the kind of guy who fucks a girl when she's not into it.

Tucking my finger beneath her chin, I rub my thumb over her delectable bottom lip. I think I'm obsessed with her lips. They're full, but not overly so. Annoyingly perfect, that's what she is. "That's up to you."

Her eyes close and she takes a deep breath, clearly sorting through her thoughts. I understand her hesitation. It's not like we've exactly been getting along, and we have a rocky past. Not to mention I don't think either of us expected this when Jaci insisted on us taking this trip.

When she opens them, I can see she's made her decision. Popping the button on my pants, she eases the zipper down while not breaking eye contact. Maybe she's like me, scared that if she blinks or looks away, this will all disappear, some wild figment of our imaginations.

She drags my pants and boxer briefs down my thighs, then sinks to her knees. My cock bobs between us, ready and eager. I clench my hands at my sides when she wraps her small hand around my dick. I have to try to hold myself together. How fucking embarrassing would it be if I blew my load this fast?

She strokes me once, slowly, almost gently, before she does it again, firmer this time.

Every muscle in my body is locked up tight. I need to keep myself in control, to take my time, to drag this out, because this can't happen again.

Tonight, I get Lennon Wells out of my bloodstream once and for all.

When she wraps that sweet mouth around my cock, I almost lose control.

Almost.

I loop her hair around my hand, controlling the speed. She gags when my cock hits the back of her throat, but she takes it. Watery eyes look up at me like she's begging me, daring me to give her more. She doesn't shy away from me, and I shouldn't like that as much as I do. Lennon would do well to be afraid of me. The only thing I'm capable of is hurting her.

"Look at you," I croon, stroking her cheek with my pointer finger, "on your knees for me. Fucking beautiful."

She practically purrs at the compliment.

I know I'm not going to last long like this—as embarrassing as that is to admit, even to myself.

"On the bed," I demand. She lets my dick go, saliva stringing from the tip to her mouth. I wipe her lips as she stands.

A voice in the back of my mind tells me it's not too late to stop this, that I could shove her out of my room without a care in the world. The easiest solution would be to end this before it even begins, but I've never liked taking the easy way out.

I have this chance to fuck her out of my system, and I fully plan on utilizing every minute I have.

Lennon lies down on the bed, legs spread, her bare pussy glistening with wetness.

I swipe up the pack of condoms I bought earlier and grab one. I rip it open, and she watches my movements as I take one out and roll it on. I purposely go slow, trying to calm myself. If she had any idea how much she unravels me, I'd never live it down.

She arches a brow in challenge. "Are you going to stare at me or fuck me?"

"Oh baby," I practically laugh, "you don't want to play this game with me."

I grab her by the hips, pulling her to the edge of the mattress. Her eyes sparkle with mischief. I line up my cock with her entrance, then slip inside her. Inch by inch. Letting her fill up with me. As much as I want to go hard and fast, I want to punish her a bit for that sassy little comment.

She whimpers as I take my time and then wiggles her hips to try to get me deeper, faster. I grab her hips, my fingers digging into her ass.

"Nice try."

"If you don't fuck me like I want, I'll find someone who will."

We both know it's an empty threat, but dammit if it doesn't work on me anyway. Fully inside her, I pull back out and plunge in. Her body quakes beneath me. I've barely touched her, and she's so wound up she's ready to go off. I like that. I like it a lot.

Her eyes start to close, and I reach for her, wrapping my hand around her throat and giving a squeeze. "Open your eyes. Watch me while I fuck you."

Her eyes shoot open, and I wonder if she remembers our first time. I knew she was a virgin, but I was too. Not that I told her. She assumed, like so many others, that I was a playboy back then, but it was far from the truth. Not that I was a complete saint: I had fooled around some, but I'd never been able to bring myself to go the whole way—every time I tried, all I saw was her.

I knew that night that I shouldn't have fucked her, but I did it anyway. I took what didn't belong to me, because I was selfish and I wanted her to be mine.

My thumb rubs her sensitive little nub, eliciting a moan from her. She arches her head back despite my hand still being around her throat. The movement pushes her body closer to mine, her taut nipples brushing my chest. Lowering my head, I press kisses along her breasts before circling my tongue around each of her nipples. She whimpers beneath me, a helpless, pleading little sound.

After pulling out of her, I encourage her to flip over onto her hands and knees, her fine ass sticking up in the air. She turns her head, peering back at me with all that dark hair spilled like drops of ink around her.

I fuck her from behind, thinking that'll be easier—that I really can fuck her out of my system.

The problem is Lennon Wells has been buried so deep under my skin for so long that, now that she's back in my life, there's no getting her out, but I'm going to have to try.

She's a shuddering mess beneath me when she comes, and fuck if she doesn't take me right along with her. I groan, lying on top of her until I pull from her body and get rid of the condom.

When I return to the bed, she's rolled over onto her back. Her chest rises and falls rapidly as she struggles to regain her breath. I lie down beside her, stroking the smooth skin of her stomach.

Breathlessly, she asks, "Again?"

I grab her face, pressing a bruising kiss to her mouth. "Fuck yes."

Chapter Eleven

LENNON

I'm sore everywhere, and from the way Beckham keeps glancing at me with a smirk plastered on his arrogant face, he knows exactly why I can't stop wiggling in the chair. I finally had to escape his room this morning so I could shower and get ready in mine. Anytime I've heard someone refer to "marathon sex," I thought it was an exaggeration, but that's exactly what Beckham and I had. I'm running on only a few hours of sleep. It shouldn't be worth it, but it *so* was. The guy still annoys me, while I also admit it was the best sex of my life.

The woman we're interviewing sits across from us, hopefully completely oblivious to my struggle.

Haley Daniels is in her late thirties, a self-made multimillionaire, and perhaps one of the most interesting people I've had the chance to meet.

Listening to her story, how she grew up with very little but always dreamed big and started her own marketing firm so young, is inspiring. She speaks of the charities her company donates to quarterly and how proud she is that the amount they're able to give is always growing.

Beckham rises from his seat, snapping some photos of Haley while I chat with her—both taking notes and recording the interview.

Shockingly, Beckham throws out his own questions now and then, adding to the conversation. I'm surprised by how insightful some of his questions are. I realize I've been judging him on the surface level too much. There's always more to people than we see.

Our hour with Haley is almost up, so I wind down my questions and begin to pack my things away.

"I have to admit," Haley begins, smoothing her already-impeccable hair down, "I was a tad disappointed when Jaci said she was sending others in her place. I've been friends with Jaci for a while now, but we've never had it work to meet in person, but I must admit you two are lovely. I'll be sure to let her know."

I smile, pleased. This is good. Great, even. This was Jaci's whole purpose in sending us, for us to learn to work together and get along, though I don't think she expected me to go to the extent of riding Beckham's cock. But what our boss doesn't know won't hurt her.

"Thank you, we appreciate it." I extend my hand to shake hers. "Hopefully the next time you're in Manhattan, we'll see you again, and of course, I hope you finally get to meet Jaci in person."

Beckham finishes packing up his camera and says his goodbyes.

As we exit the room, he places his hand on the small of my back. I wonder if it's an unconscious gesture or intentional. There's no telling with him. We take the elevator down to the first floor and head out onto the street. Our hotel isn't too far away, but I *am* wearing heels, so I'm grateful when Beckham gets us an Uber.

He holds out his arm, indicating I should slide in first. He closes the car door behind us, his leg pressed right up against mine. I stifle a gasp of surprise when his hand lands on my thigh, his fingers toying with the edge of my skirt where it's ridden up.

I shoot him a look and he stares right back, not moving his hand.

I figured last night was it for us, but the way he's staring at me says it was only the beginning. My body tightens with anticipation from the promising look in his gaze. I'm still sore, but I can't exactly say I don't want this.

The Uber driver lets us out at the hotel, and Beckham takes my hand, tugging me from the car and heading inside, straight to the elevator.

It's just us two inside, the warm wood-and-citrus smell of his cologne permeating the air. The space feels even smaller with the way he looks at me. There's a glint in his eyes, one that says he's barely holding back. Something inside him must snap because he wastes no time in pressing my back to the wall and kissing the breath from my lungs. I can still taste the hint of coffee on his tongue.

"Beckham." He skims his hands over my body like he's trying to memorize me by touch alone. I don't think any guy has ever managed to make me feel like I'm on fire like he does. My body prickles with awareness in every spot that his scorching touch has held.

The doors slide open, and he practically drags me down the hallway since it's hard for me to keep up in my high heels.

"Your room or mine?" he asks, already reaching for his own key despite not having an answer from me yet.

"Yours."

We've already debauched practically every surface in his room, so we might as well keep at it.

He curses when the door doesn't open with the first swipe of the key card. After another try, it opens, and we stumble inside.

I have a moment of thinking, *I can't believe this is happening . . . again.* Kicking off my shoes, I work my fingers against the slick buttons of my blouse. I'm absolutely insane to be sleeping with Beckham not once, not twice, but . . . how many does this make it at this point? And all in one sordid weekend, to boot.

Laurel is going to wallop me . . . after she wipes her tears of laughter away, of course.

Beckham sets his expensive-looking camera bag down on the desk in the room and strips down to only his dress pants. They hug his thick thighs, molded to him like a second skin. I can't help but wonder if he has them tailored. Surely, he can't walk into a store and buy something that fits that well off the rack.

My breath seems to catch in my throat the longer I look at him.

When I was a girl, he captured my heart, and I realize now that I've unconsciously been comparing every guy I meet to him, which is *insane* since we were so young, just teens when it all fell apart. I guess sometimes we can't help who our heart continues to pine for.

Him working for the same magazine was a shock—a complete bulldozer, if I'm being honest—but maybe this is all a good thing because I can fuck the guy into oblivion and move on. Meet the kind of man I want to settle down with. Get married. Have kids. The whole pretty picture. It's exactly the kind of thing my mom would love for me—especially if she had a hand in picking the guy.

"You're staring," he says, his voice deep and a tad breathless. He squeezes his erection through his pants, his tongue sliding out to moisten his lips.

"So are you," I argue, my blouse fluttering to the ground behind me.

He licks his lips again. "Can you blame me?"

I roll my eyes at him, closing the few feet of space separating us. "Shut up." I grab the back of his head, threading my fingers into that silky-soft hair, and tug his mouth down to meet mine. The kiss is firm but somehow soft—almost gentle when he takes my cheeks in his hands and guides my head back.

God, Beckham can kiss. It's slow, sensual. I feel it through my whole body.

One of his hands skims down my body, settling at my waist to pull me in tighter. I moan into our kiss, turned on by the hard press of his erection, specifically of what it means.

Beckham Sullivan wants to hate me, but his body certainly doesn't.

He kisses me long and slow as my hands explore the planes of his chest. Neither of us is as hurried as we were last night. It's nice, just kissing him, touching him, taking my time to learn his body.

The unhurriedness between us makes this different from last night.

We can't blame this on alcohol, or a spur-of-the-moment bad idea, or an itch that needed to be scratched.

This is deliberate.

"Turn around," he commands in that deep, sexy voice that manages to rattle my insides.

I know later I'll curse myself for thinking anything about this man is sexy, but for now I do as he says.

He slides the zipper of my skirt down, and I wiggle my hips to help him get it off. Leaning in, he presses a kiss to the back of my neck, making my breath catch. His fingers are warm against my back when he unclips my bra. I let it slide down my arms to the floor.

Beckham's hands skim my hips, his fingers toying with the smooth edge of my thong. Then it's gone, too, and he's turning me back around, taking me in.

"Beautiful." He utters the word so softly that I'm not sure he means to say it aloud.

He circles his thumbs around my nipples, my skin pebbling all over at his touch. Dipping his head down, he captures one peak in his mouth, rolling his tongue around the bud. His hands slide down my stomach, grabbing beneath the curve of my ass until he lifts me up and my legs are forced to go around his waist.

His erection presses against my aching core. I can't help myself when I roll my hips against him. I should be embarrassed to be so eager, maybe even worried that he'll use this information against me, but with my body aching with desire, I can't bring myself to care.

"Fuck, Lennon," he curses, his fingers digging into my ass so hard that I won't be surprised if I find bruises come tomorrow. "Keep doing that and this won't last long."

He lays me down on the bed, stripping the last of his clothes. I wiggle impatiently on the bed, almost shy beneath his stare, even though he's already seen everything, and at every possible angle as well.

Bending down, he grabs a pack of condoms from his pants pocket. I didn't even know he'd gone and bought more—I guess we used them all up last night and in the wee hours of this morning. It probably shouldn't please me as much as it does that he was hopeful we'd end up right back here.

"I'm sore," I warn him as he rolls the condom on. "You—please be gentle this time." I blush at my own request. I loved how rough he was before, how it was like he couldn't control himself, but if we're doing this again, then my body definitely needs tenderness.

"Gentle," he repeats, drawing a moan from me when his fingers rub against my throbbing pussy. "I think I can do that."

Gripping the base of his cock, he guides it slowly to my entrance, sinking in until I'm filled with him. His body is lying over mine, close, intimate. My breath catches when our eyes make contact. He quickly looks away, like he's scared I'll see too much there.

But I know what this is—what we are. Temporary.

He doesn't need to worry.

Chapter Twelve

BECKHAM

I pinch my eyes shut as the plane dips toward the ground back in New York. Lennon grips my hand despite my protest that I'm fine. When the plane lands and taxis to the gate, I pull my hand out of hers. I can't have her getting any ideas after this weekend.

It was just sex.

Easy. Simple. No strings.

Sure, it's on me for crossing that line, but that's why I'm going to make sure to reestablish it. When it's time to deplane, I grab my bag from the overhead compartment. Slinging it over my shoulder, I spare Lennon a one-second glance before joining the queue to leave. In that split-second look, I can see her confusion but also her acceptance. That almost pisses me off, which I have to question. Why would I want her to fight me on this?

It's not like I want a relationship with her.

I try not to grumble as people take their time getting off the plane. I'm desperate to put my feet back on the actual ground.

Hustling through the airport, I refuse to look back to see if Lennon is somewhere behind me. I need to get to my apartment and forget she exists.

Until we both show up for work tomorrow.

Outside, I head for a taxi. I had planned to drive to the airport, but after the grief Lennon gave me, I decided it would ultimately be easiest if I just took a car and got dropped off. I'm almost home free when I hear my name somewhere close behind me.

"Beckham."

I should keep moving, carry on with my mission to get out of here as fast as possible, but my feet suddenly stop moving.

"Beckham." Her voice is closer this time. I close my eyes, steeling myself. "Turn around."

Stupidly, I do. She glowers at me, somehow managing to look intimidating despite being so much shorter than me. "Just because I licked your pussy doesn't make us friends."

I wait for the gasp, the rear back, even the slap of her hand against my cheek. It's the only reason I said it. I *want* her to hate me. It's easier that way. At least for me. I'm not allowed to have this—*her*—so the best thing I can do is push her away. If she hates me, then it means she'll stay away.

But Lennon likes to surprise me, so she does none of those things.

"And just because your cock was in my mouth doesn't mean I like you, but we *do* work together, and we need to get along for this project. That means you need to work with me, not against me. That's what this whole weekend was about." She tilts her chin upward slightly, like she's daring me to contradict her. "We don't have to be friends or fuck buddies to do that."

I narrow my eyes on her. "And you think you can do that?"

She smirks at me. "Are you implying that you're so great in bed that there's no possible way I can control myself around you?" She looks me up and down. "That's a lot of faith you have in yourself."

She's trying to get under my skin, and it's working. "You weren't complaining about those multiple orgasms, were you?"

She shakes her head roughly, pressing a hand to her forehead like she needs to steady herself in order to deal with me. I might be offended if I weren't so amused.

"All I'm asking is, when we go into work tomorrow, be civil. I love this job, and I won't let you drive me away from it."

I rear back. That's what she thinks? "I'm not trying to get you fired or make you quit."

"Oh?" she challenges. "Is that so?"

"We have history," I begin with a sigh, struggling to find the words. "And I've let that overshadow things."

She crosses her arms over her chest in a challenge. "You think?"

"I'll do my best to be . . . cordial," I say, settling on the word.

It doesn't appear at first that my statement is going to appease her, but then with a breath, she lets her arms drop. She gathers her hair back and secures it in a ponytail. "I'll see you tomorrow."

And then she pushes around me and steals what was going to be my taxi. A slight smile is plastered on her lips when she looks at me through the window before the car pulls away.

Sure, there's a whole line of other waiting taxis, but we both know that's the one I was going to get, and she beat me to it.

That sneaky little devil.

Cheddar starts yowling before I even open the door. When I finally do, he's standing there with a disgruntled look that seems to say, *How dare you leave me? Give me treats.*

He walks toward the kitchen, tail twitching.

I follow, because I am nothing more than my cat's lowly servant. After dropping my bag onto the floor, I open the cabinet that houses his treats. Cheddar, as chunky as he is, hops onto the counter, meowing like he's afraid I haven't heard him.

I shake the treats into the palm of my hand and give him one and then another. I put the bag away and scratch him behind the ear, lightly scolding him. "I've told you not to jump on the counter."

He blinks his large, yellowish-green eyes at me. We both know he runs this house and merely lets me live here, so with a sigh I walk away from the fight I know I won't win.

I hear his feet plop onto the floor a moment later.

After grabbing my bag again, I unpack and sort out my things between what will need dry cleaning and what I can wash myself. When I was first looking for an apartment, one of my must-haves was an in-unit washer and dryer. Sure, I can pay to send my stuff out, but I don't want to. I guess it's this stubbornness I have, to remind myself that at my core, in my very DNA, I'm not a Sullivan. I wasn't born into the family—to the money. I was a kid from foster care who got lucky. I'm still lucky. And I don't ever want to take that for granted.

That's why, after I get the laundry going and drop off the rest for dry cleaning, I go to see my dad.

It's also why, even though I shouldn't, I tell him more about Lennon—how she lights my world on fire, and how I know if I'm not careful, she'll burn me with it.

I smell her before I even hear her. Her perfume isn't that strong of a scent—it's soft, almost skin-like—but it's all her, so it's no surprise when I look up from the photos I'm editing from the Chicago trip to find Lennon standing there.

Her dark hair is pulled back into a bun at the nape of her neck, a few stray hairs framing her face. The dress she has on is a soft pink color, and dammit if it doesn't look gorgeous on her. It has a high neck, but that does nothing to stop my treacherous mind from straying to dangerous thoughts. About what it would be like to unzip it from the back, kissing her neck and down her spine as each smooth inch is exposed.

"Are you just going to stand there?"

"Oh." She startles like she seemingly forgot where she was. "This is for you. Brendan brought everyone coffee," she says like she doesn't want me to think she got it for me, "so I said I would deliver it to you." She crosses my small office, holding out the cup.

I look at the cup, then my desk, and back again when she doesn't get the message.

She gives an annoyed huff but sets it down on the surface.

"Thanks." My tone implies I don't want to be bothered, but she doesn't seem to get the memo.

"What are you working on?"

With a sigh, I nod my head for her to take a peek at my desktop.

She bends over me, her scent even stronger than before. I inhale because I can't get enough and, apparently, I'm a masochist.

"Wow, these are looking great."

She turns her head, smiling at me. A smile shouldn't make you feel anything, but I . . . I feel *something*, and that something leads to me grabbing the arms of my chair, fingers digging into the leather.

"Thanks."

Is that the only word I'm capable of saying?

I was worried about her being the one to act differently after this trip, when in actuality I should've been concerned about myself. My pants grow tighter—and Jesus fucking Christ, I'm really getting a boner right now, all because she's so close. Talk about inconvenient.

I scoot closer to my desk, and she takes that as a signal to step away, just like I had hoped.

"I'm too busy to get together for lunch today," she says, walking toward the door. Her pencil skirt hugs the curves of her ass. "That's what I wanted to let you know."

"Who said I wanted to get lunch with you?"

She rolls her eyes, exhaling a disgruntled breath. "To talk about the project—we still need to brainstorm ideas, or have you already forgotten in that pea-size brain of yours?"

I fucking love her sassy tongue.

I—what?

No, I most certainly do not love one fucking thing about this woman.

"Tomorrow, then?" I suggest.

"It's a date," she jokes, sticking her tongue out. She flashes me the finger before she's gone, a soft peal of laughter carrying behind her.

I bury my head in my hands—and then I bury myself in my work, refusing to let my thoughts stray to Lennon.

Chapter Thirteen

LENNON

I spot Laurel in the back of the restaurant, her hand flailing to draw my attention.

When I got back from Chicago, she wasn't home. She spent the whole weekend out with some guy. Apparently, both of us needed a hookup. At least hers wasn't with her archnemesis.

Smoothing my hands down the back of my dress, I sit across from her with an excited "Hi."

"I already ordered. I hope that's okay." She lifts her glass of red wine and tips it toward mine.

"I'm not complaining. Food too?" I take a sip of the wine, and God, is it needed. Today wasn't particularly difficult, and I didn't see Beckham much except when I swung by his office to give him coffee, but I did write almost all day, so my body is feeling the hours spent sitting at the desk.

"Yes." She giggles in a way that tells me that, even though I'm not late, this certainly isn't her first glass of wine. "You always get the same thing."

This is true.

The Italian restaurant is just down the street from our apartment and boasts some of the most authentic cuisine in the area. It's a little hole-in-the-wall of a place, not somewhere my parents would ever be caught dead in, not that it matters. But I just know they'd judge the old tile floors and the photos that cover every square inch of wall space.

"What did you do this weekend?" I'm curious what my girl was up to.

She shrugs but wears a sly grin. "Nothing much."

"Laurel," I press, desperate for some juicy gossip.

"I met a guy on Tinder, we had great chemistry, so I stayed the weekend. That's it. I don't plan on seeing him again."

I gasp, practically swatting at her in exasperation. "Why not?"

"I'm not ready to settle down."

"Not even for another hookup?"

Her lips twist in disgust. "No. Do you remember that one guy I hooked up with for a few months? Justin? The sex was great, but around the three-month mark, he started getting clingy and acted like we were dating. I won't make that mistake again. I just want easy fun."

"There's nothing wrong with having fun," I agree, and I can't help the twisted little smile that graces my lips.

Laurel doesn't miss it. "Girl, what have you done—or better yet, *who* have you done?" Then she gasps, hands flying to her mouth as realization kicks in. She doesn't give me a chance to respond. "You were with Beckham!" Her high-pitched shriek is loud enough to earn us a few looks from nearby patrons. "You fucked him, didn't you? You little hussy," she says in a more hushed tone.

I take a sip of wine, feigning casual disinterest. "Maybe."

"Lennon!" She grabs my wrist. "First off, what the hell were you thinking? Secondly, tell me everything. Thirdly, do I need to murder the bastard?" She twists her lips, thinking. "Actually, don't answer the third one. I'll decide on my own once you've answered one and two. I can't have you being an accessory."

"I don't know what I was thinking," I admit, crossing my legs. My feet are aching, and I rub in vain at my exposed ankle for some relief. "We were in the bar, and I was pretending to be his girlfriend—"

She nearly spits out her drink. "Why were you doing that?"

"I was going to explain," I assure her. "Anyway, there was a woman who was being pretty persistent with him, even when he clearly wasn't interested, so when I showed up, he played it off like I was his girlfriend, and I went along with it." I give a shrug like it was no big deal, because at the time it didn't feel like one.

Laurel gapes at me, gesturing wildly with her hand for me to go on. "And?"

"We had a few drinks and slept together. It's no biggie." I smile at the waiter, then scoot my glass aside when he sets down our pasta dishes. The smell of their homemade tomato sauce hits my nose, my stomach rumbling in excitement.

"No biggie?" Laurel scoffs. "Not likely. I need details."

"Well, I mean, we had sex . . . a lot of it, and then . . ." I fight a smile at the memory.

Laurel glares at me. "This is like pulling teeth. You better finish that thought."

"After our meeting, we might've had sex again."

Her mouth opens, closes, opens again. I think I've stunned her to silence. "There was no alcohol involved that time, was there?"

I reach for my wine, trying to hide my smile. "No."

Laurel throws up her hands. "I can't believe this. A part of me wants to cheer you on, because you don't do this kind of thing, but the other part wants to ask you what the hell you were thinking. This is Beckham we're talking about."

I cringe a bit. "I know."

"But the sex was good?"

I hesitate, inhaling a breath. "The best."

"Well." Laurel raises her glass to mine. "Cheers, slut."

I burst out laughing, clinking my glass to hers. "Cheers."

Chapter Fourteen

BECKHAM

I startle awake with the realization that I can't breathe. For a split second I think that I'm dreaming, but I quickly realize that's not the case at all. I am in fact awake and suffocating because my fat cat is lying on top of my chest.

I pick him up and lay him on the other side of the bed with a groan. "Cheddar, what the fuck?"

He just blinks his overly large owlish eyes at me, not even giving me a meow in response.

Groaning, I sit up and press a hand to my aching head. I went out with some colleagues last night and drank too much. I wasn't drunk, but it was enough to make me regret my choices this morning. At least it's the weekend.

After rolling out of bed, I head to the shower, hoping that'll help me clear my head, even if I should really go to the gym. My stomach rolls at the thought of working out. Maybe later.

I wouldn't have drunk as much as I did last night if I hadn't been avoiding the temptation to contact a certain someone. A someone who should not be on my mind as much as she is. We had two working lunches this week, and it shouldn't have been as difficult as it was to resist the urge to touch her. I found my hand hovering at the small of her back while we were in line but quickly pulled my hand away like I'd touched scalding water.

All too quickly I was letting Lennon get under my skin, falling into old patterns. It had to stop.

When I get out of the shower, Cheddar is still snoozing on the bed—the traitor—despite my phone ringing incessantly from where it's plugged in.

Cinching the towel tighter on my waist, I pull the plug from my phone and answer with a gruff "Hello?"

"Ah, my favorite son." My mom's laughter fills the phone. "I haven't heard from you in a few days. I was worried."

"Sorry." I walk into my closet and grab a pair of jeans to tug on. I put her on speaker while I change. "I've been busy." Normally, I talk to my mom daily, but I've been swamped, so the one thing I haven't been able to accomplish is checking in on her.

"I know." She says it in a way that I know isn't meant to make me feel bad but does anyway. It's this soft, resigned tone that says she understands but misses me. "I'm coming to the city today. Would we be able to grab an early dinner?"

It's not that I don't want to see her, but she'll ask questions about work, life, and so on. I *should* tell her about Lennon—she might even know already—but . . .

But I need to see my mom. No matter the number of excuses I can come up with, telling her no would be wrong.

"Sure," I finally say. "Dinner would be great."

"Oh good!" I can actually hear her clap to herself, which makes me feel like a dick for even considering saying no to her. "I'll make reservations and text you the details. Love you!"

Most people wouldn't be able to get reservations anywhere in Manhattan at the drop of a hat, but once she mentions her last name, all doors will be open.

"Love you, too, Mom. See you tonight."

With the conversation over, I head to my kitchen and set out Cheddar's breakfast. It's no surprise when he comes running out of the bedroom yowling at the sound of the kibble in the bowl. Despite the diet the vet has put him on, I don't think he's lost any weight. If I'm forced to reduce his portions again, I'm almost certain he'll plot some sort of grisly murder scenario for me.

I open the fridge and search through what I have for my own breakfast. I'm sorely lacking in food supplies at the moment and need to make a run to the store or else have some groceries delivered. My head gives a dull throb—yeah, delivery it is.

I have enough to make a simple egg sandwich, and I hope like hell the food will help me feel better. I pop some ibuprofen as well. Even though it'll be hours before I meet up with my mom, I know I need to get myself together. Showing up in my current state will only disappoint her.

After sitting down on the couch with my food, something I don't do that often, I put the TV on and scroll through the news channels. Cheddar hops up beside me, rubbing his body against mine.

I glare at him. "Now you love me? You tried to kill me in my sleep."

"Meow."

"Bastard," I grunt, but can't help but smile at the cat. I really do love him. As I scratch behind his ears, he starts to purr, rubbing himself against me for more pets.

A text comes through with the details on dinner. I figure I'll go visit my bio-dad before meeting her. I'm sure if I asked, she'd come with me. Both she and my dad have mentioned wanting to meet him, but I've always felt weird about it. I'm not even sure why that is. I think maybe it comes from the part of me that's never felt worthy of them.

Maybe one day I'll feel different about my worth, but today isn't that day.

◆ ◆ ◆

The restaurant is crowded when I arrive, which I expected—doesn't mean I'm pleased about it, though. With my immense dislike of people in general, I'm not sure why I even live in Manhattan.

I give my name at the front, and then I'm quickly guided to a private room tucked away from everyone else. Holding my breath as I enter, I find my mom seated at the table. I expected my dad to be with her, even though she didn't mention him, but she's alone.

She stands from the table, arms open wide. "My boy."

I wrap my arms around her, and despite the fact that I tower above her, I always somehow manage to feel like a kid again when I hug her. "Hey, Mom." I kiss her cheek, letting her go so she can sit. "How have you been?"

"Good." She carefully smooths her dress. "I'd be better if my only son reached out more." She arches a brow. "You dropped off the face of the earth the past few weeks. It felt like pulling teeth to get you to even reply to a text message. And don't get me started on how you never come home to visit anymore. We miss you, Beckham."

I'm not surprised by her little speech, but I sigh anyway. "I've been busy with work."

"Hmm." She eyes me skeptically. "You've never been so busy before that you ignored me—what's changed?"

"Just a lot going on." *Like Lennon being back in the picture.* My eyes scan the menu. "The magazine is growing rapidly."

She sighs, adjusting her glasses on her nose so she can better give me what I've dubbed "the mom stare." It's a simple look that tells me immediately she's disappointed in me.

"And how is that an excuse to neglect your poor ole mom?" She winks, then removes her reading glasses to set them on top of the now-closed menu. "Surely you have more going on in your life than work? A woman, maybe?"

I'm saved from answering—for the moment at least—by the waiter arriving for our order. He's no more than left when she widens her eyes, a silent reminder that I'm not getting out of answering this question.

"Sorry to disappoint you, but I'm still very much single." Lennon's face pops into my mind, and I push it away. Now's not the time to be thinking of her.

"A boyfriend, then?"

"Mom." I pinch the bridge of my nose. "I'm not gay."

"Okay"—she takes a sip of water—"but it wouldn't be a problem if you were. I just want . . ." She pauses, inhaling a heavy breath that rattles out of her chest. "I want you to be happy, Beckham."

"I don't need a wife to be happy."

"I know, but the problem is you're *not* happy now, either, and don't even try to argue with me." She raises her pointer finger in warning. "I'm your mom and know you better than anyone else. You're going through the motions, day by day, but you're not really living."

"I haven't met the right person." Again, Lennon crosses my mind. I tug at the collar of my button-down. It suddenly feels a bit snug. *Is it hot in here?* "I need a drink," I grumble, rubbing my damp palms on my pants.

Why the fuck am I sweating?

"Your water is right there, dear," she says with a smirk, knowing perfectly well that's not the kind of drink I'm referring to.

"Alcohol—that's what I need."

"Beckham," she admonishes, fighting a smile at my expense. "Are you telling me that my motherly concern drives you to drink? I'm hurt, honey. Besides, how can you meet the right person when you hardly go out, or so I hear?"

"How do you know this shit?"

"Beckham," she warns, and I'm a teenager again, being scolded for vulgar language.

"Stuff," I correct.

"I know people." She smiles over the rim of her wineglass. I'm glad at least one of us has alcohol for this conversation. "I spoke with Deidre Wells this past week." *Oh fuck.* "She was telling me that Lennon is working for a magazine in the city too. What a coincidence. She couldn't remember the name." She taps her lips in thought. "Surely you remember her? You were such good friends with her, and Hunter too."

Yeah, until I took her virginity and fucked everything up.

"I remember her." How could I not? It hasn't been *that* long.

"Maybe you should reach out to her," she suggests casually, her pink nails tapping against the table despite the fact that she's very obviously meddling. "You could give her some advice."

"Advice?"

She smirks like she's caught me. "With the job."

"Right." *Why didn't I order a fucking drink?*

"I have her number. I'll give it to you before we leave. Deidre also said she's single."

"Is that the reason for this dinner? Are you trying to concoct some kind of marriage arrangement between Lennon and me?"

It might be surprising to some, but in the world of the elite, arranged marriages happen often. It's a way to connect names, build more wealth. But even I can't stand the idea of love being reduced to nothing more than a business transaction.

"No." She looks ready to throttle me for even suggesting she would do such a thing. "How could you think that?"

I shrug, reaching for my water glass since it's the only form of liquid I have access to at the moment. "You never made any secret that you liked the idea of us together." I look away before she can see too much in my eyes. The last thing I need is her seeing how I used to imagine a future for us. That version of myself feels like a ghost now. That guy wasn't nearly as jaded.

"I would've been blind not to see how infatuated the two of you were with each other. I couldn't help but root for you."

I give a gruff, irritated laugh. "That ship has sailed."

There was never even a ship to begin with. Not really.

She waves a dismissive hand in the air. "Forget I said anything. I want to know if you plan to actually make it home for the holidays this year." I open my mouth to reply, but she cuts me off. "Don't give me some vague response or lie to me like the past three years, where you said you'd come but canceled at the last second."

"Things came up." No, they didn't. I just didn't want to return to the Connecticut mansion. Being back there is nothing but a reminder of what I'm not and what I can never have.

"Don't lie to me. I may be getting older, but my mind still works. I've let you off the hook, but no more. I want you to come home. We miss you."

I rub my jaw. It's that "We miss you" that gets me. I've never ever wanted to break my parents' hearts, not when they've done so much for me, and they love me like I truly am theirs.

I count to five, taking a deep breath as I do. "Okay. I'll come home for the holidays."

Thanksgiving is still a few months off, but it's enough time that maybe something really will come up this time.

She beams, tears flooding her eyes. "Good. Thank you. It means a lot to me—having you back home."

Her words are like a stab to the heart, and I know that even if something does come up, there's no chance now that I'll let it derail me from making my mom happy.

I hope someone rolls out the red carpet, because I'm coming home all too soon.

Chapter Fifteen

LENNON

I have a love-hate relationship with New York City. I love the constant flow of movement, the vibrancy that exists all around you, but I absolutely hate the rudeness of some people.

Like the taxi driver who nearly hit me but has the audacity to honk at me like I'm the one in the wrong. I flip him the finger and finish crossing the street—on the crosswalk that clearly indicated it was my turn to go—my heart still racing.

The restaurant I'm meeting Beckham at is another block away. Why didn't I pack a change of shoes in my bag? I'd kill for some flats right about now. I love my heels, how they can completely elevate an outfit, but man do my feet hate them.

Beckham texted me this morning to say that he wouldn't be at work until the afternoon, but he would be available for lunch. That was all he said, followed by a link to the restaurant. He didn't give any explanation for why he was out, and I didn't ask. We don't have that kind of relationship, though over the last month we have become . . . not friends, but maybe reluctant reacquaintances?

Finally, I see my destination and book it a little faster since the sooner I get there, the quicker I can sit down and rest my feet.

When I open the door to the restaurant, I find that it's busy with the lunchtime crowd. I shoot a text to Beckham, asking where he's seated.

The dickhead doesn't respond despite the message showing that he's read it.

What a prick.

"Are you looking for someone?" the hostess asks me.

I sigh in relief. "Yes—he's about six foot six, dark hair, and always scowling."

She laughs. "Is he insanely good looking?"

"Unfortunately."

"He's this way." She nods for me to follow, and sure enough, she leads me right to Beckham, seated at a booth. He has his laptop set up and appears deep in thought, his phone resting beside his hand. "Enjoy your lunch." She leaves me alone with the biggest pain in my ass to ever exist.

"You seriously couldn't text back? You have your read receipts on, you know."

He rubs his bottom lip, intent on whatever is on his computer screen. "I know."

I roll my eyes. "This isn't our usual place." I cringe at my words, because in what world do Beckham and I have a usual place?

"No, it's not."

"Why here?"

He gives me an exasperated look. His eyes are shadowed like he didn't get much sleep. Even his shirt is slightly rumpled. This isn't the put-together Beckham I'm used to. It makes me curious about what went on this morning that had him unable to come to the office.

"I was in the mood for something different. That's why."

I roll my eyes yet again, because why does he have to be so rude about everything? I open the menu and search for something that sounds good.

"Where were you this morning?" I know I shouldn't ask, but I'm nosy.

He closes his laptop, crossing his arms on top of the table and then hunkering down, like he's about to fill me in on some kind of juicy secret. I find myself leaning closer to him.

"Let me ask you something." He crooks his finger, urging me nearer. Stupidly, I follow the gesture until we're practically face to face. "Why do you think you deserve to know?"

I bristle. "It's not about deserving. It was only a question." I rearrange the cutlery on the table to busy my hands. My mother used to reprimand me for my fidgety nature whenever I became nervous or annoyed. It's a habit I've never been able to break, and one that she'd comment on if she saw it now.

"Sure it was." His sarcasm isn't lost on me. He sits back in the booth. "We're not friends. Remember that."

"God, you're so full of yourself." It annoys me to no end how impossible he can be. Even a simple question makes him snappy.

"I am." His long fingers tap lightly against the table.

"At least you're self-aware."

The waitress stops by for our drinks, and Beckham surprises me by ordering an appetizer.

"Fried pickles?" I ask after the waitress has left.

"They're the best. I can't come here and not get them."

I try to stifle a laugh; at least he's acting a tad more civil. Maybe he's just hangry, and the promise of food has him feeling better.

"Anyway, we need to talk about the project. I hate to tell you, but I think we need to scrap all the ideas we've had so far." It's been tough, since Jaci is giving everyone a lot of leeway for the proposals, wanting to see where our creativity takes us. "Not that these are bad," I go on while he stays silent, "but they're not strong enough to stand out."

He pinches the bridge of his nose like he already has a headache forming. "Unfortunately, I agree with you." I school my features, trying not to show how surprised I am. I must fail spectacularly, because he says, "Don't look so shocked."

I tuck my hair behind my ear, having chosen to wear it down today in loose waves. "I didn't know you were capable of agreeing with anything I had to say."

His lips twitch with an almost-smile. "It's only because it was what I was going to say. That's why I wanted to come here instead."

"Huh?" I'm genuinely confused as to what he means.

"I needed the fried pickles to get me through in case you threw a fit."

"Ah, you've got jokes."

He shrugs. "Sometimes."

After the waitress sets down our drinks, my hands reach greedily for the sweet tea. I don't normally drink it, but for some reason I find myself craving it.

"Iced tea?" Even Beckham notices. Huh. "You never drink that."

He's not wrong. It's always coffee or water or even wine for me.

"I wanted to be different today." *Do I sound as defensive to him as I do myself?* "Your fried pickles inspired me."

"Are you guys ready to order?" the waitress asks, interrupting our conversation. Stupidly, I completely forgot she was there.

Beckham gives me a questioning look, and I nod. He places his order first, a cheeseburger, and I follow behind him with chicken and waffles.

"You're going all kinds of southern on me today, honeybee." He squeezes his eyes shut, and I have no doubt he's silently wishing he could take back that slipup.

"You picked this place," I remind him, choosing not to call him out on his use of the pet name. I'm not in the mood for a sparring match with him.

"That's true."

He opens his laptop, then fiddles with some things before turning the screen to face me. "Do any of these mood boards resonate with you? I work better with visuals." I swear there's a light stain of blush blooming on his cheeks, but it's hard to tell with the scruff there.

I can almost hear my dad scoffing at Beckham's facial hair while declaring that real, dignified men shave their beards. I happen to like the overgrown-stubble look on him. It gives him a roguish appearance. Not that I'll ever admit that.

I scoot his laptop closer, taking my time to carefully consider each one. There's five in total. I go back and forth before zeroing in on one. "I like this one."

He smiles—it's small, but it still counts. That somehow feels like such a victory.

I made Beckham Sullivan smile. I'm winning at life.

"That's my favorite too."

Before we have a chance to discuss it, the waitress is placing his appetizer on the table.

"Those look . . ." My lips curl.

"Delicious?"

"Artery clogging."

He grabs one, dipping it into some sort of house-made sauce. "Don't let that scare you away." He waves one in front of me. "Try it." He takes a bite. "Mmm, delicious."

I snag one of the pickles, following his example of dipping it first. "That's actually really good," I admit, chewing slowly as I try to savor it. "Like, *really* good."

He chuckles, his lips quirking into the briefest of smiles before he schools his features once more. "I tried to tell you."

"How'd you ever come to find this place?" I dip the pickle again. If he says anything about double-dipping, I might smack him. After everything we did just over a month ago, I think double-dipping should be the least of our concerns.

"Brendan recommended it, so I checked it out one day."

"Do you come here a lot?" I'm not sure why I keep asking him questions, why I even want to have a normal conversation with him.

"Sometimes."

I wipe my greasy fingers on a napkin. "What does that even mean?"

"At least twice a month—does that specificity suffice for you?"

I swallow a sip of tea, trying not to smile. I know he's not trying to be funny, but I can't help but be amused by him. "Yes, thank you."

We get back to brainstorming, and it isn't long before our meals are delivered. I'm not as hungry as I was, thanks to the fried pickles, but that doesn't stop me from digging in. I skipped breakfast this morning—not on purpose—since I slept through my alarm, and it didn't leave me with enough time.

Beckham watches me with barely concealed amusement. I refuse to let him bother me.

I'm almost halfway through my chicken and waffles when the nausea hits me. It comes out of nowhere, but it's so instant and persistent that I'm afraid I might projectile vomit all over the table and Beckham.

No. Oh no.

I gag, slapping a hand to my mouth.

"Are you—"

I'm gone, running from the table blindly toward bathrooms I don't even know the location of.

I'm not going to make it. I'm not going to make it. I'm not—

Restrooms. There in the corner.

I make it in the nick of time, my knees slamming against the tiled floor. I try not to think about how dirty it might be. Now's not the time.

Everything I just ate ends up inside the toilet.

I've had food poisoning one other time, and it was hell. My stomach cramps, trying to expel every last bit of what I assume is undercooked chicken. It *looked* fine, but chicken can be finicky.

The bathroom door creaks, and I feel bad for the poor woman who just needs to pee and is going to have to deal with the memory of me sprawled in an open stall, expelling everything I've ever eaten in my whole life. At least that's how it feels. Already my body is growing damp with perspiration. My shirt clings to my chest, and I try to pull it away, but it's a feeble gesture.

"Lennon?"

What the hell? The last thing I expected was for Beckham to brave the women's restroom—and to what? Check on me? Has hell frozen over?

I can't answer him, because more bile rises in my throat.

The sink squeaks, water running, and then a moment later, a cold, damp paper towel is pressed to the back of my neck, my hair gathered in his large hand.

I blink bleary eyes over my shoulder at him. "What are you doing?" Even sick, there's no missing the surprise in my voice.

"I don't know," he answers honestly. He's squatted beside me, black slacks hugging his thick thighs. "You looked like you needed help. Here I am."

I don't get a chance to respond before I'm heaving again. My stomach hurts so bad with the way it feels, like it's squeezing against itself.

Beckham shuffles beside me, my hair still held in his grip. I realize he's pulling out his phone.

"Hey, Jaci. Yeah, no, sorry. I wanted to let you know I won't actually be in today. Lennon won't be back either. We met for a work lunch, and she has food poisoning, so I'm going to take her home and make sure she's okay. Yeah. All right. See you tomorrow."

"You're not . . ." I press a hand to my head. Ugh, am I going to get a headache now too? It feels like my brain is pulsing behind my eyelids in a desperate attempt to break free. "You don't need to take me home."

"I know I don't, but I am. Give me your address—I'm getting us an Uber." He's so sure about it, not a hint of hesitation.

"No."

He stares at me, some sort of silent battle of wills. Who will give in first?

"I'm not letting you get home on your own like this. Now's not the time to be your usual stubborn self." He looks amused, which only makes me want to slap him.

"I'm not stubborn, you—" I turn away from him, back to the toilet bowl that has now become my new home, because there's no way I'm letting Beckham take me to my apartment.

I'm never eating chicken again. Not for as long as I live. It has betrayed me in the gravest of ways.

"Address?" he prompts when I'm no longer puking my guts up.

I grumble out the location. He wins the battle. Someone crown him the victor.

He smirks the whole time he puts in the request for an Uber. I've never wanted to kick a man in the balls before, but I have a feeling I'd get great enjoyment out of it with Beckham.

He sits quietly with me in the bathroom, never letting go of my hair. "The car is almost here." I haven't been sick again, so I say a prayer that I'm in the clear. For now, at least.

Beckham helps me up. The only reason I accept his help is because my body is aching from being on the floor, and my knees are throbbing. They didn't appreciate that bruising hit they took on the tile.

"Stay here," he says with a forceful nod. "Just in case. I'm going to pay our bill, and I'll be right back."

"Okay." I slowly shuffle to the sinks to wash my hands.

He could totally abandon me here. This could all be a ruse, but somehow, I think he actually wants to help me. I lean my back against the wall, breathing in through my nose, out through my mouth. I have no idea if that's the proper way to do it, but it seems to help ease the nausea slightly and quiet the pounding in my head.

It's not long before he returns with a to-go box, a paper cup of some sort of drink, and an empty plastic bucket that looks like it's probably meant to store food.

He notices me looking. "It's in case you get sick on the way." Well, that was thoughtful of him. "And this is ginger ale. It'll help your stomach." He wags the cup, ice sloshing around. I take it, sipping hesitantly. "The car should be here in a minute. Let's go. I don't trust the guy not to drive away."

"What's that?" I point to his bag.

He takes my free hand, guiding me out of the restroom. "My food. I'm not the sick one, and I'm hungry."

I'd laugh if I didn't feel so shitty.

Outside, he checks his phone and searches the street. "He's almost here. How are you feeling?"

"Better. At least I don't feel like I'm going to throw up all over your shoes."

His eyes widen in horror. "Please, don't. I like these."

"I could buy you new ones."

"But I like these." He pouts in a petulant way.

I cross my arms over my chest. "Has anyone ever told you that you're dramatic?"

He rubs his jaw, still looking for the car. "No, just you." He must spot it, because he reaches for my elbow and starts tugging me down the street. "This is it," he says, opening the back door to a red Honda Civic.

He greets the driver and waits for me to get in first. I don't think it's meant to be a gracious, gentlemanly gesture. He's probably afraid that if he doesn't get me in the car first, I'll run away from him. Normally, that wouldn't be a wrong assumption, but considering how I feel, there's no chance of me taking off.

We don't speak during the drive. I sip the ginger ale, while Beckham eyes me for any signs that I'll need the plastic bucket.

I do get a tad nauseous again on the ride, since our driver is a typical New Yorker who thinks traffic laws don't exist.

By the time the car stops near my building, my head is spinning. I feel almost faint. I'm reminded again that I didn't eat much today, and then I threw up the little I had. There's no chance that I'll risk trying to have anything right now, so I'll have to suffer through.

After offering me a hand, Beckham helps me out, his arms going around me when I teeter on my feet. "Are you okay?" His breath is warm against my forehead, the question almost a gentle caress.

I clutch the sleeves of his shirt, steadying myself. "I think so."

"Where exactly is your apartment? This way?" He points down the street.

The urge to tell him I don't need his help is strong, but since I really do feel like shit, I don't have it in me to argue. "Yeah, this way."

If you'd told me this morning that I'd willingly be leading Beckham to my apartment, I would've laughed. But here we are. The universe has a weird sense of humor.

We fall into silence again until we reach my door, where I have to dig through my purse for my keys.

"Give it here." He takes my purse and gives it a shake, after which my keys jingle at the bottom. He sticks his hand in and comes out with my assortment of keys on a pink puffball chain. "Nice key chain." I can tell he's trying not to laugh.

I lean my head against the wall beside the door. "Shut up."

After he unlocks the door for me, I push past him and head inside. Luckily, Laurel and I are in the habit of doing a nightly reset, where we straighten things up and wipe down the counters before bedtime, since neither of us likes to wake up to a messy apartment.

"This is nice," he remarks as he closes the door behind us. "Smaller than I expected."

"What did you expect?" I sip the last of the ginger ale before emptying the ice in the sink.

"Figured Daddy would've gotten you a penthouse."

I shrug as I head to the bathroom to brush my teeth. "He would have, but I didn't want that." Beckham lingers outside the bathroom door. I narrow my eyes on him. "What are you going to do? Stand there and stare at me while I brush my teeth?"

He grins, leaning against the doorway with crossed arms. "Sure."

I try to ignore him as I brush my teeth, but I can feel him watching me. After spitting out the toothpaste, I rinse my mouth and turn to him. "You can go. I'm feeling much better."

"Nah." He leans away, letting me exit the bathroom. "I think I'll stay." He says it in a light, teasing way, but I don't miss the genuine worry in his eyes.

Lucky for him, I don't have the energy to fight. "Fine. Make yourself comfortable." I gesture vaguely around us.

"Why do I have the feeling that was sarcastic?" He crowds behind me at the fridge while I grab a bottle of water.

"Because it most definitely was." I twist the cap off and gulp down some water, then sink onto the couch and wrap a blanket around my shoulders. Beckham takes a seat in the chair, looking way too big for it. He wiggles around, trying to get comfortable. "Seriously, there's no need for you to stay."

The last thing I need is him sticking around out of some sort of pity. It's not his fault the chicken was bad.

He sighs, leveling me with one of his infamous glares. "I'm fine right here."

"Suit yourself." I won't say anything else about it. Let him suffer in the chair if he's going to be stubborn about it.

"Do you care if I reheat my food?"

I reach for the remote and turn the TV on. "Knock yourself out."

He strides into the kitchen for his lunch while I search for something to watch. I also send a text to Laurel letting her know what's going on.

Laurel: WHAT?!

Laurel: You can't just drop that information on me like it's nothing.

Laurel: He's in our apartment?

Me: Yes. He won't leave.

Laurel: Do you want me to come kick him out?

Me: I can handle him.

All of a sudden, a horrendous smell hits my nose. "What is that?" I shriek, gagging while I struggle to disentangle myself from the blanket.

"I'm microwaving my burger," he answers, raising his hands innocently when I look at him over the back of the couch.

"It smells like it's rotten!" I lunge for the bathroom toilet.

I don't know how it's possible that I still have anything left in my stomach, but I do. I'm never letting Beckham pick another lunch spot again.

"My burger definitely isn't rotten," he remarks, his voice raised from the kitchen. There's obvious confusion in the way he says it. "Are you sure you don't have a bug or something?"

I flush the toilet, then pick myself back up to wash my hands and brush my teeth again.

"I don't think it's a bug. I really think it's food poisoning." I press a hand to my clammy forehead. Exhaustion settles deep in my bones.

"Lennon," he says carefully, like he's treading dangerous waters. His steps grow near, and then he's right at the door. "You didn't eat my burger—it was the smell that made you sick?"

My eyes widen in horror, because I might be loath to admit it, but he's right.

I lunge past him, digging through the blankets and pillows on the couch for my phone.

No. There's no way. We were *safe*.

"No, no, no, no," I chant, finally locating my phone and bringing up my app.

"What the hell is going on?" He suddenly looks panicked and even more out of place in my apartment than he did before. I turn my phone around for him to see. "Is that supposed to make any sort of sense to me?"

"My period," I practically cry, collapsing onto the couch. "It's late."

Chapter Sixteen

Beckham

I have to be in an alternate dimension.

It's the only plausible explanation as to why I'm in a pharmacy a corner away from Lennon's apartment, pacing the fucking family-planning aisle of all things. They should really have a family-accidents aisle for this sort of thing.

I tug at my hair for at least the hundredth time since Lennon shoved me out of her apartment with a demand to, and I quote, "Bring back a pregnancy test—all of them, not just one."

"Jesus Christ," I mutter to myself, picking up another box.

Why are there so many?

Do you really need this many options to tell you whether you're pregnant? Why can't they make one that gives a simple yes-or-no response? Doesn't that seem reasonable? Instead, there are some with smiley and frowny faces, others with lines, some that tell you five days before your missed period, and—

"Sir, do you need help?"

I turn to find a middle-aged woman with an employee badge. There's a split second where I almost drop to my knees in front of the woman and hug her legs, because she's my hero right now.

"I need . . ." I gulp. What I need is to wake up and realize that all this is some sort of elaborate dream, but I don't see that happening anytime soon. "Some of these." I waggle my fingers in the vicinity of the tests. "I don't know what to get."

"Well," she says, looking me up and down, "I don't think you're worried about cost, so ignore these. They're not very reliable." She motions to a few boxes that I already decided look questionable.

"I need reliable. I need a definite yes or no."

"I'm taking it this was unplanned?" She arches a brow, but there's no judgment emanating off her.

"Definitely."

Lennon. Pregnant. *Maybe* pregnant. With my . . . kid.

That's hard to wrap my brain around. I mean, I assume it would be mine if she's pregnant. Could it be someone else's? That thought makes me irrationally angry, which is absurd since if she's knocked up and I'm not the dad, then it means I'm off the hook. Shouldn't that be what I want?

I don't have time to sort out my feelings right now.

"Get these," the woman, Susan, according to her name tag, suggests. She pulls the box off the shelf and drops it in my basket. "There's five in there, just in case you want more than one."

"Is it easy to use?"

She motions for me to follow her to the registers. "All your lady friend has to do is pee in a cup, dip, and wait."

"Yeah, but does it spell it out plainly? Those lines look confusing."

"It'll say *pregnant* or *not pregnant*. Nothing complicated about it."

I let out a breath, suddenly feeling exhausted. It's already been a hard day—my bio-dad isn't doing well, so I spent the morning checking in on him.

"Thank you. For your help."

Susan steps behind the register, looking amused. "I get the impression you don't say thank you a lot, so you're welcome." She checks me out, wrapping the box in a white plastic bag before she hands it to me. "Good luck."

"Thanks," I say, even though I don't know which way she's hoping it'll go. I don't even know which way I want it to go. I'm not sure my thoughts have ever been so jumbled.

Pregnant.

Lennon might be pregnant.

Holy shit.

I speed-walk back to her place, then press the buzzer for her to let me in.

Perspiration dots my forehead, and it's not even hot out. That's how unhinged I am right now.

Lennon already has the door open, waiting for me. Her eyes are red, like she's been crying. That brings me up short. Sure, I've been freaking out, too, but I never stopped to think about what she might be feeling.

"Is that it?" She nods to the bag in my hand.

I hold it out. "Yeah."

She takes it eagerly before booking it to the bathroom. I lock up behind me, and even though I should give her space, I find that I can't. I stand outside the closed bathroom door.

"You know," I say, rubbing my jaw, "I never thought I'd spend so much time with you in and around bathrooms."

"Shut up, Beckham."

"Noted." I mime zipping my lips, even though she's not there to see it.

I wait, listening through the door as she flushes and washes her hands. When the door opens, I nearly fall inside.

"Jesus, were you listening to me pee like a creeper?" Her nose crinkles in mild horror.

I ignore her creeper comment. "What does it say? Are you pregnant?"

"We have to give it five minutes." She walks past me to the small kitchen and grabs a fresh bottle of water. She unscrews the cap, rolling the small plastic top around on the counter before taking a tentative sip. Wiping her mouth with the back of her hand, she stares out the window like she's searching for some sort of answers there.

"I have to ask . . . ," I start. She looks away from the window, making reluctant eye contact with me. "Am I . . . would I be the father?"

She looks halfway tempted to chuck the open bottle at me. "What kind of question is that?"

"Hey!" I throw my hands up in defense. "I'm not judging, if that's what you think. I don't know what kind of sex life you have."

"A pretty dry one," she mumbles. "Before you, it'd been over a year. Not that it's any of your business, and no, there's been no one after." She places her palms on the stone counter, her shoulders practically curling in on themselves. She starts to shake, and I realize she's crying.

She's fucking crying.

What the hell am I supposed to do with a crying woman? I'm not cut out for this kind of shit.

"I . . . um . . ." I stuff my hands in my pockets.

"You don't need to say anything." She sniffles, grabbing a paper towel to dot her eyes. "This is just—" She throws her hands up in a *What am I going to do about it?* gesture. "Life, I guess. It's ironic, hilarious, and sometimes downright cruel."

My jaw tics at that. I don't know why I take offense to her words. It shouldn't matter. I know I haven't been the most accommodating person for her, but I don't want her to view me as the villain in her story either.

For once in my life, I'm at a loss for words, so I choose to keep my mouth shut instead of letting something moronic slip through.

Lennon glances down at her phone. "It should be ready." Pushing her hair back from her forehead, she starts for the bathroom. She comes to a stop before swinging around and colliding with my chest, since I followed her. She backs up, looking down at her feet. "Will you look first?"

I gape at her. "You want me to check it?" I point at my chest.

She nods, her top teeth digging lightly into her plump bottom lip. "Go look and tell me."

I hesitate for a moment, in case she changes her mind. Leaving her standing by the couch, I walk to the bathroom like I'm headed to the gallows.

The problem is, I'm not sure which outcome I'm dreading the most. Surely, the answer should be obvious. I shouldn't want Lennon to be pregnant. We're not together, we hate each other, we're young—there's an endless list of reasons why this would be bad.

But some small part of me is wondering, *What if?*

I've never really contemplated the idea of being a dad. Marriage, babies, the whole shebang never crossed my mind, and now I'm standing before a crossroads.

One where my life is going to either stay on the path I envisioned or completely deviate to a different, uncharted route.

"Beckham," she pleads, covering her face with her hands, "look at it."

Her words remind me that I still haven't breached the threshold.

I take that final step into the bathroom and peer down at the tiny stick that holds our fate.

And clear as day, spelled out plainly just like dear ole Susan knew I needed, we have our answer.

Chapter Seventeen

LENNON

I've spent the past two weeks in a rotating state of shocked and ill.

Morning sickness is a bitch, and so is hiding it from my best friend. I'm lucky that she's a deep sleeper and too focused on getting ready for work to notice me puking my guts up. It helps, too, that I've always played music in the bathroom when I get ready in the mornings, which masks any sounds she might hear.

As I hustle down the street toward my doctor's office, I'm caught off guard by the tall, frazzled man getting out of a taxi.

Stopping dead in my tracks and nearly getting knocked down because of it, I gape at my baby daddy, who glowers at me.

"What are you doing here?" I stutter, coming out of my shock.

"You told me you had your appointment today, and I said I wanted to be here."

"I . . . I never told you where my doctor was." He has me rattled, showing up like this. It's like seeing some sort of mirage in the desert, but instead of water, it's a handsome man on the streets of Manhattan.

He rolls his sleeves up his forearms, those blue eyes of his rendering me immobile. "I have my ways."

I tug my purse back onto my shoulder. "Are you in the Mafia?"

He snorts. "Not likely. Now, are we going in, or do you want to stand on the street all day?"

I still can't wrap my head around Beckham showing up here. Does he have a tracker on me? Maybe he slipped an AirTag in my purse or something? I should probably check later. I wouldn't put it past him.

I don't have time to dwell on those thoughts, because I do need to head into the building. I've been to this practice before, but it's my first prenatal appointment, the one to confirm my pregnancy and I guess see the baby? I have no clue when it comes to this kind of thing. My experience with anything baby is zilch. That makes all this even more terrifying. I've already ordered some books on parenting, but I doubt that'll be enough to prepare for what it's actually like.

"All right." I sigh, like his presence is a complete hindrance. Though, deep down, I think I might be glad to have his support. I haven't told anyone yet. Definitely not my parents or my brother. I figure I'll tell Laurel after this appointment. As for my family . . . I want to put that off as long as possible, not because I'm ashamed but because I don't want to hear their disappointment. "Let's go."

Beckham falls into step beside me, not saying a word. I can feel his irritation, though, and it manages to make me feel bad enough that I utter a surprising apology. "I'm sorry. I should've given you the address."

"Yes," he agrees, "you should have. Neither of us asked for this, but we'll handle it. Together."

Hearing him say that warms my heart but takes me by surprise at the same time. Beckham is utterly confusing.

We reach the building, and I expect him to hold the door open for me, but he flashes me one tiny smirk before going in first and letting the heavy door fall shut behind him.

Prick.

I'm pretty sure this stuff is a game to him now.

I don't show any emotion, appearing unbothered by the gesture just to ruffle his feathers.

Inside, we take the elevator up in silence. He follows me down the hall and into the office.

It's a sleek and modern facility—I remember thinking the first time I came here for my annual exam that it seemed like the kind of doctor's office you'd expect to go to for Botox, not to have your vagina probed. Abstract paintings of babies and pregnant women line the walls. I'm not sure I'd even know that's what the art was if it weren't in an OB-GYN office.

"You can go sit." I point to a chair, hoping he'll listen and park his butt. Luckily, he does, allowing me to check in and give myself a moment to regroup after his surprising appearance.

"Hi." The woman behind the reception desk smiles. "Wells, right?"

"Good memory," I say, hoping she can't detect the nervous quiver in my voice. "Lennon Wells."

"Ah, right here. It looks like you already filled out the forms we needed for this visit online and we have your insurance on file from last time, so I'll get you checked in. Take a seat, and the nurse will call your name when they're ready."

"Thank you."

I turn to see where Beckham has snagged a place to sit. He holds a parenting magazine delicately between his fingers, like he's horrified he's even touching it.

Bracing myself, I join him. "Whatcha got there?" I tap the magazine.

He exhales a shaky breath. "Just some light reading." He shows me the cover with an expecting mother and headlines saying things like, What You Should Know about Breastfeeding to Do It Right, Is Your Baby Sleep-Regressing? We Have the Tips and Tricks You Need!, and How to Baby-Proof Your House for Your Bundle of Joy!

"Sounds stimulating."

He snorts, tossing the magazine onto the coffee table with the others. "Stimulating is how we got into the predicament in the first place."

He's not wrong. I press my hand to my flat stomach, marveling at the fact that there's a whole tiny human in there. I always wanted to be a mom, but later, after I lived *my* life and settled into work, found a great man, and got married, then lived *our* life for a while before adding a baby to the mix.

I look at Beckham, taking in his profile—the sharp jaw dotted with stubble, his long lashes and full lips. This is the man I'm having a baby with. Teenage Lennon would be jumping up and down over this news; adult Lennon feels . . . well, I don't really know how I feel.

I think I'm still in too much of a state of shock to be able to process my feelings on the whole situation yet.

"I guess this isn't what Jaci intended when she sent us on that trip," I remark.

He surprises me by chuckling. "No, I guess not. It's not what we expected either." He turns to look at me, briefly giving me a flash of the worry and fear in his eyes before it's gone. Stifling another laugh, he says, "How much you want to bet those condoms from the hotel were expired or something? I didn't even think to check them."

"It doesn't matter how it happened now." I grip the arms of the chair, my nerves settling in. "Regardless, we're in this situation." I pause then, giving him a contemplative look. "You know, I'm kind of surprised you didn't suggest I just . . . take care of it."

He rears back like I've slapped him. "Do you think so little of me? I mean, I'd support your decision, but I would never pressure you to do *that*."

My breath is shaky when I exhale. "You realize this is forever, right? No matter what, we'll always be in each other's lives."

He wets his lips, leaning back in the chair. "Yeah, I know." He almost looks more scared about that fact than us having a whole child. I should probably be offended, but I'm too stressed to care.

"Wells?" a nurse calls out a few minutes later.

This is it. Even though there's no doubt I'm pregnant, this confirmation seals it, and there's no going back.

I stand up slowly, Beckham rising alongside.

It shocks me beyond belief when he takes my hand, giving a small squeeze like he's trying to remind me that I'm not alone.

Together we make our way across the room to the waiting, smiling nurse. Beckham releases my hand when I have to step on the scale for my weight. After, I'm sent to the bathroom for a pee sample; then we're led to an exam room, where I answer more questions from the nurse. She takes my blood pressure and leaves us for me to take off my pants.

Beckham clears his throat from the chair in the corner. "Why do you have to . . . um . . . depant?"

I snort at the way he phrases it. "I'm assuming they're planning to do a transvaginal ultrasound." I reach for the button on my jeans.

"A what?"

He doesn't look away as I undress, but what's the point? He already knows what I look like naked.

"It's an ultrasound they put inside you when the baby is small." At least that's what the Google search told me when I looked up what I should expect for my first appointment.

"That's horrifying." He actually looks a bit pale at the thought.

I grab the sheet to cover my bottom half and sit down. "*That's* horrifying? You know your penis has been in there, right?"

He shakes his head. "Don't ever call my cock a *penis* again—that's offensive."

"That's the correct term." I find myself smiling. *Why is bantering with him so much fun?*

"A penis is—"

There's a knock on the door, and he shuts up.

"I'm ready," I call out.

The door swings open, revealing my doctor. Dr. Hersh is in her forties with dyed bright-red hair that usually has streaks of another color—this time it's purple. I could never pull off the look, but she does it effortlessly.

"A penis is?" she prompts, fighting a smile. The nurse enters behind her and closes the door.

Beckham blushes, adding to my previous amusement.

"How we got into the predicament in the first place," I answer for him, and he shoots me a glare. "What?" I shrug, the paper sheet beneath me crinkling. "It's true, and it's not like she doesn't know where babies come from."

Dr. Hersh laughs, her nurse also stifling a laugh while Beckham covers his face.

The doctor scoots over to my side on her rolling stool. "The urine test came back positive. Since you're here, I'm going to send in my ultrasound tech to check things out and make sure everything looks good. Overall, how have you been feeling?"

"Sick," I admit, biting my lip. "I know that's normal, but it sucks. Sometimes it hits me during the day too." I try not to think about how the smell of Ethan's tuna sandwich sent me running for the bathrooms only a day ago while we were at work.

She nods emphatically. "That's how it is for some women. If it gets worse and you can't make it through tasks, please reach out to us, and we'll talk about what we can do."

She runs through some more questions and gives me a pamphlet, and then we're left to wait for the ultrasound tech.

My eyes follow Beckham's movements in the chair. How he leans forward, leg jostling.

"Are you nervous?"

His head whips in my direction, and I swear there's a bit of sweat on his brow. "Huh? Me?"

"You seem jittery."

He leans back, rubbing his hands on the legs of his pants before crossing his arms over his chest. "It's a lot to take in. I mean, we knew, but this . . ."

"Makes it real?" I finish for him.

He exhales in a gust, tugging on the longish strands of hair on top of his head. "Yeah. A baby. That's big. Huge. How are we going to handle this? You're so calm." He sounds almost accusatory.

"Are you kidding me, Beckham? I'm *terrified*, but what am I going to do about it? This is what's happening, so I have to take it one day at a time. I can't look at the whole picture right now, or I'm pretty sure I'll have a panic attack."

He crosses one ankle over his knee. His fidgeting is amusing, since he's normally the picture of ease. "Have you told your parents?"

I snort, nearly choking in the progress. "No, definitely not."

He raises a brow. "What does that mean?"

"It means I don't want to hear their disappointment, or a lecture. I'm an adult. I made the decision to have sex with you, and while we used protection, there's always the chance of something happening, so here we are." I raise and lower my hands in defeat. "I don't think you understand my family at all."

Something flashes over his face—a shadow of pain, I think—and he looks away with his jaw ticcing. I struck a nerve. "Believe me, I know exactly what kind of people they are."

My lips fall into a frown. "What is that supposed to mean?"

There's a knock on the door, and then the tech is wheeling in an ultrasound machine. I don't take my eyes off Beckham, how tense he is now.

After the tech explains things, she gets the ultrasound probe out.

Beckham's eyes widen, but he says nothing, just rubs a hand over his face like he's trying to keep himself calm. I wonder if he's regretting coming now. I hope not. I'm actually thankful for his company. Not that I plan on admitting that to him.

The tech checks some things out before turning the screen so we can view it.

"See this black area right here?" She points. "That's the sac, and this right here"—her finger moves down the screen to a tiny gray blob—"is your baby."

There's nothing indistinguishable in that splotch on the screen, and yet I feel a fierce surge of love and protectiveness flood me.

"What the hell?" I sniffle, fanning my face. "I'm so sorry. I didn't mean to cry."

"It's okay," she assures me with a smile. "Totally normal. You see that flicker right there?" I squint to make it out. "That's your baby's heartbeat. It's too early to hear it, but sometimes you can see it."

I only cry harder, and when I look over at Beckham, I see him wiping away a tear, his lips parted in awe.

"I'll print some out for you guys. I have everything I need, so I'll get these to Dr. Hersh, and she'll pop back in before you go. You're free to get dressed."

When she leaves the room, I sit up to put my pants back on, but suddenly there's a hand in front of me holding a tissue.

I take it from him and use it to dry the last of my tears. "Thank you. This is insane, right?"

He stares into my eyes, not saying anything for a moment, which lets my mind wander. I wonder if our baby will have brown eyes like me, or blue like him.

Clearing his throat, he says, "Insane. Life changing. It's a pretty little mistake."

"A mistake?"

He nods, cupping my jaw in a surprisingly tender way. "The best one we could make."

I bite my lip nervously. "Are we ready for this?" There are so many things we're going to have to figure out over the coming months, especially since we're not together.

"Probably not," he admits, stepping away and allowing me to get up. "But we'll figure it out."

And somehow, I feel like he's right, and that in some strange way everything will be okay.

Chapter Eighteen

BECKHAM

The second I step inside my apartment, I loosen my tie enough to shuck it across the hall in the direction of my bedroom. I like dressing up—it makes me feel more together—but by the end of the day, the tie has to go.

Cheddar meows, rubbing between my legs. I bend down, pulling the ultrasound photos we got from the doctor out of my pocket. I was glad they gave us enough for me to take some too.

"Look, Cheddar." I show the chubby cat the black-and-white photos. "That's your brother or sister."

He takes one paw and bats at it before hissing and running to hide under the couch.

Standing, I chuckle. "Well, that went well." I'm sure that's close to what I can expect with an actual infant too.

In my kitchen, I stick the string of photos onto my fridge with a magnet. After grabbing a beer, I settle on my couch and turn the TV on, looking for some mindless sitcom to watch. I had dinner before I came home, because I wasn't in the mood to cook something.

Cheddar's paw slides out from under the couch, batting at my foot. "You're really not excited about a sibling." He meows in response, a small sad-sounding one instead of his usual aggressive, almost growl-like meow.

"Come on out from there." I bend over, trying to coax him out. "Ow, you fucker!" I sit up, inspecting my finger, which now has a cut on it from his sharp claws. "A baby will be a piece of cake after putting up with you."

He meows as if to say, *Fuck you.*

Trying to focus on the TV proves impossible when my mind keeps wandering. It's been hours since I parted ways with Lennon, but I find myself wondering what she's up to. I know I shouldn't do it, but I have her number now, so I send her a text.

Me: How are you feeling?

It's a few minutes before she responds. That shouldn't bother me, but I find myself wondering if she's okay, especially since she's spoken about how sick she's been getting.

Lennon: Just got out of the shower. I'm feeling fine.

Lennon: I'm kind of surprised you're texting me. What are you doing?

Me: Watching TV and sparring with my cat.

Lennon: YOU HAVE A CAT?!

Me: Don't sound so surprised.

Lennon: But I am! I didn't picture you as a pet person.

Me: Cheddar's offended.

Lennon: His name is Cheddar?! That's so cute.

Me: <picture attachment>

Lennon: He's so fluffy and cute! Is that a birthday hat on him?

Me: Yes.

Lennon: Why?

Me: It was his birthday.

Lennon: You celebrate your cat's birthday?

Me: Sure. He deserves to be celebrated. He gets the fancy cat food and everything. It was a tradition his previous owner started and I felt bad to stop it.

Lennon: Previous owner? Don't tell me you killed someone to steal their cat.

Me: You're not funny. Peter was struggling to get around and felt like he couldn't take care of him anymore, so I took him.

Lennon: Wow. That's actually kind of sweet of you.

Me: Thank you. I think.

Lennon: This is weird right? Us talking like this?

Me: We're texting. There's a difference. One's where you use your mouth to make sounds and the other you tappy-tap your fingers on the phone and type out words.

Lennon: Smart-ass.

Lennon: I'm getting in bed. It's not even late, but your spawn makes me tired.

Me: I appreciate you taking care of my pet sperm.

Lennon: GAG. You did NOT just call our BABY a pet sperm. Gross.

Me: It kind of is though.

Lennon: I hate you.

I swallow thickly, my fingers hovering over the screen as I stare at those words. Lennon has every right to hate me. I hurt her when we were teenagers, and now I've completely turned her whole world upside down as adults.

Me: You should.

Lennon: I was kidding.

Lennon: Sort of.

Lennon: I hated you for a long time.

I deserve that. To see those words. Feel them. Have them echo through my skull. I never told her, but I was in love with her. Sure, it was a young, teenage kind of love, but it was real. I didn't intend to hurt her. And even though for a long time I thought I hated her, too, it was actually me that I hated. For being weak, for listening to others.

Me: You should still hate me.

She doesn't respond right away, so I figure she might've dozed off. I flip through the channels for a few minutes, my own eyes heavy. Cheddar finally emerges from beneath the couch.

"Do you want your dinner now?" I ask him with a raised brow. He doesn't answer, but I take his glare as response enough.

Cheddar follows me to the kitchen, tail swishing. He meows when I open the can, rubbing against my legs. He starts to purr, and I take that to mean I've been forgiven.

For the moment at least.

I set his bowl down, deciding to shower and head to bed.

I've barely put my head on the pillow when my phone vibrates with a text message. I should ignore it, but curiosity eats at me, wondering if it's Lennon.

Her response is one single word: Why?

I hesitate for a moment, then start typing.

Me: Because, no matter how you look at it, I'll always be the villain in your story.

I don't want to know if she responds, so I power my phone off, roll over, and force myself to go to sleep.

I'm not the right guy for Lennon.

She needs to remember that.

And so do I.

Chapter Nineteen

LENNON

"I love this place." Laurel vibrates with excitement, picking up a plain white piece of pottery. "What do you think of this?" She holds up the small flower-shaped plate.

"Solid choice."

"Mmm." She wrinkles her nose. "I'm not sure. Maybe this?" Now she holds up a sculpted octopus.

I brought her to one of those pottery places where you paint already-made pieces and they fire them for you to pick up later. I want to tell her about the baby and wasn't sure about doing it over lunch. It's been a while since we've come here, so I thought this might be a good idea.

"Looks a bit complicated." I pick up a geometric owl. I should probably stick to something simple, like a plate, but I find myself thinking about painting something for my baby. Something I could put in their nursery, and maybe it would even be a keepsake they could pass down.

I'm getting ahead of myself, but I find it almost comforting to think about the future. Like deep down something inside me knows it's all going to be okay.

"Ugh." She stares at the octopus a moment longer. "You're right. We'd be here all day if I painted that." She moves away from me, scanning another shelf.

I put the owl back, and in the process, something else catches my eye. I pick the item up. It's a tad smaller than the length of my hand and about four inches tall. I should put it back, but for some reason, my hand closes around it, holding on.

"Is that what you're going to do?" Laurel nods to the item in my hand. She's holding a small unicorn-shaped piggy bank. It's such a random choice but somehow perfectly Laurel at the same time.

I stare at the bumblebee, realizing I don't want to part with it. "Yeah. It's cute."

We set our finds down on a table, then grab our paint colors and brushes.

"This is so fun." Laurel pulls her hair back in a ponytail, no doubt remembering the last time, when she got a chunk of black paint in her hair. "It's been way too long since we've done this." It really has. It's been difficult for us to find time to hang out outside the apartment lately. "I'm really glad you suggested this."

My breath is caught in my lungs. The whole point of this is to tell her I'm pregnant, but now that we're here, I'm terrified. Not that I think Laurel would be mad, or judge me; if anything she'll be excited. But bringing this outside the bubble where only Beckham and I know makes it that much more real.

I dip my brush in the pastel yellow. I chose a lighter yellow and gray instead of black, thinking it would be more neutral for a nursery. It's hard to believe I'm thinking about a nursery already. But I find myself contemplating all the things I'll need to take care of before the baby comes.

"I thought it would be fun," I finally answer her, concentrating on adding yellow to the stripes.

"Maybe we should go get drinks after this? We'll probably still have time to hit brunch somewhere."

"Um . . ." I bite my lip nervously. "Sure, yeah, maybe."

Laurel sets down her paintbrush, eyeing me with an arched brow. "You're weird today."

My hand freezes in midair. "What do you mean?"

Her nose crinkles in thought. "I can't put my finger on it exactly, but you seem cagey. In fact"—she frowns, her brows furrowing together—"you've been off the past few weeks."

I should've known there was no way all my behavior would go unnoticed.

Fingers trembling, I set the paintbrush down. "There is something I need to talk to you about."

Laurel pales. "Don't tell me you're moving out. If you leave, your parents might sell the place."

"What?" I blink at her. "It's not that."

"Oh." She relaxes, looking utterly relieved. "What is it then?"

Tell her. Rip it off like a Band-Aid and do it.

"Wow, I didn't expect this to be so hard." I rub my hands together, but the sound of my dry palms is nearly the equivalent of nails on a chalkboard to my ears, so I stop immediately.

Worry returns to her eyes. "What's going on? Are you okay? Like healthwise—everything is all right?"

I swallow past the lump in my throat. "Actually, there's a tiny health thing—not bad," I rush to reassure her, "but . . . it's a thing."

"Lennon," she pleads, reaching to place her hand on top of mine, "you can tell me anything."

"It appears I picked up a hitchhiker from Chicago?" I don't know why it comes out sounding like a question. I squint, gauging her reaction.

Her brows knit in confusion. "Huh?"

"I'm pregnant."

The gasp that comes from her draws the attention of the group of older ladies on the other side of the room.

"You're pregnant?" she whisper-hisses. "I knew it!"

I gape at her. "You knew?"

"I mean, I wondered." She lets go of my hand, resting her elbow on the table. "Our cycles are in sync, and I noticed your tampon wrappers weren't in the trash." I never thought about that, but since we use different brands, the wrappers are different colors. "You've also had a lot of food aversions. You made me throw away a perfectly good sub last week. The salami was not bad." She points an accusatory finger at me with a laugh.

"A baby, Lennon. You're going to be a mom." Her hands smack to her cheeks. "And that means I'm going to be an auntie. Oh my God, we're going shopping after this, forget brunch, unless you're hungry? I've got to keep you fed since you're growing my future best friend. Wait."

She frowns, a contemplative look falling on her face. "We promised we'd wait to have kids together. This is a betrayal."

"Sorry"—I point to my stomach—"the hitchhiker didn't get the memo."

She sighs playfully. "Oh well. Next time, then." She waves a dismissive hand.

My eyes widen in horror. I've barely wrapped my head around one baby, let alone thought about giving them a sibling in the future.

"Let's slow it down," I plead with her, both of us resuming our projects.

"How did Beckham handle it? Have you told him yet?"

"He knows, and surprisingly well to be honest. I have to give him credit there."

"Hmm." She hums, her tongue sticking out slightly as she adds pink to her unicorn's mane. "He lives to see another day then. How far along are you?"

She starts counting on her fingers, but I answer her anyway.

"Seven weeks now. It's all so weird to me how they calculate it."

"Have you thought about names?"

"Laurel." I laugh, fanning my face because she's making me have a hot flash from the stress of all these questions. "I'm still coming to terms with this, let alone thinking about names."

"I'll get you a baby name book," she vows, seemingly unbothered by the freak-out she's giving me. "Whatever you do, don't give the kid a boring name, but nothing too trendy either. There was a woman at Sephora the other day with the cutest baby ever, and I asked her what this child's name was. Do you know what she said?"

"Um . . . no?"

"Peanut—this kid's name was *Peanut*. I said it was a cute nickname, and she was sure to clarify that it was this child's legal name. I swear to God, these people are naming *babies* but not thinking about how that will sound as an adult. That little boy is going to have to introduce himself as Peanut. The horror."

I bite my lip to hold in laughter. "That is pretty bad."

"Oh my God!" She practically leaps out of her chair. "Please tell me this means I can plan the baby shower. Your mom will make it beyond ostentatious, and we both know that isn't exactly your thing."

I frown at the thought of my mother organizing a baby shower. It would end up not only over the top but all about her and her friends. "You can have baby shower duties."

I'm sure Laurel would do something nice. Simple. It would be *me*.

Laurel claps her hands excitedly, earning curious glances from the group of old ladies. At least they don't seem perturbed. "Have you told your parents yet?"

I stifle a laugh. "God no. I don't plan on saying anything until I'm further along. At least out of the first trimester."

"Good. No offense, but your parents are crazy."

Laurel might come from the same world as me, but her family isn't nearly as strict or pretentious as mine.

"Believe me, I know."

I focus on painting my bumblebee for as long as I can before Laurel comes up with a new onslaught of questions.

She's been quiet for five minutes max when she asks, "Does it feel weird? Being pregnant? Like, do you feel any different?"

"It's weird in the sense that there's a person growing inside me. And as far as how I feel, just sick. Today's been the best day I've had in weeks."

"I hope you know I'm here for you. Whatever you need. Late-night craving runs, some ginger ale and saltines, I'm your girl. I'm prepared to *Sister Wives* this shit."

I blame my out-of-whack hormones for the fact that I burst into tears. "Thank you." I shuffle things around in my purse, looking for a tissue. Locating one, I dry my eyes before I have mascara halfway down my face.

"Stop crying." She fans her face. "You're going to make me cry too."

"I'm sorry." My bottom lip trembles. "I can't help it. I'm hormonal."

Somehow, we manage to get ourselves together and focus on finishing up our pottery. As nervous as I was to tell Laurel, I'm glad it's out of the way. It feels good having her know, like I'm not so alone.

"So," she says, looping her arm through mine as we walk out of the shop, "can we go baby shopping?"

Excitement bubbles in my chest. I think it's the first time I've actually felt excited and not worried or scared about this. "Yes," I practically shriek.

Laurel grins, and I think somehow, she knew this would be what I needed.

Chapter Twenty

BECKHAM

Because we never know what smell might trigger Lennon's morning sickness, we've taken to using my office as our meeting space. It's good, in a way, since that means we can take as long as we want to go over things. We finally have a solid direction, one that was entirely Lennon's idea. We're going to spend the coming months interviewing as many women as we can about their careers, and what people have said to them to diminish them in getting their positions. It's above and beyond what we need to do, but we both agreed that the more fleshed out our idea is, the more likely Jaci will be to choose it.

I can't help but think this idea came to her because of my question when she started working at *Real Point*—about whether her dad had bought her way here.

Even if it is a dig at me, I can't be mad. It's brilliant, and relevant to society.

After closing my laptop, since that's where I keep the notes on the project and not the office computer—call me jaded, but while I might like my coworkers, I don't trust anyone with access to the work computers—I scoot my chair back and look over at Lennon. I've added a leather armchair to my office, and it's become hers whenever she's in here. I guess that's a good thing, since I did get it for her. Not that I've told her that. I did receive some strange looks from my coworkers when they saw me lugging it in here. I have no idea what they thought I was doing, but I guess now they know.

Lennon looks up from her iPad, the end of her Apple Pencil pressed to her lips. "Why are you stopping?"

"We need to talk."

From my tone, I'm sure she knows I don't mean about the project. Her nose crinkles like she smells something sour. "Why?"

"Why?" I repeat, incredulous. "Maybe because you're pregnant and eventually people around here are going to notice."

She taps the pencil against her lips, then slowly lowers it. "What does that matter?"

I bristle, my hands balling into fists. Her cavalier tone annoys me. "It matters because I'm the father."

With a sigh, she sets her iPad and the pencil aside. "Is this pregnancy brain?" She seems to mumble it to herself, not me. "I'm not following you."

Rubbing my jaw, I get up and pace over to where she sits. "What I mean is, people are going to be curious."

"So?" She looks at me like I'm the one who's lost my mind. Maybe I have.

"Relationships between coworkers aren't prohibited here. I want them to think we're together."

Lennon blinks, then blinks again, looking like some sort of owlish cartoon character. "Because I'm pregnant?"

Aggravated, I tug at my hair. I know I'm not making any sense, because frankly, my thoughts don't. "We're not together—"

"I know," she interjects, saying it slowly, like I'm the one who needs reminding.

"But I want them to think we are. I think it'll be the easiest route altogether."

"If our coworkers think we're an actual couple and that you didn't just knock me up?"

"Exactly." I clap my hands, pointing a finger at her in victory.

I already know I can come across as cold and unapproachable at work. I don't think it would help my image at all if they think I hooked up with Lennon and that was that.

She frowns, shaking her head. Her little confused pout shouldn't be so fucking cute, and I definitely shouldn't want to kiss her because of it. This is bad.

"I don't understand. There's nothing wrong with us *not* being together. I'm an independent woman. I can raise this child just fine on my own." I bristle at that, not that she seems to notice. "And I don't owe anyone the details on who the father is."

"Me." I point angrily at my chest. "I'm the father, and I'm telling you that I want that known. You're *not* raising this baby by yourself. I'm not walking away from this. I didn't plan for this, neither did you, but it's what's happening now, and I'm . . ." I pause to catch my breath, thinking of my bio-parents and the decisions they had to make. My adoptive parents too. How they chose to love so wholly a broken kid who was no blood of theirs. I might not have given children much thought before, but I fully plan on being there. Family is everything. Sometimes I forget that—I don't put in as much effort as I should—but I'm going to be better, and I'm definitely going to be as present in my kid's life as I can be. "I'm going to be the best damn dad to that kid, okay? And I want people to know that."

"But why do we need to make them think we're together? We're not." She mutters the last part in a hushed tone.

I squat in front of her, putting us at eye level. "Don't you think it makes the most sense? The easiest way for all of this? Besides"—I go in for the kill—"I think Jaci might be upset if she did the math and figured out I got you pregnant on the trip she sent us on, but if she thinks we're a couple now *because* of that trip, then she'll be ecstatic that she played matchmaker."

Lennon's nose crinkles with thought. It's always done that when she's not sure of something. "I'm still not a hundred percent on board with this, but if you're so certain it's better to play the part of a happy couple while we're at work, then sure, I'll do it." A barely there smirk dances over those lips I wanted to kiss only a few moments ago. "Does this mean you'll hold the door for me?"

"I guess." I mean, she is carrying my child.

"Will you bring me coffee?"

I stand up, crossing my arms over my chest. "Only if I'm getting coffee for myself—and remember, you can't overdo the coffee."

She ignores my comments. "What about lunch? Will you get me whatever I want?"

I grit my teeth. "Yes."

She hops up from the chair, patting my chest. "Then I'm in. You're going to be the best fake work boyfriend ever."

"Like you've had many?"

She scoops up her iPad case and pencil. "Wouldn't you like to know?"

Her dark hair swishes against her shoulders, and the little smirk she tosses back at me before leaving my office has me stunned.

I know this whole fake-relationship thing was my suggestion, but now I'm wondering if I've made a grave mistake.

"He's been more tired today than usual," the nurse tells me when I walk into the long-term-care facility at the end of my workday.

"That makes two of us."

She gives me a sympathetic smile. "Enjoy your visit."

I give her a nod, heading down the hall to my father's room. If he's asleep, I won't stay. He needs his rest when he can get it.

I'm not sure when or how I decided to visit him daily. It's not out of pity or anything of the sort. I want to be there for him. No one from his life before—family or friends—ever visits him. He deserves to know he's not alone.

I ease the door open, only the smallest squeak emitting from the hinges.

Blue eyes the same color as mine stare back at me from the bed. Even though he can't say much, he says all he needs to with his gaze alone.

And right now, his gaze is saying, *Why the hell are you sneaking in here?*

"I thought you were sleeping." I ease the door shut behind me. The lights in the room are dimmed, the blinds closed. "Did you get a nap?"

"I-I did."

I pull up the chair closer to his bed. He's grown frailer in the time since I've known him. Even though I don't want to admit it to myself, I'm not sure how much longer he'll be around.

"Do you want to watch anything?"

He clears his throat. "Sure."

I turn the TV on, watching him as I slowly scroll through the channels. "This," he finally says when I land on something of interest to him.

"There's something I need to tell you."

Surprise lights his eyes, his interest moving from the TV screen to focus on me instead.

"Do you remember the girl I told you about? The one who drives me absolutely insane?" He gives me his reply that he does. "She's pregnant . . . with my baby. I'm going to be a dad." I rub my jaw, still struggling to come to terms with this.

Even though I've accepted this deviation from the course my life was on, it's still strange to think I'm going to be parenting an actual human being.

"That means you'll be a grandpa."

God, I hope he gets the chance to meet my kid. He's been dwindling over the last few months. It's not something I like to think about.

Rubbing my hands on the legs of my pants, I go on, "Diapers, bottles, snotty noses, and scraped knees. That's what my future holds." I shake my head back and forth, stifling a laugh. "Me? A dad? Who would've thought?"

I talk for a while longer, about the baby, work, Cheddar, just anything and everything. When I finally shut up, I see that he's fallen asleep.

I pull his blanket up higher on his body. "See you tomorrow, Dad."

It's hard, watching him slip away.

Especially when there's nothing I can do and not enough money in the world to make it better.

Chapter Twenty-One

Lennon

Laurel steps out of her room, takes one look at me wrapped in a blanket on the couch with tears spilling from my eyes, and goes into defense mode.

"Who hurt you? Was it Beckham? I mean, obviously it has to be, he's such a jerk. What did he say? Do you have his address? I'll fuck him up, I swear to God."

Through my tears, laughter bubbles out of me. "It's not Beckham." I take a few breaths, quieting my sobs. "It was a commercial."

She stares at me, lips parted in shock as she attempts to process my words. "You're lying here having a meltdown over a commercial?"

"The puppy was so cute."

And the tears are pouring again. *Great.*

Laurel takes a terrified step away from me, toward the side table that has a box of tissues. She grabs the whole box, then sets it gingerly in front of me, like I'm a bomb that might detonate at any second.

"The puppy was cute? That brought on all of this?" She waves a hand at me. "Is this like . . . normal?"

I take one of the tissues, drying beneath my eyes. "I think so. Pregnancy hormones are weird." With a gasp, I sit up, and Laurel rears back in surprise from my sudden movement. "We should get a puppy!"

She starts to laugh. "Len, we're not getting a puppy."

Oh no. My eyes start to burn again. "Why not?"

"Because puppies are hard work."

"So are babies," I defend, fighting back tears, "but I'm having one of those. Maybe a puppy would be a good thing—you know, like training wheels."

"I can't believe you just referred to a puppy as baby training wheels." Shaking her head, she walks into the kitchen and grabs a bottle of wine and a glass. Ugh, I'm a sobbing mess and I can't even have a glass of wine with her.

"You don't get it."

Holding my blanket tight around me, I get up from the couch and waddle to my room. Waddle, not because I'm that big yet, but because I don't want to trip over the bottom of the blanket.

After closing my bedroom door behind me, I grab my phone and FaceTime the last person I should probably be bothering.

Surprisingly, he picks right up, his handsome face peering at me through the screen. His forehead is sweaty, his breath heavy over the line.

"Are you working out?" I blurt.

"Yeah." There's a beeping sound, and he slows down. "I was running."

I bite my lip. "I didn't mean to mess up your workout."

"It was time for my cooldown anyway," he says dismissively. "Are you okay?" His eyes narrow on me through the screen. "Have you been crying? Your eyes are red. Is everything okay? The baby—"

"The baby's fine." He exhales in relief. "I want a puppy."

His lips twitch the tiniest bit, like he's fighting to hold back a smile. He used to smile a lot when we were teens—it would transform his face, soften him. Now he keeps those smiles close, refusing to unleash them. Perhaps that's a good thing. He might obliterate my heart with a smile alone.

"You didn't answer my question, honeybee. Once you do that, we'll circle back to the puppy thing."

"It was a commercial with the cutest puppy. A little dachshund—"

"I said forget the puppy."

"But that's what made me cry."

He adjusts his AirPods, like he's not sure he heard me right. "You cried because of a puppy?"

"It was so cute! I think I should get one. I've never had a pet. It would be good practice for the baby, right?"

"Do you have time for a puppy right now?"

I frown, not liking that he's hitting me with logic right now, when I just want him to agree with me. "No, not really."

He steps off the treadmill. "Then you don't need a puppy."

"B-but they're so cute."

"And so is Cheddar. You can come over to my place and babysit his cranky ass anytime you want." He looks a bit surprised at his own proposal. "I mean, only if you want."

"You'd let me watch your cat?"

"I'm sure he'd love the company." He grabs a towel, wiping his face. "He loves treats and belly scratches. See, he's like a puppy already."

"Can I come over now?"

"Uh . . ." He steps through a door. "Yeah. I guess so. Sure. I just need to shower. Have you had dinner?"

"No," I admit. I hadn't even thought about dinner until he mentioned it, but now that he has, I'm starving.

"I'll order delivery then."

"Text me your address?"

"Sure."

"And Beckham?"

"Mmm?" He's stepping into an elevator now. "What?"

"Thank you."

He stares back at me through the rectangular screen. "Anything for you." He swallows thickly, his eyes darting away like he didn't mean to say that.

He disconnects the call, and I almost expect him not to send me his address, but he does, and then I'm doing the craziest thing of all and slipping out into the night to see him.

No, not him.

The cat.

I'm going to see the cat. Yep, that's right.

Almost an hour later I'm standing outside Beckham's lair.

I mean, his apartment.

He swings the door open, and I can't help but take him in. His hair is still damp from the shower, curling against his forehead. A white T-shirt clings to his chest, hugging every delectable muscle. A pair of loose athletic shorts hangs off his hips. It's such a dressed-down look for him, and he has no right looking this hot in what I assume are his pajamas. Especially when I'm pregnant with his child and surprisingly horny.

His brows furrow. "Did you just moan?"

"Shut up." I shove past him and into his apartment. "I smelled food."

"The food isn't here yet." He closes the door. "But nice attempt to save." He turns to me, crossing his arms over his chest with an infuriating smirk on his lips.

"Well, then someone on your floor is definitely cooking." I stick my nose haughtily in the air, daring him to contradict me.

"Whatever you say. Do you want a drink?"

"Some water would be great." He heads into the kitchen, and I follow. "This place is nice." His apartment appears large by New York City standards, and his kitchen even has a dishwasher. What a luxury.

"Thanks," he says, just as a scream flies from my throat. A big orange cat jumped onto the counter right beside me, seemingly out of nowhere.

I press a hand to my racing heart. "Where did he come from?"

Beckham points to the top of the fridge before opening it. "He hangs out up there a lot."

"Oh." I reach out, scratching the cat behind his ears. "Hi, Cheddar." He immediately starts to purr. "I can't believe you actually have a cat."

Beckham fills a glass with water from a filtered pitcher. "Why wouldn't you believe I have a cat?"

"I don't know." I pet Cheddar's head. "It just doesn't seem like you."

He returns the pitcher to the refrigerator. Leaning his butt against the counter in front of me, he meets my stare. "Why? Because you think I'm an asshole?"

I take a sip of the water, stalling. "I guess. I mean, a pet is a responsibility. It seems like it wouldn't be something you'd want."

"That's where we don't really know each other. Not anymore."

I drop my gaze first because he's right. We're different people now than who we were before. Who we've become is strangers. I don't know the real Beckham any more than he knows the real me, and what a sad fact that is. We're going to be raising a child together. Whatever happens, moving forward, we're in this together in some shape or form.

Finally, I manage to find my voice. "I guess that's something we should work on."

I can see the shutters go up behind his eyes. "I don't think that's really necessary."

"How is it not? We're having a baby together."

He glowers at me, and I bet right about now he's regretting inviting me over into his domain. His tongue presses against the inside of his cheek. "What is it you want to know?"

So many things—why he disappeared from my life after he took my virginity, why he has such a chip on his shoulder, how he really feels about the baby.

"Anything," I whisper into the air between us. "Anything you want to give me."

And I mean it. I don't want to push him too far, too fast. He's handled my surprise pregnancy well so far and seems to want to be in our child's life. It wouldn't be fair to the baby if I pushed their father away, even unintentionally.

"That's the problem, Lennon." His shoulders rise and fall with a deep breath, like he's steadying himself. "I have nothing to give, and you'd do well to remember that."

My heart breaks a little—not for me, but for him.

He really thinks he has nothing to offer, that *he* is nothing.

He has no idea that once upon a time, he was my everything.

Chapter Twenty-Two

BECKHAM

I never should have invited Lennon over. It was a moment of weakness at the sight of her tears and pleas for a pet. I convinced myself it wouldn't be so bad, but then she had to push me, question me.

When the food arrived, we ate in awkward silence.

All because I'm an idiot.

"Are you sure this is okay?" I ask for the millionth time, pointing the remote at the TV, ready to change it the moment she gives the word.

"Yes." She laughs lightly, petting Cheddar, who's curled in her lap. The traitor. "This is a cute movie."

"But it's a Christmas movie." I sound appalled because I am. It's not even Halloween yet.

She stifles a yawn, resting her elbow on the arm of the couch and her head in her hand. "It's always Christmas at Hallmark Channel."

"I wouldn't know."

"Well," she says, stifling another yawn, "now you do."

"Are you tired? Do you want to lie down? I can move."

"Beckham," she groans, "please, just shut up and let me watch this movie and pet your cat, okay?"

"I . . . okay." This is the weirdest fucking night of my life. "All right. I can do that."

She shushes me. "Watch the movie. You might like it."

I doubt that. Sappy love shit gives me hives.

Crossing my arms over my chest, I watch the movie like she requested. I observe her from time to time too. If she notices, she ignores me.

When a commercial comes on, I ask her, "Do you really want a puppy?"

She snorts. "Why? Would you get me one?"

Maybe. "No, I'm just curious."

"I don't think so, not really anyway. I guess I'm just feeling really unprepared for this whole thing. I thought I'd have kids someday, just not . . . now, you know? I didn't grow up around babies, and it's not like my parents were very nurturing. How do I know I'll be good at this thing?"

"You will be."

"But how do you know?"

"Because you wouldn't be worrying about this if you weren't going to be a good parent."

"I'm not sure I believe you, but thank you."

"Maybe we should take some classes. Surely, they have classes on changing diapers and keeping kids alive."

She laughs, and fuck if it isn't the most beautiful sound. She's got to stop doing that. It makes my chest feel funny, almost warm.

"I think it's so crazy the hoops you have to jump through to adopt a pet, let alone a child, but one that's biologically yours, they just send you on your way from the hospital." She stifles a yawn, leaning a little heavier on her arm.

"Should I get you home?"

She turns to glare at me. "Stop trying to get rid of me. The movie is back on. Pay attention." She points a bossy finger at the TV.

133

Helplessly, I sink deeper into the couch to focus on the screen.

Hours later, I jolt awake on the couch to find Cheddar curled in my lap and the spot on the couch where Lennon was empty.

I set Cheddar off my lap, then get up and call out her name.

"Lennon?" I head toward the bathroom, but it's empty. I spin around, searching the guest room and my bedroom.

She's gone.

That should relieve me, I think, that she left and went home, but instead I feel panicky inside.

I ring her phone and she doesn't answer, which only makes me spiral further.

Me: You better answer your phone.

I wait a moment.

Me: LENNON.

Me: I'm calling again and if you don't answer I'm calling the police.

Me: Don't think I won't.

I ring her again, and she answers after five rings. "Relax, *Dad*. I was in the shower."

I nearly choke. "You're talking to me naked right now?"

"I have a towel on since someone was so incredibly impatient. It's not my fault you fell asleep. You snore, by the way. You might want to get that checked out."

"I don't snore," I bite out through gritted teeth, swiping a bottle of water from the fridge. Cheddar follows me from the kitchen and back to the bedroom before leaping onto the bed.

She laughs, and it sounds like she puts her phone down on the counter. "Trust me, you do. Mouth hanging open and everything."

"I don't believe you."

"You don't have to believe me, but that doesn't mean I'm not right."

I pinch the bridge of my nose. "You should've woken me up. I would've taken you home."

"I hate to tell you, but I've lived in New York for years now. Getting home at a late hour is nothing new." I choke on water—why I chose to take a sip at that moment is beyond me. "Are you okay?"

"I'm fine," I gripe.

I'm not fine at all, because now all I can think about is Lennon heading home from late nights with other men. That shouldn't infuriate me, but it does. She doesn't belong to me, and yet it feels like some part of her has always been mine. Selfish, that's what I am.

"Well, if you're fine, and I'm fine, then I'm going to finish putting my lotion on and go to bed."

"Don't do that again."

"Do what?"

"Leave and not tell me."

"Oh, so you think there will be another time?"

"That's not what I—"

She hangs up.

I stare down at the phone screen, tempted to ring her back and chew her out.

As much as I love arguing with her, it's late and she needs to go to bed. She has my kid to take care of.

My kid.

It's still a weird thought—that I'm going to be a parent, a dad.

"Do you think I'll be a good dad?" I ask Cheddar. He peeks one eye open from the pillow I sleep on. The bastard always tries to take it. "What do you think?" He closes his eyes. "Thanks for the vote of confidence. It's not like I've managed to keep you alive."

Yanking back the covers, I climb into bed and lie there with my hands crossed on my chest, thinking.

My life has been upended in the short amount of time since Lennon came back into it, and it's about to change even more, in the most monumental way.

I would never admit it to anyone—I don't even like thinking it to myself—but I'm scared.

A child isn't a cute accessory, no matter how some people treat them. I know there's no such thing as a perfect parent, but I don't want to fuck up my kid. I want my son or daughter to love me, trust me, and always feel like they can come to me with anything, but *how* do I do that?

I press the heels of my hands to my eyes, exhaling a frustrated breath.

Cheddar gives a matching frustrated meow. I should've known better than to dare disturb his beauty sleep.

Rolling over to my side, I squish my eyes closed and will myself to fall asleep.

And when I do, I dream—a rarity for me. In it, Lennon walks down a long aisle covered in petals toward me in a white dress.

It's a cruelty, that dream, because bastards like me don't get the girl.

Chapter Twenty-Three

Lennon

I spot Beckham up ahead, leaning against the building of my doctor's office. He has no right to look so casually handsome, especially not when I'm mad at him.

"You stole my taxi!" I yell, jabbing his chest with my finger when I finally reach him.

He raises one brow. "I needed it more."

"For what?" I poke him again. I really need to pee and shouldn't be here arguing with him. But it's not like I can use the bathroom yet anyway. I was told to come to my scan with a full bladder, since it makes it easier for the ultrasound photos.

"To get coffee before the appointment." My lips part, trying to process his words. I cannot believe he's using a need for coffee as an excuse for swiping my taxi right out from under me. "Don't worry, I got you one, too, sweetie," he says in an almost playful but mocking tone. He holds the cup out to me. "It's decaf."

I smack the cup out of his hand, and it drops on the ground, the lid popping off and the contents spilling everywhere. "You better throw that away," I tell him, like I wasn't the one who knocked it to the ground. "I don't like litterers."

He laughs, and it's such a robust, hearty sound. I'm pretty sure he's so screwed up that this might be some kind of sick and twisted foreplay for him. Not that I'm ever sleeping with him again. Look where that got us.

"Fuck, you're amazing." He scoops up the now-empty cup and tosses it in the trash.

Ignoring him, I storm inside the building to the elevators, willing one to let me on before he catches up. No such luck—he's by my side in an instant.

He leans down, lips brushing the curve of my ear. "That was a perfectly good coffee you wasted."

"You can afford to buy me another." The doors slide open, and the traitor presses his hand to the small of my back when we step on. "Don't touch me."

His hand stays firmly on my waist, just to prove a point, I'm sure. "You're in a mood today."

I hiss at him—well, it's the closest thing I can think of to describe the sound that comes out of my mouth. "You stole my taxi! Of course I'm pissed. Then you got coffee and still somehow beat me here."

His lips quirk in a half smile. Pressing his free hand to his chest, he says, "It's a gift, truly."

I wonder if he'll think it's a gift when I shove my foot up his ass.

Despite Beckham's proposal to pretend to be in a relationship for our work peers, we still haven't said a word about the baby or being a so-called couple. Though I'm sure we'll have to say something soon. Jaci gave me a funny look when I requested this particular afternoon off, since Beckham had already asked for the same.

"You can stop touching me," I say when we get off the elevator and start down the hall with his hand still on my waist.

"Maybe I like my hand there."

"And maybe I'd like to cut it off? Hmm?"

"You're in rare form today." He finally lets his hand drop. "I like it."

"You're . . . you know, I don't think a word exists for what you are."

We reach the door for the doctor's office, and I head inside first and check in. When I turn around, I steadfastly ignore the seats Beckham has chosen, instead opting to sit on the complete opposite side from where he's sitting.

Out of the corner of my eye, I watch him—the little smirk on his lips and the way he places his hands on his knees before he stands, sauntering over to me like I didn't just insult him.

He sits down beside me, his arm brushing mine, and even through the fabric of my sweaterdress, I feel the heat of him like a physical burn.

"I love it when you play with me."

I mock-gag. "That sounds so gross."

He rubs his jaw. "It's nice to have a worthy opponent."

I turn to him with narrowed eyes. "You're so weird."

"I'm aware."

"And so hot and cold," I go on. "I'm pretty sure Katy Perry was inspired by you for that song."

"Who?"

I roll my eyes. "You're ridiculous."

I shouldn't let him bother me so much, but something about Beckham manages to just grate on me.

Somehow, I'm able to ignore him from the time my name is called all the way up until I'm settled in the room waiting for the ultrasound tech.

"I don't want to know the gender."

My head whips in his direction, *Exorcist*-style. "What? First off, it's too early for us to know that unless I do a blood test. Secondly, I'm the mother, and I'm growing your so-called pet sperm, so if I want to know, I'll know—which I do. I'm a planner. I want to buy baby clothes and decorate the nursery and—"

He has one leg crossed over the other, and with his brow arched at me, he looks like some kind of evil villain. "Can't you do all those things in a gender-neutral fashion?"

I hate the challenge in his tone. "I could, but I don't want to."

"As you implied, it's *my* pet sperm you're housing, so shouldn't my opinion matter as much as yours? Maybe even a little more?"

"I . . . you're . . . you have to be kidding me right now." I cross my arms over my chest, staring at the opposite wall and the diagram of a fetus. I can't keep my mouth shut, so my head swings back in his direction. "Why don't you want to know the gender?"

He lets his leg drop to the floor, pressing his hands together as he leans forward. "I'm happy whether it's a girl or boy—so why not let it be a surprise? I think it would be cool to wait, and I guess . . ." He sighs, rubbing a hand over his jaw. "I don't know, I like the idea of being the one to know first and get to tell you."

Normally I would think this was just him being a controlling dick-wad, but there's a sincerity in his eyes, and I can tell that for whatever reason, he really wants to keep this a surprise.

I don't answer him right away, instead pondering what he's said, and I have to admit that it does sound kind of nice—even if I'm certain the wait will be torture.

"Fine," I begin, and he lights up, looking ready to celebrate, "for now. But if I change my mind, we'll discuss this again."

He holds his hand out to me. "Deal." We shake on it. "It feels like we've been waiting in here forever."

"Welcome to the doctor's office, where they take all your money and all your time."

He gives a soft chuckle, sitting back. "You're not lying."

It's another five minutes before the ultrasound tech enters the room. My nerves become jittery. I've been looking forward to this appointment, hearing the heartbeat, but it just hits me, what if I *don't* hear a heartbeat? It's irrational to think that way—things have been great, no

140

spotting, and I'm maybe even a tad less sick. And yet I can't help but feel that worry grow.

Mentally, I check out, giving in to my panic. I feel Beckham's fingers loop through mine, and even the shock of that doesn't bring me back from my stupor.

And then my panic fades as the most glorious sound I've ever heard fills the room. I want to record it, play it on repeat, maybe even stick it in one of those cheap Build-A-Bears.

Tears flood my eyes, spilling over. I can't even feel embarrassed.

"That's our baby." I touch the fingers of my free hand to Beckham's cheek. He places his over mine, giving the hand he holds a squeeze.

A tear falls down his cheek. "That's our baby," he echoes.

It's a weird feeling, staring at that screen, knowing in a matter of months we're going to be holding a baby that's a mix of the two of us. I know our situation isn't ideal, and not that I'll admit it to him, but if I was going to get knocked up by accident, then I'm glad I'm doing it with Beckham.

My phone starts ringing from inside the confines of my purse almost the second I've walked into the apartment. I groan the moment I see those three little letters that spell out *Mom*.

Reluctantly, I accept the call and press the phone to my ear. "Hey, Mom. I'm just walking in the door from work." No way in hell can I mention I was actually at a doctor's appointment. "Can I call you back later?"

"No," she snipes. "You've been ignoring my calls and texts. We'll talk now."

I know it's better to get this over with, so I set my stuff down and settle onto the barstool while I listen.

"Okay." It takes a ridiculous amount of effort to keep the sigh from my voice.

My parents are exhausting, both of them overbearing in a way that isn't about love or caring but image and control.

"If you hadn't been ignoring me, you would know I've set up a date for you—"

"Mom." Disbelief floods me. No matter how many times I've told her to stop setting me up on blind dates with her rich friends' sons, she hasn't gotten the memo.

"—tonight."

"Tonight?" I blurt out, choking on air. My eyes shoot to the clock. "I can't tonight." Not that I have plans or anything, but I'm *not* going on a date with a stranger.

She goes on like I haven't said anything. "His name is Spencer. Spencer Whittling III."

"Mom."

"I've already made the reservations and scheduled a car to pick you up at six sharp. You should wear that lovely plum-colored dress I got you for your birthday last year."

"You didn't even ask me if I was able to go on this date?"

She huffs in exasperation. "Well, I tried to, but you weren't responding now, were you?" Accusation drips from her words. She's placing blame solely on my shoulders. I should have answered her, but she should also stop her meddling. "Spencer is expecting your presence. It's too late to back out now." There's a warning edge to her voice.

Despite being in my twenties, I know when she uses that tone not to push her buttons anymore. It's this long-ingrained fear that if I don't do what she wants, then I'm a major disappointment. I wish I could stop craving her approval, but I'm worried I'll always be trying to please my parents. Some part of me still feels like a little girl just begging them to love me, and I seem to think the only way I can do that is by being agreeable, even when it's the last thing I want to do.

"All right. I better hang up, then, so I can get ready."

I can practically hear the smile in her voice when she speaks next. "Good. Enjoy your date."

She ends the call, leaving me staring at the blank screen.

My eyes dart to the clock, silently cursing. I don't have much time to shower and get ready. I need every second I have. I dash into the bathroom, taking the quickest shower imaginable before I hop out and start on my makeup.

The front door opens, Laurel slipping into the apartment with a tired yawn. "I'm exhausted. Movie night?" Before I can answer she appears in the open bathroom doorway, where I'm working to carefully apply my lipstick. "Are you going out?"

"My mom set me up on a date."

She rolls her eyes. "Your mom is something else."

"Tell me something I don't know." I dab at the red lipstick with a tissue to keep it from transferring later. "A car is picking me up at six."

We both turn to look at the clock shining from the microwave. I have thirty minutes.

"Let me do your hair." She swishes her finger through the air, motioning me to turn around.

"Are you sure? I know you're tired."

"I'm fine."

She takes my hair down from the messy ponytail I tossed it up in and rakes her fingers lightly through the strands. Brushing it out, she grabs a section on each side of my head and braids them, so they meet at the base of my skull under the rest of my hair. After grabbing a clear elastic, she ties those together before making a bun. She pulls out some strategic pieces to frame my face. It takes her no time to create the cute, effortless style, when it would have taken me forever.

She pats my shoulders. "There. You look great."

I throw my arms around her in a hug. "Thank you. You're the best."

In my room, I dig through the closet for the purple dress my mom referred to. Not because I'm taking her advice, but because I'm not putting it past her to find out if I wore it. I slip it on, tugging it up past my hips. It's tighter than it used to be, but I guess that's to be expected. There's the smallest swell in my stomach. I touch it gingerly. I wonder when the awe will fade that there's a baby in there. Even with the bump, I manage to get the dress on and zipped.

I grab a pair of heels, then dance around my room in an attempt to put them on.

My phone vibrates on the dresser, and I know my time is up. With my heels on, I check the text message, and sure enough, it's from an unknown number, the driver letting me know he's here. He's a tad bit early, but since I'm ready, I say my goodbyes to Laurel and head down.

The driver is a gray-haired man with kind eyes. He opens the door to the back of the SUV with a polite hello.

Settling into the seat, I try to catch my breath.

I don't mean to, but my thoughts drift to Beckham, wondering what he'd think if he knew I was on my way to a date right now.

He wouldn't care, because you two aren't together, my conscience practically growls at me.

Even still, he's possessive enough for me to believe he wouldn't be happy about this.

Not that he'll ever know.

The drive to the restaurant isn't a short one, but man does it feel like it anyway. When the driver parks the car and gets my door, I nervously swipe my hands down my dress as I offer him a small smile of thanks.

I have no idea what this Spencer person looks like, so when I enter the restaurant, I give his last name. When the table isn't under that, I try mine instead, and that does the trick.

I sit down at the empty table, grateful he hasn't arrived yet, since it gives me a moment to catch my breath and get myself under control.

The wait isn't long. A tall, handsome man with sandy-brown hair dressed in a sharp suit is being herded back to my table. He's clean shaven, with a more wholesome look than I expected. Still, I can't help but compare him, even when I know I shouldn't. His eyes are a dark blue, like the deepest parts of the ocean, nothing like the icy blue of Beckham's eyes. When he smiles it's almost shy, unlike the confident, downright cocky at times, smirks Beckham tends to give.

"Hello, it's nice to meet you, Lennon." He holds his hand out to me. I can't help but compare even the sound of his voice to Beckham's. It's slightly higher in tone, not as raspy.

"Hi, Spencer. It's great to meet you too." I take his hand as he pulls out the chair in front of me. "I'm sorry about all this," I whisper conspiratorially. "I'm sure you were roped into this like I was."

He gives a soft, amused laugh. "Your mother pries into your love life too?"

"You have no idea." I pick up the menu, trying to decide on what I want to eat. I know I better stick with something safe. My sickness from the pregnancy has vastly improved but can still be triggered at times.

"Would you like to share a bottle of wine?" He holds the drink menu loosely in his fingers.

"Oh no . . . um . . . I'm on a break from alcohol." *You're on a break from alcohol? Did you really just say that?* "Please, order whatever you want."

His brow arches curiously. "All right."

After we've ordered, and before it can get too awkward, I ask him, "So, what is it you do for work?"

It's a basic question, but I know literally zilch about this guy.

"I work in finance."

"Ah," I say while thinking, *Of course you do*. It's not that he necessarily fits the mold, but these days it seems like almost every man in Manhattan is involved in finance somehow. "That's . . ."

He starts laughing. "Predictable?" he finishes for me.

I laugh, too, feeling a bit more at ease. "Yeah."

"It's okay. I didn't plan to follow in my dad's footsteps, but here we are. My mom mentioned something about you being a writer."

"I'm a journalist." I shoot a smile of thanks at the waiter when he drops off a basket of thick-cut french bread. "I recently started working for *Real Point*. It's a magazine. I'm not sure if you've heard of it."

"I think maybe I have." He grabs his wineglass, swirling the liquid.

"It's a young publication, but I'm enjoying it so far."

He then asks me about my family, and we volley questions back and forth throughout our dinner. At the end of the night, he walks me out to the waiting car and presses a kiss to my cheek.

"It was nice meeting you, Lennon."

"Nice meeting you, too, Spencer."

He shoves his hands in his pockets, hesitating. "I'd like to ask you on another date, but I'm kind of getting the feeling that there might be someone else you're interested in."

I bite my lip. I'm not sure how he got that vibe. I thought I was doing well at engaging in the conversation, and Spencer clearly isn't a bad guy.

"It's not that," I say, though my treacherous mind immediately thinks of Beckham. "I just have a lot going on in my life right now, and dating . . . well, dating isn't a priority at the moment."

He nods in understanding. "I get it. Well, if you ever change your mind, you know how to get a hold of me."

I give him a hug before slipping into the back seat of the car.

Spencer watches the car pull away from the curb, raising his hand to wave.

Silently, I curse myself. I might hate my mother's meddling, and the guys she normally sets me up with are so self-absorbed, but Spencer isn't that bad. I think, in another world, he'd be good for me.

But regardless of being pregnant, with Beckham back in my life, my stupid heart has made room for him, and right now I know I'm not capable of squeezing in anyone else.

Chapter Twenty-Four

BECKHAM

"Are we really going to do this?" Lennon whispers, walking along beside me to Jaci's office.

Her shoulders are stiff with tension. I itch to reach out and massage her worry away, but I keep my hands firmly at my sides. She's not mine to touch. I got slapped in the face with that reminder when she told me this morning that she'd been on a date. One set up by her mother, but a date nonetheless. She said she hadn't planned to tell me, and even in my annoyance, I wondered what had made her change her mind.

But once she told me, I decided we needed to put the truth out there once and for all, at least here. Maybe it would make her think twice before agreeing to a date if the entire staff thinks we're dating.

"Yes." I try not to sound as perturbed as I feel. When she screws up her face in annoyance, I know I've failed.

"It feels like lying."

Because technically it is.

"We have to tell her at some point."

She presses her lips together in a thin line, giving a single small nod. "All right. Fine. Let's do it."

I knock on Jaci's door, and it's only a moment before she calls for us to come in. I grip Lennon's hand before we enter, not just to make a point but also because I think she needs it.

And maybe I need it a little too.

Jaci's brow arches at our clasped hands.

"Hello," she greets us, standing up from behind her desk. "I guess I can imagine what this visit is about." She tries to hide her smile, eyeing our joined hands.

Lennon's grip starts to wiggle in mine, nerves and whatever else. I tighten my hold, reminding her it's too late to back out now.

"Yes," I begin, giving her hand another reassuring squeeze, "we wanted to tell you first, since it's you we have to thank for this." I give Lennon the most loving look I can muster. It must work because Jaci has hearts in her eyes when I turn back to her. "We've been dating since the Chicago trip." I tug Lennon a little closer to my side, sending up a silent prayer that it doesn't look like I'm holding her hostage.

"Oh." Jaci's eyes light up. "This is wonderful news."

Lennon's eyes widen, and I pinch her side to keep her from saying anything ridiculous, but I must not do it soon enough. "Really?"

She sounds so fucking shocked that our boss would be happy for us that I'm mildly offended.

Jaci gives her a funny look. "Of course! I've sensed the chemistry between you two from the start. I didn't send you on that trip thinking this would be the outcome, but I'm also not surprised."

"Chemistry?" Lennon murmurs under her breath. In the small office there's no chance that Jaci didn't hear her.

"There's more." I speak up, hoping my voice will carry over Lennon's. It's a futile hope, though, since apparently she's determined to self-sabotage us.

"I'm with child!" She slaps a hand over her mouth dramatically.

Jaci's brows furrow in confusion. "You're with . . . oh, you're pregnant! You're pregnant?" I have to give a small chuckle at the surprise when she said it the first time and the complete confusion in the next instant.

Lennon nods. "Yep, we're having a baby." She gives me a cautious smile, no doubt knowing she's turned this into a complete disaster. Apparently, Lennon can't keep her cool under pressure.

"This is great news! Wonderful!" Jaci's enthusiasm seems to startle Lennon, and she gives me a surprised look when Jaci pulls her into a hug, our hands finally letting go.

See, I try to say with my eyes, *I told you everything would be fine.*

Jaci releases Lennon to hug me, smacking a kiss on my cheek. "This is great news. I'm so happy for you, Sulli."

"Sulli," Lennon mouths behind Jaci, pretending to gag. I give her the finger.

"Does anyone else know yet? Brendan?"

I move back to Lennon's side, wrapping an arm around her. She stiffens at first, then slowly relaxes against me. I swear she even sniffs my shirt. I give her a funny look, but she ignores it.

"No," I say, turning my attention back to Jaci. "We wanted you to be the first to know."

She puts a hand to her heart. "I'm honored. I must say, Jaci is a great name for a girl." She winks.

"We'll keep that in mind." *No, we won't.* "Anyway," I begin, wanting to end this conversation before Lennon says anything else to jeopardize us, "we should get to work."

"Yes, right, of course." Jaci gives each of us another hug, which is a bit awkward since I won't let Lennon go. "Congratulations, again."

"Thank you, we appreciate it." Lennon's smile is tired, a bit forced, and I get the impression that she has more on her mind than just this conversation.

Is she thinking about that guy she went out with? Did she actually like him? Is she regretting that, thanks to the baby, she's stuck with me?

We leave Jaci's office, with Lennon almost trying to sprint away from me.

"Not so fast, honeybee." I tug her hand, pulling her into a darkened corner. She squirms, wanting to get away. With a gentle chuck under her chin, I urge her head up. "What's going on? Talk to me."

I cannot believe I'm begging this woman to talk to me, but here we are. I don't like her being in her head, especially if it's about another man.

"It's nothing."

"Then why are you trying to run away from me?"

She sighs heavily, pressing her kissable lips together. Despite my annoyance at her going out with another man, I can't take my eyes off her mouth. "It's not you I'm running from. It's . . ." She looks on the verge of tears. "I freaked out telling our boss," she hisses softly, panic written plainly on her face. "How the hell do I think I'm going to tell my parents? And why should it even matter?" she goes on. "Why do I care what they think of me when I can never do anything right anyway?"

My whole body relaxes, relieved that this isn't about the guy. This, I can handle.

I hold her wrist gently in my hand, circling my thumb against her pulse point. Anger on her behalf is slowly building inside me. "What do you mean?"

"Jesus." She sniffles, wiping beneath her eyes with her other hand. "It's not like you don't know how my parents are. I never was good enough in their eyes. Not like my brother. Hunter is their golden child. And this"—she points at her barely showing stomach—"will be another reason for them to say I'm a failure. And I don't . . ." She clears her throat, fighting to keep her emotions in check. "This wasn't a part of the plan, but this baby doesn't make me a failure."

"No," I agree, trying to hold back my irritation—not at her, but her family.

"I'll get over it." She gives me the side of her face, like she doesn't want me to see too much in her eyes.

Gripping her chin, I force her head back, refusing to let her hide from me. "There's nothing you should have to get over. They shouldn't treat you like that."

Despite how close I was to her, to her family, I didn't realize that they treated her poorly. Maybe on some level I realized, but I was so young, blinded by my own beliefs, that I just . . . didn't notice.

She closes her eyes, swallowing thickly. "I hate to ask you this—"

"Ask me anything."

I hate to admit it, but anything she'd ever want, I'd go to the ends of the earth to make sure she got.

"Will you hug me? I really need a hug right now." Her lower lip starts to wobble, and it's nearly my undoing.

"Yeah." I clear my throat, trying to rid myself of how choked up I sound. "I can hug you."

I hold my arms open wide, and she dives into my chest, wrapping her arms firmly around my torso, the side of her face pressed between my pectoral muscles. She fits seamlessly right there, like my body was cut out to be the perfect nesting spot for her.

I close my eyes, wrapping my own arms around her so she feels safe. Protected. Resting my chin on top of her head, I give myself a moment to simply exist in this space and time with Lennon. It's selfish, really, as I let my imagination run wild, to consider what it might be like if she were mine and I could hold her like this anytime I wanted.

After a minute, maybe longer, I say, "We should go tell everyone else."

"Yeah." She lets me go, stepping away and gathering herself. I can see her putting bricks back up, erecting those walls that exist between us. "Let's do it."

Chapter Twenty-Five

LENNON

"Laurel!" I call out in desperation, on the verge of tears. "I need your help."

She pokes her head in my open doorway a moment later. "Hey, what's up?"

"My dress," I hiss, trying to squeeze the back closed. "It doesn't fit!"

There's a charity event tonight, one Jaci got me an invite for so I could write an article. I knew it was black tie, but I wasn't worried about it since I have plenty of dresses that fit the criteria. Or so I thought. My bed is currently covered in a graveyard of all the options I've tried on that don't fit. My last-ditch effort of a dress clings to my body in desperation, the zipper refusing to budge.

I've gained only a few pounds so far. Apparently, that's just enough to ensure that none of my dresses fit.

I'm going to lose my mind.

Laurel, bless her, doesn't laugh at me.

"Do you need me to zip you in?"

"Please!"

Don't cry, don't cry, don't cry, I plead with myself. I already have a full face of makeup. I can't afford to mess it up now. I'm sweating, so that's bad enough.

Laurel tugs on the zipper. "Uh—"

My head whips around. "Don't say *uh*. Get it zipped, girl! Put some oomph into it!"

She gapes at me. "If I do that, the zipper is going to break."

"Don't say that." I stamp my feet impatiently. "You have to try."

Is it the end of the world that my dress doesn't fit? No. Do I care about the weight? Also no. I'm growing a fucking human, for Chrissake. I should be allowed to expand. But I am in desperate need to leave this apartment and get to the event. There is no time to go shopping for a new dress.

"Suck it in," Laurel declares, cracking her knuckles. "I can do this. We're getting you in this dress."

I suck my stomach in as much as I can, trying to help, too, by holding the zipper as close to closed as I can.

"It's. Not. Working." She bites the words out through gritted teeth. "Hold on." She braces her hand against my back. "I can do this."

And.

Then.

The.

Zipper.

Breaks.

Silence descends on my bedroom.

"Lennon," she whimpers. "I am so sorry."

I take a deep, bracing breath, squeezing my eyes shut. I cannot afford to get upset about this. It's not worth it. It's just a dress.

"It's okay." I count down from ten in my head, giving myself that short span of time to feel what I need to—mostly panic and dread.

"What can I do? I might have a dress that works. I can go look."

She starts to leave, but I say, "We're the same size." Which has always been a convenient thing up until now. "Were," I correct. "We were the same size."

Laurel looks close to tears on my behalf. Bless her. "Let me run to a store. I can find something."

"Maybe I can make a skirt-and-blouse combo work."

"I thought you said earlier this was a black-tie event."

"I-it is."

"You have to have a dress, a gown, something."

Beckham is going with me as the photographer: since Jaci thinks we're a real couple, she figured she might as well team us up for this event.

"I'll call Beckham and let him know I'll be running late. And then I'll swing by somewhere and get it sorted before I go to the event."

"Are you sure? I have no problem going out."

"You're already in your pajamas," I point out. "And you should get to enjoy your evening. Not have to hunt down something for me to wear. It'll be fine."

Maybe if I tell myself that enough times, I'll start to believe it.

She clasps her hands beneath her chin. "I'm so sorry."

"There's nothing to be sorry for. It's not your fault nothing fits me." I have Beckham's pet sperm currently incubating in my body to thank for that. Buying some clothes is going to be a must this weekend.

When Laurel leaves my room, I reluctantly pick up my phone and call Beckham.

"What?" he barks into the phone upon answering, the sound of the chaotic New York City streets blaring behind him.

I decide to cut to the chase. "I'm going to be late. I don't have a dress."

He guffaws. "What do you mean, you don't have a dress?"

"Not one that fits." I reach up to run my fingers through my hair in frustration, but I quickly stop myself before I spoil the updo Laurel spent so long perfecting.

He sighs heavily. "You need something to wear?"

"Obviously," I huff, sitting on the edge of my bed. Now I'm going to have to put all these clothes away before I can go to sleep.

"Text me your size."

"What?" I blurt out into the phone. Is he crazy? "No, I'm not giving you my dress size. That's private information."

"Your vagina is private, not your dress size, and you let me fuck that. Text me your fucking dress size."

My jaw is on the floor. "And then what?"

"Then sit your ass down and wait for me to get there."

"You're so bossy."

"And you don't want to admit it, but you like it."

The call ends because he loves to have the last word.

That leaves me to have to actually listen to him and wait, which I'm certain is exactly what he wanted.

Beckham stands on the other side of the door looking like some sort of fallen angel. The tuxedo he wears is cut and fitted to his body like a second skin. There's no doubt that it's a custom-tailored tux. No rentals for Beckham Sullivan—not that Sullivans would ever have to consider such a travesty.

His camera bag is slung over one shoulder, a garment bag clasped in his opposite hand.

"Are you going to let me in or eye-fuck me all night? We have places to be."

"Get in here," I grumble. He's always ruining everything. "Let me see it." I reach out with grabby hands for the bag.

"Greedy little thing, aren't you?" he says in a husky sex-promising voice.

Laurel squeaks from her spot on the couch, a blanket wrapped around her shoulders.

"Ignore him," I hiss at her.

"I see why he got you pregnant."

"Laurel."

"What? He's . . . potent."

Beckham's grin grows. I've never seen him smile so big. "Don't you say a word." I point a warning finger in his face. "And you"—I swing toward Laurel—"keep your thoughts in your brain."

She throws her hands up, accidentally shucking her blanket off in the process. "No promises."

"I need the dress," I remind Beckham. "We're already running late."

"We're fine. We have thirty minutes."

"And city traffic to contend with," I remind him, snatching the bag when he won't hand it over.

I hurry to my room and shut the door behind me. After hanging up the garment bag on the back of my closet door, I carefully unzip it to reveal the most stunning dress I've ever seen in my life. It's like something straight from my imagination. Thin spaghetti straps attach to a champagne-gold dress with a sweetheart neckline. It seems to shimmer in the light, but it's not made of sequins. The fabric is almost soft, velvety.

Knowing I can't afford to waste any more time staring at the gown, I quickly take off my lounge clothes and slip into it. It fits like a glove, but I'm still going to need help with the zipper.

"Laurel," I call out. "I need help."

The door opens a second later like she was waiting for this very thing.

Only, when I look over my shoulder, it's Beckham slipping into my room like the devil himself come to tempt me to the dark side. Butterflies take off in my stomach.

Obviously, it makes sense that I would be attracted to the father of my child, or else I wouldn't have had sex with him in the first place, but something washes over me where I'd much rather ditch the event and tug him onto my bed.

Hormones—it has to be, because there's no logical way that I actually want to fuck this man again.

He arches a brow, and I realize I've been staring far longer than is socially acceptable. "You needed help?"

"Y-yes," I stutter, hoping I don't sound as horny as I feel. "The zipper. I can't reach it."

"Turn around." His tone is raspy, commanding. I can't help but listen. A shiver races down my spine when he ever so lightly skims his finger over the back of my neck. He finds the zipper at the base of my spine, then drags it all the way up. "Perfect fit." The words are almost a whisper. I gasp in surprise, my body falling back into his when he kisses the top of my shoulder. He steps away, leaving me cold. "Do you have shoes that will work with the dress?"

It takes me a moment to gather my wits. "Yes."

He waits by my dresser, looking around my room while I grab heels from my closet. "Your room is different than I expected."

"How so?" I sit down to fit my feet into the heels.

"It's . . . mismatched."

I look around, trying to see it through his eyes. "You thought it would be like my parents' house? Cold, white, and sterile?" I shudder at the very thought. "No way." My room is a mix of earth-toned colors with furniture that doesn't match the next piece. Don't get me wrong: they all work together, but nothing is a set.

I grab my clutch off the bed. It has my phone tucked safely inside, along with a small notepad I'll use to take notes. I'm not sure I'll ever outgrow my love for paper and pen. "This dress . . . how'd you get it?"

He looks at me like I'm insane. "I went into a store and picked it out."

"You picked this out?"

"I didn't shuck the duty off on some employee, if that's what you're implying. Besides"—he opens the door to the rest of the apartment, eyeing me over his shoulder—"I know what you look good in. They wouldn't."

Chapter Twenty-Six

BECKHAM

I'm supposed to be photographing the event, not Lennon, but it's not my fault my camera continues to seek her out. She's magnetic, the way she carries herself through the massive room. I'm not sure if she's aware of the way I follow her like a lost puppy.

The charity fundraiser is to gather funds from some of New York's elite to help fuel children's cancer research. I can't help but be a skeptic and wonder how much of that money will truly help anyone, but I hope I'm wrong.

Lennon speaks with one of the directors of the organization. The man is clearly enraptured with her. It shouldn't bother me—I have no reason to care, and he's old enough to be her grandfather—but sometimes there's no rational explanation for our feelings.

Ever since she told me about going on the date, I've found myself becoming more irrational when it comes to her. I don't want to admit it, not to her, definitely not to myself, but I'm beginning to feel things for her. Not love. It can't be that. But I do care.

Forcing myself to turn away from them, I take photos that I can actually use that aren't focused on Lennon. I'm positive Jaci wouldn't be pleased if all I had to show for tonight were pictures of the woman she believes me to be dating.

Dinner will be served soon, with some people already finding their seats.

After exploring the room for another five minutes, snapping some photos here and there as I go, I finally let my eyes find Lennon again, and she's *still* talking to the man. Annoyed, I allow myself to head in their direction.

She laughs at something he says, making my lip curl with displeasure. I know that old man didn't say anything nearly so funny to merit this response.

I reach the two of them, trying to contain my glower at the man. I don't know his name, and after watching him converse with Lennon for what I've deemed an inappropriate amount of time, I don't care to know.

I get into their personal space, forcing their conversation to an end. Shoving my hand at the man, I introduce myself. "Beckham Sullivan."

"It's nice to meet you. I'm—"

"I don't care."

Lennon lets out a squeak of surprise, like she can't believe I'm being so rude. Does she not know me at all?

"Babe," I say, stepping between her and *the man*, as I've dubbed him. "You need to sit down. You're pregnant. Food's being served soon anyway. Take a break." Turning my back to her before she can respond, I face *the man*. "That's right, she's pregnant. I'm the father, in case that wasn't clear."

Grabbing Lennon's hand, I guide her toward a table.

It's not surprising at all when she fights me the whole way.

"Beckham." She says my name through clenched teeth in a hushed tone, probably not wanting to draw attention our way. "What are you doing? I was interviewing—"

"You interviewed him long enough."

"You're ridiculous."

"And you need to sit down."

I already located our seats previously, so I find them easily enough. With my free hand, I pull out the chair for her to sit down. She doesn't fight me on it, so that tells me she does need the break. Just as I suspected.

Sitting beside her, I don't let the glare she sends my way bother me. I got her away from the old guy, and that's all that matters to me.

Her fingers brush against my shoulder, plucking something off my tux jacket. She holds it up, letting the light catch the orange cat hair.

Fighting a smile, she says, "Cheddar dust."

"Smart-ass."

"What's the real reason you didn't want me talking to Mr. Martin?"

"I didn't like the way he was looking at you. He's old and it was creepy."

A burst of laughter flies out of her lips. "He's not that old. He's in his fifties."

My hackles raise. "Like I said, he's old."

She shakes her head. "You're ridiculous."

Only when it comes to her—not that I'll admit it. "How are your feet?"

We've been here awhile already, and I can't imagine it's too comfortable as a woman to wear heels in any circumstance, let alone while pregnant.

"My feet are fine." I don't believe her. "Find something else to worry about." She's my favorite thing to worry about. "Really, I'm fine," she adds, apparently noticing the doubt I don't bother to hide from her. Across the room, someone calls for everyone to find their seats for the dinner. "Although," she goes on, "food does sound great right about now."

"Do you have what you need? As far as interviews."

She gives me a horrified look. "No. I have a whole list of people Jaci wants me to speak to, and I've barely made a dent in it."

"Oh, come on," I plead, looking around to see where the food is. My pet sperm needs to be fed. "We can ditch after the dinner. She'll never know." I keep my voice hushed now that we're not alone at the table.

Lennon's jaw drops slightly. "Are you crazy? Do you want to get me fired? I'm going to be a single mom. A job is more important now than ever."

My hackles rise. "You're not a single mom—I'm a part of this. I'm helping you in any way you need."

I refuse to be a deadbeat parent. I can't guarantee I'll be a good one, since God knows I haven't got a clue what I'm doing, but I'm going to try, and I'm willing to learn. That has to count for something.

"Technically, I am. We're not together."

I shouldn't need the reminder—I know we're not a couple—but hearing her say it almost feels like a slap in the face, because somewhere along the way, I started to think of us as a team of sorts. I didn't mean to—it's an accidental development—but the reminder that we're not anything stings.

"It doesn't bother you if I say I'm a single dad?" I retort, noticing the minuscule tic of her cheek that gives away the fact that she is annoyed by it.

"No."

"Why do you always lie to me?"

She sighs as the food arrives at our table. "I'm not lying to you, Beckham."

"You just did it again."

She smiles at the waiter setting the plate in front of her. "You're in rare form tonight."

"I'm always like this."

"And yet, somehow you're even worse than usual."

She reaches down, trying to be inconspicuous about it as she rubs her right ankle.

"Give me the shoes," I demand.

Her face morphs into horror, eyes bugged out, mouth gaped. "Ew, no."

"Take them off while we eat. Give your feet a break."

"I can't do that," she hisses in horror.

We're locked in a battle of wills. "Do your feet stink?"

"I-I don't think so?"

"Let your feet rest. No one will even notice." The black tablecloth drapes against the floor. It would be easy enough for her to tuck her feet beneath it, and no one would see that she'd ditched the heels.

"Fine," she reluctantly agrees. I smirk at the fact that she's giving in. "Don't act so smug." She bends slightly, taking a heel off. "My feet are killing me."

"I'll rub them for you later."

"You will?" I should probably be annoyed that she sounds so surprised that I'd even offer. I know I can be . . . *me*, but I don't think I'm a bad guy.

"Sure."

"Sure?" she repeats, brown eyes narrowed like if she squints hard enough, she could see right through me. "That sounds very reassuring."

"Lennon." I say her name slowly, carefully, making sure I have her full attention. "You're growing my child, you're working, and you're wearing heels that are what? Six inches? I have zero problem massaging your feet if it makes you feel better."

Her lips tremble like she's either trying not to laugh or cry. I'm not sure which is more horrifying.

"I can't believe we're talking about my feet at a table surrounded by other people."

I look around, and they're all locked into conversation with each other, not paying attention to us. "I don't think they care."

She places her hand absentmindedly on her belly. It's an unconscious gesture, and even though there's the tiniest bit of a swell beginning to show in her stomach, it's still strange to think of her growing

163

even bigger. Being able to feel the baby move. Having the baby *here*. In only a matter of months, I'll be holding my kid.

"I need to tell my parents soon," she mutters, more to herself than me. She bites down on her bottom lip. "God, I'm scared. It's so silly. I'm an adult."

"When do you want to tell them?"

I'm following her lead on this. I haven't peeped a word to my parents, who I know will both be thrilled, because if they know, then my mom will definitely spill the beans to the Wellses.

Fuck, that thought makes *me* scared, and suddenly I'm a teenage boy intimidated by this wealthy family all over again. I knew I didn't belong in that world, and when her brother found out about what Lennon and I had done, Hunter wasted no time reminding me of it.

I rub a hand over my jaw, waiting for her response.

"Not yet," she answers softly, almost pleadingly.

Beneath the table I place my palm on her knee, giving it a squeeze. When she doesn't shove my hand away, I leave it there. I think I need this physical contact as much as she does. "Whatever they say, whatever they think, I hope you know it doesn't matter."

"I know." It's a wooden answer, an automatic response.

What did they do to you? I ask with my eyes.

She blinks at me, her answer reflected back at me. *It doesn't matter.*

But it does. It does to me.

Chapter Twenty-Seven

LENNON

Halloween is around the corner, only a few days away, and I'm freaking out a bit. Or a lot.

Because this means I can't put off the inevitable much longer—telling my family about the baby. I should just do it, rip it off like a Band-Aid, but pathetically I'm not sure I can. I know I'll be seeing them for the Thanksgiving holiday, and Beckham will be headed back to Connecticut as well, so maybe it's best to wait until then and do it in person. I'll definitely be showing, but I think with an oversize sweater I'll be able to hide it temporarily.

"Are you nervous about the interview?"

My head swivels in Beckham's direction. I forgot he was beside me, which is quite a feat since his presence is so potent. Not that I'll ever be telling him that.

"Huh? What? No."

"Oh." He types something in an email. "You seem distracted. Worried, almost." He lifts a mug of coffee to his lips, peering at me over the rim.

We're seated inside a diner, not far from the office, to meet our first interviewee for our project. Her job is nearby, this location being her suggestion, which worked great for us.

"It's not about the interview." I mouth a thank-you to our waitress when she delivers my glass of sweet tea. I don't know what it is about the drink, but it's become my first real pregnancy craving. I can't get enough. It's one I don't give in to often—too much sugar and caffeine wouldn't be good for the baby—but right now I need some.

He clicks "Send" on his email. "Then what's it about?" He drapes his arm over the back of the booth behind me, using the gesture as leverage to lean closer to me. I am effectively caged by his body.

I know he means nothing by it, at least nothing sexual, but tell that to my body, which doesn't seem to know better.

Apparently, I've hit not only the craving stage but the sexual-yearning one as well.

My vibrator is getting a workout tonight.

"Why are you looking at me like that? Are you okay? You're breathing funny."

I shake my head roughly, trying to rid myself of the internal tangent I've gone on, not to mention the mental flashbacks of everything he did to me in Chicago.

"I'm fine, I swear." Heat is rising to my cheeks. I hope he can't tell I'm blushing.

"Are you sure? You're worrying me."

And to his credit he genuinely does look concerned. "I'm fine," I reiterate. "Truly. Just have a lot on my mind."

Not a total lie.

I do have a lot on my mind these days. It just so happens at this particular moment that I'm thinking about him.

Naked.

Mouth on—

"Here's that cinnamon bun for you. Your sandwich will be right out." The waitress sets the plate in front of me, and I immediately forget about my sex-ravenous thoughts, because this cinnamon bun looks like the greatest thing I've ever seen in my whole life.

"That looks good."

I glare at the man beside me. "If you even think about stealing a bite, I'll gut you like a fish with my fork."

His eyes widen in surprise, lips threatening to curl in amusement. "You're feisty today."

"I suppose I am." I dig into my cinnamon bun, watching the door for Cassie Locke to arrive.

Beckham closes his computer before tucking it back into his bag. I'm not even sure why he's here for the interview. He brought his camera, but we spoke about doing one massive photo shoot with all the women we interview at the end, if our proposal is the winner. We wanted to have some interviews complete already, to round out our pitch. Despite his presence being unnecessary, I haven't given him any shit about it.

Oh my God, does that mean there's some part of me that wants him here?

I shudder at the thought.

"Is the cinnamon bun that good?"

I give him a mystified look. "Huh?"

He shakes his head. "You're way too lost in your thoughts today." He's not wrong.

"I'm fine."

Just then the door to the diner chimes, and Cassie enters. I lift my hand in a wave, flagging her toward our table.

She smiles as she weaves her way through the tables to reach the booth we snagged in a corner.

"Hi, so sorry I'm late." She extends a hand to each of us before sliding into the booth. "My meeting ran over."

"It's no problem at all. It's nice to formally meet you."

"Likewise."

"This is Beckham," I say, introducing the man at my side. "I've mentioned him in our chats. He's a photographer at *Real Point* and my partner on this project."

"Yes, yes," she chants, unzipping her jacket. "I remember you saying that."

"Why don't you go ahead and order. Then we'll get to it." I pull out my notebook and pen.

"That would be great. I'm starving."

After she's placed her order, I turn on the recorder and start my questions. I feel Beckham's eyes boring into the side of my face the entire time. It's distracting, but I do my best not to show it. I don't want to give him the satisfaction of knowing he's thrown me off my game.

"You're currently leading a major PR firm. It's a huge accomplishment you should be proud of, but we know with success oftentimes comes critiques. Can you tell me about some of the worst comments you've had?"

Cassie tucks a piece of dark hair behind her ear. "Yeah, sure. As a woman it can be tough in almost any industry to be taken seriously, especially as an authority figure." She reaches for the soda she ordered. "I worked hard for my position, as much as anyone else. I went to school, started from the bottom, and moved up in the company over the years. But it didn't stop the rumors, the whispers from my fellow coworkers—particularly the men—that I was sleeping my way up the corporate ladder." She laughs humorlessly. "Despite the fact we all had the same degrees, similar work experience. They didn't take into account that I put in more hours, and frankly had better ideas than them. They couldn't comprehend that maybe I was merely good at my job—no, I must be fucking the boss to get there." Rubbing a hand over her face, she gives us a small smile. "I'm sorry. It's a sore subject, but that's why I agreed to do this." Her pointer finger flicks between us. "I think it's important to bring to light the injustices women can face in the workforce. That's not to say there aren't good people out there that would never say those kinds of things, but we should hold the ones who do accountable."

Beckham stiffens beside me. I think I know why, but I won't comment on it. It's not the time or place.

I move on to more questions for Cassie, and before I know it, our hour is up and she has to head back to work. As do we. Beckham did snap some photos, explaining he thought Jaci would appreciate some candid interview shots along with the more editorial-style shoot we have planned for the end of this project, if we get chosen. I have to give him credit: it's a good idea.

Before we leave the diner, I ask for a to-go cup of sweet tea.

"Is this a craving?" He pulls out his wallet and lays some loose bills down on the table to cover the tip. "I've watched you down at least two glasses of the stuff since we've been here. Is that even good for you? The baby? Isn't there a lot of sugar in sweet tea?"

I gape at him. "It might be," I hedge. "Okay, it isn't the best for the baby if I have too much, but please don't judge my craving. Let me enjoy my tea. It's the only thing bringing me joy at the moment. I promise not to overdo it."

He snorts—well, he comes as close to the sound as he's capable. "That's all that's bringing you joy? I thought pregnancy was supposed to make you glow with joy?"

"I'm pretty sure the glow is just sweat." I accept the to-go cup from the waitress so we can finally leave. "Seriously, I've never sweated so much in my life."

He looks at me over his shoulder before exiting the diner. "I didn't need to know that."

"You got me pregnant—that means you're obligated to hear all the gross details. Speaking of gross details," I continue on, dodging people speed-walking in the opposite direction on the sidewalk, "I'm so constipated. I haven't pooped in like three days."

He chokes, rearing back. "Lennon. Jesus."

"I know, it's terrible. Maybe I should get a pumpkin-spice latte? Those always make me go to the bathroom." I start to turn in the opposite direction, to head to where I know there's a Starbucks, but his hand loops around my arm, holding me prisoner.

"Let's wait until after work for that. I can't let you destroy the work toilets. I'm not sure they could handle both you and Brendan when he has his Chipotle."

I bite my lip, trying to hold in a giggle. "Good point."

We head back to the office, and he nearly shocks me speechless when he actually holds the door open for me.

"Don't look so flabbergasted. I'm capable of being a gentleman when I want to be."

Damn him, those words make me think about how very ungentlemanly he was in the bedroom. Not in a bad way, but it's Beckham. He's going to be dominant. It's in his nature. He's always had this commanding way of carrying himself. Even when he was young.

He falls into step beside me, heading for the elevator bay. "Are you cold?"

"Huh?" I give him a confused look.

"You shivered."

"Oh . . . um . . . I'm not cold." Am I blushing as much as I think I am? I hope not.

"But you—"

"Drop it," I plead, pushing the button repeatedly to call the elevator, even though I know that won't make it go any faster.

His eyes narrow, no doubt taking in my flushed state. "Are you turned on right now?"

"No!"

He gapes at me, looking both surprised and intrigued. "You definitely are."

"I am not."

He looks me in the eyes. I can't help it when I start to wiggle uncomfortably. "I'm going to help you."

"What?" I blurt out, but he's already pulling me away from the elevators. We've just turned the corner when it dings its arrival. I was so close to escape. Beckham glances around, then opens a door and tugs me in after him. "What are you doing?"

"Like I said, helping you out." He flicks the lock closed on the door, and we're inside some small empty office space with desks and computers. "If you think for a minute I'm going to let you find someone else to take care of you, think again." He shucks off his jacket and tosses it onto a chair, then loosens his tie and the cuffs on his shirt. Rolling the sleeves up his forearms, he arches a brow at me. "Don't just stand there. Hop up." He pats the table like he wants me to sit on it.

"Beckham, this is ridiculous. I'm fine. I don't need . . . you don't need . . ." I hide my face in my hands.

"Lennon." He says my name like he knows I'm moments away from running from the room. "Does it look like I'm feeling any sort of hardship at the thought of pleasuring you?"

He points to the crotch of his pants, where it becomes painfully obvious that he's turned on.

"I . . . oh."

"Now, please, for the love of God, get your ass on this table and let me lick your pussy."

I don't argue with him further and instead just listen to the man.

I've barely sat down when he encourages me to lie back. Blood roars in my ears. I don't want to want this, but I do. He pushes at my skirt, rolling it up my hips. I rise to help him, and soon it's bunched around my stomach.

His blue eyes hold me frozen for a moment. I can't take my eyes off him when he slides my panties to the side. My breath catches when he rubs two fingers over my folds. A slow grin spreads over his lips.

"You're wet, Lennon."

"I am?" Of course I am. I've been struggling most of the day, and even though I don't want to admit it, this man does something to me. Something dangerous that consumes me in a way that terrifies me.

"Mmm." He rubs again, letting his fingers slide in just a little. Not enough, not near enough, but I moan anyway. "You want me."

I shake my head. "N-no. It's not you."

Annoyance flashes across his face. "Don't lie to me." He presses his thumb against my clit, my back bowing off the table. "You can hate me and still want to fuck me."

"I don't hate you."

He arches a brow. "You sure about that?" I give a broken cry in response when his fingers curl inside me. "It's okay if you do," he goes on, eyes dilated as he watches the pleasure on my face. "It doesn't mean I can't still make you feel good."

He swipes his tongue over my clit, eliciting a surprised gasp from between my lips. My fingers delve into his hair as he works me with his tongue and fingers. I grip those strands of hair roughly, pulling, tugging. He groans at the bite of pain but doesn't ask me to stop. If anything I think it turns him on even more.

My hips rock against his mouth, begging and demanding. My orgasm is right there on the cusp. I know it won't take much to set me off, to fall over that cliff into bliss.

"Yesyesyesyes," I chant, my words blurring together. "Don't stop." I can feel sweat dampen my skin. I'm not sure how I'm going to collect myself enough to go back to the office, but I can't dwell on that right now, since there's zero chance of me stopping this. "Beckham," I beg, practically crying with need.

His groans and moans fill my ears. I feel myself grow wetter just listening to him.

"You taste so good, honeybee. So fucking good. Here, have some."

I mewl in protest when his fingers leave my body. Then they're nudging at my lips, pushing inside my mouth. I wrap my lips around his fingers, tasting myself on him.

"Good, right, baby?"

He doesn't wait for me to answer. He takes the hand whose fingers were just in my mouth and wraps it around my throat, applying a hint of pressure. His tongue laps at my pussy, my body squirming again on the table.

"Please," I beg, my nails scraping against the fabric of his shirt. "Fuck me, Beckham. Please."

He strokes himself over his pants but doesn't pull his cock out.

I want it, I want it, I want—

My orgasm shatters through me, his hand moving from my throat to my mouth to cover my cries. My breaths are ragged as pleasure rattles inside me, my body shaking with aftershocks.

"Holy shit," I finally mutter, slowly coming to in time to see Beckham straightening his clothes. "You . . . ?" I gesture vaguely to his crotch area, where the erection tenting his pants is still painfully obvious.

"Are fine." He shocks me speechless when he places a gentle kiss on my forehead. "I'll head upstairs first while you clean up." He picks his jacket up from the chair, draping it over his arm.

"Okay." My voice still sounds breathless, shaky.

He excuses himself from the room, leaving me alone with my skirt still around my stomach, my pussy on display to any hapless person who might be unlucky enough to happen by and open the door. I shouldn't be surprised that he'd leave me behind like some trussed-up turkey. I give a small laugh and wiggle my skirt down as I hop off the table. I didn't realize my heels fell off, but they lie haphazardly on the ground. After putting them on, I fluff my hair and slip from the room to the restrooms on the main floor to wash up.

By the time I make it up to the office, at least ten or fifteen minutes have gone by.

Beckham is talking to Brendan, somehow managing to look completely put together and not like he had his head up my skirt only a little bit ago.

His jaw moves back and forth, chewing gum.

When he catches me staring, he winks.

With a shake of my head, I settle back at my desk and force thoughts of him from my brain so I can finish the article I was working on before we left to meet up with Cassie.

Beckham Sullivan is dangerous—for my mind, my body, but most importantly my heart.

Chapter Twenty-Eight

BECKHAM

"Trick or treat!"

I stare at the woman on the other side of my door. "What the fuck are you supposed to be?"

She balks at me. "Seriously? You don't know?"

I blink, stepping aside so she can enter. Cheddar is already yowling with excitement at a new person to love and pet him. "No, I don't. Hence me asking."

She sighs in a way that shows her complete and utter disappointment in me. "I'm a Dementor from Harry Potter. Duh."

"How was I supposed to know that? You look more like the grim reaper."

"I'm truly offended right now."

"Um . . . sorry? Don't most people dress up as, I don't know, Harry Potter himself or Hermione?" I wave a hand at her black, hooded garb. "I hate to break it to you, but my brain didn't go to Dementor."

"You're a party pooper." She scoops up Cheddar into her arms, which is quite a strange sight with her in costume. She cocks her creepy head to the side. "Do you have sweet tea?"

I ease toward the kitchen. "I might," I lie, pretending to search the fridge before coming up empty. "Um . . . bad news?" I turn around to find her watching me with crossed arms. Cheddar purrs, rubbing his body between her legs.

"Why did you frame it as a question?"

"Because there are other liquids?" I grab a bottle of water and hand it to her.

She takes it, twisting off the cap. After a few swallows, she asks, "You definitely don't have sweet tea?"

"No, I don't like it."

Her mouth gapes, equal parts shocked and annoyed. "Then why did you pretend to look? You might not like it, but you'd think you'd at least have it on hand for the woman who is carrying your child."

"Um," I say, feeling a tad chagrined, "I didn't think to buy any." I close the fridge, rubbing my jaw. "I can run down to the store and get some if you really want it."

"I really want it, Beckham."

"Okay, then." I swipe my wallet off the kitchen counter. "I'll be right back. But I'm cutting you off after one glass. Eight ounces—I'm measuring it."

She narrows her eyes on me but surprisingly doesn't argue.

"Before you go, can I use your shower? And maybe borrow something to wear? As fun as this all is"—she does a spin in her gray-and-black robes—"my face is itchy, and I want to be comfy."

Tucking my wallet in my pocket, I stifle a sigh. "Yeah, come on."

She follows me to my bedroom. I wonder what she thinks, how it adds up in her mind to what she'd expect of me. Her room certainly wasn't what I predicted.

Searching my drawers, I find an older tee that shouldn't completely drown her and a pair of lounge pants that she'll be able to tighten with the drawstring. I carry them to the bathroom, and she follows behind me.

We haven't spoken all that much since I went down on her at work, which makes her showing up here all the more surprising. Or maybe that's why she's here? She wants a round two?

I don't think I've felt this rattled by a woman since . . . well, since her, back when we were both clueless teenagers and feelings were weird.

"Everything you need is in here. Try not to destroy my bathroom with your—"

She glares at me, hands on her hips. "Stop hating on my costume. You know it's brilliant and just don't want to admit it."

"Yeah, yeah. Let's go with that." I just know I'm going to come back to my white sink covered in black-and-gray face paint. "Is there anything else you want besides tea?"

"Popcorn. Some chocolate too. And maybe pizza? Yeah, pizza too." At my shocked expression, she pouts. "Don't judge me, I skipped dinner."

"I'm not judging." I totally was. I mean, she can have whatever she wants; I don't care. But it's a weird combination of things.

"Sure, you're not. Now go get my drink and all the other stuff." She shoos me from the bathroom.

I think I've become Lennon's bitch boy.

Surprisingly, I don't even mind it.

Is this what it means to be whipped?

I struggle to hold on to everything in order to let myself inside the apartment. I'm not about to set something down either. That's for quitters.

When I finally manage to get inside, the lights are dimmed and a movie plays in the background.

"I'm so glad you've made yourself at home." Sarcasm drips from my voice.

She tosses a pillow from the couch in my general direction. It lands nowhere near me. "I knew you'd want me to get comfortable."

I sigh, scratching at the stubble on my jaw. I *did* invite her over. It surprised me when she started texting me earlier in the evening. At first it was just randomness that was kind of amusing, mostly texts about what everyone was up to at the party she was attending, but when the messages kept pouring in steadily, I deduced that she was bored and invited her over.

I'm not sure what it is about this woman that possesses me to do such stupid things as invite her into my home. I never have anyone over except my parents.

I carry everything into the living area, where I set the pizza box and the bag of other things on the table. "I'll go pop some popcorn."

"Wait." She grabs my fingers loosely before I can walk away. "Thank you. For letting me come over, for feeding me."

I stare at her for a moment, something sappy on the tip of my tongue. I don't let it slip. "You have some face paint caked around your nose," I say instead.

She gasps, launching her body from the couch to hurry down the hall to the bathroom.

I only seem to know how to ruin moments. Self-Sabotage should be my middle name. I bet a therapist would have a field day with me, not that I'd ever give them the chance.

After removing the plastic wrapper from the popcorn, I stick the bag in the microwave. Cheddar hops up on the counter, meowing. I swear he's telling me how much he likes Lennon.

"Me too, Cheddar." I scratch him behind the ears, then dig through my cabinets for a large enough bowl.

Lennon's been the one girl who's ever gotten to me, and there are a multitude of reasons why. She's insanely brilliant and quick witted, a talented writer, confident, and beautiful inside and out. It sounds cheesy, but it's true.

I remember the first time I saw her after I was adopted. There was this instant recognition, like I'd known her forever, when in reality I had never met her. But she made me feel at ease immediately. When I saw her, I knew everything would be okay.

As I'm emptying the popcorn, Lennon tiptoes into the kitchen, carrying the pizza box. "God, that smells amazing. I'm so hungry."

"You could've had a snack while I was gone."

She lifts the lid of the pizza box and plucks out a slice. "I didn't want to go through your stuff."

"You know I wouldn't have cared."

She arches a brow. "But wouldn't you have?"

"Maybe a little."

She laughs as I follow her into the living room. "At least you admit it."

"What are we watching?" I sit down on the couch, peering at the screen to try to figure it out.

"*Beetlejuice*," she responds, sinking into the couch cushions. "It's one of my all-time favorite movies."

"Wow, I haven't watched this in . . . a long time."

"I can tell. You didn't even remember it."

"There's a lot I tried to forget from that time in my life."

She watches the side of my face, not the movie. "Why is that?"

Because it hurt too much.

"A lot of reasons."

"We had good memories."

"We did." Almost all my good memories center around her.

"Do you remember . . . ," she begins before trailing off, almost like she's scared to know the answer to whatever it is she wants to ask. Finally, she must decide to just go for it. "Do you remember that camera I got you for your fifteenth birthday?"

I'm mildly offended she thinks I could forget. "I remember."

That camera has a place of honor on my bedroom dresser. I'm surprised she didn't spot it when she followed me in, or maybe she did but thinks I forgot she was the one to give it to me.

"You kept saying you wanted to take photos, to be a photographer."

"And you got my first camera. Well, film camera anyway." I stuff my face with popcorn. "There were things I wanted to forget, but that was never one of them."

"How did things end up like this?" She looks at me with pleading brown eyes, trying desperately to understand how things fell apart, but looking back now, it's difficult for me to put it into words.

Sure, I never felt welcome in that elitist world she was born in, and her brother had no problem reminding me of my place the minute he noticed I was interested in Lennon. But it all seems so trivial now that I sit beside her in my apartment. I was young, a fool. I didn't know better and had so much to learn about myself and the world.

"Life, I guess." I don't have another explanation for her.

With a wistful smile on her face, she says, "I can't believe I'm sitting here right now with you. Pregnant, of all things. Twelve-year-old me would've been stoked. Of course, she thought we'd be married."

I can't believe she's telling me all this. It's like she's swallowed some sort of truth serum. It's interesting to hear what she has to say, how different it is from the assumptions I've had.

"You thought you'd marry me?"

She rolls her eyes. "I'm not surprised you're flattered by that." She adjusts the pillow behind her back. Cheddar cracks an eye open to check out what she's doing but goes back to sleep as soon as she's still. "I was a kid, and you were my brother's hot best friend. How could I not make up some fantasy happy ending for us?"

She places her hand on her stomach. I watch the gentle way she splays her fingers over the tiniest bump. "Have you felt her move yet?"

Lennon's brows shoot up in surprise. I can't help but grin. "Her?" she accuses.

"Her. It's a girl. I feel it."

"And if it's not?"

"I'll love a boy just as much. I don't care what our baby is, but I have a gut feeling it's a girl."

She rubs her hand in small, slow circles over her belly. I know that shouldn't fill me with so much satisfaction, but knowing I did that, that I put my baby in her, makes me feel powerful.

"How can you have a gut feeling, and I don't? I'm the mother. What happened to mother's intuition?"

"I guess you're lacking, honeybee. Time to catch up." I snap my fingers.

Her hands shoot out, capturing mine before I can snap again. "Don't rub it in my face."

I give her a funny look. "You're really upset about this?"

"Yes!" Her eyes fill with tears. "What if I have no motherly instincts at all? God knows my parents weren't the loving, caring people they should've been, so what if I'm somehow defective?"

"You're not." I say it with the utmost confidence.

"How can you be so sure?"

"My gut."

She pokes my side. "If you say something about your gut one more time . . ." She leaves the warning hanging in the air, not letting me know what the threat is.

"What?" I laugh, grabbing her hand before she can poke me again. "I'm being honest. You're kind, and caring, and so many other things. You're everything our kid will be lucky to have."

Her hand stills in mine, her lower lip trembling slightly. "Don't you dare make me cry. I'm already hormonal enough."

I chuckle, amused. "What if I kiss you instead?"

Her eyes widen in shock. I don't spare a breath before I loop my hand behind the curve of her neck, drawing her lips to mine.

She sinks into me with a slight mewl, like she's fighting against herself, fighting against wanting me.

I beg her with my tongue to give in.

To give in to what, I'm not even sure.

I'm not good for her.

I'm not boyfriend material.

Certainly not the kind of guy who could be the husband she deserves.

But we have this attraction, and right now, can't that be enough?

"Beckham." She gasps my name. It has me grabbing her by the hip to haul her onto my lap. Her breath is shaky as my erection presses against her core. I can't help it when it comes to her.

I cup her cheek, rubbing my thumb over her soft skin, still reddened from when she scrubbed her face clean of that atrocious makeup. "What do you need, baby?"

She sits back on my lap slightly, hands on my chest. Her eyes are hooded, lips pink. She hesitates, not sure if she wants to voice what we both know to be true. "You."

I look her over, searching for any sign of regret at her admission. "Are you sure?"

"Yes. But for the record, this isn't why I came over." Her eyes flick down to my lips and back up. It's so quick I don't think she meant to do it. I can't help but smile, drawing her eyes to my mouth again.

"For the record, I don't fucking care." With my arm around her waist, I grab on to her ass and haul her up and into my arms. "I've needed to be balls-deep inside you since I tasted your sweet pussy this week."

She laughs, kissing my neck, then sucking the skin there. "You could've fucked me on that table. I wouldn't have minded."

I groan at the memory of her spread on the table, and how easy it would've been to sink inside her. "Don't tease me like that."

She kisses the other side of my neck. "It's not a tease when it's true."

I kick my bedroom door closed behind us. Cheddar's going to be pissed, but the orange demon will have to deal with it.

As I lay Lennon down on the bed, I take a moment to look at her. She's in my T-shirt and baggy pants, and the word *sexy* shouldn't be what comes to mind, but it's exactly what she is.

"Why are you looking at me like that?"

"Because you're gorgeous."

She sits up on her elbows, looking me over with a challenge in her eyes. "Then show me."

I take my time undressing her, which is difficult since she's completely bare beneath the shirt and cotton pants. It helps me to go slow by kissing every inch of skin as it's gradually unveiled to me.

"Beckham." Her fingers curl against my shoulder, her nails biting into my skin through the fabric of my shirt.

"Lennon." My mouth curls around the letters of her name with amusement. I spread her thighs, pressing an open-mouthed kiss to the inside of each leg.

"You're torturing me."

"If this is your idea of torture . . ."

"Shut up," she says in a needy, begging kind of voice. I fucking love hearing her so desperate for me.

"Are you sure you want me to shut up?" I stroke her folds. "Fuck, baby, you're so wet. You love for me to touch you, don't you?" She wiggles beneath me, but I use my shoulders to keep her in place. "Do you want me to put my mouth here?" I slide my fingers inside. "Do you want me to make you come with my tongue?"

She rises up, peering down at me between her legs. "Stop talking and put your mouth to good use."

I grin up at her. "Yes, ma'am."

I put my tongue to work, and in no time she's squirming beneath me. I'd like to think it's a compliment of my skills, but something tells me that being pregnant has her way more sensitive down there. Her thighs squeeze against my head, but I refuse to let that deter me.

Within a shockingly short amount of time, only a few minutes, her body is shaking as her orgasm shatters through her. She covers her eyes with the crook of her arm. While she's recovering, I yank my shirt off, and then my jeans are gone. Stroking my cock, I wait for her to peel her arm away.

Her eyes widen, watching me touch myself.

"You want this?" She nods, eyes hooded from that postorgasm glow. "I need you to say it. I need you to tell me you want my cock."

She whimpers, wiggling on the bed. "Beckham."

I stroke myself harder. "Say it."

"I need you to fuck me." Her voice is broken, pleading, desperate, just like I want her to be. "I want your cock."

"Good girl. That's all I wanted to hear."

I pull her closer to the edge of the bed, lining my dick up with her entrance. Sinking inside her, I moan at the feel of her warmth wrapped around me.

My hips pump into her, and I try my hardest to keep it slow, to be gentle and not be too much.

Her nails dig into my ass cheeks, pulling me into her harder. My strokes are rough as my self-control begins to slip.

"Give it to me," she begs, the words ending in a moan. "I want it."

"I've never been in a woman bare before," I admit, my breaths choppy. "This is . . . fuck, it's so fucking good, Len, you have no idea."

Her cheeks warm. I'm not sure if it's from my words or the nickname that I haven't used in so long, and only once before now. I was inside her then too. We were young, clueless. But now I fuck her like I mean it.

Her cries of pleasure fill my room, spurring me on.

I get lost in her.

I'm drowning.

And I don't want to come up for air.

Chapter Twenty-Nine

LENNON

I turn off the desktop computer, then slide back my chair to grab my purse. The workday is over, and while I should be tired, I feel surprisingly energized. That might be thanks to all the sex I've been having with Beckham the last few weeks. Is it a bad idea to sleep with him? Absolutely. Does it feel oh so good? Again, absolutely.

Besides, it's just sex. There's no chance I'll let him break my heart a second time.

After slipping my purse onto my shoulder, I make my way through the open space toward Beckham's private office. He sits behind his desk, shoulders hunched, his eyes squinted at the screen.

"See you later, Lennon," Brendan says, passing by me. "Sulli, the day's over!" he hollers before he rounds the corner.

Beckham lifts his head, finding me standing just outside the door. "I'm busy." He's gruff, dismissive.

Instantly, my hackles rise. I'm not some lost puppy who trails desperately after him. I don't enjoy being treated as such.

"I was going to ask you if you wanted to go shopping for the baby. There's a store a few blocks from here."

He looks up at me, lips pursed like he's sucked on something sour. "As I said, I'm busy. I don't have time to go shopping for baby things."

It shouldn't offend me, his casual dismissiveness, but it does. If he's like this with me, what will he be like with our child?

"All right." I'm not going to argue with him or attempt to force him to go with me. I'm not so desperate for his attention that I feel the need to do that. I knew the minute that pregnancy test came back positive that I was doing this on my own. "Enjoy your evening."

I don't know how I manage to keep my tone diplomatic.

After taking the elevator down, I pause before I go outside to shrug my coat on. It's a blustery November day, gray skies but no hint of rain, thankfully.

I've bought only a few things for the baby, which, as someone who loves to shop, has been a difficult feat, but there have been other things on my mind. This pregnancy was a surprise, and it has me thinking about a lot of things. Like what kind of parent I hope to be—it's not like I had the greatest example. Or what the future might look like—will I stay in the city or eventually leave so my child has a house and a yard?

When I reach the store with all things baby, I step inside out of the cold air and take in all the soft color tones, blankets, furniture, and everything else one could possibly need for their little one.

"Hi!" An employee comes out of nowhere—I swear it's like she pops up from behind a rocker, just waiting for some innocent expectant mom like myself to wander in. "Is there anything I can help you with?"

I stand there for a moment, flustered by her sudden magic-trick-like appearance. "Um . . . I don't think so."

"Anything specific you're looking for?"

"Oh." I scratch behind my ear nervously. "I was just going to browse."

"Sure." She smiles, nodding almost robotically. "If you need me, I'm Cindy."

"Thanks, Cindy."

Luckily, she disappears. Probably to hide behind more furniture to frighten someone else.

The store is three entire stories of all things children, which is both overwhelming and exciting.

I never knew babies needed so many things—clothes, blankets, pacifiers—and that's only the tip of the iceberg, since apparently there are even baby-specific nail trimmers. It seems way too easy to mess up a child. I think of my own parents, their lack of maternal or paternal skills. I don't want to be like them. No one is a perfect parent, but I want to be as good of a mom as I can be.

I reach the section with things like strollers and car seats. There are so many options I can't help but wonder how you ever decide what the best choice is. I read the information on one of the car seats, baffled at what some of the things mean. Clearly, I'm going to have to spend the night googling stats on everything so I can make my decision on what to get.

I'm on the second level, looking through tiny clothes, when I feel a presence behind me. I nearly jump, expecting to find Cindy lurking, but it's Beckham.

"What are you doing here?" I ask, taking him in like he's some apparition. His hair is windswept, his cheeks a bright red from the biting cold.

"Looking at baby stuff," he replies in a dry tone. "What does it look like I'm doing?"

My hands fly to my hips, a defensive gesture. "It looks like you're creeping behind me."

"Really? Because I was more interested in these . . . whatever these are, than you." He snatches a zippered beige footie-pajama set from the rack, holding it up triumphantly in front of him.

"Whatever you say." I'm annoyed with him. I shouldn't be, I know that, but sometimes being rational is hard to do. I start down another aisle, fully intent on ignoring him, but I can't. I whip back around and glower at his looming presence. "Why are you being such a jerk?" I blurt out, steeling my spine. "Do you get off on being so hot and cold with me? Need I remind you, I've never done anything to you." I poke him in the chest, fully aware I'm literally poking the bear. "You're the one who broke *my* heart. You took my virginity and fucking ran." My voice is getting louder. I can't bring myself to care that we're gaining attention. "You don't get to waltz back into my life, knock me up, and berate me like I hurt you, when we both know that isn't true. I didn't ask for this"—I point at my growing stomach—"but I'm taking it in stride. I refuse to let you make me feel bad for inviting you to look at baby stuff. Forgive me," I say, my voice dripping with venom, "for thinking the father of my child *might* be interested in that."

He stands there, looking properly chagrined. "I'm sorry." Begrudgingly, I have to admit to myself that his apology sounds entirely sincere. He ducks his head, but not before I see a range of emotions swirling over his face. The one that stands out the most is vulnerability. "My problem is entirely mine." His jaw tics with the admission. "It's wrong of me to keep taking it out on you."

I blink in astonishment at him. This might be the most honesty he's ever given me. "And what is it . . . your problem, I mean?"

He rubs a hand over his face. "I'm not good enough for you." It's barely a whisper. In fact, it's so quiet I'm not sure he meant for me to hear him.

Even still, I say, "That's not true, but I know I can't convince you of that. You're the one who has to realize it."

I turn my back on him and return to browsing. Beckham trails me through the store, not saying a word. I pick up a few gender-neutral outfits, looking them over before deciding to get them. There's still a chance that I'll change my mind and find out the gender regardless of what he says, but for now I'm surprisingly content to wait.

He continues to hold on to the one outfit he chose. It has tiny bees on it. I know I shouldn't read into that, since it seemed like an accidental choice, but I can't help it.

Back downstairs, I look at the furniture, pointing out things I like and don't. I mean, if he's going to tag along, he might as well listen to me ramble.

Cindy ends up cornering me to try out some strollers. The one I fall in love with has a million different pieces you can switch out and is able to be used from baby to toddler to even a small child.

Beckham watches me walk past him, pushing the stroller with the bassinet attachment.

There's something in his eyes, a hunger almost, but not of the sexual variety.

I park the stroller back, and Cindy beams. "Would you like to take it home today?"

I shake my head. "No, not today. I'm so sorry. I want to do some more research before I decide." Especially considering the cost of these things. I swear the stroller alone practically requires a down payment. I might've grown up with money not being an issue, and even I can admit that I was spoiled, but that doesn't mean I haven't learned to be careful with my own money.

"No problem. When you're ready, just ask for me." She passes along a business card. Who knew people made commissions on baby products? I'm learning so much just from getting pregnant.

Beckham holds the door open to the street, letting me exit first. I'm not used to him actually being a gentleman. I almost expect him to smack my ass to remind me that he's not.

He shoves his hands in the pockets of his coat, shoulders hunched as he falls into step at my side. "You wanted that stroller."

"I liked it, yes."

"You wanted it," he corrects.

I shoot him a glare. "It was nice, and I liked it. But it's pricey. I want to research it and see reviews from other moms first."

"Reviews? Really? It's a stroller."

"You're giving me a migraine," I gripe, trying to speed-walk away from him.

What a silly notion, considering his long legs. "Am I wrong?"

"I'm new at this," I snap, dodging out of the way of a man who refuses to move aside. Beckham shoots a glare at him over his shoulder. "Just because I like how something looks, or that it's expensive, doesn't make it a good choice for the baby. I don't want to be a bad mom before the baby is even here." It feels like a big confession I just handed him, but I don't know if he sees it that way.

He scoffs. "You could never be a bad mom."

"How do you know?" I counter. "Huh?" Tears prick my eyes. I'm blaming it on the wind burning my eyes. It's definitely not because I'm upset. "My mom treated my brother and me like accessories. I don't know what I'm doing with any of this."

"And you think I do?" he counters, gesturing wildly.

I'm thankful we're in the city and that to these seasoned pros, our behavior is normal. When walking these streets, you get used to seeing people in any kind of state, from annoyed to carefree, to sobbing to raging, or even just flat out looking like they've crash-landed from another planet.

"Lots of people have kids all the time with little to no experience, and they do just fine," he continues, slapping the top of his hand against the palm of his other to drive home his point. "Not that we won't struggle or make mistakes, but this kid is always going to know it has two parents who love them. Got it?" Oh Jesus, I'm a puddle of tears, and why? Because of a stroller? Anxiety? "We're doing this thing together," he reminds me. "You're not alone. And if you ask me, a lot of this is coming from you being scared to tell your parents. Well, I've got news for you—fuck them. If they're mad about this, that's on them. I know my parents are going to be ecstatic to be grandparents. Regardless of them being your family, nothing says you have to keep shitty people in your life. Remember that."

"You have a weird way of giving pep talks."

"At least I try." I guess I do have to give him credit there. In the middle of the busy street, he grabs me and tucks me against his solid chest, where he rests his chin on top of my head. "We're going to get through next week just fine."

Next week, when we go home for the holidays.

When my time is up, and I'll have to tell my parents about the baby.

I don't tell him, but it's a promise I'm not sure he can keep.

Chapter Thirty

BECKHAM

When I pull up in front of Lennon's apartment building, she's already outside waiting, nervously biting at the side of her thumb.

I roll down the window, sliding my sunglasses down the bridge of my nose. "Why are you pacing?"

She lets out a little scream, evidently startled that it's me. I chuckle, amused, though I should've warned her I was driving us, not just taking the train to Connecticut.

"Why are you in a . . . boat?" She wrinkles her nose at my Tahoe.

"Because it's my car."

"This is not a car. This is a whole-ass yacht."

I cover my mouth with my hand, trying to hide my laugh. "At least it has room for the pet sperm. Are you getting in or not?"

She takes a deep, bracing breath and opens the back passenger door to toss her bag inside.

She then climbs into the front seat beside me with a heavy sigh. "I don't want to do this."

I look over my shoulder, waiting for traffic to pass before pulling out. "I know you don't."

Perhaps I should be offended that she's so reluctant to tell her family about the baby, but if anything, I'm angry *for* her. She's an adult; we had sex; sometimes babies happen. She shouldn't feel like she's headed to the firing squad because of something like this. She didn't do anything wrong.

"Do your parents know I'm going to be with you?" She fiddles nervously with the hem of her shirt, waiting for my response.

"Yes, I already told you they do."

Lennon told her parents that she'd be staying with a friend for the holiday. I know they're not happy about it, but as nervous as she already is, I extended the invite before I even said anything to my mom—I knew she'd be ecstatic—because Lennon shouldn't have to stay under the roof of people who make her so visibly ill.

We'll have a Thanksgiving dinner with my parents tonight and with hers tomorrow evening, on the actual holiday.

"Okay, good." She tucks her hair behind her ears, wiggling restlessly in her seat. "Just wanted to confirm."

"By the way . . ." Her eyes shoot in my direction at my tone. "I told my mom we're together."

"Obviously we're together. We're in the same car."

"No," I say slowly, fingers flexing against the steering wheel, "I mean I told her we're a couple."

"You told your mom we're dating? Beckham!"

"What?" I keep my tone innocent. "It makes the most sense to say we're together. We're having a baby, Lennon."

"You don't need to remind me that I'm currently incubating your offspring. Your mom is already planning our wedding. I hope you know that."

"It's just one weekend, Lennon."

She sputters, arms flailing. "No, you idiot, it isn't only one weekend. This baby makes it *life*, and you just told your mom we're a couple."

"It's not that big of a deal."

"I think it is. First you wanted everyone at work to think we're together, and now your parents? I'm starting to think this is some kind of pissing contest, or maybe you really do want to be together." She gasps, hand slapping to her mouth. I keep my eyes focused on traffic, refusing to let her dramatics thwart my attention. "Oh my God, is that what this is—are you trying to convince everyone we're together so that we're so deep in this lie it just makes sense to actually be together?"

"Jesus, Lennon. No. I'm an asshole, but I'm not manipulative."

"Then please, elaborate on why you told your *mom* I'm your girlfriend?"

I chew my gum more forcefully than necessary. "Because I knew it would make her happy."

"You're . . . you . . . baffling, that's what you are." Groaning, she buries her face in her hands. "You do realize your mom talks to mine, right? That means there's no doubt she didn't tell her, and now not only have I kept the baby a secret, but a whole relationship too? A relationship that, mind you, isn't fucking real!" She's in hysterics now. I did this to myself, but in my defense, it seemed like a good idea at the time.

"I think you're blowing this out of proportion."

It's like an icy wind whips through the car at my statement, and I know I've fucked up.

"I know you did not just say that to me."

"Lennon, it's a done deal now. What do you want me to do about it?"

"I don't know—why don't you start by telling them you lied?"

"Mmm." I press my lips together, pretending to think about it. "No, not doing that."

She crosses her arms over her chest. "I'll tell them."

"Think about it. Doesn't it make the most sense to play it off like we're together? It's what they'll want, and with the baby, they'll assume it anyway."

She arches a brow, tapping her lip. "Mmm, you're not selling me on this, I'm afraid. I might have to tell your mom what a liar you are." There's a playful smirk on her lips, so I *think* she's kidding.

Wiggling uncomfortably in my seat, I clear my throat and change lanes. "Can't we just play family for one extended weekend?" I hope I don't sound like I'm begging, but I'm afraid I might. "Would that be so awful? We might as well try, right? We need the practice."

She grows quiet, minutes passing as she ponders my question. I don't dare utter a word while she thinks. I turn the volume up on the radio a smidge.

Finally, after what feels like an eternity, she says, "You have a point."

"See?" I point a finger in the air triumphantly. "I have good ideas sometimes."

"Only sometimes. Don't let it go to your head."

I'm already grinning. "I definitely won't."

With a sigh, she curls her arm against the window, resting her hand on her fist. "I'm taking a nap."

"Okay."

There's a yowl from the back seat. She sits straight up and peers into the back. "You brought your cat?"

I scoff in offense. "You thought I'd leave Cheddar behind? Never. That's my cat son."

"I shouldn't be surprised, and yet I am." She seems almost pleased that I brought my cat. When I go on work trips, I have a neighbor who looks after him, but since I'm going to be at my parents' place, it made the most sense to bring him. "I didn't even notice the carrier when I put my bag in."

"I'm full of surprises. I'm not the guy you think I am." The guy I try to make her think I am.

She curls back up to go to sleep. "That remains to be seen."

With a sigh, I turn the radio up even louder.

◆ ◆ ◆

I pull into the circular paved driveway of the stone mansion. It's the kind of place that's more castle than home—a display of wealth, not warmth. But I know I lucked out that the two people who adopted me are some of the kindest people out there.

Even if their house is showy as fuck.

The SUV isn't even in park when the massive front doors swing wide, and my mom runs out with open arms.

Lennon sputters awake, wiping drool from her mouth. After a bathroom break about an hour ago, she went right back to sleep. I wasn't even going to make any stops since the drive is a relatively short one, but Lennon said the baby demanded she had to pee. I wasn't about to deny the pregnant lady a bathroom.

My mom stands nearby, clapping excitedly while she waits for us to get out of the car.

"Showtime," I tell Lennon.

I don't give her a chance to respond before I get out of the car, then grab Cheddar in his travel carrier from the back. After making my way around to the passenger front, I open the door for Lennon. My mom positively beams.

The look Lennon shoots me isn't angry, not anymore; she just looks worried.

"We'll be fine," I say low enough there's no chance of being overheard.

Taking a deep breath, she nods before taking my hand to help her out of the vehicle.

"I'm so happy to see you two."

Lennon gives a small, awkward wave. "It's so good to see you, Tracy. It's been way too long."

"Oh, you have no idea. I had to practically beg this one to come home for the holiday." She motions to me as if it isn't already obvious enough I'm the one she's referring to. "Can I have a hug?"

"Jeez, Mom, what am I? Chopped liver?"

From inside his carrier, Cheddar yowls in agreement.

"You are when you bring home Lennon as your girlfriend. Why didn't you tell me you two had gotten together? I gave him your number, you know." Finally, she pulls her into an embrace. Her lips part in surprise and she pulls back, holding Lennon at arm's length. "Please, don't take offense—it's just . . . are you?"

I step up behind Lennon, wrapping my arm around her shoulders. She stiffens for half a second before she sinks against me. "You're not imagining things, Mom." The excitement is already building on her face. "Lennon's pregnant."

Her mouth forms a perfect O as she jumps up and down. "A baby! I'm going to be a grandma!"

"And there's more—"

Her eyes widen with excited wonder. "Is it twins?"

Lennon nearly chokes on her own saliva at that preposterous accusation.

"No, not twins," I tell her. "It's just that Lennon and I were together already when I had lunch with you that day, so you can't exactly take credit for this."

She's stunned into silence. It's a miracle. My mother is never lacking for things to say. "Why didn't you tell me?"

There's genuine hurt in her voice. I feel like even more of an asshole, since it's all a lie anyway.

I tilt my head down to Lennon, and she blinks up at me, curious as to how I'm going to explain this one. "It was so new," I say, staring at her and not my mom. "We made each other promise to keep it secret."

"My parents don't know either. About us or the baby," Lennon hastens to add, panic infusing her voice.

My mom covers her mouth. "Oh, thank God I didn't let it slip to Deidre. I spoke to her this morning, but I got distracted and didn't mention it."

Lennon's shoulders relax at this development. "We were going to tell all of you in person, but this one"—she pokes my side—"got a little overzealous and told you ahead of schedule. Well, at least about us."

"That's my Beckham." She beams from ear to ear. "He can't keep secrets from me."

I grab our things out of the car—weighed down between our bags and all Cheddar's things—and finally head inside. Meanwhile, my mom chats with Lennon about anything and everything. If Lennon's bothered by her rambling, she doesn't show it.

Because the house is so big, it takes a ridiculous amount of time to get to my bedroom. It's still pretty much the same from when I was a teen—heavy black furniture, gray wallpaper with a subtle design I never was able to pinpoint, and thick carpet that I swear is more cushioned than some mattresses.

My mom follows us up, still talking Lennon's ear off.

"I'll leave you two to get settled in for now. Your dad and I will be in the drawing room when you want to find us."

She eases the door shut behind her. It latches with a soft click.

"The drawing room," Lennon repeats, shaking her head, with her arms crossed under her breasts. There's a soft, almost annoyed smile on her lips. "Sometimes I forget how rich our families are, and then I come home."

I set our bags down on the couch in the corner. Sunlight streams in through the floor-to-ceiling windows. "I don't." My back is to her so I can't see her reaction.

The bed creaks. "You don't what?"

I turn around to find her sitting on my bed, taking in every detail of my room. There's not much to see. I never was big on personal items.

"I never forget how much money they have. Sometimes I think you forget that I grew up under very different circumstances than you before I was adopted."

She looks down at her hands, studying her nails. "I don't mean to."

I know she doesn't. But growing up in the literal lap of luxury as she did, she has trouble relating to other people who didn't. It's not her fault for being born into the family she has. I know Lennon has a good heart, but when you grow up in a family so wealthy that a million dollars is spending change, then it's hard to understand the real world, how bad things can be, that children are beaten and go to bed hungry.

I cross the room to her, then gently encourage her to look up with my finger beneath her chin.

She blinks those big brown eyes at me. I've always loved her eyes so much, the dark warmth of them, how easy it is to get lost in their depths. I overheard someone say once that brown was the ugliest eye color. I disagree. I find it to be the most beautiful, downright fascinating in the way the color shifts in different lights. From nearly black to a color that's almost golden. There's nothing boring or ugly about brown eyes. Especially not on Lennon.

"I know you don't mean to, but the fact remains that you were born into an incredible life some people only dream of. I'm not saying it was perfect for you—I'm only beginning to see that, and I'm sorry I didn't realize it sooner—but you being able to forget that you come from a life with all this?" I swing an arm to encompass my massive bedroom, which I know for a fact is smaller than hers at the Wells mansion. "That's a privilege you can't deny."

She nods, no doubt understanding what I'm saying.

I let my finger fall from her chin, and my hands go to her belly, hidden beneath an oversize sweater. She's grown so much, and according to her, her belly has popped. Whatever that means.

"Can you believe it?" I murmur, awed.

"That you knocked me up? Definitely not."

"I don't want to fuck this kid up." I hate the vulnerability that rings in my voice, but the words are out there between us, and I can't take them back now. I'm always assuring her that she's going to be a great mom, but I've never voiced my own fears to her.

"You won't." She puts her hand over mine.

My eyes flick up to hers. "How do you know?"

She gives a small, amused smile. "Because if you were, you wouldn't be worried about it."

I chuckle, shaking my head. "Throwing my own words back at me, honeybee?"

Her smile grows. "Always."

Heaviness hangs between us, the weight of our combined futures.

"We better go find my parents."

She doesn't respond right away. "Okay." She slips off the bed, shocking me when she stands on her tiptoes to kiss my cheek. "This baby is lucky to have you as its daddy."

I smile to myself, letting her take my hand and pull me from the room.

Chapter Thirty-One

LENNON

I'm exhausted by the time we return to Beckham's room after our early Thanksgiving dinner with his parents. I've always loved the Sullivans. They're both kind people, warm, unlike my parents. Beckham's mom hugged me so many times tonight that I lost count. His father was thrilled about us being together, and about the baby.

I can't help but think about how they're going to feel when they find out we're lying about being a couple. I'm not like Beckham: I don't like lying to people I care about.

Stifling a yawn, I riffle through my bag for pajamas.

Beckham stretches his arms above his head, his belt already undone. My mouth waters at the slip of stomach revealed above his pants. I swear pregnancy has turned me into some sort of sex-crazed demon.

Before he can notice me practically drooling after him, I sprint to the attached bathroom to shower. I set my change of clothes on the counter, then reach over to turn the shower on.

I tear my sweater over my head and let it drop to the floor. The door opens behind me, outlining Beckham. He stares at me in the mirror, hunger in his eyes.

"You ran away awfully quickly, honeybee."

"I want to shower." I sound stronger than I feel.

"I don't think that's what you want." He steps fully into the bathroom before shutting the door behind him. Steam begins to fill the room almost immediately.

I flip around to face him. "How do you know what I want?"

In a blink he's in front of me, my face gripped in one of his hands. The pressure is almost painful—*almost*. "Because I know you better than anyone else."

He doesn't give me a chance to argue that fact before he kisses me. Rough and deep, his tongue plunges into my mouth, claiming ownership. My butt hits the back of the marble counter. Grabbing me beneath the ass, he positions me on top of it. He pulls away slightly, his eyes hooded and lips puffy. His fingers dig into my skin, tugging at my leggings to yank them down. They keep getting stuck, and he curses when they wrap around my feet. When they're finally off, he sinks to his knees on the tile floor, looking up at me like some sort of knight kneeling at his queen's feet.

"You want me to lick this pussy?" I nod, practically whimpering. "What about your clit?" His thumb hovers over the sensitive nub, not touching but so close that it's impossible not to imagine how it would feel to have him touch me there. "Want me to suck it, baby? I can make you feel so good. I know you want me. I know you need me."

Something vulnerable fills his eyes at that last comment, like maybe he's worried I don't need him. I'm too turned on to dwell on it. He followed me in here, after all, and he's the one on his knees. How can anyone expect me to have a rational thought in a moment like this?

He turns his head, kissing the inside of my right knee. Then the left.

"Please," I beg, my back arching. My breasts heave with every breath I take. I swear I can't get enough oxygen into my lungs.

He looks up at me, blue eyes surrounded by an enviable fan of black lashes. "I love it when you beg."

He buries his head between my legs, a cry flying out of me. I slap a hand over my mouth, thinking of his parents, which is downright silly, since this house is so massive and their room is nowhere near this one. I can scream as loud as I want. There's no one to hear me.

He licks and sucks, bringing me to the brink and backing away, then doing it all over again.

My fingers delve into his hair, holding him there so I can ride his face. From the way he moans, I can tell he doesn't mind it one bit.

Finally, he lets me come. I'm still shaking from the power of the orgasm when he stands up and gets rid of his pants. There's nothing graceful in his movements. He's just as desperate as I am, and the faster he gets his pants off, the sooner he's inside me.

Gripping his cock, he lines it up with my entrance and slams inside without preamble, his arms wrapping around me to hold me steady when my body rocks back.

His breath fans against my ear, and I love when he goes deeper and moans. It lets me know that I'm not the only one lost in us.

"You're so fucking good." His fingers dig into my hips, forcing me to meet his thrusts. "I love fucking you." He kisses my neck. "You're so hot." Each word is practically panted in my ear with every thrust.

Then he's pulling out, my mewl of protest echoing in the bathroom. He strokes himself, up and down in rough, hard pulls, his dark brows drawn.

"Get off the counter and turn around."

My legs are shaking, but I do as he says. With a hand on my back, he pushes me down against the counter so my ass is in the air. The marble is ice cold against my chest. My nipples pebble against my lace bra, my eyes meeting his in the mirror a second before he slaps my ass, slamming back into me.

"Oh my God!" I cry out, hands sliding against the stone counter in a desperate search for something to hold on to. "Beckham. Yes. Please. Oh. God. Yes."

He fucks me, holding nothing back, just the way I want and need. My pussy is aching, pulsing, another orgasm building.

My eyes squeeze shut, stars dancing behind my closed lids, when I come.

Beckham's moans grow louder, his fingers digging into my hips. I won't be surprised if I'm bruised tomorrow, but I can't bring myself to care. His body collapses over my back, his hands braced on the counter by my hips, so I don't feel the entirety of his weight pressing into me.

He pulls out, his semen sticking somewhat to the inside of my thighs.

"Fuck." His voice is low, gravelly. I watch his reflection in the mirror. A shiver runs down my spine when he gathers the liquid slowly leaking out of me and pushes it back into my aching pussy. A growl rumbles in his chest. "I've made a mess of you." His eyes meet mine in the mirror. "Time to clean you up."

A surprised laugh tears out of my throat when he grabs me around the waist, dragging me into the shower.

He makes good on his promise of cleaning me—after he dirties me up again.

We're forced to share a bed, since it would seem odd if we didn't. I wake sometime in the night, my body stiff and hot thanks to the fact that he has me spooned against him, his arm tight around my middle.

I don't pull away, not at first.

Instead, I give myself a moment to think about what it would be like if this were my reality. If we were a real couple expecting a baby. It's not as terrifying as I thought it might be. It's sort of nice.

But that's not our reality, and I have to accept that it never will be.

Beckham is going to help me raise this baby and be an amazing dad, but that's it.

The two of us will never be, and I need to dash that foolish hope before it gets out of hand.

The problem?

I think my feelings for him have already grown and I was oblivious to them, and now it's too late to do anything about it.

Except get my heart broken.

"You know," Beckham's dad begins over breakfast the next morning, "I always knew you two would end up together." He peers at us over the top of his newspaper, wire-rimmed glasses perched on his sharp nose. "Gut instinct, you might say."

Richard Sullivan smiles at us, smile lines crinkling around his eyes. He looks so happy seeing us together, just like his wife, that I can't help feeling like the worst person on the planet for going along with this lie.

Beckham rubs his jaw, looking a tad uncomfortable. Maybe lying to them isn't as easy for him as I thought.

"Do you have any names picked out for the baby?" his mom asks, setting down her cup of tea.

I sip at my glass of water, stalling. "No, not yet. Since we didn't want to find out the gender, it hasn't been something we've really discussed."

"What about moving out of the city? With a baby, you should really consider a house. I can get my real estate agent to look into it. I'll put in a call to her."

"Mom," Beckham interjects, "that's really okay. We're still figuring things out. On our own." He tacks the last part on in a soft tone. I'll give him credit for being firm but not wanting to hurt her feelings.

She frowns anyway. "Oh, of course. That makes sense. But if you two decide to move, please let me know. I have connections."

"Thanks, Mom. We appreciate it."

That seems to appease her. My parents wouldn't be so easily deterred.

"Breakfast is lovely," I say, changing the subject to the fluffy omelets and fresh-baked scones.

"I'll tell Martha you loved it."

Beckham clears his throat. "Yeah, Mom. This is delicious."

She laughs lightly, her eyes sparkling at her son. "I'm sure it's definitely better than whatever you feed yourself for breakfast."

"Mostly protein shakes."

"See? This is much better. Back to the baby for a moment: Lennon, do you plan to quit your job? Will you need a nanny? I can start interviewing some candidates to narrow it down for you."

I shoot a panicked look at Beckham. I love his mom, but a nanny? Really? I know it's normal—my brother and I had a nanny—but I'm not my parents. I don't want to shuck my child off on someone else full time. When I'm at work, I know I'll need help, but that's the most I want to accept.

"We don't need a nanny." Beckham's almost scarily firm. "If we need your help with anything, we'll ask." Hurt flashes across her face this time, and I can tell that he feels marginally bad. "I appreciate it, Mom, I do. But we want to do things our way."

She gives a tiny smile and nods. "I can respect that, but please know you both can come to me with anything. I'm more than happy to help."

"They get it," his dad interjects, setting his newspaper down with a smile. "You're stressing them out more than necessary. Can't you just be excited to be a grandma?"

She dots her lips with a napkin. "I'm thrilled. Truly. I hope you're both ready for me to spoil this baby silly. It's a blessing."

I wonder if she's thinking at all about her struggles with infertility. My heart aches for her. I can't begin to imagine what that was like. I overheard enough as a girl growing up about their trials and failures to get pregnant. They had the money to afford any and all methods to conceive, but it just wasn't possible for them. I remember them talking about adoption for years, how hard and long the process was, and then they got Beckham. He was older, obviously, barely a teen, but even from that first time I saw them with him, how they beamed with pride, I knew they thought of him as their son in every way.

Beneath the table, Beckham squeezes my knee. His silent way of checking in. I give him a small, closed-lipped smile to let him know I'm fine.

His parents' questioning (well, mostly his mom's) doesn't bother me because I know it comes from a good place.

But it's also a reminder that tonight, when we have dinner with my parents, it'll be a whole different ball game, and not nearly so supportive.

Chapter Thirty-Two

BECKHAM

Lennon's hand is sweaty in mine, her nails digging bitingly into my palm. When I turn to look at her at my side, it's impossible not to notice her pulse jumping in her throat, how her panicked eyes dart around the outside of the ivy-covered mansion. She appears two seconds away from running back to my car.

I'd gladly follow.

"Is it really going to be that bad?"

Her eyes scurry up to mine. "No." It's an unconvincing answer, considering she draws out the word skeptically. Fucking great. "It'll be fine." She swallows, smoothing her hands down the front of the oversize sweater that hides her growing belly. She sounds like she's trying, and failing, to convince herself.

There's no point in lingering in front of the door any longer. I reach out and push the doorbell to ring it.

Lennon's teeth dig into her bottom lip.

The door swings open what feels like an eternity later, revealing a housekeeper. She lets us in, collects our coats, and takes us straight to the lavish dining room.

"You're late," her father's voice booms from the head of the table. Caspar Wells has always been an intimidating man—big and burly, with a constant angry brow. As a teenager, I was scared shitless of him. As an adult, I'm merely annoyed.

"You told us seven," I reply coolly. "It's six fifty. That's early. Unless we were given the wrong time?" I arch a brow in challenge, looking from him to his stiff-as-a-board wife, to Hunter and the woman at his side.

Caspar makes a noncommittal sound. "You both might as well sit."

"Lennon, you didn't tell us you were bringing a guest." Her mom has a high-pitched voice, her mouth barely moving as she speaks. I'm not sure if that's from fear of wrinkles or Botox or some shit.

I want to shoot Lennon a look, annoyed that she didn't tell them, but I refuse to show them that I was just as in the dark as they were. Besides, I've learned enough about Lennon to understand that her reluctance to tell them anything isn't about me. It's all them and the way they've treated her.

Lennon and I sit side by side. I end up across from Hunter, who seems surprised to see me. I suppose he should be, since he said I was never welcome here again. Just wait until he finds out he's stuck with me for life.

"I didn't think it was necessary. There's always more than enough food, especially on Thanksgiving. Besides, you all know Beckham. He was practically family at one point."

"How is it you two reconnected?" The question comes from Hunter.

"We work together," Lennon answers, sending me a small smile. Beneath the table I can't help but notice how much her hands fidget. I wrap my fist around her hands, holding them in place. She gives me a grateful smile. "It's a small world, huh?"

"Small indeed." I can't quite get a read on Hunter, but I guess it doesn't matter. Things are going to go to shit soon enough anyway.

"I'm hungry," their father interjects, my presence unimportant to him, it seems. "Let's eat."

Deidre calls for the food to be brought out. Lennon wasn't kidding. It's a big enough spread for at least twenty people, let alone the six of us. This has to be the most joyless Thanksgiving table I've ever seen, despite the delicious spread of stuffing, turkey, and my personal favorite, homemade macaroni and cheese.

As we eat, random questions are thrown out, things they probably already know about me through my parents, like where I went to college. But I answer anyway, trying to keep things diplomatic. Lennon's clearly uncomfortable, and I don't want to make this unnecessarily difficult for her. She barely eats, mostly pushing her food around the plate.

Fuck, was it always like this? Was I really so oblivious to how they treated her?

When our plates are cleared and dessert is in the process of being brought out, I give her a look, silently communicating that she needs to speak up.

She looks close to throwing up.

I'm here, I try to tell her with my eyes. *You're safe with me.*

I trust you, her gaze says back.

Steeling her shoulders, she nods, clearing her throat. I think her mother has already noticed something is up from the way Lennon turned down wine with her dinner. She's been watching her daughter with a curious look ever since.

"I have some news to share with all of you." The table grows quiet, all eyes going to Lennon.

There's only a breath of silence before her dad's voice booms, "Did you get fired? I told you that place was a waste of time. It's time for you to settle down—"

"Speaking of settling down," she interrupts, looking to me for reassurance, "Beckham and I are together, and we're expecting."

She blurts the words out there. Quickly, but in a clear voice so there's no mistaking what she said. I have a feeling that if she didn't just say it, our kid would be an adult and out of the house by the time she got the courage to confess to them.

"Expecting?" Her mom titters, swaying in her seat like she might faint.

Hunter rears back.

And her dad just looks downright confused. "Expecting what?"

"I'm pregnant."

The words go off like a bomb. I never knew ten letters could come together to be so detrimental. Her mom shrieks in horror, pressing her napkin dramatically to her lips. Caspar sputters, turning red, his fist striking against the table. Hunter chokes, seemingly on nothing, while his date, whose name I can't remember, looks like she wants to crawl under the table, or maybe flee out the front door.

"You are a Wells," Caspar bellows, his voice echoing through the room. "This is not how we do things. You are to be married before you have a child. How will this look to our friends? To our family?" He swings toward Hunter, sausage finger wagging. "You were supposed to take care of this."

"Take care of this?" Lennon sounds small, confused. Frankly, so am I.

"Of you two!" he yells, while Diedre grabs up her wineglass, downing the last of the liquid inside. She motions for one of the staff in the corner to come forward and pour her more. "He's not like us, Lennon."

Once upon a time, his words would've felt like a hot brand pressed against my skin. I would've let them eat at me.

"You're right," I interject, drawing his anger to me. "I'm nothing like you, and thank fuck for that." At my f-bomb, he looks ready to go into cardiac arrest. "I would never talk to my child the way you've spoken to Lennon. What are you really angry about?"

"You're from bad blood." He wags that finger at me that was just swinging at Hunter only moments ago. "You're—"

"Why?" I counter, my voice calm. I'm the picture of unbothered, which only makes him angrier—I can tell in the way his eye begins to twitch. "Because I'm adopted, that makes me bad blood?" Beside me, Lennon physically recoils, like the idea of that being the cause of so much hatred is blasphemous to her. Lennon isn't like her parents, though. Where I came from has never mattered to her. He sputters, mouth opening and closing as he searches for words, any explanation. "Is that how you always viewed me?" I look to his wife and back to him. "Did you always think I wasn't good enough to be your son's friend? To be with your daughter? I bet you never voiced that to my parents—oh, let me correct myself, adopted parents. Since I'm not their blood, it's irresponsible of me to call them my parents, right?"

Lennon stiffens, her hand seeking out mine beneath the table. I reluctantly take my eyes off the sputtering head of the table to look at her. Her eyes are sad, but there's pride there, too, like she's happy I'm finally standing up for myself.

I'm not even angry; if anything, this whole thing is hilarious to me. Belatedly, I begin to realize that, compared to Lennon and her brother, maybe I'm downright lucky, because this is insane.

"That's not what I meant," he finally says, still red faced.

I tap my finger against my wineglass. It's mostly full. "Isn't it?"

With an annoyed growl, he pushes back from the table, leaving the room. Deidre is quick to follow, calling after him.

There will be no congratulations from them.

Lennon sniffles at my side. "I don't know why I'm crying," she says to me, dabbing her eyes with her napkin. "I knew this was going to be bad. I'm so sorry you had to be here for that. Bad blood," she sputters over what her father said. "How could he say that to you? It's not true, Beckham. I hope you know that."

I quietly shush her, hating the fact she's crying on my behalf, for things her parents said that I realize now mean something only if I let them. With a hand on the back of her head, I pull her in for an awkward hug at the dining table.

Across the table, Hunter and the woman watch us.

"Ellie, give us a moment?"

Ah, Ellie. That's her name.

"Sure." She shoots an apologetic smile our way and excuses herself from the table.

A few minutes of silence pass while I comfort Lennon. When her tears are pretty much dry, she faces her brother.

"Surprise," she says, making me smile when she does some sort of awkward jazz-hands movement. "You're going to be an uncle."

"An uncle," he repeats. "That's going to be interesting. I don't even like kids." She stiffens at that. He smiles slowly, genuinely. "But I'll love this one. So, you two, huh? I can't say I'm all that surprised, and yet I am. I didn't even know you were in contact." He sounds almost accusing to me.

"I didn't seek her out, if that's what you're implying," I say. Lennon's nose wrinkles, looking between the two of us. "I certainly didn't expect to walk into work one day and see her, but there she was. It was like my world was finally centered again."

Our eyes meet, surprise evident in her brown orbs. It's not like we've discussed that first day, what either of us thought. Despite my anger at her waltzing back into my life, there was a strange sort of peace, too, one that I've only ever had around her.

Her tongue swipes out, moistening her lips.

That first day when I got off the elevator, the funniest feeling washed over me. I'll call it a gut instinct, but I knew she was there. The air particles seemed to be charged, drawing me right to her. And when I looked, there she was.

Lennon reaches for the glass of water to her right, taking a hearty sip. It breaks the spell I didn't even know we were under. I wonder how long we've been staring at each other.

She clears her throat, shaking her head slightly in an effort to refocus herself. "What did Dad mean when he said you were 'supposed to take care of this'?"

Hunter rubs his bare jaw. His dark hair, the same shade as Lennon's, is slicked down with some sort of product. I guess that's the Wells way—not a hair out of place. His eyes bounce between the two of us, a sigh rattling his chest.

"I'm not sure either of you are aware of how you looked at each other back then." Lennon stiffens beside me. "It was probably more obvious to everyone else than either of you. He'd already told me previously to keep you away from Lennon, but that was hard since you were always around." Turning to me, he adds, "I didn't see what the big deal was. I mean, yeah, it would be a little weird—my best friend and little sister—but not the end of the world. That's not how Dad saw it, though."

Lennon and I both wait for him to go on.

"Someone on the staff saw you two go to the pool house. It didn't take a genius to figure out what went down, and they told Dad. He was . . . disappointed in me, for not doing something more about you two. I confronted you," he says to me, leaning back in his chair in an almost-casual gesture, like this isn't a conversation we've avoided for years. "I was angrier than necessary because of how Dad had cornered me. I took that out on you. Said things I never meant. But it worked. After that, we weren't friends anymore, and you stayed away from her."

Lennon starts sniffling again. "Sorry," she whispers. "Hormones." She fans her face with her hands. "That's not entirely true. This whole thing sucks. It's not fair that Dad played you against each other." Teary eyes meet mine. "I wonder how different things would've been if none of that ever happened."

I see her unspoken question in the soft way she looks at me.

Would we have been together long before now?

Hunter clears his throat, and I can feel him shifting his feet back and forth under the table. His face twists with remorse. "I never wanted to lose you as a friend."

Inhaling a breath that's shakier than I expect, I reply, "You chose your father over me."

He winces like I physically punched him, nodding sadly. "I did."

I'll give him credit: he doesn't balk from what happened.

"Was it worth it?"

His lips twist, his fingers adjusting the oversize watch on his wrist. "I don't know." To Lennon, he says, "Mom and Dad will come around."

Her eyes drop to the ground. "It doesn't matter."

But it does. I can tell she cares what they think of her, even if she wishes she didn't.

Hunter nods in a way that says he doesn't believe her. That makes two of us. "I'm sorry," he says to me. "I mean that."

A part of me, the part that's always held a grudge, wants to continue being angry. That would be the easy way. Anger is so much easier to hold on to than it is to extend forgiveness. But I think of Lennon, of our baby, and how I need to make better choices. Be a stronger person. Staying angry is the coward's way out.

"I forgive you."

He rears back. I guess I always did have a chip on my shoulder, even back then, so he's probably surprised that I'm choosing to be a bigger person.

"Wait," Lennon says suddenly. "Did you break his nose?" She asks the question of me. To Hunter, she says, "You said it was a lacrosse accident."

I flick my fingers lazily at Hunter, letting him take the lead on this one. He clears his throat. "Yeah, he broke my nose." To me he says, "I lied to my parents too. If they'd known you were the one to break my nose . . ."

"Yeah, well, your hard-ass nose bruised my fingers."

"Broken nose." He points to his face. "I win."

I can't help but laugh, and he joins in. Poor Lennon looks flabbergasted. "I'm going for a walk." She pushes away from the table, paler than normal. From the downturn of her lips, I can tell this conversation is getting to her. "I need some fresh air."

We both watch her leave. The urge to go after her is strong, but I sense that she needs a moment to herself.

I don't exactly want to have this conversation with Hunter. Normally, I don't mind confrontation, but something about being back in this place makes me feel incredibly young again—the boy who didn't know how to stick up for himself.

"You were pissed that night."

"I was." He grabs his wineglass, frowning when he realizes it's empty. "I'd just been reamed by my father, and now you've seen how he is, so imagine that, only a hundred times worse. This family . . ." He pauses, shaking his head. Sitting up straighter, he goes on. "It's all about appearances. I'm the male, the heir, so to speak. I carry on the family name, the legacy. Lennon? To our parents, she's nothing but a pawn. My father has been trying to arrange a marriage for her for years now, basically since she turned eighteen. He wants her to marry someone in our circle, with a powerful name, and push out children so she can continue this cycle." He spins a finger in the air. "That's not Lennon. Her going to college and working for a magazine? That makes her practically a traitor in his eyes. She's meant to sit and look pretty—that's all he thinks she's good for."

"Fuck him," I snap.

"Yeah." He laughs humorlessly, eyes dropping to the table. "Fuck him. It's not that easy, though, you know? This life. Don't get me wrong, I'm aware of our privilege—but that privilege is constantly dangled overhead, with scissors threatening to snip the threads at any time. This life comes with strings to most of these people. Not everyone is the Sullivans."

"You threw away our friendship."

His jaw tics, and he nods. "I did."

"You chose money over me."

He hesitates. "I thought I had no choice."

I stand from the table then. I'm not even angry, just resolved. I didn't know I needed to have this conversation with him, but now that I have, I feel lighter. A weight has been lifted.

"We always have choices."

With those parting words, I go to find my girl.

Chapter Thirty-Three

LENNON

Lights twinkle through the mazelike garden. It's one of the only things I ever liked about this home. The lush greenery is at arm's length as I pass through, the air smelling of jasmine. At least, I think that's what it is.

Dinner was . . . explosive. I expected it, but that didn't make it any easier to witness. I've always known my parents aren't great people. They're too focused on the wrong things. Money. Status. But that didn't make hearing the things my father said about Beckham any easier. It was a slap in the face to know that's what he thinks of other people. The number in your bank account doesn't make you any better than someone else. If anything, it's rotted their hearts.

Even Hunter didn't stand up to him. He spoke up only once they'd left the room. Despite his confession, it feels hollow since it only came once our parents weren't there to witness it.

It pisses me off and breaks my heart in equal measure knowing that my father and brother were behind Beckham disappearing from my life. They didn't care about my feelings at all. When it comes to my dad, all that's ever mattered is what benefits him.

Beckham handled tonight with more grace than any of them deserve. If I were in his place, I'm not sure I could've forgiven my brother for his actions. Despite what Beckham thinks of himself, he has a good heart. He cares about people way more than he lets himself realize.

My hand goes to the small swell of my stomach.

My baby.

I want to love, support, and protect my child, unlike my parents. I want to be the first person my kid tells everything to. As much as my lack of knowledge when it comes to kids scares me, I suppose I have a perfect handbook on everything not to do.

With a sigh, I sit down on the next bench I come across. The hand-carved stone benches are dotted throughout the entire garden.

Tilting my head back, I look up at the night sky. The stars are bright, the moon nothing more than a sliver. A perfect little slice.

So much beauty can exist out here, quiet and peaceful, while inside that mansion, anger and harsh words are slung around.

When I hear footsteps, I know it's him. I knew he wouldn't leave me alone with my thoughts for too long, but I appreciate him giving me a few moments of privacy.

"That went well, huh?"

Beckham sighs, standing across from me with his hands shoved in the pockets of his pants. It's his classic pose, one that suits him well. He's not wearing his coat. He should be. It's cold enough to need one.

"Are you okay?" Worry furrows his brows. He shouldn't be worried about me. He was the one who was treated like crap tonight. *Embarrassed* hardly feels like a strong enough word for how I feel over this turn of events.

I purse my lips. "Yes."

Those blue eyes narrow to thin slits, his mouth flat. "Don't lie to me."

"I'm not lying." I look away from him, messing with my hair. With an annoyed sigh, I say, "I'm not surprised, and yet . . ."

"You're disappointed," he finishes for me.

I rub my hands together, trying to get some warmth back into them. Even though I did grab my coat before coming out here, the chill is beginning to set in. "I know how they are, and I still keep expecting a different outcome. The things my dad said . . . it makes me sick. I hope you know I don't think that way. I never have and I never will."

"I know that, honeybee. And I understand too: they're your parents. You want them to be different, to prove you wrong." He holds out his hand for mine, pulling me up from the bench so we can continue on through the opulent gardens. Even in late November they still manage to be lush. "It's natural to want their approval, even when you know it isn't likely."

"I'm a fool." I watch the tendrils of my breath fog the air, fading into nothingness.

We walk a few steps before he says, "No, you're not. You're a daughter who loves her parents and wants them to love her the same way in return. It doesn't make you a fool, just . . . too good for them."

"My brother . . . ," I start, swallowing past the lump in my throat. "I can't believe he did that to you. To *us.*" I shake my head in annoyance. "You two were so close . . . all of us were, and in the end that must not have meant much to him, or he wouldn't have done what he did."

Beckham sighs. "I guess he felt like he had no choice."

I crack a small smile. "You're too nice, and he doesn't deserve it."

"Too nice?" He snorts, shaking his head in amusement. "Can't say I've heard that one before."

I lay my head against the side of his arm. "I'm glad it's you."

"Me what?"

"That got me pregnant."

He laughs, Adam's apple bobbing. I wonder if he knows how beautiful he is when he laughs. He lights up from the inside out. It's a sight to behold.

"Laugh all you want, but I don't think I could do this with anyone else."

He gives me a serious look. "You could. You're stronger than you give yourself credit for." He pulls me toward him, placing his hand on my belly. I've only begun to feel the stirrings of what I think might be the baby moving, but it's all too subtle to be certain or to be felt on the outside. "But you do have me, and we're going to do right by this kid, way better than your parents did you. You don't need their approval. You shouldn't even want it. People like that . . ."

He doesn't have to go on; I know what he's saying. In order to get their approval, I'd have to be like them, and that would basically be like going to the dark side, which I have no intentions of doing.

We round the corner where the pools are. In the distance is the pool house, both our eyes going to it. Neither of us says anything. I rest my head against his arm as we take in where it all began.

"I want to take your picture," he says suddenly.

"What?"

"With the pool house in the background."

I fight a smile. "Really?"

He nods, pulling out his phone since he doesn't have his camera. "For nostalgia's sake."

He poses me how he wants me and snaps the photo. Then he leans in beside me, taking a selfie of the two of us. Except we're both looking at each other and not the phone screen.

When I shiver, he says, "We should head inside." He shoves his phone back in his pocket.

"Yeah, we should."

I'm desperate to head back to his parents' house. At least I feel comfortable there. This night has already been long enough.

Inside, we search out my family to let them know we're leaving. We could leave without doing that, but with silent communication we both know that would be a bad idea. We find them in the formal living area, my brother sipping at some sort of dark liquid while my dad smokes a cigar. My mom paces in the corner, lips pinched.

When we approach it's like everyone freezes.

My father's eyes narrow on us. Standing slowly from his favorite leather chair, he plucks the cigar from between his lips. "Your mother and I have discussed it, and we've figured out what we're going to do."

I give him a funny look, wondering what he's getting at. Beckham squeezes my hand, and I can't help but wonder if he knows what this is about.

"You're going to get married," my mom pipes in from the corner, turning away from the window. Her shoulders are stiff, chin held high.

Hunter watches us, his worry palpable. I wonder where his girl went, if she went to bed or got the hell out of here when she saw how crazy this family is.

I look between my parents, waiting for them to laugh, take it back, say something. They don't. Of course they don't; my parents don't joke. This is deadly serious.

I start to laugh uncontrollably. I'm not laughing because it's funny. I'm laughing because if I don't, I might cry.

Beside me, Beckham stiffens. I don't know whether it's over the suggestion of marriage or because of my own hysterical reaction. Shock courses through my system when I feel his pinkie brush against mine before loosely curling around my own finger.

"You have to be kidding me," I blurt, appalled that they think it's acceptable to force us into marriage.

"We're not." My father takes a puff of the cigar. "It's the only thing that makes sense to keep our image clean."

"Image," I repeat, stunned.

I shouldn't be shocked right now, and yet I am.

Stupid, naive me.

"You know how important our image is," he goes on. I can feel myself shutting down. Beckham must notice how unsteady I am, because his arm wraps around me, holding me against his side. "A child out of wedlock isn't a good look. We'll have a wedding planned quickly, by Christmas, and make an announcement that this is only the formal ceremony and there was a small service just for family over the summer. Hence, the . . ." He waves his hand at me, at my stomach, at my baby.

I feel my brother watching us. I want to scream at him to be a fucking man and stand up to our dad, to tell him this isn't okay, but he just sits there sipping his scotch or whatever the fuck it is. I'm enraged by the fact that he stepped in on our father's behalf all those years ago, and he's not even making up for it now. He's sitting back, letting it happen. Complacency is a choice.

"We're not getting married." My chin wobbles, fingers curling into fists.

My mom scoffs. "Why not?"

"Because I don't want to. Because a baby doesn't equal marriage. Because—no." I shake my head, a humorless laugh escaping me. "I don't have to justify this to you. To either of you."

The most ironic part of all this is that Beckham and I aren't even a real couple.

A vein in my dad's temple bulges and pulses. I don't think I've ever seen him this angry.

"You"—he points a finger at me, like he can cast a spell that will force me to listen—"will not defy me on this, Lennon."

My heart is breaking in half. It's no secret, even to me, that I don't have a great relationship with my parents. But staring me in the face is the fact that maybe I don't have any real family at all, not anyone who truly cares.

"Dad—" Hunter tries to speak up.

"Silence," he snaps back.

Hunter zips his lips, and that's that. My big brother, whom I've always loved and admired, who took me under his wing growing up, sits back and says nothing more because that's the easy way out.

"You do realize we're both adults, correct?" Beckham's voice is eerily calm as he addresses my parents. There's power in that—in being the one who doesn't raise his voice. "You can't force us to do anything, so this is a moot conversation. We'll be going now."

He tugs me away from them, from the room, from my father yelling after us.

He speaks to me in a low, kind tone, but I don't hear anything he says.

It's not until I'm buckled in the front of the Tahoe that I let the tears fall.

Wrapping my arms around myself, I murmur to my baby, "I'll always love you. I'll always protect you. I won't be them. I promise."

Beckham places a gentle hand on my knee, and then the house disappears behind us.

I have a feeling I won't be seeing it ever again.

I'm not even sad about that fact, only relieved.

I wake sometime in the night, tears streaming down my face.

I don't know why I feel so sad. Why I'm even crying. Those people, my parents, don't deserve my heartbreak.

Sitting up in bed, I wipe my tears away on the back of my hands.

Beckham must sense my movement because he reaches for me. "Whasgoinon?" His words are slurred and groggy. He pushes his sleep-mussed hair out of his eyes, stifling a yawn. "Are you okay?"

"Yeah."

"You don't look okay."

I'm sure I don't. "I don't know why I'm sad."

He knows I'm talking about them without me even clarifying it. "You're sad because you're not them, because you care. You have love in your heart, and you're mourning something . . ."

"Something that was never real to begin with." I cry harder.

Stifling a curse, he shoves the blankets off his body and sits up with me, pulling me into him. His chest is bare, my tears soaking into his skin. He doesn't say anything, doesn't even seem to mind. His fingers gently stroke my hair in a calm, soothing gesture.

"You're so much better than them, Len."

Sniffling, I say, "Maybe so, but it doesn't make it hurt any less."

I hate that I want their acceptance, their love, even though deep down I know I'll never get it. How pathetic is that?

I don't mean to say that out loud, but I must, because Beckham replies, "You're not pathetic."

Clinging to him, a buoy keeping me afloat, I ask, "How do you know?"

My body shakes with his chuckle. "Because I know *you*. There's nothing pathetic about you. I promise. I'm just sorry I didn't see how they were when we were young."

"I don't think they were always this bad. I think as we got older, they got worse, wanting to force us to fit their expectation. Hunter complied. I didn't."

My eyes begin to grow heavy again from the gentle rubbing of his fingers in my hair.

"Go back to sleep." He kisses the top of my head. "They're not worth losing sleep over."

I let him lay my body back down.

I let him hold me.

And because I love to torture myself, I let myself imagine what it would be like if this were real.

Chapter Thirty-Four

BECKHAM

I don't think I've ever been so glad to see the city in my entire life, but when the skyline appears ahead of us, I relax.

Home.

This holiday weekend was a clusterfuck—well, I mean, things with my parents weren't too bad, but Lennon's family is certifiable.

I wasn't going to tell my mom and dad about what happened at the Wellses' residence, but Lennon told them anyway. *Horrified* doesn't even begin to cover their reaction. My mom cried, while my dad sat in stunned silence before grappling for his phone to call Caspar and chew him out. Luckily, I stopped him before he could. I don't want more time wasted on those people.

Suffice it to say, their decades-long friendship is over.

I can't help but wonder how Lennon came from people like that. She's nothing like them. Her brother is baffling as well; it seems like he sees their parents for what they are, and was apologetic, but he didn't come to his sister's defense. Fucking pathetic.

"I'm sorry," Lennon says, breaking the silence.

I sigh, adjusting my grip on the steering wheel. "I've told you, stop apologizing. You didn't do anything wrong."

"I feel like this was my fault."

"It takes two. I think it's safe to say we're both responsible for this situation."

"My dad is probably going to cut off my access to the family money," she says softly, looking out the window. "Not that it's the end of the world, but . . ."

"And what? You think I'm going to let the mother of my child struggle? You'd move in with me. But I don't think he's going to do that."

"Why not?"

"If he's so worried about appearances, think about what it would look like if his only daughter was cut off and struggling." I shake my head, merging into the left lane. "He won't want that."

"I guess you're right."

"I'm always right."

I can feel her glaring at me. It's hard not to smile. I fucking love riling her up.

"I'm glad to see you're back to your normal cocky self."

"You thought that went away?"

Her sigh is her only answer.

Thanks to the typical bumper-to-bumper city traffic, it's a while before I'm able to reach her apartment building.

"Don't waste any more time thinking about them," I tell her, getting out to grab her bag.

"I wish I could promise I wouldn't." She tries to take her bag from me, but I refuse.

"What if I said every time you think about them, you have to pinch yourself?"

"It might work," she concedes, again trying to tug the bag out of my grip. "Give me my bag."

"I'm taking it up."

"No, you're not."

"Why not?" I narrow my eyes on her, my gaze shooting toward the building. Annoyance floods me. Is someone there that she doesn't want me to see? "Are you hiding someone up there?"

Lennon gasps. "God, you're ridiculous. *No*, I am not hiding anyone upstairs except Laurel, if she's back yet. She hasn't responded to my texts."

I glower at her. "Then I'm definitely coming up."

"You'll get a parking ticket. That's fifteen-minute parking," she argues.

"I can afford the ticket."

She knows I won't give up, so she walks away into her building, leaving me to follow.

She says nothing to me on the elevator ride up to her floor. I know she's not actually mad at me; this is just . . . our thing.

It's weird to think of us as having any sort of thing, but the more time we spend together, the more I realize how in tune with the other we are and that there are these little games we play.

The elevator opens, Lennon fumbling with her purse to find her keys.

"Do you need help?"

"No, I've got it."

Her tone is snappier than normal. I know the past few days are catching up with her, so I don't call her out on it. With how everything went down with her parents, she has every right to be snappy.

She finally locates the keys, then unlocks the door to the apartment. I carry her bag in and head straight to the bedroom. When I come out, she's already pouring herself a cup of sweet tea, looking at the glass like it better fix all her problems. She didn't have any the whole time we were gone, so I'm sure this must feel like a much-needed treat.

"Laurel's not back yet."

"The whole dark, empty apartment tipped me off."

She rolls her eyes at me, sipping her drink. "Smart-ass." Tucking her hair behind her ear, she leans her arms against the counter and says, "This baby is going to be here before we know it. God, that's so clichéd." She stands up straighter. "But it's true, and we have a lot to figure out. We should probably see a lawyer."

"A lawyer?" I blurt out, taken off guard. That's the last thing I was expecting her to say. My brain isn't sure how to process this turn of events.

"Yeah—I mean, we're not together. We need to figure out custody. I imagine it's going to be difficult at first. I plan on breastfeeding for as long as I can, so they'll need to be with me. But I would never stop you from visiting."

I shake my head rapidly.

It strikes me then, that maybe her dad was onto something with the whole marriage thing. Not that I'll ever give that man credit for anything.

It's stupid of me, but despite us not actually being a couple, it never occurred to me how little I would actually be able to be involved initially with the baby. We don't live together, and she's right: the baby will need to be with her more, since she's the mother.

Fuck.

I don't like this one bit.

"I can't think about a lawyer right now." I hate how fucking vulnerable I sound, but the idea of getting a lawyer involved, talking about visitation and custody, makes me feel ill.

A wrinkle forms between her brows. "Why not?"

Because we're already faking this for our coworkers, for our families— maybe we need to make it real.

I don't say any of it out loud. I know if I did, it would have her spiraling. She's not ready to hear it, and I need to be certain of my feelings before I say anything.

"I don't think we need one," I say instead. "At least not right now."

She presses her lips together, thinking. "Okay. If you're comfortable with that."

I wouldn't say *comfortable* is the correct term for it, but for now I don't want to get a lawyer involved.

"I better go. Cheddar's probably yelling in the car, and even though I left the engine running, I don't want anyone to think I kidnapped someone."

She smiles, a genuine one. "I love Cheddar."

"He loves you too."

And I think, maybe, I might too.

Chapter Thirty-Five

LENNON

My fingers are flying across the keyboard, the article I'm working on nearly wrapped up, when a stack of papers slams down in front of me, startling me so badly that I feel some pee slip out. A new perk of pregnancy.

"What was that for?"

"I said your name three times. You were ignoring me."

My teeth smash together, molars grinding. This man, I swear. "So you thought fit to scare the literal pee out of me?"

Beckham's mouth twists with disgust. "You peed yourself?"

In a soft voice, I mutter, "Only a little," cheeks heating.

He rubs his jaw. "Jaci said to give that to you."

"Cool. Why are you still here?"

He pulls out the chair beside me—stupid, freaking communal workspace. "I booked us a trip."

My fingers stutter over the keys. I save my document, then swing my chair around to face him. "What did you say?"

A trip? What is he talking about? And I just know that he's only bringing whatever this is up now because he knows I can't argue with him in front of our coworkers and give away the fact that we're not a real couple.

Already Claire and Layla are exchanging giddy glances.

"It's at an inn in Virginia."

"Virginia?"

Baffled doesn't even begin to cover how I feel.

"It looks very nice," he goes on. "It's on a farm, between the mountains, newly renovated. I rented out the whole thing, so you don't have to worry about anyone hearing you scream."

Layla squeaks at that. She sends me a wide-eyed look and pretends to fan herself.

To her I say, "Not the kind of screaming you're thinking of. He means no one will hear me when he murders me."

I'm not expecting Beckham's laughter, and apparently no one else is, either, because when it booms out of him, the entire floor falls silent.

Beckham—or Sulli, as everyone else in the office calls him—is always so serious. He rarely smiles or laughs anywhere, and I have the impression that this is the first time some of them have ever heard him let loose like this.

"You keep me on my toes." I shrug, trying to appear unaffected, even though inside I'm dancing a jig at having made him laugh so profusely.

Standing, he taps his fingers against the tabletop. "I'll give you more details over dinner."

Is this his way of inviting me to dinner?

"All right," I say as he walks away.

Claire leans over, biting her lip to tamp down her smile. "You guys are so cute."

"I . . . um . . . thank you?" *Why do I have to frame it as a question?*

"It's good to see you guys so happy. He's a great guy—don't get me wrong, you know some hearts were broken around here when we found out he was taken now." Layla nods in agreement at this, hand pressed achingly to her heart. "But we've never seen him like this before. You're good for him."

It's on the tip of my tongue to say, *I am?* But I manage to bite back the words.

The idea that we're good for each other should be preposterous, but the more time we spend together, the more I think we're just right.

◆　◆　◆

It *was* his way of inviting me to dinner.

Our waitress walks by with a mouthwatering pepperoni pizza for another table. I'm downright salivating, my stomach crying out with hunger. I need that greasy, cheesy goodness right now.

"You're drooling."

My head swings away from the pizza. "Huh?"

He taps the corner of his lip. "Drool."

I think he's kidding, but I touch my mouth where he pointed, and there *is* drool. How embarrassing. I wipe it away with a napkin, not meeting his gaze.

"I'm hungry."

"I gathered that." He looks at something on his phone. The Coke he ordered is already halfway gone. I don't think I've ever seen him drink soda before. "Anyway, we'll leave on the twentieth and return on the first."

"Wait." I pick up the wrapper to my straw, ripping it to shreds to busy my hands. "You were serious about that?"

"Why wouldn't I be?"

"I thought you were just saying that for the benefit of everyone else to think we're spending the holidays together."

"I don't need to do that. They already see the way you look at me, so that does all the work for me on convincing them this is real."

He says it so seriously that I'm not sure he's lying—and if he's not, it's horrifying to realize I display my emotions so plainly.

My jaw drops. "I don't look at you in any particular way."

He arches a single brow, amusement dancing in his blue eyes. "Trust me, you do."

"And what about how you look at me?" I counter, sticking my chin haughtily in the air.

"Tell me, how is it I look at you?"

"Like you want to eat me."

He thinks it over, nodding in a way that seems to say, *Fair enough*. "I do love the taste of your pussy."

A little shriek flies out of me. I cannot believe he just said that in public. Leaning across the table, I slap my hand against his mouth. "Don't say things like that in front of strangers."

He licks my hand, forcing me to yank it back. "Why not? It's true. Besides, nobody is listening." He brushes the ripped pieces of paper from my straw wrapper into a pile. "Back to Christmas, I assume you don't want to spend the holidays with your parents, and mine are going to Italy. We can spend it together—we might as well get used to it."

"You never asked me. What if I have plans with Laurel?"

"Do you?"

"Well, no—"

"That settles it."

This man makes me want to rip my hair out. "You didn't even ask me."

"Because you would've said no."

I don't confirm. He's right. The problem is, the more I'm around Beckham, the more I *like* him. Sure, he can be bossy and rude, but he can also be incredibly kind and go out of his way to help people. I even like the stupid games we play with each other from time to time. But he's said enough that I know he doesn't want to be a real couple. That's fine—but my heart doesn't want to get the memo, and it's starting to get those treacherous things called *feelings*.

The horror.

"If you think for a minute I'm going to spend any holiday or birthday not seeing our kid, think again, so consider this a trial run."

"I would never tell you that you can't see our child."

I hate that he even thinks that of me. I know coparenting isn't easy, but even if one day in the future, we meet other people and get married, I want us to be able to get together and be civil for the sake of our child. This baby is innocent in all this and deserves two parents who can get along, not go at each other's throats.

Even if I really like it when he chokes me a little.

"Why is your face getting so red? Are you having an allergic reaction?"

There's no way I'm telling him where my thoughts have strayed, so I blurt out the first thing that comes to mind. "I really have to fart."

He gapes at me, clearly startled by this development. I'm glad I'm capable of keeping him on his toes. "Do you need to go to the bathroom?"

"No. I'll be fine."

He looks skeptical.

"I swear if you smell something bad, it's not me. Lady farts don't smell." They totally do, but I have to cover myself since I'm not actually gassy.

"Sure," he says slowly. "All right."

Blessedly, our pizzas are finally brought to our table. My stomach growls its approval. At least the restaurant is loud enough that no one can hear it.

"Ow! Hot! Hot! Hot!" Stringy cheese is burning the roof of my mouth as Beckham looks on in horror. Tongue flapping, I manage to disentangle myself from the cheese, setting the pizza down on the small plate the waitress brought earlier.

There's no saving the burned roof of my mouth.

"Jesus, Len. Was the steam coming off the pizza not warning enough to let it cool down?"

"I was hungry!" I defend with a whimper. Hot cheese hurts like a bitch. "I told you we should get those breadsticks."

"Are you okay? Do you need anything?" Our waitress rushes to our table.

I flap my hand to get rid of her, but Beckham says, "More water for her and an order of breadsticks."

"It's too late to bribe me with breadsticks." My voice is hoarse, the roof of my mouth throbbing.

I don't even want my pizza now. It did me dirty.

Beckham sighs, running his fingers through his hair. Somehow, despite it being the end of the day, it still manages to look impeccable, lying in soft, supple waves. He needs to drop the hair-care routine so my hair can look just as good. Sadly, I think I could learn a thing or two from him.

"You'll still eat them," he says, removing a slice of his own pizza from the serving platter and putting it on his plate to cool.

Smart man.

I was not so smart.

Lesson learned—bring more snacks to work, and don't eat hot cheese.

"You're right. I will." I don't even feel ashamed. Breadsticks are the superior bread—everyone knows that—and my pregnant self can't get enough carbs. And sweet tea. I've been trying to limit myself, because I know it isn't the best thing for me to crave, but damn, it can be hard.

"I think you'll enjoy the inn." I'm blaming pregnancy brain for the fact that somehow, I already managed to forget we were discussing that. "It'll be a good chance to discuss expectations for when the baby comes."

I frown, pondering his words. "What do you mean?"

"Nothing." He waves a dismissive hand, refusing to meet my eyes. "We'll talk about it then."

"You're forcing me to go on a trip to talk about things? This sounds sketchy. You *are* trying to kill me, aren't you? I knew it."

"Don't be dramatic, Lennon."

The waitress returns with that glass of water and a basket of breadsticks. I immediately take one of them, still not trusting my pizza.

Beckham watches me with a knowing look.

Smug asshole.

"Is Cheddar coming with us on this trip?"

"No, not this time. We'll be taking the train."

"I like your cat."

He chuckles. "I know you do."

"I still find it surprising you have a cat."

He bites into his pizza. It doesn't burn him since he waited for it to cool.

"I'm full of surprises."

"This trip . . . ," I hedge, carefully. I can't believe I'm giving in to this, but a getaway sounds kind of nice, and we do have a lot of things we need to get sorted. "What should I pack?"

A sly grin curls his lips. He knows with that question he's got me on board.

Chapter Thirty-Six

BECKHAM

We left behind snow in the city for more snow in the country.

Outside the window, the sky is already dark. Winter and its early nights. Snow flurries speckle the sky. In the reflection of the window, I see Lennon behind me, wrapped in a blanket on the couch, holding a mug of hot chocolate.

"It's beautiful here," she says to me when I join her on the couch. "I hate to admit it, but you picked a good place. I wouldn't mind seeing it in the summer."

The inn is pretty much a massive farmhouse situated between the mountains with a working vineyard.

"I'm sure it's beautiful," she goes on. "The deck is amazing. Something like this would be nice to . . ." She gets a wistful expression, her words trailing off.

"Nice to?" I prompt.

She shrugs, her blanket falling off her shoulder. I push it back up into place so she can stay warm. I'm surprised she's even chilly, considering the fireplace is going.

"It's the kind of place that would be nice to raise a family. A decent-size house, privacy, lots of property. It's big without being ostentatious."

"Would you want to leave the city?"

Her lips twist back and forth, thinking. "I never thought I'd want to leave this soon. I wanted to focus on my career, and I love New York, but I also didn't think I'd have a kid until I was at least thirty. But yeah, I'd like to leave sooner than I'd planned. I want this baby to grow up in a home, have a yard, a golden retriever."

"You're describing the quintessential American dream right there, Len. You can do better than that."

She swats at me, nearly spilling hot chocolate, but somehow she manages to save it from spilling on the white couch. "Don't make fun of me. It sounds nice. Happy."

"It sounds normal."

"And what are you proposing?" she counters with a laugh.

"Move in with me." Silence. The only sound filling the room is the crackling of the wood in the fireplace. "Lennon?"

"Like in your apartment?"

Did she hit her head on something, and I missed it? Why is she not computing?

"In my apartment, yes."

"But it's an apartment, not a home."

I pinch the bridge of my nose. This woman. Beautiful, infuriating, and so fucking dense to the fact that I want her, need her. Not just her, but this baby. My feelings are all kinds of mixed up, but somehow in my brain it makes the most sense for us to live together.

"First off, it's the people who make a place a home, not the dwelling itself." Her family should be proof enough of that. "Secondly, yes, my apartment. This is our kid. Half you. Half me. That means it is both of our responsibilities. I don't like the idea of you doing this alone." She opens her mouth to argue, so I quickly shush her. "I don't mean from a sexist standpoint, just that I should help as much as you do. The baby wakes up screaming? Let me rock her back to sleep. She's hungry in the night? You want to breastfeed? You sleep, and I'll stuff your breast in her mouth. See, I have this all figured out."

"You keep saying *her*."

I throw my hands up in exasperation. "That's all you got from that? Yes, her. I already told you, it's a girl, I have a sixth sense with my pet sperm. A psychic connection, if you will. It's a girl."

"It could be—"

"Stop deflecting. Move in with me." Fuck, I sound like I'm begging her. I guess I am.

Frowning, she sets her mug down on the table behind the couch. "You can't just demand that I move in with you. What would I do? Sleep on the couch?"

"Don't be ridiculous. We're adults. We can share a bed without me mauling you. Unless you want me to—then I'm more than happy to oblige."

"We're not even together. Not for real anyway."

We could be. It's on the tip of my tongue, those words, but I bite them back because I don't know if she's ready for that. I don't know if *I'm* ready for that.

"We don't have to be. Not everything needs a label. There's nothing wrong with two adults living together to coparent their kid."

"Most people can't do that."

"We're not most people."

She rubs her face, nervous. "I'm not going to answer right now. I need time to think about this, and I think you need time to make sure that's something you actually want."

"I have thought about it, and it is. I wouldn't broach the topic if I wasn't certain."

"Okay." She nods, wetting her lips with her tongue. "Obviously you've had time to think about this and come to terms with it. I want you to allow me the same privilege."

I'm not a patient person. The idea of having to wait for her to make up her mind is brutal. But somehow, I'll do it.

"I'll try, but we don't have a lot of time."

"I know." There's fear in her eyes.

She wiggles around on the couch, finally lying back and putting her feet in my lap. My hands automatically grab on to them, massaging. A half sigh, half moan leaves her. Eyes fluttering closed, she mumbles, "That feels so good. Don't stop. You know"—she laughs suddenly—"I guess if it were up to my parents, we'd be married right now, and this might be our honeymoon."

I choke, turning the sound into a cough. The inn I chose is a honeymoon hot spot. No kids or pets allowed here.

Poor Cheddar.

"Married." I sigh, mulling over the word and how I might feel if we were. "How is it that *that* sounds weirder than having a kid?"

"Right?" She giggles, the sound turning into a moan when I rub my thumb into the arch of her foot. "Don't stop. That feels so good." She stifles a yawn. "Do you have any baby name ideas?"

"Beckham Jr. is an obvious choice if it's a boy," I joke, grinning when she glowers at me. Fuck, I love riling her. "But it's not a boy. I like Alice for a girl."

"Alice?" she scoffs. "Ew, no way."

"What? Why? It's a good name, old fashioned. Solid."

"I can't believe you just described a name as *solid*."

"Because it is. What's a name you like, if you're going to judge my suggestion?"

"I don't know, maybe Olivia."

"Olivia?" I scoff. "Hell no. That's way too popular. Do you want our kid to introduce herself, and there are five other Olivias in the class? I don't think so."

She pinches her brow. "You're going to make this incredibly complicated, aren't you?"

"Yes." I'm not going to pretend otherwise. "A name is an important part of a person."

"Maybe we shouldn't talk about this right now."

"If it's going to lead to an argument, I guess not." Standing up, she presses a hand to her belly. "I'm going to go take a bath. My back is aching. I can't imagine how it's going to feel when I'm at the end of this pregnancy."

"I'll rub your back for you."

She smiles, her eyes sparkling with appreciation. "I know you will."

She doubted me on the foot rubs, but now that I've proven my worth, she knows I'll follow through on my promise.

"I'll fix the bath for you. You can't have the water too hot."

"I know. I'll be fine."

"Still, it'll make me feel better to do it."

Throwing her hands up in exasperation, she then gestures for me to go on ahead of her. The bathroom of the room we chose has a huge soaking tub, large enough for three people, not that I'm going to invite myself to join her. I start the water, adding a few spoonfuls of the epsom salts into the water from a jar beside the tub.

"Thank you," she says when I finish.

I touch her waist. "You're welcome." I bend down, placing a quick kiss on the corner of her mouth.

I don't know what I'm doing. I barely understand what I'm feeling, but what I do know is that I'm finding myself longing for this. The little moments. Just being with her.

Apparently, I'm not as coldhearted as I thought.

Chapter Thirty-Seven

LENNON

I haven't been in the bath long when the door creaks open. Beckham slips inside with a tray of something. The lights in the bathroom are dimmed, creating a cozy glow with the candles I lit before sinking into the warm water.

"Did you miss me already?" I joke, the water sloshing when I sit up.

"I thought you might want a snack." He sits down on the floor beside the tub, balancing a tray of cheese and crackers on the ledge within grabbing distance for me.

"In the tub?"

"Yes."

"Beckham." I try my best to suppress a smile. "You can just tell me you missed me."

"I didn't miss you. I wanted to be with you."

I'm not sure he's aware, but I think Beckham's love language is quality time.

"Thank you for the cheese board." I pick up a cracker and stack a piece of cheese he cut up.

"You're welcome."

We're silent, snacking. I'm sure we're a sight, me in the bathtub, him sitting on the floor with his long legs stretched out.

I've come to crave these small pockets of time with him. It's a dangerous thing, putting my heart at risk of getting too attached.

I think about what Beckham said, about moving in with him.

It should be a preposterous idea, but I understand where he's coming from. When the baby gets here, they're going to need me the most, and I'm going to need help. As the father, he should be the one doing the helping, and he can't exactly do that if we're not under the same roof.

I suppose I could look at it as a temporary thing—maybe for only the first year after the baby arrives. We get along surprisingly well. It might not be such a bad thing.

But I'm not going to tell him that yet.

I want to think on it some more to myself, and if I give even a hint that I'm considering it, he'll jump all over me to do it, and I want to be sure it's my choice.

The baby moves, a sharp kick. It's been happening more lately, but Beckham is rarely around when I feel it. With a startled gasp I shoot my hand out, the cheese board he so sweetly put together tumbling to the bathroom floor. I wrap my wet hand around his wrist, tugging his hand into the water and onto my round stomach.

"What the hell?" His question is muffled around a cracker.

"The baby kicked." I move his hand around my stomach, hoping the baby does it again so he can feel.

"She did?" His eyes light up, and he sits up on his knees so he can better reach my stomach in the water. He puts both hands on me, feeling for himself. "Where?"

I don't argue with him on the girl thing. I think it's kind of cute, actually, how certain he is, even if I am jealous my mother's intuition hasn't told me one way or the other. Apparently, he wants to be a girl dad.

"Over here." I show him the spot.

"Get her to do it again."

"It doesn't work like that." I laugh.

I wonder if it's the laughter that does it. When I giggle, I feel the baby give another sharp jab. Since Beckham's big hands are splayed out over my entire stomach, he feels it. His lips parting in wonder, awe fills his eyes.

"Lennon," he gasps. "There she is." I put my hand over the top of his, watching him experience this. The baby moves again, and he laughs. "Wow, this is amazing."

It truly is. A miracle.

"That's our baby."

A tear spills from his eye. Grabbing me by the back of the neck, he pulls me forward, our lips meeting as water gushes over the top of the bathtub.

Letting me go, he presses his forehead to mine, echoing my words. "That's our baby."

A few nights later, on Christmas Eve, I wake up to the sight of blood in the bed.

Chapter Thirty-Eight

BECKHAM

Helpless.

It's the only word to describe how I feel.

Lennon woke me roughly, shaking me desperately. I was about to grumble over the rude awakening when she pointed to the bed, the blood on the sheets. Not a lot, but it was there, it was red, and I've never been more scared in my entire life.

I threw on my clothes, grabbed the rental car's keys, and hauled her to the nearest hospital. It was twenty-five minutes away. I made it in less than fifteen.

Lennon lies in the bed in the emergency room, each section curtained off. They had her change into a gown before they started running tests. She stares straight ahead, her color pale. She hasn't spoken in the last ten minutes, like if she opens her mouth and utters a single word, it'll break some sort of spell.

I can see it, her shutting down from the fear.

"Len—"

"Shh," she begs, her gaze never wavering from straight ahead of her. "Don't say anything. Please?"

The problem is I don't know *what* to say. But I want her to know I'm here.

I slip my hand into hers, entwining our fingers. "I'm scared too."

"Beckham, I'm begging you. Just be quiet." Her words end in a choked sob.

I hate this, that she won't let me comfort her. Her hand is stiff in mine, but I keep holding on because I need the touch. If I hold on tight enough, I can make things better. I have to.

We've been here for hours already and haven't seen a doctor, only a nurse who occasionally drops by.

We might be losing our baby, and they're not treating it like an emergency.

"That's it," I growl, letting her hand go. I shoot to a standing position, swatting the curtain aside. "Someone send a doctor in here *now* to look at my wife," I bellow. Sure, she's not my wife, but I don't give a shit right now. If a fake marital status will get her seen faster, so be it.

"Sir." A nurse I haven't seen before speaks up. "I'm going to need you to—"

"No." I slash my hand through the air. "I have the utmost respect for medical professionals, but this is beyond ridiculous. You took blood work from her when we first got here and said someone was going to do an ultrasound. It's been two hours." I wave two fingers through the air. "And the blood work isn't back, and no tech has been by. This is—"

"We're very backed up tonight. There was an accident—"

Is this how we're going to play it? Constantly interrupting each other? Fine.

"Did the people in this accident require an ultrasound?"

"I can't speak to you about other patients." She smooths her blonde hair down, getting ruffled.

"The answer is no, Tina," I say, reading her name tag. "I'm betting there's a very low chance they needed an ultrasound tech. Stop bull-shitting me and get something done. We might . . ." My throat closes up, not wanting to say the words. "We might be losing our baby, and you're all doing *nothing*."

"Beckham," Lennon says softly behind me, "please."

I turn around to her. Small. Frail. Her hands clasped protectively over her stomach like she can make everything okay if she holds on tight enough. I shake my head. I won't be thwarted from my mission.

"Get someone down here. Now."

Tina shakes her head, annoyed. I'm sure if I were in her position, I'd feel the same. They probably deal with people like me all the time, but this, forcing shit to get done, is all I can do right now to help, so fuck it all, that's what I'm going to do.

I leave the curtain open so I can make sure they actually get something done and take my seat back by Lennon's side.

"You didn't need to make a scene."

I touch her belly, rubbing my thumb in slow circles. "Yes, I did. It's not just you I'm trying to look out for. It's them too."

She looks at me then, mouth wobbling, and then she just breaks down crying.

I wrap my arms around her. Like her cradling her stomach protectively, I do the same to her. I doubt it'll be enough, but I'm damn sure going to try.

◆　◆　◆

Bed rest.

No flying.

No sex.

Lots of checkups.

That's Lennon's future until the baby arrives, but it could be a lot fucking worse.

We still have our baby. That's all that matters.

Preeclampsia, the doctors said. It was sudden, and the bleeding was terrifying. They said it could've been a placental abruption. Thankfully, it wasn't, but I chewed them out for not tending to Lennon sooner. She could've died or gone into multiple-organ failure due to their negligence.

I help her into the bed at the inn. The sheets are new and the place has been tidied up. I let the owner know what was going on and that I'd appreciate things being nice when we got back.

Mostly I just wanted the bloodied sheets gone.

Though it wasn't a lot, I never want to see them again, and I'm sure Lennon feels even more that way.

Once I have her in bed, pillows behind her so she's sitting up, blankets squished in around her, I level her with a stern stare. Hands on my hips, too, so she knows I mean business.

"As soon as we're back in New York, you're moving in with me. No arguments."

"Are you crazy? No—"

I mime zipping my lips. She falls silent. "You're on bed rest until you go into labor. You have months until that will happen." Unless the baby comes early, but we don't want to talk about that. We're not at the viable stage yet, so I'm taking every precaution necessary. "I can take care of you at my place."

"I'm not helpless."

I sit down on the end of the bed by her feet. "I know you aren't, but you *do* need someone through this, and that someone is going to be me. You'll have Cheddar to keep you company. It won't be so bad. You'll see."

"Oh no, the magazine!" she cries out, trying to reach for her phone. I grab it before she can get it. "Jaci is going to fire me."

"I highly doubt it. You can work from home. Now, stop stressing. Remember, the doctor said stress isn't good for the baby."

With a sigh, she lies back as far as the mountain of pillows will allow. "Okay."

"Do you want to stay here or head back to New York and get the ball rolling on moving your things in?"

She shakes her head. "I want to stay. If I'm going to be locked in a proverbial prison with you for the foreseeable future, at least my scenery is different here."

As much as I know she's upset about being put on bed rest, I know she'll do anything to make sure the baby is okay. When we got word that the baby was fine, I don't think I'd ever known relief like that.

"Try to take a nap. I'll bring you some water."

Neither of us has had any sleep in . . . I don't know how many hours. It feels like we were at the hospital for six days.

When she doesn't protest the nap comment, I know she's truly exhausted.

It doesn't take me long to get her a glass of ice water and bring it back to the bedroom.

She's got her arms wrapped around herself, cradling her stomach protectively, just like she did in the hospital.

"What if we'd lost this little nugget?"

I set the water glass down. "We didn't."

"But what if we had?" she protests, her voice hoarse from all the crying she's done. "We're not together, Beckham. We're not a real couple." As if I need the reiteration. "It's not like we can just try again in a few months. This was never supposed to happen anyway."

"Don't talk like that." I shake my head roughly. "Don't say that shit."

"Why not? It's the truth. This was supposed to be a one-night stand, not this . . ." She gestures around her. "You don't even like me."

"I like you just fine." So much so that I might even love her. "But you need to stop going down this path, thinking like this. Little nugget, as you called her, is just fine."

She nods woodenly. "I think I do need that nap."

"Okay. Let me fix your pillows."

After some minor grumbling on her part, she lets me move some of the pillows so she can lie back more.

"Thank you," she says, grabbing my wrist so I can't run away. "You don't have to do this. Take care of me."

"I take care of the people I . . ."

Love.

Care about.

I think of my dad back in New York. How his health is failing. How I've never really gotten the chance to know him, but I'd still do anything for him.

I guess I have a heart after all.

Lennon saves me the embarrassment of finishing my sentence by kissing me. Her lips are chapped from being in the hospital. The stale air can't be good for anyone.

"I know," she says, meeting my eyes for only a millisecond. "I feel the same."

It's dark out by the time I finish making all the arrangements to have Lennon's things moved into my apartment so they're already there when we get back. Laurel wanted to give me hell for it. Once I explained the situation, she agreed it would be for the best if Lennon was with me. I also sent an email to Jaci, informing her of the situation and that Lennon would need to work from home for the foreseeable future and that, by extension, I'd need to be home as much as possible. As a photographer, I do have to go out more than Lennon would normally need to, but I'll make it work, reschedule shoots so some are the same day. Fuck, I'll get Cheddar's cat sitter to check on Lennon if I have to. I'm not sure she'd really appreciate knowing that she has the same sitter as Cheddar, but what she doesn't know won't kill her.

"Beckham," she calls out from the bedroom. "I need a break from this room. I'm coming to the couch."

I hop up from the kitchen stool, sprinting to the bedroom. "Not without my help, you're not."

She rolls her eyes, already halfway out of the bed. The nightgown I bought her from the local Target, covered in gingerbread men, hangs down past her knees.

"I'm on bed rest. That doesn't mean I'm incapable of getting around on my own, just that I need to be seated most of the time."

"And like I told you, I'm going to help you."

"God, you're a tyrant."

I wrap an arm around her, guiding her to the couch in the living room. She's right, she's able to get around just fine on her own, but it makes me feel better to help. Like at least I'm doing something.

I don't like feeling useless, like I can't fix something.

This entire situation has me feeling inept.

Once she's seated on the couch, she grabs the nearest blanket to drape over her legs. "Let's watch a movie."

Since I just spent the last I don't know how many hours getting everything set up for our return to Manhattan, watching a movie sounds like a great idea to me.

Fuck, we spent all of Christmas in the hospital. I was so stressed about her and the baby I forgot.

"Pick a movie," I tell her, heading back to the bedroom.

I riffle through my luggage, pulling out the gift. I don't know what made me get it, think it would be a good idea, but when I saw it, I knew I had to buy it for her.

The box is small, smaller than the palm of my hand.

She's scrolling through the Christmas movie options when I return. I sit down on the coffee table in front of her and hold the box out.

"Merry Christmas, honeybee."

Her eyes dart from the box to me. "You . . . you didn't have to get me anything."

"I know."

"I didn't get you anything," she whispers, almost like she's ashamed. "I didn't think we were doing that."

"I don't need anything." I shake my hand, wiggling the box. "Take it, Len."

She does, ripping off the bow so she can remove the lid to reveal what's inside.

"It's beautiful," she gasps, pulling out the dainty gold necklace with a tiny bee charm dangling from the end of it. Beside the bee charm is a small blank gold disk charm. "Thank you, Beckham. I love it."

"When I saw it, I knew it was meant for you. I had them add the other charm so I can add the baby's initial when she comes."

"Again with the *she*." After removing the necklace from the box, she holds it out to me, then turns around to lift her hair off her shoulders. "Put it on me, please."

I drape the necklace around her collarbone, struggling with the clasp until I finally secure it. "We've been over this. My gut says it's a girl. My gut has never steered me wrong before, so I'm not going to stop believing it now."

She turns back around, settling herself into the cushions. Her fingers go to the necklace, rubbing at the charm.

I like it there. My honeybee wearing a honeybee. My mark on her.

I'm falling in deep with her, and it scares me shitless. Caring about people gives them the ability to hurt you. But I don't know how to stop this. Not when it comes to her.

Chapter Thirty-Nine

LENNON

"Why are we outside your apartment?" I stare in horror at the building, not because it's a bad place but because I know exactly why we're here. I still need him to say it.

"Because you're moving in with me. Thanks for the ride, and happy New Year," he says to the Lyft driver while urging me to slide out the back of the car. Now I know why he insisted on us sharing a ride after we dropped off the rental car. "I should've gotten you a wheelchair," he mumbles to himself.

"Oh, for fuck's sake," I groan. "It's called *bed rest*, not *bedridden*. I need to stay off my feet, but I can still get around some throughout the day."

"Still." He rubs his stubbled jaw. "I think I'd feel better if you had a wheelchair."

"Just get our bags, Sullivan," I grumble in annoyance. "I'll sit down in the lobby."

"Sullivan." His nose wrinkles with distaste. Apparently, he doesn't like me calling him by his last name. Good to know. But right now, Sullivan it is, since he thinks I'm moving in with him.

In the lobby of his building, I find a big, cushy leather chair to sink into.

God, I'm already so tired of all the sitting and lying. I don't know how I'm going to do this for *months*. I know I'll find a way to endure it for the sake of my baby, but that doesn't make the reality of it any less daunting.

Beckham comes in with our bags, eyes searching frantically for me. I should let him suffer, and maybe I do wait a purposeful few seconds too long before I lift my hand in a wave. Relief floods his face as he makes his way to me.

"Let's go home," he says softly, almost pleadingly.

"This is your home," I remind him.

His lips purse like he wants to argue, but by some miracle, he decides to keep his mouth shut. Resolve floods those baby-blue eyes. He sees this as some challenge of sorts. I have a feeling that's about to be very dangerous for me.

Since his hands are full, he offers me his elbow, which I steadfastly ignore. I know it's a sweet gesture—I'll give him credit there—but I do not want to be coddled.

We take the elevator up to his floor. It's almost comical watching him waddle down the hall with all the luggage.

"Keys," he grits out through his teeth, "in my front-right pocket."

I stick my hand in his pocket, riffling in the deep space until my fingers close around the keys. Women's pants would never be able to hold the keys to begin with.

After unlocking the door, he dips his head for me to go in first. I've barely taken three steps when Cheddar flies out from under the couch, yowling excitedly.

"Cheddar!"

I'm about to bend down and scoop up the floof when Beckham yells out in a panic, "No bending over!"

I cringe. "Right."

Beckham moves past me, headed down the hall to his room.

I figure while I can, I might as well stand as long as possible. He'll be forcing me to sit or lie down soon enough.

That's when I notice the additions to his apartment. My special bound copies of Jane Austen's collection sit pretty on the coffee table. My favorite cheesy Christmas blanket with dancing elves and snowmen is draped over the couch. I spin around, and on the bookcase in the corner is my snow globe with the Empire State Building inside. It was a gift I got for myself when I was fifteen, a reminder that one day I'd live here.

I tiptoe into the kitchen and open the cabinets, where I find my plates and cups filling the shelves alongside his.

I should be mad, panicking. Instead, tears spring to my eyes because he went out of his way to make sure I had my stuff, my comforts, and as much as living with him scares me, I know it makes the most sense with me being on bed rest. Beckham will be able to look out for me far better than Laurel would.

He appears in the doorway of the kitchen. "You've been up long enough."

"All my stuff is here."

He wets his lips, pressing past me to the fridge. He swipes a bottle of water from within the depths, then grabs one of my pale-pink glasses with flowers on them. "It is." He fills the glass and slides it over to me. "Did you think I'd insist you live here and not allow you to have your stuff?"

I take a tentative sip. "I don't know what I thought."

"You continue to underestimate me."

I set down the glass. "I suppose I do."

I don't mean to, but sometimes—scratch that, all the time—I find him hard to read.

He presses his body in front of me, caging me in to the counter. He ducks his head low, his hair tickling my forehead. "Before you move that cute ass down the hall to bed, can I kiss you?"

"Are you seriously asking for permission right now?"

"It seemed like the right thing to do."

I put my hand on his chest. "Since when do you ever do the right thing?"

He grins, that devastatingly handsome smile that makes my stomach somersault. "You're right."

Fingers delving into my hair at the back of my head, he yanks me forward in a possessive gesture that somehow still manages to be somewhat gentle with the way he holds my hip with his other hand.

He kisses me slow. Deep. I feel it all the way to my toes.

It isn't long, and yet I'm somehow still left breathless.

"Now"—he smacks my ass—"bed for you."

When Beckham said he took care of everything, he meant it, even going so far as to secure things with Jaci for me to work from home. The work-issued laptop sits on the bedside table, waiting for me to pick it up.

It doesn't keep me from feeling disgruntled at being cooped up inside. I know what I'm doing is the best thing for the baby, but man, I'm already going stir crazy.

"I'm heading into the office for two hours." Beckham holds up two fingers, wiggling them back and forth just in case I need the reminder on what *two* means. "I'll be back, and I expect to find you here, or on the couch, and no—"

"Going to the bathroom or kitchen without notifying you of when I get up and when I return." He clears his throat, waiting for me to finish. "And no checking out the mysterious door in the hall."

"Good." He shrugs his navy coat on the rest of the way, then picks up a gray-and-blue scarf to wrap around his neck.

In another world I'd grab that scarf and yank him into bed with me.

But alas, no sex.

"I'll text you when I get to the office." He looks at me in the bed. I'm sure I'm a ridiculous sight, pillows and blankets stuffed around me. The TV in the corner of the room plays a morning news channel, and Cheddar is asleep on top of the dresser.

I love that Beckham has let his cat take over the apartment. Cheddar does whatever he wants, including sleeping in the strangest of places.

Stress radiates off Beckham, from the tightness in his shoulders to the obvious way he's clenching his jaw.

"I'll be fine."

He grabs his watch and fastens it onto his left wrist. "I really think I should hire a nurse to stay with you when I have to be gone."

"That's overkill."

"But is it?"

I make a shooing gesture with my hand. "Get out of here. I'll survive a few hours without you. Besides"—I reach for the laptop, and he's there in an instant, passing it over—"I have work to do myself. You worry too much."

He grunts out a noncommittal response. "Use your phone. Check in with me. I mean it." He points a finger at me in warning as he edges toward the bedroom door. "And text if there's anything you want me to bring back for lunch."

"I will."

That seems to appease him. With a nod, he raps his knuckles against the door, and I watch him disappear down the hall. A moment later the main door opens and shuts.

"Well, Cheddar"—the orange cat cracks an eye open—"it's just me and you." The baby chooses that moment to give me a sharp kick in the ribs, reminding me they're there. "And you too, baby."

257

When I get up for a potty break, I use my allotted time to check the forbidden room, as I've dubbed it. Beckham has labeled his guest room as off limits. Color me curious. But when I try the knob, the door is locked.

Damn him. Of course he suspected I'd try to get in here. What's he hiding? A dead body? Am I the next victim?

I should get out while I can.

Instead, I tiptoe back to bed.

Cheddar has moved from the dresser to the chair in the corner, watching me as I slip back into bed. I shoot a text to Beckham letting him know I've returned from the bathroom.

Evil Baby Daddy: You were in the bathroom for 6 min and 28 seconds.

Me: You TIMED it?!

Evil Baby Daddy: Yeah. Why were you in there so long?

I wasn't . . . I was trying to find a way into the Narnia room.

Me: I was taking a shit if you must know.

Evil Baby Daddy: I don't believe you.

Me: You don't have to. It's the truth.

It's a few minutes before I get his next reply.

Evil Baby Daddy: You were trying to get into the room, weren't you?

Me: Absolutely not. You said it was off-limits. I'm a good girl. I listen.

Evil Baby Daddy: We both know you're not a good girl.

Is it only me who senses a sexual innuendo there?

Me: Aren't you supposed to be working?

Evil Baby Daddy: I'm walking to the subway. I need to shoot for Jaci in Central Park. I dropped by the office first.

Me: That means I have the pleasure of being annoyed by you until you get to your destination then?

Evil Baby Daddy: You catch on quickly. How are you feeling? I'm being serious.

Me: I feel fine. And I'm being serious too. I know I have to be careful, and I will be. I don't want anything to happen to this baby, but I feel good.

After we left the hospital, we never took the time to discuss what happened—what *could* have happened—and how we felt about it. I think we've both been avoiding the conversation because it's scary.

Evil Baby Daddy: I don't want anything to happen to the little nugget. Or you.

Me: I know. I don't either.

Evil Baby Daddy: I'll leave you alone. Movie night, tonight?

Me: I'm pretty sure it's movie night every evening for me now.

Evil Baby Daddy: I guess that's true.

Me: But yes, I'm down

Evil Baby Daddy: It's my turn to choose.

I smile at my phone. Me: Better pick a good one.

Evil Baby Daddy: Are you implying I don't have impeccable taste? I did choose you to take care of my pet sperm.

Me: That was an accident and we both know it.

Evil Baby Daddy: But it was the best accident.

"Do you hear that?" I say to my belly, gently caressing it over the fabric of my oversize shirt—well, Beckham's shirt. "Your daddy says you were the best accident. Don't tell him I said this, but he's right."

The baby kicks like they agree.

Me: Focus on work. I need to do the same. I'll check in. Promise.

He sends back a heart emoji.

A.

Heart.

Emoji.

I smile goofily at it, reading into it even when I know I shouldn't.

Chapter Forty

Beckham

"I can't believe I have to present this proposal from your couch," Lennon gripes, trying to put on mascara. I'm not sure why holding her mouth in an O shape is going to help all that much.

"I'll be right beside you," I remind her.

I could've gone into the office while Lennon had to call in for the meeting with Jaci, but we're teammates on this project, and I want to do it together.

"I know." She sets down the mascara wand and reaches for a tube of lipstick, or maybe it's gloss. It looks to have some sort of glitter in it. "But somehow you'll manage to look impeccable, and I'll look like me."

"Do you have any idea how fucking hot you are?" Lennon is the most gorgeous woman I've ever laid my eyes on. Even when we were young, I knew she was a special kind of pretty. "You're gorgeous, Len. You make me fucking crazy."

"I don't know if that's much of a compliment. You're already crazy."

Pinching the bridge of my nose, I growl in annoyance. "I'm trying to be nice."

Her lips twitch in amusement. "Try harder."

Somehow, we both manage to finish getting ready and park our asses on the couch for the meeting. I turn on my computer, logging into Zoom to wait for Jaci.

Lennon nervously picks at the edge of her thumbnail. "What if she doesn't like our proposal?"

"Then we did the best job we could." I shrug like it's no big deal, even though I'm feeling the nerves as well.

Jaci is meeting with every team individually over the next week; then she'll deliberate about which proposal she's going to choose. This whole thing feels very much like a test, one I hope we pass. As much as I want this win for myself, I find myself wanting it for Lennon even more. Who the fuck am I becoming?

Is this growth? Or is it a dad thing, since I'm going to be a parent soon and now my brain is suddenly hardwired to care about another person's success?

Lennon wiggles around on the couch, trying to find a comfortable place to sit. She already spent five minutes this morning grumbling that her ass is sore from not being able to move around enough. I feel bad, but what else can I do?

She ceases her wiggling just in time for Jaci to start the meeting.

"If it isn't my favorite couple." She beams from the screen. "How are you feeling, Lennon?"

"So far, so good. I have a long way to go, so we'll see how I hold up."

Jaci clucks her tongue in sympathy. "I hope you have everything together. I can't wait to see what you have for me."

I launch into my spiel on what we want to do, the people we've already interviewed, and the others we have on tap should our project get chosen. Jaci doesn't give anything away as she listens to us. I have no way of knowing if she's connecting with our idea or not.

"This is a really important public issue that needs to be addressed in a big way," Lennon says from my side, her eyes intent upon our boss. "Women are constantly overlooked for promotions, even when they're more qualified, not to mention when they *are* in a position of power, it's usually degraded by someone around them. We're more than our looks or, dare I say it, our vaginas." I have to cover my face at the word *vagina*, because I have the sense of humor of a prepubescent boy. "It's wrong in this day and age for women to be told they only got where they are because they're pretty, or sleeping to the top, or, on the other end of things, being told they'll never amount to anything because they don't look the part." Taking a breath to slow herself down, she adds, "Women even face questions regarding if they plan to have kids. Men usually aren't asked about that. It's why I think this idea is worthy of its own stand-alone spring issue."

We finish up our presentation. Jaci smiles, tapping her pencil against her desk.

Tap. Tap. Tap.

Is there a hidden meaning in that tapping? Morse code? I don't know Morse code. What if she's telling us we're the winning proposal, and I can't even tell because I don't know the fucking code?

"Thank you for sharing with me. I have a few more teams to listen to before I make my decision. Have a great day and get some rest, Lennon."

She ends the meeting, leaving Lennon and me in silence.

A few minutes go by, the two of us frozen, before Lennon says, "Do you think she liked it?"

I run my fingers through my hair. "I have no fucking clue."

We'll just have to wait and see.

I lock up the guest room behind me, peeking to make sure that Lennon hasn't decided to take this moment for a snack or bathroom break. Even though I keep insisting that she ask for my assistance, she refuses. Stubborn woman.

After double-checking that the door is locked, I mumble a greeting to Cheddar, who's lurking in the hallway. He gives me a look that says I'm up to no good. This might be true.

On the couch, I find Lennon typing away on her computer. She stops when she sees me, lifting her blue-light glasses to the top of her head. She's taken to wearing them recently, and I haven't told her, but she's giving me a glasses kink. I've jerked off at least five times in the past week just to the thought of her wearing those glasses and nothing else.

"Why is there paint on your shirt?"

"Huh?" I pull my shirt away from my body, shocked to find a smear of cream-colored paint across the gray fabric. And here I thought I was being so careful. "Would you look at that?" I stride into the kitchen, on a mission for some water, and a fleeting hope that she'll forget about what she saw.

"You didn't answer my question," she singsongs.

The bottom of the fridge sees the annoyed face I pull. "I enjoy painting," I call back.

"You're telling me that you, Beckham Sullivan, are an amateur artist?"

I swipe a bottle of water, returning to the living area. There's no point in hiding since she's like a dog with a bone. She isn't going to drop this conversation.

"Uh . . . yeah. I'm a creative guy. Painting is a great outlet."

"You keep that door locked to hide your art?" She doesn't believe me. Not surprising since I'm lying through my teeth.

"It's private."

Her eyes narrow on me. "If you're painting yourself nude, that's both weird *and* I have seen your penis, so I'm not sure why you'd be hiding it."

"I'm not painting nudes."

Her nose crinkles adorably. Finger wagging at me, she says, "I'm onto you, Wazowski."

"I think someone's been watching too many Disney movies this week."

I toss my now-empty water bottle, then swipe a bag of chips from my pantry cabinet.

"It's not my fault *Monsters, Inc.* is a masterpiece."

"I'm aware—you've made me watch it twice this week and the sequel once."

Her mouth drops with indignation. "It's a prequel! Did you not pay attention? I'm putting it on again." She slaps her hand against the couch. "Sit."

I'll gladly watch the movie again if that means she'll forget about the paint on my clothes.

"Put the movie on, I'll be right back." I practically sprint down the hall to change out of my shirt so that the paint stain can't serve as a glaring reminder of what I was up to.

After stuffing the shirt in the laundry basket, I yank out one in a similar color from the drawer. The dresser and closet are overflowing with my stuff and Lennon's.

I used to think something like that would send me into a panic, the mixing of two lives; instead, I find myself liking seeing her stuff interspersed with mine. Beckham of a year ago would not believe where I am now, but I don't find myself wishing for it to be any other way.

Lennon has the movie starting when I enter the room. I take her laptop from her, setting it on the coffee table before I pick up her feet and place them in my lap when I sit down. It's become automatic for me to massage her feet when she's like this. The tiny little noises of pleasure she makes are the sweetest kind of torture, and I know I'll be spending more time with my hand later. I haven't jacked off this much since I was fifteen.

With a gruff meow, Cheddar jumps up on the coffee table, tail swishing.

"Come here, Cheddie." I can't believe she's given my cat a nick-name. "Lay with me."

He gently pounces onto the couch, curling himself on top of her. "I think my cat is in love with you."

She pets him behind the ears, his purr loud enough to be mistaken for a freight train. "That's because he's a good boy who has taste."

"I don't know about that," I joke, cursing when she pinches the hair on my arm. "Hey," I scold, "I'm rubbing your feet here."

"And I'm pregnant, so you wouldn't dare stop." She shoots a beam-ing smile my way. With a gasp so loud my heart drops to my feet because I think something's wrong, she says, "We should do that!"

"Do what?" I growl, trying to calm my out-of-control heart. This woman is going to be the end of me.

She swishes her hand dramatically at the TV. "For Halloween next year with the baby! Since everyone we work with calls you Sulli, you'll be Sulley." She sounds so pleased with herself. "It's pretty perfect since his last name is Sullivan, too, and that's where he gets his nickname. The baby can be Boo—even if it's a boy, I think that could work. I mean, who cares?"

"It's a girl," I say emphatically. "And what would you be?"

She gapes at me. "Mike, duh."

"I should've known."

"Yes, you should've."

She was a Dementor this year, so a one-eyed green monster makes perfect sense.

I don't tell her, but hearing her talk about things in the future, like Halloween, gives me hope that maybe I won't fuck all this up. I don't want to ruin us, but sometimes it feels like good things aren't meant for me.

Chapter Forty-One

LENNON

It's the longest I've been left alone in the apartment since Beckham moved me in. But I should've known he wouldn't leave me without a babysitter. Laurel calls me to be buzzed in, and I unlock the door, positioning myself in the rocking chair recliner that's now in his living room. He said it was for when the baby comes, which is believable enough, but I think he got sick of me griping about only having the couch and the bed to lie in. I will say, the chair is nice—a cream, faux-shearling material, and comfortable enough that since it was delivered three days ago, I've already fallen asleep in it once. Okay, five times, but who's counting.

"It's unlocked," I call when there's a knock on the door. Laurel lets herself in, balancing a pizza box and—

"Is that a cat?" I shriek at the dirty orange ball she unleashes in the apartment.

She's out of breath, panting like she's run a mile. Laurel and cardio don't mix. I learned that the one time I dragged her to a spin class.

"You have no idea how long it took me to catch that thing and not drop the pizza. Your boyfriend owes me."

"For what?" I practically scream at her, the cat zipping past me to hide under the couch.

Cheddar watches everything play out from his perch on top of the bookcase.

She looks at me like I've grown an extra head. "For catching his cat." She sets the pizza box down in front of me, flips the lid up, and hands me a slice, then takes one for herself.

The slice dangles loosely in my hand. "That's not his cat."

"What do you mean?" She snorts, setting her piece down on the box so she can shrug out of her coat. "That's definitely his cat. You've sent me pictures. It needs a bath, by the way."

"Laurel." I'm flabbergasted at my best friend right now. I don't know whether to laugh or cry. "I'm telling you, that's not Cheddar. That," I say, pointing to the top of the bookcase, "is Cheddar."

"I know." She plops on the couch, pizza in hand. Her cheeks are red from the cold. "I'm the one who rescued him from the streets."

"He hasn't left the apartment. You just brought in a random cat off the streets."

"No, I—" The random cat chooses that moment to dart out from under the couch, making her eyes shoot from the orange furball streaking across the floor to the one perched on the bookcase. "Oh my God, I did!" She slaps a hand to her mouth. "Your boyfriend is going to kill me!"

I didn't say anything the first time, but this time I do. "He's not my boyfriend."

She snorts. "Does he know that?"

"Um . . . I'm pretty sure he does. Now, are you going to catch that cat or not?"

"Nope, that's your not-my-boyfriend's job."

I sigh, wondering where the poor kitty disappeared to now. At least Cheddar seems unbothered.

"Anyway"—Laurel passes me another slice, since I've polished off the first—"we have lots to catch up on."

"We do?" We talk and text almost every day, so I have no idea what I might've missed out on. "Fill me in."

"I met a guy."

"Since we talked last night?"

"Mmm." She chews the end of her crust, nibbling on it like some sort of woodland creature. "This morning I was getting coffee, you know from that little hole-in-the-wall I love?" She waits for me to nod before she goes on. "Anyway, he ordered the last blueberry scone, and you know those are my favorite. I said something like, 'Oh, come on, dude, I wanted that.' He turns around and looks at me, and Lennon"—she grabs on to my arm, a dreamy look in her eyes—"I kid you not, this is the sexiest man I've ever seen in my *life*." She makes a noise like she wants to eat him up. "Dark hair, gray eyes—I didn't even know gray eyes were a thing, Lennon!—these full, kissable lips, and he says to me we can share the scone, but the caveat is I have to sit with him. Like I was going to say no. We have a date planned for Friday." She kicks her legs excitedly.

"That's so amazing."

"I'll send you the deets, in case he's a serial killer."

Gotta love being a woman in the dating world and having to cover your bases in case the guy you're seeing is a monster.

"What's his name?"

"Crew—is that not the hottest name you've ever heard?" She dramatically swoons into the couch cushions. "I think I'm in love."

"Don't get ahead of yourself now."

Laurel is famous for this, falling hard and fast, and then getting bored by the third date. I want her to find love, to be treated like she deserves.

"I know." She straightens the pillows. "But I'm excited. The last I don't know how many guys I've been out with have all come from a dating app. This felt like something out of a movie."

I point a finger in mock warning. "You better keep me updated. Since I'm bedridden, I have to live vicariously through you."

She snorts. "You don't have to worry about that. You know I'll be giving you a play-by-play as soon as the date is over."

Just then the mysterious cat she picked up off the streets of New York goes whizzing past, sending both of us screaming at the top of our lungs.

There's never a dull moment when Laurel is around.

It's late when Beckham gets home. I've already moved myself back to bed, a book clasped in my hands. It's some of the raunchiest smut I've ever read, and I don't know whether it's helping or hindering my sexual frustration.

I peek over the top of the book, waiting for him to notice our new companion, who is now fluffy and clean thanks to the mobile grooming service I was able to pay an emergency fee to.

He hangs his coat up on the back of the closet door. "How are you feeling?"

"Great." I draw out the word, watching him sit down and remove his shoes and socks. "How was your day?"

"Spectacular. Froze my balls off, but I got some decent photos. Spoke with Jaci, too, and she'll be holding a meeting at the end of the week to announce what team's story she's chosen." He loosens the buttons on his shirt. No tie today. "I'm exhausted. I haven't had a day this long in a while. I want to shower and—Lennon, what the fuck is that?"

I force a smile, setting my book down on the bed. "What do you mean?"

"That!" His blue eyes nearly bug out, finger wagging accusingly at me. "On the bed, beside Cheddar, that thing that looks mysteriously like a cat."

"It's a cat."

He scrubs both hands down his face. "Why is there an extra cat in my apartment?"

"Um . . ." I bite my lip. "Because Laurel rescued it off the streets thinking it was Cheddar." His jaw drops, incredulous. "I know, I know.

269

I love her, but sometimes she can be a bit zany. What's another cat when you already have one?"

"Laurel is about to be the proud new owner of an orange cat." He eyes the new cat with his hands on his hips. His lips are already beginning to soften the longer he looks at the sweet kitty.

"About that . . . I already named him, so he's kind of mine. Or, I guess, ours."

"You named him?"

"Yeah," I reply, but it comes out sounding more like "Yuh."

"What's his name?" He says it like it's a challenge.

"George Sanderson."

"George—what?"

"He's the orange monster from *Monsters, Inc.* Do I seriously have to put the movie on again, so you'll actually pay attention this time?"

He shakes his head, looking frustrated yet somewhat amused. "That thing could have rabies."

I scratch George Sanderson under his chin. "Do you have rabies? No, you don't. You're just a cute wittle baby."

"He could be feral."

"Does he look feral?"

"Well, no, but—"

"No buts." I mime closing a mouth with my hand. "He's a good boy. He deserves a loving home. I had a vet check him out already. I promise he's fine."

He huffs a breath, hands on his hips. "And you think we're a loving home?"

"I mean, I'd hope so—I am eventually going to have to evict your pet sperm from my body."

He points a finger at me in warning. "Not too soon. That's why you need to stay off your feet."

"Yeah, yeah."

He eyes the new addition for a moment longer. "He can stay as long as Cheddar is okay with it."

"They're cuddling," I point out.

He smiles, looking at the two cats. "Like I said, as long as he's okay with it."

He grabs some sweatpants from the dresser and goes to shower.

I put the movie on, since clearly he's already in need of a refresher.

By the time he's returned from the shower, I've read another chapter in my book. I set it aside for now because it's getting me a little bit too worked up.

"Your cheeks are flushed," he accuses, plugging his phone in to charge for the night. "You weren't up, were you?"

"What? No?"

Oh Jesus, why did it come out as a question?

"No?" He arches a brow. "Is there something you should tell me?"

"N-no," I stutter.

I can tell he doesn't want to let this go, but he asks, "Do you need anything from the kitchen? I'm getting some water."

"Water would be great."

He leaves the room, both cats hopping off the bed to trot after him.

I think Cheddar and George Sanderson are going to be the best of friends.

Beckham strolls into the room with the waters, sweatpants slung low on his hips, and I *moan*.

All it takes is a man holding water bottles and wearing sweats to get me going these days.

He pauses midstep. "Did you just—"

"Don't say it," I beg, squishing my eyes closed. "I'm just . . . really, really horny, okay, and that book isn't helping." I point accusingly at the paperback. "And you're being attentive and wearing those sweatpants that I can literally see the shape of your dick in. I'm just sexually

271

frustrated at the moment." I grip the sheets in frustration. "We can do other stuff. I mean, it's just penetration that's off the table."

Oh my God, am I begging this man for oral and just used the word penetration *out loud? I'm hopeless. A complete disaster.*

He arches a brow as he gently sets the bottle down before backing away from me as if I'm a bomb ready to detonate. "Are you asking me to go down on you?"

"Not asking," I squeak. "Suggesting? Or maybe you could, um, do yourself and I could watch? That might make it worse for me, though."

I can tell he's trying to hold in laughter. Bless him for attempting to keep it together, but I still want to smack him.

"Babe, I might be flexible, but not even I can bend over and suck my own dick."

"That's not what I meant." I press the heels of my palms to my eyes.

Suddenly, he's there, warm hands wrapped around my wrists to tug my hands away.

"I'm sorry," he says, sobering. "I'm not trying to make fun of you. I think it's cute."

"Cute?"

"Mmm." He rubs his nose along my cheek, my whole body shivering in response. "I don't want to hurt you."

"Y-you won't." I'm a stuttering, shaky mess. "Dr. Hersh said oral was okay. Touching. Just no—"

He slaps his hand over my mouth. "Don't say *penetration* again."

When his hand falls away, I give a soft, "Okay."

"Okay," he repeats, kissing along my jaw.

A pleading moan slips out of me. I don't think I've ever felt so desperate in my entire life.

I need this so bad.

"I'm going to be gentle with you. You have to be okay with that."

"Do whatever you want with me."

He laughs darkly. "Say that again when I can fuck you the way I want."

My pussy clenches at the delicious promise in his words.

Wrapping a hand loosely around my neck, he rubs his thumb over my bottom lip. "So pretty. So perfect. So fucking *mine*," he growls, diving in for my mouth.

My lips part, my body melting into the pillows. I'm so worked up I feel like he barely has to touch me and I'm likely to go off.

He gently moves the blanket aside, grabbing more pillows to use to prop up my hips after he's gotten rid of my pajama pants. Parting my thighs, he kneels on the bed between my legs.

"Fuck, baby, you're so wet. Is this all for me?" I nod vigorously, biting my lip to hold in a whimper. "I didn't realize you needed me so bad."

"I do." A small cry escapes me at the feel of his hands rubbing my inner thighs. "I was trying to be good."

"Mmm," he hums, lowering himself between me. "Let me take care of you." At the first swipe of his tongue, my hips buck against his face. He chuckles, amused, and loops his arms around my legs to keep me in place. He's both gentle but firm in his touch. "You taste so good, baby."

He flicks his tongue over my clit, and I swear I see stars. My fingers delve into his hair, holding on, tugging. If it hurts, he doesn't say anything. "Yes, yes, yes," I cry, rocking my hips against his face.

It doesn't take me long before my orgasm crashes over me, but it's not enough, and Beckham must sense this, because it's not much more than ended when he's back at it, working me up to another.

I've never considered myself someone who *needs* sex, but with Beckham it's so good that I find myself wanting it more than I ever have before. It doesn't help that pregnancy hormones have turned me into a raging hornball. Is this how teenage boys feel? Like if you don't come, you might spontaneously combust?

He rubs at my clit with sure fingers, and that does it. My back arches, sweat dotting my skin as the orgasm rocks through me.

He wrings one more orgasm out of me before my body is spent. I lie there, my shirt askew, my legs weak.

"Let me clean you up," he says, climbing off the bed.

"But you—" I reach for him, for the erection tenting his sweatpants. He pushes my hand away gently. "Are fine."

"Clearly not," I protest, trying to sit up. Somehow the mountain of pillows behind me is dislodged. My hair is plastered to my forehead. "Let me—"

"No," he says more forcefully this time.

"Fine." I try to fix my hair with my fingers. "Then let me watch."

He gapes at me. "What?"

I wet my lips. "You're going to take care of that, right?" I challenge, my breath still short from the workout he gave me.

"Yeah, but—"

"Let me watch you. I want to see what you do to yourself. Please."

His Adam's apple bobs. I expect him to shut me down, say no, and that will be that. "I'll clean you up first." He grips his cock through the fabric of his sweats, staring at me, still spread out on the bed, the feast he just devoured.

Shaking himself free, he pads into the bathroom, returning a moment later with a warm white cloth that he uses to gently clean me up. After tossing the cloth into the bin, he watches me, his eyes dark and stormy.

He strokes himself like he did before, over his pants. Such a fucking tease.

"Take it out," I practically beg, my mouth watering.

If I can't fuck his cock, I can at least watch him fuck himself. It's not the same but still sexy as hell.

"Where do you want me?"

I'm surprised he's asking. "The chair," I half gasp, half beg. Perhaps this is a bad idea. There's no way I'm making it out of this without turning into a needy, wanting mess again.

He shoves the sweats down his thighs, his cock springing free. Grabbing the base, he strokes upward, twisting his wrist on the end. His eyes stay locked on me, watching me. I can feel him. But my eyes stay glued to his hand, his dick, watching with rapt attention as he jerks himself off.

His ab muscles contract, and I know he's holding himself back. His movements become jerkier, unsteady.

"Wish this was you that I was fucking," he groans through clenched teeth, squeezing his cock so hard I'm sure it must hurt. "Your mouth, your tits, your pussy. Anything but my hand."

"I wanted—"

"I'm not fucking your mouth or tits tonight." He closes his eyes, jaw clenched. "I have to be careful with you, and I'd be too rough. I know it." His head falls back, and he moans, hand speeding up.

I know he's close.

I lick my lips in anticipation.

And then he's grunting, and groaning, and moaning, thick spurts of cum covering his stomach as his hand milks every last drop from his cock.

Holy fuck.

My heart is beating out of control like I just went three rounds with him. Apparently, the organ didn't get the memo that I'm just lying here.

When he recovers, he yanks the sweatpants up and grabs the damp cloth he used on me from the bin and uses it to wipe himself off. "Did you like the show, honeybee?"

"You have no idea."

He gives me a dark chuckle, then helps to fix my pillows before climbing into bed beside me and holding me close.

That's when he sees the TV.

"Not this movie again."

Chapter Forty-Two

BECKHAM

Lennon and I are seated at my small kitchen table to call into the office for the meeting that will determine our future.

That's a bit dramatic of me, but the way Jaci has framed this thing, it sure feels like it.

Which is crazy, considering it's not like we get any sort of prize or anything.

I think her motivation was to force us to work in teams, to get creative, and since she can be a bit off the wall, it wouldn't surprise me at all if she said this was one giant experiment she conducted to see how her staff handles group projects.

"You look stressed," Lennon whisper-hisses, despite the fact that we haven't been connected to the meeting yet. "You're turning red."

I let out the breath I was holding. "I'm fine." I reach for my cup of coffee.

"Hey." She places her hand on top of mine. "Whatever happens, it'll be fine."

"I know."

It's funny that she's the one reassuring me when our whole proposal was her idea, and I know what it would mean to her to be chosen.

"Regardless of what happens, we make a good team."

I look at her a moment, letting her words sink in. "We do, don't we?"

Jaci chooses that moment to connect us to the meeting.

"Ah," Jaci says, clicking something on the screen, "it's so good to see your faces. How are you feeling, Lennon?"

"Doing good." She forces a smile, giving her a thumbs-up.

The meeting gets underway, and I don't know if it's because she's purposely trying to drag it out or if Jaci is just that oblivious to the fact that everyone wants to know who's won this not-really-a-competition.

She discusses elements she wants revised for next month's magazine, photos she wants to see other shots of because she's not sold on the current selections, and then finally, blessedly, she says, "Now, on to the spring print issue."

Beside me, Lennon grabs for my hand, her nails digging into my skin.

Jaci touches on each team, lightly going over what they proposed.

"Everyone's ideas were brilliant, and I feel like you all got into the spirit of things—thinking deep, outside-the-box thoughts. You all have put me in a tough position, because there is no bad or wrong choice here; in fact, I think many of these ideas can be used in future editions. I have this vision, you see"—she paces away from the camera, where we can still hear but not see her—"of *Real Point* becoming something big. More than a magazine. I want to be a staple that people talk about." She breezes back in front of the camera, speaking animatedly with her hands. "And that is why I'm choosing Lennon and Beckham's proposal for the spring issue."

Beside me, Lennon's hand falls away from mine. She gasps, slapping her hands to her mouth. On the computer, Jaci laughs, beaming at us when she appears back on screen.

"You both presented such a compelling idea, and it's so pertinent to the world we live in. I want you to focus on your interviews and compiling everything. I want the whole issue to revolve around this concept, down to the brand deals we make."

Lennon vibrates with excitement beside me. Judging by Jaci's knowing smile, she notices her excitement.

She goes on for another ten minutes or so about how many interviews she wants us to include, as well as ones that we've already done that she wants us to refine more, and then she touches on a few other things before the meeting ends and Lennon and I are alone once more.

Unless you count Cheddar and George Sanderson. In that case, we're never alone.

She wraps her hand around my neck, pulling me down to her level. "We did it." She crashes her lips into mine.

"You did it," I remind her. "This was all your idea."

"You agreed."

"Because it was a fucking great idea. Now, come on." I slide off the chair. "We need to get your feet up."

With a sigh, she stands, hand to her belly. "You're so lucky you're worth it, little nugget."

"She wants to be dramatic like her mom."

Lennon's eyes narrow on me, and I'm pretty sure she's seconds away from hissing at me like one of the cats. "More like her father."

My eyes widen. "You said *her*." A slow smile tugs my lips as I help her into the rocker that takes up a large amount of real estate in my living room.

"It was a reflex because you're always saying it," she gripes, adjusting her shirt over her expanding belly.

"Are you sure your mother's intuition isn't kicking in?"

She purses her lips in thought. "No, sadly it was just an automatic response. I think I'm broken."

I grab her cup of water and set it on the table beside her within easy reaching distance. "You're not broken."

"How can you be so sure? Have you ever been a mother?" Her eyes twinkle with laughter.

"No, can't say I have." Her favorite blanket is on the back of the couch. I pick it up and cover her legs with it.

She cradles her stomach, sighing heavily. "This sucks. I can't even properly nest."

I nearly trip over Cheddar—no, that's George Sanderson—when I take a step back. "What do you mean, nest?"

"You know, nesting." She gestures with her hands. "It's where you get everything ready for baby. I haven't gotten anything yet. The baby will be here before we know it. Summer is around the corner."

"It's the beginning of February," I point out. "You have plenty of time."

"I really don't." I see the stress rising inside her. "A lot of stuff, like furniture and whatnot, takes time to get here, and where am I going to send it anyway? Here? What if you decide you don't want me to stay? And I need things like a stroller, and a car seat. I mean, even though this is Manhattan, you do have a car, and just in case I'd need to take a taxi, I should definitely have one, right? And—"

I put my hand over her mouth, silencing whatever she plans to say next. "I want to show you something."

I let my hand fall away. "Show me what?" She eyes me skeptically.

Wiggling my hand in front of her to help her up, I say, "Can't you trust me?"

She gives me a curious smile. "Okay."

I slide her hand into mine and help her up from the rocker. "I wasn't going to show you this yet." I lead her down the short hall, yanking the key from my pocket as we go. "It's not ready, not just yet. But . . ."

I unlock the door to the spare bedroom, the one I've kept her out of, and let it swing open. Afternoon light filters into the room.

Shocked, wide brown eyes blink at me, her pink lips parted.

"Go on," I encourage her. "Take a look."

She takes a tentative step forward, then another. I'm right beside her. Logically, I know she isn't at risk of falling, at least not yet, but I can't help but hover. Especially since she's not on her feet a lot and is getting weaker because of it.

"You . . . you did all this?" She turns, my hand hovering at her side. "The . . . the paint on your clothes? You painted this? The room?" She points to the cream-colored walls.

"I can be handy when I want to be."

"And . . . and the crib. It's the one I said I liked at the store that day. The sheets too. You listened."

"I did." I look around, trying to see the room through her eyes.

I've been working on it ever since that day she went to the baby store, and I joined her. At the time I wasn't thinking about her living with me, and when I placed the order, I was just going to give everything to her, but things changed, and now she's here. I always planned to turn this space into a nursery for the baby, but with her living here, I wanted it to be the room she dreamed of.

"Did you put all this stuff together?"

"The crib and stroller. The dresser was delivered built."

"You did all this for the baby?"

"For the baby and you," I correct. "Once the baby comes, I'll move the rocker into this spot." I point to the blank space in the room. "I thought you might like it by the window so you could look out and rock the baby at the same time. I haven't gotten clothes yet or anything like that. The dresser is empty. You can order whatever you want. I'll even give you my credit card."

She cracks a smile, her eyes filled with tears. "You've done more than enough. This is . . . this is amazing, Beckham. It's beautiful." She rubs her fingers over the fabric of the striped curtains. The lady at the store helped me pick them. She said they matched the bedding. "I couldn't imagine a more beautiful room for our baby if I tried."

"Please, don't cry. I don't want you to cry, honeybee." I tug her into my arms, kissing the top of her head.

"I'm happy, I promise. This is so beautiful, Beckham. I can't believe you did all this for our baby. I can't wait to bring them home from the hospital to this amazing room their daddy made for them."

Daddy. I haven't let myself think too much on how that's what I'll be soon. Someone's father. I just . . . fuck, I just want to be a good one. Not perfect, that doesn't exist, but good.

"Thank you." She wraps her arms around me, chin resting on my chest. "You're incredible."

"Pretty sure you didn't think that when you hated me."

"You broke my heart," she reminds me. "It was easy to hate you— but need I remind you, you hated me too. Why was that? I didn't do anything to you."

"No, but your family did, and I think you got the brunt of my anger because I felt like if I hadn't liked you the way that I did, then none of it would've happened. I would've still been friends with your brother and in your life in some way."

She stiffens at the mention of her brother, pulling away from my body. She grips the railing on the crib, knuckles paling. "I'm so angry at him," she hisses softly. She looks over at me with pain etched into the lines of her face. I want to smooth them away, take the agony from her. I hate that I ever hurt her, and I wish I could keep anyone else from doing the same. "What a fucking weasel."

I shouldn't laugh right now, but hearing Lennon refer to Hunter as a *weasel* sends me into a fit of hysterics.

"What?" she asks innocently, starting to giggle. "He is! You know he is. He cares more about saving face for our father than standing up for the right thing."

Sobering, I clear my throat. "Maybe one day he'll get his priorities straight."

"Yeah, and his head out of our dad's ass." She snorts, making me laugh again with her.

Once we collect ourselves, she takes in the room again. I still need to patch some spots on the walls, and hang a mirror by the closet, and there's the bookcase I want to build, too, but—

"I can't believe we're going to bring our baby home here. Think of all the memories they'll make in this room."

I hadn't even thought about that, which seems ironic, since I put together this bedroom for our kid, but thinking about them living in it, growing, is a crazy thing to wrap my head around.

"Do you think she'll like it?" Fuck, I sound idiotic asking that.

Lennon doesn't say that, though. Instead, she smiles, hugging me again. "Trust me, they're going to love it . . . and love you even more."

I lay the side of my cheek against the top of her head and smile.

This, I realize, is what I've always wanted but was too blinded by other things to realize: a family.

Chapter Forty-Three

LENNON

Fuck bed rest. It's mid-March, and I'm over this. This baby isn't due for another two months. I have *weeks* of this left, because despite my numerous appointments, every time they say I need to keep doing what I'm doing. I'm going stir crazy, downright insane. At least I have been given a longer amount of time that I'm allowed to be on my feet throughout the day, but it's still not much.

Manhattan is the worst place in the world to be put on bed rest, since you have to walk everywhere.

It's for the baby, I remind myself. That's the only thing getting me through at this point. Mothers deserve a round of applause for bringing babies into the world. This shit is hard and not for the faint of heart.

It's a cool day, but I sit outside on Beckham's balcony anyway, inhaling as much fresh air as I can get.

"You, little nugget, are trouble," I tell my stomach. The baby kicks in response. "You just want to keep Mommy on her toes, don't you?" Another kick. I smile to myself.

Sometimes I find it hard to find joy in these little moments, since there's so much I can't do. Beckham reminds me I'm growing a human, and therefore, I'm doing plenty, but in the back of my mind, it doesn't feel like enough.

It's like the interviews that will go to print for the May issue. I've been having to conduct them via Zoom instead of getting out there and meeting these women in person. The most I get out of the apartment is doctor's appointments or the one time Beckham gave in to my pleading and took me out for breakfast.

My phone rings, and I already know who it is.

My brother.

He's been calling all week, and I've been ignoring him.

The only time the phone has been answered is when Beckham picked it up and promptly told him to leave me the fuck alone. Not exactly eloquent but to the point, and I appreciate that.

The call cuts off, a text message popping up on the screen a moment later.

Hunter: We need to talk.

I don't want to talk to him, but I also want to talk to him. It's quite the conundrum. He's my brother and I love him, even if he's a big idiot.

But I don't reply.

I need to see more effort from him than just endless phone calls and a cryptic text message.

Starting to feel the chill, I head inside to find Cheddar and George Sanderson snoozing on the giant cat tree—a purchase from Amazon. There are lots of online purchases overflowing Beckham's apartment. Turns out I'm a boredom shopper.

Boxes of diapers crowd the space beside the front door—once I read about how many diapers babies, especially newborns, go through, I panic purchased a ridiculous amount. But the idea of running out in the middle of the night terrifies me.

I settle myself back on the couch and pick up the latest book I'm reading. That's been another source of endless online purchases. Paperback books are stacked in the corners of the living area and

Beckham's bedroom. I still can't seem to make myself think of any of this as being mine—ours.

Since Beckham is gone for another hour or so, I occupy myself with reading. I haven't kept count, but I'm fairly certain I've read at least fifty books since my bed rest started. It isn't long before the cats abandon their perch on the tree to snuggle with me on the couch. I've always heard about cats being standoffish, but not these two. They rarely leave me alone for long.

Beckham arrives a little while later with a clatter of keys and a curse when he drops them outside the door. He finally enters the apartment, hair windswept and his nose red from the cold. He carries five grocery bags, dumping them onto the kitchen counter the second he reaches it.

"Are you okay?" I ask at his huffing and puffing.

"Fine." He riffles through the contents, unpacking and sorting them into sections. "My lungs don't like the cold air."

"Oh, they told you that?"

He turns around, a can of soup clasped in one hand. "Do you hear this wheezing?" He demonstrates the almost squeaky sound he makes when he inhales. "Yeah, they told me. How long have you been on your feet today?"

"Not too much. Why?" I can feel my hackles rising—he's like the steps police.

"I thought we could make dinner together."

I deflate, fighting a smile. Considering how strict he's been that I not breach the parameters of my bed rest, it means a lot that he's including me in something that will give me a chance to be somewhat active. "That would be great."

To feel useful for a little while will be nice. I ease off the couch, careful not to disturb the slumbering kitties, and join him in the kitchen. It's a decent size by the city's standards, but still a tight squeeze for two people.

"How are you feeling today?"

"Stir crazy," I reply, pouring myself a glass of water.

"You say that every day," he counters, lining up ingredients for dinner. It looks like we'll be making cheese-stuffed tortellini with home-made sauce.

"Because it's true."

"I'm sorry."

I know he means it, but it doesn't make me feel any better. I think the only thing that will is getting this baby to full term and being able to function like a normal person again. Preeclampsia is scary stuff, for me and for the baby. Following my doctor's orders is a must, but it's definitely affecting my mental health.

"What do you want me to do?" I ask, eyeing everything he's left on the counter.

"Want to chop up the garlic?"

"That should be fine."

I grab a cutting board and knife, then get to work while he dices up a shallot.

We work side by side in companionable silence, the picture of domestic bliss. It's nice, just doing things together. When I started at *Real Point* and he waltzed back into my life, I thought I'd continue to hate his guts forever. What people forget to tell you is that love and hate can feel a lot like each other.

Beckham finishes with the shallot, then adds both it and the garlic to a pan. "Stir that around some," he tells me.

I do as I'm told, happy to be able to actually do something.

He puts some music on for background noise, and my hips begin to sway to the beat.

He groans, grabbing my hips to still them. "That, that right there is what got me into trouble with you."

"My hips?" I laugh the question.

"These hips. Your ass. The way you walk. Talk. Smell." He brushes my hair over one side of my shoulder, nuzzling into my neck, arms wrapped around me from behind. "You drive me crazy."

"I don't mean to."

"I know," he murmurs, his breath warm against my skin. "You don't even have to try, and that makes it even worse."

He lets me go, and I instantly miss his warmth. He grabs a small carton of cream before pouring it into the sizzling pan, along with some parmesan cheese to make the sauce. Simple, but it smells like heaven.

He gets started on the pasta; since it's the refrigerated kind that takes no time to cook, it's ready about the same time as the sauce.

We plate our pasta, and he curses. "I forgot to get garlic bread."

"It's fine. We don't need any. This will be amazing." I sprinkle some parsley onto each of our dishes.

"Are you sure?" He sounds so worried.

"Positive."

The song changes, and Beckham holds out a hand to me. "Dance with me."

"What?"

He shrugs, hand still hanging in the air. "Dinner needs to cool some. Dance with me. Please?"

It's the *please* that gets me. I'm such a sucker.

I slide my hand into his, letting him pull me into his body as we sway to the song. It's awkward, my belly firmly in the way now, but he doesn't seem to mind. He places one hand on my waist, the other holding mine in the air as he moves around the small space.

Cheddar hops up on the counter, watching us with a curious flick of his tail.

"I love this song," I admit, smiling at him.

"It's a favorite for me too."

"You didn't strike me as the love song ballad type of guy."

"What can I say? I'm full of surprises. I have to keep you on your toes some way." He kisses my forehead.

"My brother called again today. Texted too."

He stiffens. I know my brother is a sore spot for him. "Did you answer?"

"No. I feel bad ignoring him," I admit, letting him guide me in the most pathetic twirl ever since he won't fully let me go, "but I don't want to talk to him. Not right now."

Beckham sighs, his face shadowed. "I won't be mad if you want to talk to him."

"I'm not avoiding him because of you. I just have nothing to say to him."

I'm pretty sure if I did speak to him, I would tell him he's a spineless weasel wrapped around our father's finger.

"I wanted you to know that, though, that it won't bother me."

I reach my hand up, curling in his soft hair at the base of his neck. "You're a good man, Beckham."

He mock cringes. "Not the kiss of death."

"What?" I laugh.

"Good guys don't have any fun. I'll take being the villain any day."

I roll my eyes in pretend annoyance. "You always have to go against what I say, don't you?"

His lips lift in a small half grin. "Only because it's fun."

The song ends and we sit down with our meal, both cats perched at our feet watching us. I don't know why; it's not like they've ever been given a morsel of people food.

I realize how much I love this. Being together. The domesticity of it all.

I could get used to this with him, and that terrifies me.

We crashed and burned before. What's to say it won't happen again?

Chapter Forty-Four

BECKHAM

I enter the care home with the same sense of foreboding I've had for months.

Watching someone you care about slip away and get weaker day by day is a hard pill to swallow. Especially for someone like me, who just wants to fix everything. This is one thing I can't do a damn thing about.

"Today's a better day," Anna, one of the nurses, says when she spots me striding into the building.

Good days have been few and far between, and even those aren't great.

I settle myself in the chair in my father's room. He's sleeping, his skin pale and almost translucent in areas, the blue of his veins standing out starkly in the fluorescent lights.

I turn some music on in the background and sit with him while he sleeps. I like to think he knows I'm here, but it's probably a ridiculous hope.

One of the nurses stops by to check in on my dad. She shoots me a sympathetic look. I hate the pity I see in their eyes now. They've worked here long enough to sense when someone's time is near. Being bedridden is hard on the body, and he's had two different infections in the past few months. It's all taken its toll, and his body is shutting down.

"How are you doing?"

I have to bite my tongue not to snap at her, that I'm not in the mood for small talk. "Fine," I say instead. I know she's just trying to be friendly, but sometimes it's hard to remember that when I'm so close to losing control.

I hate feeling so fucking helpless.

"Do you want me to bring you a drink while you're here?"

I shake my head. "That's okay. I won't stay long."

"If you need anything, don't hesitate to ask one of us."

She leaves the room, and once again I'm left with my thoughts and the man in the bed.

He stirs, eyes slowly peeling open.

I hate that I didn't find him sooner. Maybe he wouldn't be dying right now if I had. The other facility did a number on him, not really caring for him, and they haven't been able to do much here because of his already-weakened state.

"Hey," I say when he finds me in the chair. I swear there's a smile in his eyes. "You look good." His eyes narrow like he's telling me I'm full of shit. He couldn't talk much before, and the last infection left him without a voice. When he tries to speak, it's more of a wheeze than anything else. "Lennon's doing well. The baby too. I wish you could meet them." I leave out the part where I haven't told Lennon about him. I don't know why I haven't. I know she'd be happy for me, that I found him, but a part of me feels like, what's the point? I know it's the wrong way to think. "Would you want to meet them? Well, her. The baby's not here yet."

He blinks once.

That means yes.

We've developed our own secret language to be able to communicate with each other now that he doesn't have any words at all.

"Okay. I'll ask her." And I will if that's what he wants, which clearly it is. He deserves to look at someone else besides these nurses and me day in and day out.

I settle more comfortably into the chair, knowing I'll be staying now until he drifts back out.

My stay ends up being two hours long.

A good day, indeed.

◆ ◆ ◆

"Are you sure you don't want one of these, Sulli?" Brendan digs into an apple pie at a diner near the office.

Since I'm hardly there these days, I wanted to catch up with my friend.

"I'm sure."

He grins, oblivious of the crumbs around his mouth. "That's right. You have to stay in shape. Some of us"—he pats his stomach—"don't care."

"If I wanted the pie, I'd eat it." Which is true. I'm not much of a pie person. I prefer ice cream as my dessert of choice.

"Sure you would. How's the wife?"

I roll my eyes at his joke. "She's fine."

I wonder what he'd think if I told him that we're not even a real couple. We act like one, but we've still never defined those lines.

"She's fine? That's all I get?"

I sigh, grabbing a fry from my half-eaten plate of food and then shoving it in my mouth. "She's tired of being stuck in the apartment, and she's growing a literal child in her body, so that makes her irritable."

"But you're surviving?"

"Yep." I grab another fry.

Brendan shakes his head, an amused smile curving his mouth. "I have to say, I'm surprised at seeing you settle down. Not that you dated

291

much to begin with, but in case no one's ever said this to you, Sulli, you can be kind of scary."

"I just have one of those faces."

"Huh?"

"The intimidating kind."

He polishes off his apple pie. "You do," he agrees. "How do you feel about becoming a dad? I don't have any experience on that front, but I have to say I think I'd be terrified."

I relax into the booth. It feels good to get my mind off my dad for at least a little while. "I wasn't expecting to become a parent yet, maybe not ever, but I'm looking forward to it."

"Are you having a baby shower? My girlfriend told me to ask."

"Oh." I scratch at the stubble on my cheek. "That's a real thing?"

"According to her, yes."

"I haven't thought about it. Lennon hasn't mentioned it either."

"You should ask her about it. You know these women: sometimes they keep things to themselves as a test to see if we'll figure it out." He chuckles obnoxiously.

"Lennon's not like that," I defend, getting pissed off on her behalf.

"Trust me, all women are." Brendan might be my friend, but right now I want to punch him. I won't. I have better control than that. Plus, he does have a point. Does Lennon want a baby shower? "Ask her." He wipes his fingers on a napkin before dropping it onto the crumb-laden plate. "I'm sure Tiffany wouldn't mind putting one together," he says, referring to his girlfriend.

I've met her only once, and even I know she very much would mind.

"I'm sure if she says she does that she'll want her friend to organize it. Plus, if my mom catches wind, she'll want to be involved." I want to get poor Tiffany off the hook.

"Ah." He nods. "That makes sense."

The waitress drops our bill off at the table, and I scoop it up before he can. The least I can do is pay for it, since he's had to put up with my rude ass.

"Let me give you some money," he insists, sitting up to reach for his wallet.

"I got it."

I pass the cash to the waitress the next time she's nearby, insisting on no change. She smiles in thanks and tells us to come back soon.

I shrug into my coat before heading out into the cold.

I can't fucking wait for the weather to break. Maybe one day I'll live somewhere warmer. As much as I love the city, I'm not a fan of the winters.

"See you next time, Sulli," he calls, heading in the opposite direction. "And don't forget to ask Lennon about the baby shower."

I lift my hand in a wave, then tuck my head down against the wind on my trek to the nearest subway station.

When I get back to the apartment, I shrug off my coat and hang it on the rack beside the door.

"What are you doing?"

Lennon's on the couch with a pad of paper and a pen, baby clothes stacked in neat piles in front of her on the coffee table.

"Taking inventory," she says in a tone like it should be obvious.

"Of what?"

"What baby clothes I have—style and size, so I know what I need to get more of."

I hesitate beside the couch. "Is this that whole nesting thing?"

She scratches the tip of her nose. "I think so. I want everything to be perfect."

I don't think now is the time to preach to the mother of my child how perfection doesn't exist.

"I had lunch with Brendan. He asked about you."

She smiles, folding some kind of footie pajamas before proceeding to tick something off in her notebook. "How is he?"

"Good, he's good. He said his girlfriend mentioned something about a baby shower. If you were having one or not."

"Oh?" She sets her notebook aside, sitting back.

"Do you want one?"

Her lips turn down in a frown. "I haven't really thought about it. I suppose I should. One of the first things Laurel asked when I told her I was pregnant was if she could plan a baby shower. I kind of forgot about it. But if we're doing one, it's not going to be one of those no-guys-allowed things. You're the dad. You should be there too."

I chuckle at her rambling. "I'm sure my mom would love to come, maybe my dad too. We could invite the office."

"Wow." She laughs, shoulders shaking. "We have a real lack of friends and family." She toys with the ends of the blanket in her lap, a forlorn expression clouding her face. I hate that her parents suck so bad, and that her brother is just like them.

"We have each other. It's not about the amount of people you have but the kind of people you do."

She looks at me with a softness in those big brown eyes that have always been my undoing. I find myself wanting to take her picture, so I do.

"What was that for?" She tries to pluck my phone out of my hands. "I look terrible."

"You're beautiful. Like always."

She softens. "I think you like me."

I hold up my thumb and index finger a millimeter apart. "Only a little."

"I'll say something to Laurel about the baby shower, see what she says."

"Okay." I sit down on the coffee table near a pile of clothes, and she gives me a look, just daring me to knock down her organized stack. "There's, uh . . ." I rub my hands over my jeans. "There's something else I wanted to talk to you about."

Wariness settles over her. I wonder what she thinks this is about. "Okay. What is it?"

"It's nothing bad. I want to tell you about my dad."

Her brow knits in confusion. "I know your dad."

I shake my head. "My biological dad." She gapes, her mouth wide open. I've taken her by surprise, which I expected. "I want to tell you about him, and then maybe you'd like to meet him?"

She nods vigorously. "Yes, tell me. Please."

So I do. I start from the beginning and tell her all about my search to find my birth parents and all that I learned. She listens with rapt attention the entire time, never once making me feel crazy for wanting to find out about my birth family.

When I'm done, having spoken more than I think I have at one time in my entire life, she hugs me. It feels good, that simple human touch of being held. For so long I've denied myself this, convincing myself I don't deserve it.

I was wrong.

If there's one thing we all deserve in life, it's to love and be loved.

And I think I really love Lennon. So much that it terrifies me.

Chapter Forty-Five

LENNON

When I mentioned the idea of a baby shower to Laurel, she immediately went crazy planning it—even though at the time I still wasn't sure if I wanted one. But she'd hear none of it, insisting that I had to have one, and she knew if our roles were reversed, I'd be organizing one for her. She wasn't wrong.

The baby shower is being held at a swanky restaurant in Manhattan. Beckham's parents insisted. I didn't think the splurge was necessary, since they rented out the whole restaurant, but who was I to tell them what to do with their money? It's not like they'd listen to me anyway.

"Do I look okay?" I turn away from the mirror, fixing one last piece of hair that insists on sticking straight up.

Beckham steps around the corner, holding a gray T-shirt in front of his chest. His nice, sculpted chest immediately has me drooling. Since living with him, I've learned that he works out a lot at his building's gym and that he utilizes their indoor pool for laps almost daily. That hard work has certainly paid off. His body is basically a work of art.

It's May, and I still haven't been cleared for all activities and sex is still off the table, but I am finally allowed to be on my feet more. Thank God. Every day, Beckham and I have been walking down the street to a café for coffee. It gets me out of the apartment, and I manage to get a little bit of exercise in. I feel like I'm going to have a hard time regaining my strength after the baby is here.

"Did you seriously just ask me if you look okay?" He tugs the shirt on and hides his half-naked body from my greedy eyes. "You're always beautiful, honeybee, you know that."

"I don't need you to flatter me, but thank you."

He cups my cheeks in his hands and places a chaste kiss on my lips. "You're stunning, Lennon. Truly. I think we both know I'm brutally honest enough to tell you if you looked like shit."

I laugh, because he's right. Standing, I smooth my hand down my belly, which has grown to a size I didn't think was possible. The baby could come most any time, which is crazy to think about. Anywhere between now and the start of June, just two weeks away. If I make it to June, my doctor wants to induce me, rather than letting me get to full term, because of the preeclampsia.

"I like the yellow dress," he says.

"I have no idea what Laurel has planned. She just told me to wear yellow."

"She told me too," he admits with a sheepish smile, "but I don't own anything that color."

I pat his chest, walking by him. "Of course you don't. It would be way too happy of a color for your dark soul."

His eyes glimmer with amusement. "I'm so happy you get me."

I love when he jokes with me. As much as I was against the idea of moving in with him, I think it's been the best decision for us. I've gotten to know him so much better because of it.

An open and honest Beckham Sullivan is almost too much for this world. He's scarily perfect, at least for me. We still haven't had a talk on what we are exactly, if we're a real couple now, or still playing pretend. I think we're both avoiding the conversation, afraid of what the other might say.

It doesn't take us long to finish getting ready. I'm both excited and nervous. A little sad, too, since none of my family will be in attendance. My brother has stopped trying to contact me. I've decided it's better that way.

There are some people you don't need in your life. Blood or not.

Beckham drives us to the restaurant, a surprising stirring of nerves in my stomach. It's silly that I feel worried about this at all.

"How's your dad today?" I ask, trying to distract myself.

I've been by the care home three times now with Beckham to see his dad. I hate witnessing what it does to Beckham, watching his biological father deteriorate before his eyes, but I also know he's glad to have had this chance to be with the man, and I'm thankful he decided to share it with me.

Beckham parks near the restaurant in a parking garage, then eyes me warily the entire walk. I don't know whether he's worried since I haven't been moving much or if he thinks my water might break. I've tried to tell him it's not nearly as crazy as movies make it out to be and that many first-time mothers don't even have their water break naturally.

Has he listened?

No.

Everything I tell him goes in one ear and out the other.

The restaurant looms ahead of us, and Beckham grabs the door when we get there and ushers me in first. The main interior space has been transformed into a yellow, white, and cream theme with little bees.

Beckham's lips touch the curve of my ear, his hand light on my waist. "I told them to do something with bumblebees."

I smile up at him, pleased that he had some hand in this. "This is . . . wow. It's perfect."

The restaurant prepared a buffet that's laid out on a long serving table with a balloon arch behind it that matches everything. Fresh flowers cover nearly every available surface. Everywhere I look, no detail has been forgotten. Even the cupcakes have some sort of candy on top that looks like a honeycomb.

I'm so busy taking everything in that I miss Laurel barreling toward me until her arms are thrown around my neck.

"Happy baby shower!" she shrieks, letting me go to pass me a drink from a nearby table. "Is that what people say? 'Happy baby shower'? I don't know." She shrugs, handing Beckham a drink too. "Come on, come on. You two are the guests of honor, after all."

She ushers us to a table with just enough room for the two of us. Along the way, Beckham's mom stops us, giving each of us a hug and planting a loud kiss on his cheek that has him saying, *"Mom."*

Some of the faces in attendance I don't recognize. I suppose I should be bothered by that, but I'm just thankful that anyone wanted to take time out of their busy lives to celebrate us.

Beckham's mom takes my hand and pulls me away from the others. He lifts a brow in question. I shrug, not sure what she wants.

"I wanted to ask you how you are?"

"Oh." Her question isn't exactly odd, but it still catches me off guard. "I'm good."

"I just wanted to say I'm so sorry about your parents, sweetie. How they've treated you . . . both of you." She looks over my shoulder; no doubt Beckham is lingering somewhere behind me. "I've tried talking some sense into Diedre, but it's been to no avail."

"It's okay." I squeeze her hand lightly since she hasn't released her hold on mine.

"They should support you," she insists. "They should've been here. We invited them." That bit stings. They knew about my baby shower, and they just didn't come. I know it's better that they aren't here, who knows what kind of drama they might have stirred up, but even knowing that, it still hurts. "I guess what I really want to say is that I'm sorry they are the way they are."

I don't bother saying it's okay this time, because in reality it's not. But I'm learning to deal with it and move on. They're not worth my heartbreak.

"Thank you."

She pulls me into another hug, one I sink a little deeper into. She's a good woman. I'm so happy that Beckham found a home with her and Richard.

"Games!" Laurel claps her hands together to get everyone's attention. Beckham's mom releases me, giving me a reassuring smile before I take a seat at the table. "Let's play games first. I found all these on Pinterest, so they better be good." Laurel whispers the last part so only I can hear when she passes by me. "First up, everybody, we have the water-breaking game—at least that's what I'm calling it. I'm going to pass out these small cups with a baby frozen in them—okay, that sounds bad, but it's a fake plastic baby, I swear." I stifle a laugh. I can't help but be amused when Laurel goes off on one of her tangents. "Keep an eye on your baby throughout the festivities, and whoever's baby comes free from the ice first will shout out that your water broke. Got it?" She waits for a collective agreement, then proceeds to pass out the cups, even giving one to Beckham and me.

He turns the clear cup around and around, staring at the small naked plastic baby trapped inside. "That thing is terrifying."

"Don't let Laurel hear you. She had fun doing this."

Seriously, I think the girl could have a future in party planning if she wanted.

Beckham mimes zipping his lips shut, then sets the ice-encrusted baby as far away from him as possible.

"It's not going to hurt you."

"Are you sure about that? They're freaky looking." He points at my baby in front of me, face up, eyes black beneath the ice. "Look at it. It's disturbing."

"Be nice." I set my cup aside like he did. With the amount of water that's frozen around it, I'm not sure anyone's is going to "break" before the shower ends.

Laurel, playing hostess, points out another game where everyone can guess how many Honeycombs—the cereal kind, not the real stuff—are in a jar.

"I have prizes for the winners," she singsongs, "so if you need motivation to participate, there you have it." Cupping her hands around her mouth, she mock-whispers, "There are guy-themed prizes as well, so don't think just because you have a penis that you're excluded from this."

The next game is one where people have to cut a string at the length they think would fit around my stomach. I'm mildly offended by how big people think I actually am. It's an insult to all pregnant women everywhere. I'm carrying one child, not five.

The person who comes closest to guessing right is Beckham's mom, who accepts her prize with a gloating victory dance.

There's a break from games to eat. I pile the food onto my plate, eager to try a little bit of everything the restaurant whipped up. When I sit back down, Beckham has a laugh at my comically overflowing plate.

"Are you having fun?" Laurel balances a plate in her hand, stopping beside my chair to chat.

"This is amazing, Laurel." I give her arm a light squeeze of thanks. "I so appreciate you doing all of this."

"Beckham's mom helped a lot. Not only did she pay for everything, but she wanted to be here to help with setup too."

"Thank you. You're already the best auntie to this baby."

Her eyes light up, then get watery with tears. "I get to be called *auntie?*"

"Laurel." I gasp, forgetting about my food for the moment. "You're my best friend. That automatically gives you aunt privileges."

She sniffles, wiping a tear away. "I'm going to be the best aunt ever to your little baby. Just you see. I'm going to spoil them silly."

She walks off then, possibly in search of a tissue.

"She's not pregnant, too, is she?" Beckham's question surprises me. "She seems pretty emotional today."

I gape at him in horror. "A woman can be emotional and not be pregnant."

He throws his hands up in surrender, his face the picture of innocence. "I didn't mean it like that."

"You've already dug your grave, buddy. Stay there."

He ducks his head with a chagrined smile and digs into his food. Good. As long as his mouth is full, he can't say anything stupid.

The rest of the day passes in a blur. By the time we say our good-byes, I'm in a sugar coma from the two cupcakes I had back to back. In hindsight, that was way too much sugar at one time, but they tasted so good I couldn't stop at one.

My eyes are heavy on the short drive back to the apartment. I want to take this dress off, shower, and go to bed. I'm pretty sure I'll be zonked the moment my body touches the mattress.

"Did you have fun?" I ask Beckham, my head heavy against the headrest.

He signals to change lanes. "More than I expected."

"That's good, I guess."

"Did you have fun?" he volleys back.

"Yeah, but now I'm exhausted." I stifle a yawn.

"Laurel sure knows how to throw a party." He chuckles, glancing at me practically melting into the seat.

"I didn't know a baby shower could be such a rager."

"Or that Brendan could go so low in a conga line."

I snort, poking his side. "You mean limbo?"

He shoots me a puzzled glance as we pull into the apartment's underground parking garage. "Isn't that what I said?"

"No," I say, laughing harder. "Definitely not."

In the elevator, I lean against Beckham. "I'm so tired," I groan, letting my eyes drift shut momentarily. "And my body aches. This is the most I've gotten out in so long."

His lips press tenderly against the top of my head. "Do you need help showering?"

I can't help but grin up at him. "Just say the real reason you want to help—you want to see me naked."

He snorts, seeming surprised by the sound. "I always want to see you naked. That's a given."

The doors slide open onto our floor, Beckham wrapping an arm around my side as we walk.

Inside, we're immediately greeted by the two ginger cats, both demanding cuddles and treats.

"Ugh." I wince, pressing a hand to my back. "My back is killing me."

"Want me to rub it for you?" The fact that he's dead serious makes me smile. He's been incredibly generous with all the back massages and foot rubs.

"After I shower." I pull my hair to the side, off my neck, and turn around. "Unzip me?"

He slides the zipper down, his warm knuckles grazing the skin of my back. I shiver, which elicits a chuckle from him. He kisses the curve of my neck, then lightly swats my ass.

"Get in the shower. I'll be there in a minute. I'm going to feed the cats."

Waddling down the hall, I use one arm to hold the dress to my front. I don't know why I'm bothering with modesty—it's not like he hasn't seen everything there is to see—but considering sex is off the table and I'm exhausted anyway, what's the point in trying to be coy?

The shower warms up quickly and I step inside, letting the water uncoil my stiff muscles. Beckham doesn't appear, and it doesn't take that long to feed the cats, so I start to get a bit worried. After squirting some of my soap onto my loofah, I suds up my body, the bathroom soon filling with the scent of rose. I'm rinsing my body free of bubbles when Beckham steps into the bathroom.

I take one look at his crestfallen face and know something is majorly wrong.

"What is it?" I ask through the glass.

He opens the door, stepping inside still fully clothed. His eyes are red, tears streaming down his face, now mixing with the spray from the shower. "My . . . uh . . . my dad just died."

"Oh baby." I pull him to me, and he lays his head on my shoulder, wrapping his arms around me.

Sometimes there's nothing you can do but hold on to someone. Just be there for them.

So that's what I do.

Chapter Forty-Six

BECKHAM

I can't sleep.

My mind is occupied with thoughts of my father. He's gone now, and there's nothing I can do to change that. But it still fucking sucks. Beside me, Lennon is restless. I'm not sure if she's actually sleeping, but if she is, it can't be good sleep. She has her body wrapped around a pillow, holding on to it for dear life.

She goes to roll over, her eyes cracking open slightly. Seeing me awake, she opens them fully. "Hey." She rubs her eyes groggily. "You're not sleeping." There's an accusation in her tone.

"Thinking about my dad."

She frowns, then sits up and scoots closer to me. She doesn't say she's sorry, which I'm thankful for. Looping her arm through mine, she leans her head on my shoulder. Sometimes nothing at all needs to be said. "Do you want to talk about it?"

"No," I answer automatically. Hesitating, I sigh, running my fingers through my hair. "Yes. I think I should, at least."

Sitting up, she rests her cheek on my shoulder. "I'm listening."

"It's just that . . . he's gone. Truly gone. I'll never have a chance to tell him how much he meant to me, and I should have done that.

I don't know why I didn't. I've always been bad at that. Keeping my feelings to myself."

She rubs my arm soothingly. "Sometimes it's hard to say the things we mean. Words can be scary."

It's such a simple way to put it, but she's right. Words are terrifying. Once you say them, put them out there, you can never take them back.

But some things should be spoken and not kept like a closely guarded secret.

I brush my lips over hers and speak into existence the words that I've been struggling with for months. "I love you."

Surprise fills her eyes, a tiny gasp falling from her lips. I want her to say it back, of course I do; I want her feelings for me to be as strong as mine are for her.

But Lennon never does anything I expect. "You do?"

I laugh, cupping her cheek. "Yeah, I do."

"That's cool." I laugh harder at that response. "Because I love you too."

Now it's my turn. "You do?"

"Yeah." She grins goofily. "I do." She pulls my head down so our lips meet in a kiss.

I think my dad, wherever he is, would be proud of me. I hate that it's taken getting that call to have this realization, but sometimes we all need that thing that wakes us up from the box we've put ourselves in.

For the longest time I didn't think I was good enough for this—for love, a family—but we're all worthy of the things we want, and Lennon is the thing I want most in this world.

◆ ◆ ◆

I manage to scrape by with a few hours of sleep—three tops—and finally get out of bed at seven to make breakfast. The cats devour their food, then circle between my legs begging for more.

I plate up the scrambled eggs, toast, and bacon and call for Lennon, since I heard her stirring in the bathroom.

I'm surprised I even feel like eating. Getting that phone call last night was expected but rough. My mind has been spinning ever since.

Life is scarily short, and anything can happen, and loving someone can lead to unimaginable pain but a joy that is unlike anything else. I'm angry at myself for holding back from the people I care about, for not giving them every last piece of me that they deserve. All this time I should have been telling them how I feel.

Lennon strolls into the kitchen, looking paler than her normal golden complexion, instantly putting me on alert. She slides the chair out, plopping in front of me.

"Are you okay?" My eyes dance over her face: her eyes are dilated, and there's a thin sheen of sweat above her brow.

"Mmm," she hums, wiggling uncomfortably in the chair. "But I need you to time my contractions."

Silence settles between us, my fork hovering halfway to my mouth. "What did you say?"

"My contractions." She bites into a strip of bacon. "Time them." She wiggles her pointer finger at my phone sitting on the table.

"You're in labor?"

"Pretty sure. It could be Braxton Hicks."

"Braxton who?" I recall reading about those, but now that she's telling me she believes she's in labor, it's like my brain is leaking out all the information it has stored away on pregnancy and birth.

"The fake kind of contractions. Now start timing—I just had one." She taps impatiently at the table for me to pick up my phone.

"Are you sure you should eat?"

Her eyes widen like I've hurled a massive insult at her. "I'm eating before we go to the hospital. You know why? Because hospitals starve mothers before birth, and I need my strength if I'm going to have to push a whole-ass human out of my vagina. And chances are, since this child is half yours, that their head will be huge."

"I think I should be insulted."

"I can't help it. I'm mean when I'm in pain."

I start the timer on my phone, letting it go until she tells me she's having another contraction. "Twelve minutes and forty-four seconds."

"They're getting closer together."

"Do we need to get to the hospital?" My panic is rising. I'm ready to drag her to the car and speed there if need be. In my mind, the baby is coming right this second.

"No," she laughs. I'm panicking and she's laughing. I might need a drink to get through this. "I'm going to call Dr. Hersh and see what she says. Since this is my first baby, it's probably too soon to go in."

"Jesus." I rub my hands over my face, stubble rasping against my palms. "When do you go in? When they're three minutes apart?"

"Probably six, I think."

"This is stressing me out."

She finishes her breakfast before pushing her plate away. "I'll call the doctor, and we'll go from there."

"Okay." I tug at my hair. "The doctor. Right."

Is this what a panic attack feels like?

She's the one having the kid. I need to keep my cool and be strong for her.

Cheddar rubs himself against my leg, and George Sanderson hops up into the chair Lennon just vacated. George seems to be judging me for my internal meltdown, while Cheddar is trying to comfort me.

"Beckham?"

I nearly fall out of the chair, on instant alert. "What?"

"Do you have a bag packed for the hospital?"

I abandon our plates in the sink to come back and wash later, then find Lennon in the nursery, riffling through the baby bag.

"Should I have something packed?"

She pauses her ministrations. "Uh . . . yeah."

"Fuck," I curse. "How much do I need?"

"I don't know." She throws her hands up in exasperation. "In case you need the reminder, I've never had a baby before. Pack some clothes and your pillow if you want it."

"Do we need to go to the hospital? Like right now?"

She sighs, frustrated with me, or maybe that's just the pain. "No. Dr. Hersh wants me to wait a bit longer to see if the contractions get closer together or stop. She said it's very likely they won't continue and not to get my hopes up, but we should be ready to go just in case."

"Right." I tap my fingers against the doorframe. "I'll pack some things and call the cat sitter so she's on standby."

And try to get myself together, because I need to be strong right now. Lennon needs to know she can lean on me if she needs me, not that I'll crumble at the first sign of stress.

I shove a few shirts and pants into a duffel bag, as well as my phone charger, camera, batteries for my camera, and my laptop. Hopefully I'm not forgetting anything important. The call to the girl who checks on Cheddar for me—and now George Sanderson—goes well, and she's thankfully okay with being put on standby.

When I come out of the bedroom, I find Lennon on the couch, eyes closed, and taking deep breaths in through her nose, out through her mouth.

"How are you feeling?" I pace around awkwardly, not sure what to do with my hands, my legs, anything.

She cracks one eye open. "It's like bad period cramps."

"I don't know what that feels like."

"It hurts like a bitch, that's what it feels like."

I start timing her contractions again, and it's slow going, but two hours later they're close enough together that her doctor says it's time to come in.

I feel completely bewildered. I knew this day was coming, but there's a vast difference in knowing it and experiencing it. I'm not sure I'm ready for this—to watch Lennon go through this kind of pain.

But I have no choice.

This is happening.

Chapter Forty-Seven

LENNON

I'm riding a high. The epidural high. Any woman who chooses to go completely natural—wow, you're a fucking badass. I tapped out and said, *Give me the drugs.*

"Whoever invented the epidural, I love them. They're brilliant."

Beckham's knee bounces nervously in the blue plastic hospital chair he's dragged over beside my bed. His hand still bears the brunt of my pre-epidural pain, the crescent-shaped indent of my fingernails now faded from a pink to a white.

He arches a brow, tapping his lips. He forgot to shave before we left, so his cheeks are scruffier than normal. His hair is getting long on top, falling into his eyes, so he continuously has to flick it away. "I thought you loved me?"

I smile dreamily at him. "I do, baby daddy, and you love me."

"Baby daddy." He snorts, rubbing his fingers over his mouth in an attempt to hide his amusement. "You're high."

"Am not." I pout, cradling my stomach. Soon my baby won't be in there anymore. I want to hold it for as long as I can. "I just feel *great.*"

Those contractions were no joke, so yeah, I guess technically I am high—high on not being in pain any longer.

Beckham reaches over, smoothing my sweat-dampened hair off my forehead. I smile in appreciation. It really is the little things. "I do," he whispers.

"Do what?" My brain is too tired to function at this point.

He grins, clearly entertained by me. At least one of us is amused by all this. "Love you. I should've told you sooner, how I felt, but I was scared."

"Why would you be scared?"

He doesn't answer right away, thinking about how he wants to phrase his answer. "Loving someone means they can hurt you, and that has always terrified me. I've done my best to avoid pain in any shape or form, but giving your heart to someone—yeah, it's at the risk of being brokenhearted, but would you rather have never loved the person at all? I . . . I wish I would've told my dad that I loved him. He might not have been able to say it back, but at least he would've known. I regret that now. I don't want any regrets with you."

I cup his cheek. "What happened to the grumpy bastard I encountered, oh . . . about what? Ten, eleven months ago?"

He places his hand over mine. "He's still here, just matured. And don't worry: I won't hold the door open for you every time, just to remind you."

I laugh, shaking my head. "I appreciate it. You know, we still haven't decided on a name. Time is running out. They're going to expect us to have this figured out. I think parents are supposed to be more put together than we are."

"We're failing at this already."

"What about Rose for a girl?" I suggest, deciding to start somewhere.

"Rose Sullivan." He mulls it over. "Not bad."

"Rose Wells sounds good too."

Eyes narrowing, he shakes his head. "Don't test me, woman."

"What about boy names?"

"It's not a boy," he protests vehemently.

"It could be."

"It's *not*."

"We should still have a name."

He sighs, rubbing his jaw. "If it's a boy, how about Wells?"

I wrinkle my nose. "Wells Sullivan. I kind of like it, but I don't know." As much as I joke about giving the baby my last name, I don't know that I want those ties connecting back to my family. Not after how they've acted. My brother has started up calling and texting again. His last text was kind of rude. He told me to stop being a little bitch and answer him. No fucking thank you. "Any other ideas?"

He rubs his jaw. "Fuck, Len, I think I'm failing at this whole dad thing already. This is hard."

"Who would've guessed there was so much pressure in naming a human?"

"I think anyone could've told you that." He kisses my knuckle. "Let me google some names." He sits back in the chair and slides his phone out of his pocket. Tapping the screen, he says, "For boys it looks like we've got Liam, Noah, Oliver—"

"Are you listing off the most popular names?"

"Yes?"

"Is that a question?"

"Um . . . yes, I was."

"I don't want to give our kid a name that's completely out there—like . . . I don't know, Puzzle, or something super crazy—but I'd like it to be different somehow. Unique. Personal to us."

"Okay." He scratches his jaw. "Mind if I ask where you came up with Puzzle?"

"It was the first random word that popped into my head," I say defensively.

"I'm going to brainstorm some more names." He stands up from the chair. "I . . . I might have an idea for a girl, but I don't know."

"Say it," I beg.

"Nope." He shakes his head adamantly. "Not yet. I'm going to grab some coffee. You want anything?"

"More ice, please."

"You got it. But only because you said please." He drops a kiss on my head. "I'll hurry."

While he's gone, I check my phone, finding a string of text messages from Laurel.

Laurel: YOUR IN LABOR?!

Laurel: *YOU'RE—TOO EXCITED TO TYPE

Laurel: You better tell me the second that crotch goblin flies out of your coochie

Laurel: I want to meet my niece or nephew right away.

Laurel: I'm dead serious. I'll show up at 3am if I have to.

It's five in the evening. I've been in labor for more than a full day now if I started contracting when I suspect, which would've been yesterday morning, before the baby shower. I woke up not feeling right, but I naively didn't think too much of it at the time.

Laurel: Are you okay? You're not replying.

Laurel: Right, you're in labor. I'm not important right now. Ignore me.

I can't help but laugh at her rambling antics while I type out my own response.

Me: Hi. Sorry. Finally got an epidural. Feeling MUCH better. I'll let you know as soon as this nugget decides to make an appearance.

Laurel: YOU'RE ALIVE

Laurel: I was getting worried your vagina got ripped to shreds and you were bleeding out somewhere.

Me: Nah, just waiting now. I was 6cm dilated the last time they checked. They should be back soon.

Laurel: Keep me updated as much as you can or get Beckham to do it.

Me: Will do. Beckham went to get coffee from the cafeteria. I'm going to try to get a nap. I think even if it's only twenty minutes I'll feel better.

Laurel: Oh my God, yes! I'll shut up. Get some sleep. Love you!

Me: Love you, too, girly.

I set my phone almost out of my reach, so I won't be tempted to grab it. The lights are already dimmed in the room, but I don't see any point in trying to get some rest until Beckham returns.

A few minutes later he strolls into the room with his coffee and my ice.

I take the ice from him greedily, popping a cube into my mouth. It's not much, but at least it's something.

"I'm going to try to get a nap in. I'm feeling tired."

He settles back in his chair, wincing at his first sip of coffee. "Is there anything I can do to help you sleep?"

"Just stay."

He flashes me a small smile. "Don't worry, honeybee, I'm not going anywhere."

I feel like I've only just closed my eyes when the nurse comes in and flicks on the bright overhead lights, blinding me. I wake with an annoyed groan. The lights? Really.

"It's time to check you." No apology for disturbing my rest. Figures. At least this time I don't feel her probing me. "Oh." Her eyes widen. "It's go time."

"What? What does *go time* mean?"

I know exactly what *go time* means, but somehow, I seem to think making her spell it out will make it an easier pill to swallow.

"It means it's time to push. I'll get the doctor."

"Push?" I shriek at Beckham the second the nurse is gone. "Am I going to be able to do this?"

He stands up, comes to stand by my side, and takes my hand. "You can do anything."

"How do you know?" I start to cry, feeling extremely overwhelmed. This is a big deal. I'm about to bring a whole new human into the world. One who will be dependent on me to take care of it, teach them and guide them into being a good person.

"Because, Len, you're the strongest person I know."

"Fuck." I cry harder. "That was really sweet. And I don't know why I'm crying. I didn't think I'd do that until the baby actually came."

He reaches for the tissue box and grabs one for me. I expect him to hand it to me, but instead he wipes my face dry himself.

"You're a badass. Don't forget it."

"In case I haven't told you lately, I'm really happy that it was you who knocked me up."

He laughs, amused. "You might not be saying that soon."

"It's okay. I can't feel anything below my waist, so you're safe."

It feels like an eternity passes before my doctor is in the room, along with two nurses. I've never had so many people all seeing my vagina at the same time, but I can't bring myself to care, since I'm about to meet my baby.

My baby.

I push and I push some more, and then, nearly an hour later, a screaming and squirming goo-covered baby enters the world.

Dr. Hersh puts the baby on my chest with a "Congrats, Mama."

I'm shaking and crying, and I realize Beckham is too.

"You did so good. Look at her."

I gasp. "Her?" I stroke my finger over a plump pink cheek, then trace the most perfectly shaped lips I've ever seen.

"It's a girl," he confirms, kissing my forehead, my cheeks, my lips. "We have a daughter."

I close my eyes, holding my little girl to my chest, the realization that we're a family now washing over me.

Nothing else in this world will ever matter as much as her.

She is everything.

Chapter Forty-Eight

BECKHAM

Holy fucking shit I'm holding my daughter.

I was so sure the entire time it was a girl, but having it confirmed is surreal. That's not to say I wouldn't have been happy with a boy—I would be fucking ecstatic no matter what—but if I was wrong, it would've left me confused, since my gut was so certain.

I rock her back and forth in my arms, never wanting to put her down. She's in only her diaper, my shirt gone so I can do skin-to-skin with her. Lennon watches us with sleepy eyes from the bed.

"Look at you two. My second-favorite person holding my favorite person."

I snort, looking down into the beautiful face of our baby. She has a headful of dark-brown hair and small pink lips. Her skin is still pinkened from birth, her face a bit squished. I can't wait to stare at her some more and figure out who she looks more like.

"The only person I'll ever accept second place to is this little thing." I kiss her nose. "Fuck, Lennon, she's so perfect. I never want to stop looking at her."

"I can't get enough of her fingers and toes. They're so cute I want to eat them."

"Sounds like I need to keep her away from you," I joke.

"Don't even try. Besides, I have the boobs."

At the reminder, I eye her chest. She's mostly covered by the hospital gown, but I'd swear her tits have somehow managed to get even bigger in the past hour or so.

"I love her so much it's overwhelming."

She laughs at me, wincing slightly. "Ugh, laughing feels weird. Anyway, I was going to say I guess it's a good thing you've accepted that loving someone isn't such a bad thing after all."

I rock my precious angel in my arms, dancing more than walking to Lennon. "I never thought it was a bad thing. I just didn't want to get hurt. But this one?" I stare down at her, milk drunk in my arms. "I love her so much I don't think she could ever hurt me. Does that make sense?"

"Sort of. I think. I don't know. I'm really tired."

"Go sleep. Rest as much as you can. I don't mind hanging out with our daughter."

Our daughter.

I want to say it over and over again. Shout it from the rooftops. I already sent my mom a bunch of pictures with the caption *Our daughter.*

Lennon adjusts the pillow behind her head, lowering the bed some. "We still have to come up with a name."

"I know. It'll come to us."

"I appreciate your confidence in this." She stifles a yawn. "You two be good while I nap."

While Lennon gets some sleep, I rock my little girl in my arms, unable to take my eyes off her. How is it possible that someone like me was able to be a part of creating something so overwhelmingly perfect?

I kiss the top of her head, her downy-soft hair. It's probably past time that I should dress and swaddle her, but I love the feel of her skin against mine. So new. So perfect.

I'm a bastard who doesn't deserve this, but fuck if I'm not going to spend every day of my life trying to be the best dad possible.

The door starts to crack open to the room. I make a *shh* motion to the nurse, then cross the room to meet her at the door.

"It's time for baby to have her first bath—well, sponge bath. Do you want to help?"

I nod vigorously, not just because I want to but because I have no clue how to even give a baby a bath. I need all the lessons I can get before we leave the hospital.

The nurse takes me down the hall to a different room. "All right, Dad, she can't have a real bath until her umbilical cord drops, so for now we're just going to sponge her off and wash her hair."

She walks me through the steps, letting me hold her the whole time. It's pretty straightforward, but I'm finding that everything with a newborn as a first-time parent is terrifying. Once she's clean, I dress her in an oatmeal-colored onesie—I only know it's called that because Lennon got offended when I called it beige—and the nurse then shows me the proper way to swaddle. I doubt I'll remember all the steps, so I fully plan on asking her to walk me through it again before we leave.

Back in the room, Lennon's still asleep. I should put the baby in the clear bassinet thing, but I don't want to. I just want to hold on to her and never let go. It's like a part of me is scared that if I set her down, she'll disappear.

Lennon manages to get another thirty minutes of sleep before I have to wake her up to feed the baby. She's groggy and exhausted from giving birth. I just want to let her sleep as much as she needs, but since she wants to breastfeed, that means the baby needs the boob.

She takes the baby, getting her into position with some kind of curled pillow around her middle. "I'm getting hungry too. Do you mind getting me something?"

"I'll get you whatever you want."

She smiles tiredly. "You're surprisingly good to me."

"Surprisingly?" I scoff playfully.

"Well, we both know you like to act like you're too good for everyone. The ice king, if you will, but you're a big softie under all that."

"Only for you."

She rubs her finger over the baby's cheek. "Not just for me, but you're not ready to admit that yet."

"What do you want to eat, Len?" I ask, trying to get her back on track.

"Listen, I know it sounds insane, but I want a spicy chicken sandwich. I don't care where it comes from. I'm so hungry I think I could eat two, but that's my stomach being confused since it's been so long since I ate."

"A spicy chicken sandwich, you got it. Anything else?"

"A Sprite. But only a McDonald's one. If I can't have that, then I'm good."

I pretend to add it to my list, making a scribbling motion on my palm. "I'll fetch the food and the Sprite. You hold down the fort while I'm gone."

"I think I can handle it. I have the nurse call button if I need it."

I stare at the two of them a moment longer, my girls, my little family. I don't want to leave them, but Lennon needs food, and I want to make sure she's fed.

"What are you doing?" she asks.

"Taking a mental picture."

"You have your camera—that'll last longer."

She's right. Why didn't I think of that? I unpack my camera, and she smiles for the photo. I look at the screen, and I'm sure I'm grinning like a fool. I set my camera on the tray table so that it will be handy when I get back.

I lean over, pressing a kiss to her lips. "I love you." I say it because I want to, because I can, because it doesn't scare me anymore.

"I love you too. Now, quit stalling and get my food. I'm starving."

I chuckle, then swipe up my phone and pat my pocket to make sure I have my wallet. "You've got it."

◆ ◆ ◆

"This is the most beautiful baby I've ever seen." Laurel gasps, peering at our sleeping bundle in her bassinet. "You guys did good."

Lennon smiles tiredly. I wonder if she'll ever feel rested again. Probably not. "I think she's pretty perfect, but as her mother, I have to also admit to being biased."

"Nah, no bias here, she's so cute. Most newborns look like angry old men, but not this one. What's her name?"

Lennon cringes. "We don't have one yet."

Laurel's head swivels back and forth between the two of us. "You don't have a name yet? How is that possible? You didn't discuss this?"

"I mean, we did, it just never got anywhere," I say, picking up my camera to get some shots of Laurel with the baby. "You can hold her. She sleeps like the dead."

"Are you sure?" She eyes the burrito-wrapped bundle nervously.

"Oh yeah, go for it." Lennon waves her fingers toward the bassinet. "She's seriously unbothered."

Laurel carefully picks up the baby, being mindful to hold her head. "She's so little. Can you believe this thing was inside you?"

"Trust me, I can believe it since I had to push her out."

"Women are such badasses."

"I have to agree." I circle Laurel, taking photos.

"How many pictures have you already taken?"

I snap another photo, a close-up of the baby's face. "A ridiculous amount I will not be disclosing."

Laurel sits down, bouncing the baby in her arms. "Has she cried a lot?"

"Not really," Lennon answers. "I'm not sure she's figured out that she's in the world yet."

"I can't blame the girl for wanting to remain in disbelief a little longer. I'm sure it's way nicer where she came from than out here. Has anyone else been by?"

"Just you." Lennon stifles a yawn. "Sorry, I'm still sleepy."

"Good, I'm glad I'm the first. It gives me bragging rights."

"Laurel loves bragging rights," Lennon informs me.

"It's true."

Laurel doesn't stay much longer, and when she's gone, I grasp the railing on the bottom of the bed, watching Lennon as she feeds the baby again.

"I have an idea."

Her hand stills where it was brushing the baby's hair. "What kind of idea? I feel like you and ideas are a dangerous combination."

"I have a name to propose, one I think is perfect, but I want you to have an open mind and not say no right away."

"Okay?" It comes out as a question, her dark-brown eyes skeptical. "What do you have in mind?"

"I was trying to think of something that's personal to us, something with meaning, even if it's something only we understand."

"Can you just spit it out?"

"Open mind," I remind her. "I think her name is Bee."

It's been speaking to me all day, but I wanted to feel certain in my gut that it was the right name. A name is such an important part of a person. It's also why I frame it as *I think her name is Bee* instead of *I think her name should be Bee.*

"Bee." She says the name softly, testing the weight of it on her tongue. "It's sweet. Simple." She looks down at the nursing baby. "Is your name Bee?"

The baby makes a happy humming noise. I'm pretty sure it's just excitement about the milk, not the name, but we both smile anyway like it's a sign from Bee herself.

"You don't think I'm crazy?"

She shakes her head. "No . . . Bee, this feels right."

And just like that, our baby finally has a name.

I move to their side, placing my hand on her tiny head. "Welcome to this crazy world, Bee Sullivan. I hope you shake things up."

Chapter Forty-Nine

LENNON

We've been home with Bee for a little over a week now. It's been a surprisingly easy adjustment, mostly because Beckham is such good help, but I still have moments throughout the day where I find myself thinking, *Holy shit, I'm a mom.*

I crack my eyes open, my internal alarm clock alerting me to the fact that it's time for Bee to eat. But when I look into her bassinet, she's gone, and so is Beckham.

With a groan, I rise from the bed. My shirt is askew, a boob nearly popping out. I right the fabric, which is pointless since I'm just going to yank a boob out anyway.

After tiptoeing out of the room, I find them in the nursery.

Beckham is seated in the rocker, using his foot to lightly push them back and forth. He holds the baby in one arm, a kids' book in the other, reading to her.

"What are you two doing?" I ask, even though it's pretty obvious.

He closes the book and sets it on the small table by the chair. "She woke up early, so I thought I'd keep her entertained for a bit."

He gets up so we can switch places, then puts Bee into my arms.

"I'm not sure I'll ever get used to this," I admit, rubbing her cheek, then her fingers. I help her latch on, wincing a bit.

Beckham sits down on the floor by my feet. "Me either." He rubs my knee in a gentle, massaging motion. "I can't believe it, but I fucking love being a dad."

"Speaking of dads . . ." I hesitate, not sure he wants to, or is even ready to, have this conversation. "You haven't told me what you decided to do with your dad. You have decided, haven't you?"

He's been tasked with making the decision on what to do with the body, since his father didn't have any sort of plans or wishes in place to be executed. That's put the decision-making squarely on Beckham's shoulders.

He rubs his jaw, letting out a weary sigh. "My birth mom was buried, but there's no burial plot available anywhere near her, so I decided to have him cremated."

"You can talk about it with me. I want you to know that."

"There's not much to say. He's gone now, and I can only hope that he's been reunited with my birth mom."

"I wish he could've met Bee."

"Me too." He leans his head back to look at us. "He would've loved her. I know it. I mean, look at her. She's perfect. Who wouldn't love her?"

My parents, I want to say. I bite my tongue, not wanting to give voice to those words, because their opinion doesn't matter. I've always known they weren't the best parents, but it was *okay.* Now I realize how truly awful they are, and I don't want them in my life or Bee's.

"You're thinking about them, aren't you?"

I sigh, tracing the shape of Bee's ear with my index finger. Long, dark lashes fan her cheeks as she gulps down the milk greedily. "Yes. I know I shouldn't give them a second thought, but it's hard not to when I look at her. I would never want to be like them. I could never say the things they have to her."

"That's because you're a good person and they're not."

"Thanks." I know I shouldn't need to hear that, but sometimes the reminder is necessary that I'm not like them.

When Bee is finished feeding, I pass her off to Beckham to burp her.

She belts out a burp loud enough for a grown man, and Beckham laughs. "That's a ten out of ten, Bee. Good job."

The baby snuggles into his neck, going right back to sleep. He carries her back to the bedroom, then lays her in the bassinet. George and Cheddar watch us with annoyance for daring to disturb their beauty sleep.

"Come on," Beckham says, urging me toward the bed. "Try to get some sleep while you can. She'll be hungry again before you know it."

He's right. She nurses all the time, and since I'm her sole source of food, it's exhausting.

I settle into bed, Beckham soon joining me. He scoots over, wrapping an arm around me to spoon me against him. His lips press against my neck in a soft kiss. A lot of times with these feedings, I find myself having trouble going back to sleep, but this time, I shut my eyes and don't open them until it's time to feed her again.

Chapter Fifty

BECKHAM

Standing outside the building, I have to give myself a moment before I head inside. I didn't expect to be back here, but the front desk called this morning to tell me there was a box of my dad's things I hadn't picked up yet.

How fucking pathetic is it that I didn't even know he had any personal items?

When I moved him from the first care center to this one, I didn't help with transport. All I did was organize the change.

With a deep breath, I push inside and make my way to the front desk.

"Hey, Sulli," one of the girls who's usually at the desk when I visit says. "I assume you're here for this?" She turns around to a small, waiting box. It's barely large enough to fit a few books inside.

"I am, thanks."

She holds the box out to me with a forlorn smile. She doesn't say she's sorry for my loss, and for that I'm grateful.

I turn on my heel, leaving behind the smell of disinfectant when I exit onto the street. As I stare down at the box, my curiosity is piqued.

What was so valuable to him that he managed to keep it with him all these years?

I head toward my car a few blocks away, waiting until I'm inside and the AC is running before I riffle through the small number of contents. There's a worn braided leather bracelet, a notebook, a jewelry box, and a photo.

My fingers go to the photo first. A zap runs up my arm, electrifying my entire body, when I look at it.

It's my dad with his arm around a woman in a hospital bed. They're young. Smiling. Clearly happy, but there's fear in their eyes too. My eyes study her the longest, thick dark waves of hair that frame a pretty round face with brown eyes that can't help but remind me of Lennon.

In her arms is a baby who can't be anyone but me.

In my search for my birth parents, I never found any photos of us together, and when I reached out to other blood relatives . . . well, they didn't want anything to do with me. At first, that stung, but now I don't give a shit.

But this photo is a treasure I didn't know I was searching for.

After putting it back in the box, I pick up the notebook next. Flipping through the pages, I find it filled with poems. Most of them love poems that he must have written for my mother. I read through a few of them, my chest getting tight with emotions I struggle to keep at bay. They were so in love, and their lives didn't turn out the way they had planned. They deserved more.

That just leaves the bracelet and jewelry box. I slide the leather cord onto my wrist. It's well worn, clearly loved. I wonder if he made it or if it was something my mom got for him. Regardless, it must have meant a lot to him for it to be in his things.

The last item I pick up is the box. Opening it, I find a small pear-shaped diamond engagement ring. I stare at it for a moment. Like the poems, it's a reminder that my bio-parents were real people. Clearly, he was planning to propose to her, or maybe he already had, and when she passed in the accident, he somehow got her ring back.

It makes me think of Lennon. Our futures are always uncertain. Many things can happen to change the course we're on or end it altogether.

I wonder what would've happened to them if there had never been an accident. Would they have had more kids? Is there an alternate future out there where I have biological siblings? Maybe they would've moved away from New York. I wonder if they would've reached out to me.

But all those thoughts are futile.

There is no changing the past, and speculating on it does me no good.

I snap the ring box closed, then put it back alongside the other few items.

When I walk in the door, Lennon is cooking dinner. Music plays on the speakers, and she sings along, putting on a performance for Bee. She's so into it, singing into the wooden spoon and shaking her ass, that she hasn't heard me come inside.

I set the box down on the side table, crossing my arms over my chest with a smirk, just watching her.

Even the cats are enraptured by the performance she's putting on.

I clear my throat to make my presence known, but she goes on dancing, completely oblivious.

Finally, I move away from the doorway and grab her by the waist. She yelps, jumping in fright, but immediately settles when she realizes it's me. Spinning her around, I'm not surprised to find the fire in her eyes. I'm sure she has a few choice words for me, but I silence them with a kiss, and then I dance with her.

It makes me think of the evening we cooked dinner together and danced just like this, Bee between us, still in her tummy. I already find myself missing her pregnant belly. I hope sometime soon, in the next three years or so at least, she'll let me put another baby in her. I want all the babies with Lennon.

I think of the ring sitting in the box, and how one day I want to get down on one knee and propose to this woman. I'll even stand in front of hundreds of people and give my vows, if that's what she wants, even if I'd much prefer to run away and elope.

I want the little moments like this with her: dancing in the kitchen, watching movies together, or just sitting and watching Bee sleep.

She looks up at me with those big brown eyes, love unmistakable in their depths. She doesn't have to say the words for me to know how she feels, even if it's nice to hear her say them. "How did it go?"

"It was fine. There wasn't much."

"Anything important?"

I let her go and walk over to the box. "Not really. There was this, though." I hold the photo out to her, and she takes it.

Her eyes widen, darting from the photo to me and back again. "Wow, you look so much like them. I guess I never stopped to think about what they looked like." She traces her fingernail over the shape of my newborn body in my mom's arms. "Do you care if I hang this up? I'd like to put it in the nursery."

We have a similar photo of us with Bee, hanging on the wall above the bookcase that holds all the children's books.

"I'd like that a lot."

She smiles up at me. "Good."

Bee starts to cry, reminding us of her presence, like we could ever actually forget. I let Lennon go, bending down to scoop up my squirming girl from the bassinet we keep in the living room.

"Hey, little one," I croon, swaying her in my arms. "Don't cry. Whatever it is, Daddy will make it better." She starts to quiet, looking up at me with curious wonder. "That's right. Daddy's got you. I've always got you." I kiss the top of her downy-soft head. Turning around, I find Lennon watching us with tears in her eyes. "Come here."

I tug her into my side, and she places her hand on Bee's chest. She's wearing the bumblebee outfit I first picked out for her.

We've come far from the people we were all those months ago when she started at *Real Point*. Sometimes that guy feels like a stranger, like I was seeing in black and white all that time until Lennon walked back into my life. Now, all I can see is color. Lennon and Bee bring life to the world around me.

"What are you thinking about?" Lennon asks me.

I answer honestly. "How much I love you both."

She smiles beautifully, her eyes crinkling at the corners with happiness. She squeezes her body in impossibly closer to mine.

I'm content to stay right here, in this moment with my girls, for as long as I can.

Chapter Fifty-One

LENNON

I was so worried about motherhood, and now I wonder why.

If I didn't love my job so much, I would choose to be a stay-at-home mom. Spending time with Bee is my favorite thing in the world. I know when the time comes and I have to go back to work, I'll miss all this time with her. Who knows, maybe I can work something out with Jaci where I work from home several days a week.

"Are you Mommy's pretty girl?" I croon, changing her into a clean onesie. She might've just had a massive blowout that required giving her a bath in order to get her fully clean, but she's still the cutest thing I've ever seen.

Bee kicks her legs excitedly. Scooping her into my arms, I inhale her clean-baby smell. It's hard to believe she smelled like a sewer only ten minutes ago.

"Is she clean yet?"

I look over my shoulder to Laurel standing in the open doorway of the nursery, sniffing the air.

"She's squeaky clean and smelling nice."

Laurel grins, opening and closing her hands in the air. "Then gimme that baby." With a laugh, I hand her over to my best friend. Bee immediately grabs on to Laurel's finger when she holds it out. "Who's the prettiest girl in all the land?" Bee coos in response. "That's right, you."

Laurel is the best auntie for my little girl.

"Do you mind keeping an eye on her while I clean up the bathroom?"

She scoffs in disbelief. "Do I mind?" That's all she says before turning and heading toward the living area. Her soft hum carries behind her.

Shaking my head at her antics, I head back across the hall to the bathroom. It'll never cease to amaze me how one tiny human can manage to make such a mess. I disinfect the bathtub and hang up her towel on the hook by the door. After grabbing her baby shampoo, I go to put it away but accidentally open the wrong drawer.

Beckham's drawer.

On the very top, in plain view, is a ring box.

A million emotions flood me, but the most crippling and unexpected is fear.

I've joked about marriage, and there's no denying my younger self definitely imagined marrying him once or twice—or a hundred times—but seeing that box sends me spiraling.

I know I shouldn't do it, but I just need to confirm. My fingers close around it, my panic building second by second. I flip the lid up, and a ring sits comfortably in the velvet. It's a small pear-shaped diamond. I stare down at it, confused, because it's clearly an engagement ring but not at all what I would expect Beckham to choose for me.

I snap the lid closed and shove it back in the drawer, which I close a little too forcefully.

"Is everything okay?" Laurel calls out.

"Just fine," I holler back.

My hands are shaking. I clasp them together in an effort to still the jitteriness. Why am I acting like this over a ring? Shouldn't I feel excited?

I love this man. I don't see myself with anyone else. We have a daughter. A beautiful life we're creating together.

"Lennon?" Laurel's voice is closer this time, and I look up to find her approaching me. "Whoa, what's going on? Are you okay?"

I don't say anything. I open the drawer and pull out the ring box. She manages to open it while still rocking Bee in her arms. Her mouth opens, and she looks at me with shocked eyes.

"I know," I reply to her unspoken question.

"Beckham's proposing?"

I run my fingers through my hair. "I guess so." I wave madly at the jewelry box. "I mean, that seems like pretty damning evidence."

She wrinkles her nose, closing the box. "The ring doesn't seem like you at all."

"That's the least of my concerns," I admit. Sure, the ring seems off in some way, but normally I wouldn't care. I don't get as hung up on those kinds of things as, say, my mother would.

Laurel blinks at me, expression stunned. "Are you . . . mad?"

I try to assess how I feel, and I wouldn't say anger is present. "No." I bite my lip, thinking it over. "I feel scared."

"Scared?" she repeats. "Why?"

"I don't know."

"You've always talked about getting married one day, so . . ." She hesitates, clearly unsure if she should say whatever is on her mind. "What's different now?"

"I don't know," I say again. "Come on," I plead, trying to step around her out of the bathroom. "I can't think about this right now."

She follows me to the kitchen, where I get started on making dinner. We have the ingredients for quesadillas, so that's what I decide to make. Bee falls asleep in Laurel's arms, but she doesn't look like she's going to put the baby down anytime soon.

"I can't believe you're cooking to avoid talking about this."

I look back at her over my shoulder. "I'm not avoiding anything."

"So then, let's talk about this. Wouldn't you rather talk about this to me than flat out refuse his proposal?"

I set my hands on the counter, desperately searching myself to understand my feelings. "Laurel, what's there to talk about when I don't understand it myself?"

She frowns, finally setting Bee down in her bassinet. "You love him, right?"

"Of course I do," I scoff, focusing on my task. "But it feels too soon."

But is that really the reason?

I don't think it is. At least, timing doesn't feel like the source of my panic and confusion.

"I think you need to talk to him."

I whip my head in her direction, stunned. "And say what? 'I found the ring and had a panic attack'?"

"I mean"—she almost smiles, no doubt amused—"I'd try to frame it more eloquently than that. Men have fragile egos."

She's not wrong there.

"I'll talk to him," I concede, biting my lip. At this rate I'm going to make it sore.

"Good." She seems relieved by my easy agreement. She points at one of the quesadillas I'm preparing. "Can I have one of those to go, please?"

I stifle a laugh. "Sure. Now, tell me more about this Crew guy."

She's been on a few dates with him now, and I'd much rather hear about her dating adventures than think about the difficult conversation I need to have with Beckham.

Laurel lights up, excited to talk about him, and I let her words distract me for as long as they can.

Chapter Fifty-Two

BECKHAM

I don't know what it is exactly, but there's an ominous feeling when I walk into the apartment. I shut the door behind me and turn the lock. The lights are dimmed, both cats asleep on the couch.

"Lennon?" I call out.

It's so quiet inside the apartment that I'm worried she's not here. But where would she have gone, and why wouldn't she have told me?

"Back here," she calls from the bedroom, relief flooding me.

I find her lying propped up in the bed, nursing Bee. The TV hums softly in the background. She looks tired. I can't help but kick myself for not getting home sooner.

"I'm sorry. The shoot ran late."

"It's okay. Leftovers are in the refrigerator."

I don't care about food right now. All I care about is getting close enough to kiss my girls.

I bend down, kissing the top of Bee's head before I move in to press my lips to Lennon's. I freeze before our lips touch, noticing how stiff she's holding herself.

"Lennon?" I prompt. "What's wrong?" I stand up straight without kissing her, looking her over in the hopes that I can figure it out myself. "Is it your brother?"

"No." She shakes her head. "He's stopped trying to reach me. It's not that."

It's not that, meaning I was right and it is something.

"I feel out of the loop here. What's bothering you?" I toe off my shoes, then loosen my tie before I sit on the end of the bed. I turn to face her. "Talk to me. I can't fix what's wrong if you don't talk to me."

Big brown eyes pool with tears, her teeth digging into her bottom lip, which already looks like it's been nibbled on a bit too much today. "I found it." She whispers the three words like the ultimate confession.

I stare at her blankly, wondering what I'm missing. What could she possibly mean?

My puzzlement only grows when she doesn't elaborate. "Honeybee, I really don't know what you mean."

She huffs out a breath, her cheeks reddening from embarrassment. "The ring," she hisses like it's some dirty little secret. *The ring?* I think to myself. *What is she talking about?* "And I'm so sorry, I just . . . I didn't *mean* to find it, it was an accident, and I . . . I'm not ready to get engaged. At least, I don't think I am because I saw it and I froze. Completely panicked, and I don't even know why."

She starts to cry. I itch to reach forward and wipe away her tears, but I get the impression she wouldn't want me to do that right now.

"Baby," I say softly, "not to sound like an idiot, but I don't know what you're talking about. I don't . . . I'm not proposing. I haven't even bought a ring, and since that's not something we've discussed, I haven't even thought about it."

She blinks, lips parted and stunned into silence. "But I saw the ring. In your drawer."

My brows furrow. "In my drawer?"

"The bathroom."

The light bulb finally goes off. "Lennon." I try not to smile. "That's not an engagement ring." She opens her mouth to protest, so I quickly go on. "I mean, technically it is, but it's not one I got, and it's not for you. It was in my dad's things. It was my bio-mom's, or it was supposed to be hers. I don't really know if he'd proposed yet or not." I shrug like it's not a big deal, but it's just a reminder of all the things I'll never know about them.

"Oh. *Oh.*" She wipes at her tears. "Wow, I feel like such a fool, and here I've been panicking all day." Bee finishes nursing, and like we're a well-oiled machine already, I take the baby from her and grab up a burp cloth to drape over my shoulder.

I'm not offended by what she's said. I can sense there's something deeper going on, something that maybe she herself doesn't even understand.

"Do you not want to marry me?" I ask casually, hoping she knows I'm merely trying to understand and not pick a fight.

The me of a year ago would've been pissed by what she's saying. I would've taken it personally and been hurt. Now, I can read her well enough to know that while seeing a ring might've been what set her off, it's not the real problem at hand.

"I do . . . I think I do . . . no, I know I do. But . . ." She hesitates, her eyes dropping to the blanket bunched around her lap. "I'm scared."

That's not what I was expecting her to say. "You're scared? Of what? Me?"

"No, it's not that." She shakes her head, clearly floundering to make sense of her feelings. "I always pictured myself married, but I think when I saw that ring, it made me think, 'Do I even really know what marriage is?' Look at my parents. I didn't get the best example there." She lowers her head. "I'm scared, Beckham."

"Like you were with Bee?"

It takes her a moment before she speaks. "Yeah."

338

"You're not your parents, Len. *We* are not them. You need to remember that. For yourself, but mostly for her." I hand Bee back to her. Lennon's eyes drop to our daughter, a wistful smile touching her lips. "We owe it to her to break these generational traumas. We have to be stronger for her. She doesn't need to be weighed down by our past."

She brings her gaze back to me. "How is it you managed to talk me out of a near panic attack?"

I shrug like it's no big deal. "Because I know you. But make no mistake, one day I'm going to get down on one knee and ask you the most important question of our lives, and when you say yes, there won't be a single doubt in your mind of how much I love and respect you. No one's ever going to treat you as good as I can, honeybee, I can promise you that." Her breath catches, but I go on. "And when you walk down the aisle and look in my eyes, you'll see how you're not just the love of my life, but my whole fucking world. There is no me without you."

Some people go their whole lives never finding "the one" and then settle for something that doesn't come close to the real thing, and we were lucky enough to find it as kids.

We might've gotten lost along the way—mostly me—but we ended up back here with each other, exactly where we were always meant to be.

"You still think you're going to marry me even after I freaked out seeing a ring?"

I shrug, indifferent. "Now's not the time, but yes, I'm still going to marry you one day."

I don't know when that day will be, but I do know we'll both be ready. Lennon still has things to work through when it comes to her family. I'm not sure she'll ever want to reconcile with her parents, but her brother is a different story. I know she keeps ignoring him, but I have a hard time seeing her do that forever if he keeps reaching out. And me? God knows I have a shit ton of stuff to work through myself, but we have each other, and we have Bee to motivate us to be the best versions of ourselves.

Looking at the love of my life holding our daughter, I know that despite it all, I'm without a doubt the luckiest man alive.

I used to think that *forever* was just another word for time, but in actuality it's a state of being.

Forever begins when you start living for yourself and stop answering to other people.

This is my forever.

Chapter Fifty-Three

LENNON

A week after my embarrassing meltdown, Beckham pushes the baby stroller down the sidewalk toward the office of *Real Point*. Jaci has been begging us both to come by the office.

Today, she bribed us with the promise of an early look at the print copy of our magazine. She ended up pushing the launch date back. I'm still not sure exactly why, though her reasoning was simple enough: it needed more time to be refined. Still, that just didn't seem like the real reason, not that I was about to question my boss on her decisions with her publication.

When we reach the building, I hold the door open so he can maneuver the stroller in without trying to balance the heavy door too.

"Just so you know, if you weren't pushing Bee, I would've let it shut on you."

He throws his head back with laughter, steering the stroller toward the elevators. "Taking lessons out of my book now, are you?"

"You need some of your own medicine now and then."

The doors slide open to the elevator, and we hop on to head up to the office floor. I'm excited to introduce the baby to our colleagues. It's weird, having a baby, and how you want to show them off. It's basically a crying trophy that says, *I had sex.*

Almost immediately when we reach the floor, we're crowded by our coworkers, who want to ooh and ahh over the baby. I can't help but watch with a smile while Beckham proudly tells them all about Bee, how good of an eater, sleeper, and pooper she is.

He takes the Proud Papa Award for sure.

"Oh my God, she's precious," Jaci croons, wiggling her finger at Bee. "Look at all that hair and those rosy cheeks. Do you just stare at her all the time?"

"More than I'd like to admit." I laugh, unable to take my eyes off my daughter.

Jaci coos over the baby for a minute longer before straightening and smoothing her hands down her skirt. "Let me grab that sample for you. Again, great job, guys. I'm proud." She gives my arm a light squeeze, then pats Beckham on his shoulder and exchanges a look with him before her heels clack down the hall to her office.

I give Beckham a questioning stare, but he shrugs it off. I can't help but narrow my eyes on him. It feels like something more is going on here.

"Sulli, don't tell my girlfriend," Brendan begins, peering down at Bee, "but I think I might want one of these."

"Dude, I'm not telling her a thing." Beckham laughs with a shake of his head. He exchanges a look with me that seems to say he thinks Brendan is crazy.

"Have you had a hard time adjusting?" Layla asks.

"Not too bad. She's a pretty good baby, but you definitely don't get much sleep."

"She's worth it," Beckham adds, making a silly face at Bee. I don't tell him that she's too young to understand what he's doing. I just let him do his thing.

Jaci returns, holding out a stack of flat sheets of paper. "Let me know what you guys think." She tacks on a wink at the end, and again my curiosity is piqued.

Beckham pushes the stroller over to one of the community tables, then spreads out the papers so we can take a look at what the cover and some of the inside spread will look like.

I stare in awe at how it's all come together, all the hard work we put into it over months while still managing our regular workloads.

"Your photos are stunning." I can't stop staring at all the black-and-white images of the women I interviewed, how elegant and powerful they look, how Beckham managed to capture so much behind their eyes with just his lens.

"Your writing is impeccable."

And we're both so grossly in love that, apparently, we can't stop showering each other with flowery compliments. I could puke from the sickly sweetness of it all if I weren't so happy.

Jaci claps her hands together, then clasps them under her chin. "I'm so thrilled you both love how it's turning out. It's going to print this month. I think this is going to be huge for *Real Point*. Truly. Everyone, can we give these two a round of applause?" I blush, hiding behind Beckham when our coworkers start clapping. I don't do well with attention. "Once the issue is out, we're going to have a party. A baby-friendly one, I promise."

"As long as there are mimosas, I'm down." Beckham shakes his head, amused. I look through the spread, my brow crinkling in confusion when I note there's a prominent blank space in both the article and photos. "What's this about?" I point. "This shouldn't be blank."

When I look up, Jaci is giving a head nod to Beckham.

What is going on?

Beckham clears his throat. "I approached Jaci and told her there was a noticeable absence in our article."

"An absence?" I blurt out, looking from the sheets of paper back to him. "Did we forget someone? I—"

"We did."

"Who?"

He stares at me significantly. "You."

"Me?" I point to my chest. "What are you talking about?"

His blue eyes are both somehow sad and full of love at the same time. "When you started here, I said something pretty awful to you about how you must have gotten this job. Do you remember?" I swallow thickly at his words, nodding. "I'm sure that was a contributing factor in giving you the idea for all of this." I nod again. "So it only seems fitting that I interview you and you're included."

"I . . ." I'm at a loss for words. "How long have you been planning this?"

"A few weeks now. I had to get it okayed with Jaci, and—"

"And of course I said yes," she pipes in with a smile. "I think readers will be intrigued by the two of you, and even though I was angry at first to learn of Beckham's treatment toward you, I think it helps prove the point of this special issue. This happens everywhere." She spreads her arms wide. "It even happened here."

"You can say no, honeybee, but I think we should do this."

Everyone around us is enraptured with what's going on. I wonder if they were aware of all this beforehand or are just learning about it like I am.

"All right," I answer, nodding with a certainty I'm not positive I really feel. It's nerve racking thinking of my story being printed alongside these others, my picture included. "I'll do it." My voice sounds stronger this time, my spine steeling.

Beckham smiles, his eyes crinkling at the corners. "Good."

"Why are you so happy? Everyone's going to know what an asshole you are now." He throws his head back with laughter. There's no missing the shocked expressions from those around us. "Are you really going to interview me and write this portion up? I can't exactly write my own interview. That would be . . ." I wrinkle my nose at the very thought. "Weird."

He chuckles again. "I already told you, baby—I'll be interviewing you, and so that means I'll be writing the article. Taking your photo too."

I look around, feeling my nerves return, but everyone looks so encouraging. "When are we doing this?"

"Right now." Jaci claps her hands. "We've got the baby. You two go on." She shoos us away.

I look back over my shoulder at her as I follow after Beckham, feeling a weird sense of déjà vu, reminded of the day when he came to collect me at my computer and chewed me out in his office for snitching on him.

God, how things have changed since then.

He closes the door behind us and sits down behind his desk, motioning for me to take the chair in front, just like he did all those months ago. After rolling up the sleeves of his button-down, he cracks open his laptop and brings up a new document.

Those intense blue eyes meet mine. "State your name . . . for the record."

"For the record?"

He grins. "Yeah, isn't that what all you writers say?"

I laugh, feeling more at ease, which I realize is exactly what he was going for. "No, that's court."

"Well"—he spreads his arms wide—"welcome to my courthouse then. Shall we begin?"

It's such a simple question, but I smile in response because it feels like so much more, as if he's asking whether we should begin the rest of our lives. I might not be ready for marriage, and there's baggage I need to work through, but I do know I'm ready for whatever comes our way.

He said to me once that our baby was a pretty little mistake, but I think it's a better description for us. We tend to think that mistakes are messy, things that need to be fixed, but sometimes they can be beautiful. That's us.

So I give him the only answer that matters.

"Yes."

Epilogue

LENNON

October

"I'm not coming out."

Beckham has been hiding in the bathroom for the past twenty minutes. It's pathetic really.

"Don't be such a wuss," I say through the door, making a silly face at Bee, who watches me from her carrier, since I already have her strapped in, ready to go. "Everyone's waiting on us to go trick-or-treating."

"I can't be seen in this costume."

"Have you seen what I'm wearing?" I counter, knowing he hasn't.

"No."

"Trust me, I look ridiculous. No one will be looking at you. Be a good sport, please. It's Bee's first Halloween. She'll have these pictures to remember forever."

"Pictures?" He sounds panicked. Maybe I shouldn't have mentioned there would be photos, but I thought that was a given. "You didn't say there would be pictures."

"Calm down. Just come out here and show me. You're doing this for Bee."

"No, Bee can't talk yet. She didn't request this. This is all you."

He's right. But can't he humor me?

"If you don't wear the costume, then you're not going to match Bee and me."

He grumbles some more, unintelligible strings of words, before I hear the click of the lock. It swings inward, revealing him in the Sulley costume from *Monsters, Inc.*

"I look insane."

I point to my face, painted green to blend in with the giant round one-eyed monster attached to my body. "No, that would be me, but it's all for fun. It's Halloween! And look, isn't Bee cute?" She's dressed in the monster costume Boo wore in the movie.

He tries not to smile. "She is pretty cute. You know"—he goes to put a hand on my waist and realizes he can't, so he pulls me closer by my wrist instead, smiling triumphantly at the ring he slid onto that finger just a few weeks ago; I didn't even have a panic attack this time—"we could always make another one."

I pat his chest mockingly. "Nice try, but we're going to give it a few years. There's no way I can go through a pregnancy that tough again so soon."

"You never know—it could be fine this time."

"I'm not jinxing it. Now, quit your stalling. We need to go. Everyone's downstairs waiting for us."

He scoops up the carrier and opens the bedroom door. Voices carry up the stairs. I can't help but smile, happy that our friends and family are together with us. We bought the brownstone less than a month ago, and we're only halfway moved in, but it's already been so nice to have people over and have space to move around and not be right on top of each other. Not to mention a full kitchen. Although I was sad to say goodbye to the nursery Beckham had so lovingly decorated. Bee's room is the only one we've fully completed in the house.

Everyone—and by *everyone*, I mean Beckham's parents, Laurel and her boyfriend, and my brother with the latest girl he's seeing—is in the living room and quiets when they see us, hopefully not out of horror, but instead processing the sheer awesomeness of our costumes.

My brother called and came to see me one day, having grown tired of my silent treatment. I gave him Beckham's address, figuring it was time for me to stop acting petty. We talked for a long time and hashed out a lot of things. We're working to repair our sibling relationship. I know we'll never be as close as some siblings, but I appreciate him trying when I wasn't willing to. That means something. He and Beckham are even getting closer. I think they realize that for all our sakes, and especially Bee's, we need to set the animosity aside.

My parents, however? I don't have any plans to try to mend that relationship. I realize now it was never one to begin with. More of an ownership than anything else.

I take in everyone else's costumes with a smile.

Laurel is dressed as a witch, with Crew as some sort of grim reaper. My brother isn't in costume, but his date is a sexy angel. I'm pretty sure her bare legs are going to freeze outside, but who am I to warn her? I grin at how much Beckham's parents went all out with their Morticia and Gomez costumes.

"Your costumes are amazing." Laurel stifles a giggle, hand over her mouth.

"Sulli as Sulley. Interesting." My brother tries not to laugh, but I think Laurel's laughter makes him succumb to his own.

Beckham gives him the finger. "At least I'm wearing a costume."

I put my hand over Beckham's, pushing his arm down to make the vulgar gesture disappear. "Not in front of the baby," I hiss.

"She didn't even notice. She's half-asleep."

Sure enough, Bee's eyes are little slits. She wants to stay awake so bad but is giving in.

"Okay, then we better go, because Bee is already wearing out, and we haven't even left yet."

Our group heads outside to walk down the block to where there's normally a farmers' market but tonight there's a mini carnival for Halloween instead, complete with game booths and food.

"I like your costumes," one guy compliments my little family of three.

"Great family costumes," says a woman a few minutes later.

"See?" I bump Beckham with my elbow. "Aren't you glad you wore the costume now?"

He gives me a reluctant smile. "I guess, Wazowski. But next year, I pick the costumes."

"Ooh"—I do a little shimmy—"so you're already planning on participating next year?"

"Only if I get to pick them."

"Deal." I shake on it with him. I doubt he can make me dress up as anything too crazy, considering some of the costumes I've done in the past. "I like that you're already thinking of the future with me."

He chuckles, Bee cradled in his arms since she got a little fussy. "I did put a ring on your finger, or did you forget already?"

"That you did. You must like me."

"Or," he says, capturing my chin between his fingers and tipping my head up, "I might even love you."

I grin like a woman who's gotten everything she's ever wanted—my dream job, the guy I always crushed on, and the cutest baby in the world. What more could I ask for?

He kisses me then, and I make a silent promise to myself that I'm going to make this a tradition, that he must kiss me in this spot every year for Halloween.

Bee begins to fuss.

"Shh," he croons. "Tell Daddy what's wrong."

If he keeps talking to her like that, I might be convinced to give him another one sooner rather than later.

I loop my arm through his. "I see some candy apples over there calling my name."

He comes with me, entertaining all my indulgences on my favorite night of the year. Who would have thought when I showed up at his place a year ago, dressed as a Dementor, that this is where we'd be twelve months later? Life is funny like that: you never know in the moment how things will end up. I guess that's the beauty of it, the choices we make, and I choose Beckham over and over and over again.

ACKNOWLEDGMENTS

To my wonderful family, for always being incredibly supportive of my books and dreams. I'm so lucky to have such a huge support system rooting for me.

I have to single out Grammy, without whom I wouldn't be the person I am today. Thank you for always being there for me and pushing me to follow my dreams. And to my aunt Janiece, my angel, you deserve to be celebrated for your selfless decision to give me life via organ donation. I aspire to always be as incredible as you two women.

Emily Wittig—you've been one of my biggest cheerleaders from practically the start. I'm so grateful you sent that message on Goodreads all those years ago. We've gotten to grow in our careers and as people together. I'm so lucky to have you.

Stephanie Phillips, you're an incredible person and an amazing agent. I'm so blessed to have you on my side. You've always believed in me, even when I didn't believe in myself, and I can't thank you enough for that and for pushing me to put myself out there.

To Angela James—working with you on this book was an incredible pleasure. Your advice and insights helped shape this book into a better version of itself, and I also know you've given me immeasurable knowledge moving forward. Thank you so much, and I hope we get to do it again.

Maria Gomez, and the entire Montlake team, thank you for believing in this book and me. I'm so excited to see what's to come for us.

To my doggos, Ollie and Remy, every book is written with you two by my side, and I think you deserve the biggest acknowledgment for that fact. You two keep me sane, and I love being your dog mom.

Lastly, to you, dear reader: None of this would be possible without you, and I hope you know that. All your support and kind words make me want to do this again and again. Readers are truly incredible, and I have so much love for you.

ABOUT THE AUTHOR

Micalea Smeltzer is the *USA Today* bestselling author of *The Confidence of Wildflowers* and *The Resurrection of Wildflowers*. She hails from northern Virginia, where her three dogs, Ollie, Remy, and Roo, are her constant companions. As a kidney transplant recipient, Micalea is dedicated to raising awareness around the effects of kidney disease, dialysis, and transplant as well as educating people on living donation. When she's not writing, you can catch her with her nose buried in a book. For more information, visit www.micaleasmeltzer.com.